MW01138810

TOTALLY *and* COMPLETELY FINE

TOTALLY

and

COMPLETELY
FINE

A NOVEL

ELISSA SUSSMAN

DELL · NEW YORK

Dell

An imprint of Random House

A division of Penguin Random House LLC

1745 Broadway, New York, NY 10019

randomhousebooks.com

penguinrandomhouse.com

A Dell Trade Paperback Original

LIBRARY OF CONGRESS CATALOGING-IN-PUBLICATION DATA

Names: Sussman, Elissa, author.

Title: Totally and completely fine: a novel / Elissa Sussman.

Description: New York: Dell, 2025.

Identifiers: LCCN 2025015573 (print) | LCCN 2025015574 (ebook) |
ISBN 9780593725177 (trade paperback; acid-free paper) |
ISBN 9780593725184 (ebook)

Subjects: LCGFT: Romance fiction. | Novels.

Classification: LCC PS3619.U84 T68 2025 (print) |
LCC PS3619.U84 (ebook) | DDC 813/.6—dc23/eng/20250411

LC record available at https://lccn.loc.gov/2025015573

LC ebook record available at https://lccn.loc.gov/2025015574

Printed in the United States of America on acid-free paper

randomhousebooks.com

2 4 6 8 9 7 5 3 1

BOOK TEAM: PRODUCTION EDITOR: *Cara DuBois* •
MANAGING EDITOR: *Saige Francis* • PRODUCTION MANAGER: *Meghan O'Leary*
• COPY EDITOR: *Sheryl Rapée-Adams* • PROOFREADERS: *Julie Ehlers,
Alissa Fitzgerald, Catherine Mallette*

Book design by Barbara M. Bachman

The authorized representative in the EU for product safety and compliance
is Penguin Random House Ireland, Morrison Chambers, 32 Nassau Street,
Dublin D02 YH68, Ireland. https://eu-contact.penguin.ie

FOR BASIL
A VERY GOOD BOY

ALL TRAGEDIES ARE FINISHED BY
A DEATH. ALL COMEDIES ARE ENDED
BY A MARRIAGE.

—*Lord Byron*

YOU KNOW I LIKE MY GIRLS A LITTLE
BIT OLDER.

—*The Outfield,*
"Your Love"

TOTALLY *and* COMPLETELY FINE

CHAPTER 1

NOW

"I HATE YOU! I HATE YOU! I HATE YOU!" LENA SHOUTED, before running up the stairs and slamming her door.

Over the years, I'd compiled a lengthy list of reasons why it truly fucking sucked to be the widowed mother of a teen girl, but at the top of the list was being unable to turn to Spencer right now and ask: "Do you think she means it?"

He would have laughed. It would have been exactly the right response. Because I would have been asking him as a joke but also seriously.

He would have put his arms around me, pulled me close so my head could go right to the crook of his neck where it had always fit. He would have kissed my forehead. And then my butt would get a firm, supportive squeeze that was usually more for him than me.

"We can always send her back," he would have said. "Do you remember where we put the receipt?"

And if I had cried a little—because even though I knew

logically that my teenage daughter was in the throes of the worst hormonal years of her life, and I had done and said far worse to my own mother at that age, it would still fucking hurt—Spencer would have taken my face in his hands and swiped the tears away with his thumbs.

"Pizza will solve this," he would have said.

Then he would have dug around in the freezer, humming to himself, probably Blink-182 or some other frat boy nineties song, and eventually exclaimed "aha!"—literally, "aha!"—when he found the ball of dough that he'd hidden there.

We'd have homemade pizza that night.

Now there was one ball of dough left.

More often than not, I'd get the desire to deep clean the whole house, and I'd take everything out of the fridge, tossing old lettuce, frosted ice cream, and sad, forgotten leftovers. The dough stayed. Untouched.

We had the recipe. Even if we didn't, making pizza wasn't rocket science.

But there had been a system. One that only Spencer knew. It had been born out of his years working at King Cheese Pizza during high school. He never did the whole tossing it up toward the ceiling and catching it—something he'd always refer to as a cheap trick—but he had a specific way of doing it.

He'd offered to teach me. Multiple times.

"That's what I have you for," I'd say.

It had been clever then. It was just tragic now.

I looked up at Lena's door, forever surprised that there were no cracks in the walls from the force of her repeated slams, and missed my husband so much I wanted to scream.

That was the problem with small towns, though. No-where to scream.

I picked up the phone. It wasn't the same—it wasn't even close—but I knew that when Lena realized I'd ordered pizza—from King Cheese no less—she'd come down. We wouldn't say anything about the fight. We'd eat and pretend that what had just happened had occurred in an alternate reality.

Because this was *all* a dream—a sick, warped, normal-but-not dream—that I knew we were both still expecting to wake from. I didn't take her temper tantrums seriously because part of me truly, stupidly, dangerously believed that it wasn't real. That it wouldn't stick.

Everything was forgotten. Forgiven.

Sometimes, my mother would come over, and I'd see her notice the empty pizza box—or boxes, depending on how bad the week had gone—in the trash. She'd say nothing. She wouldn't have to. Everything unsaid she pressed down in the thin, tense line between her lips. But I could see it. The disappointment. The worry.

This wasn't my first time at the grief rodeo.

I knew my therapist would probably have some better suggestions for how to deal with the horrible whirling vortex of a teenager in grief, but I could barely talk about my relationship with my daughter, let alone outline all the various ways I was failing her.

Three years in therapy and I was just now starting to talk enough to fill the entire hour.

My therapist knew how I felt about my mother-in-law (mostly annoyed, sometimes pitying). She knew how I felt about my job (I got to play with yarn and craft supplies every day, what wasn't to love?). She knew how I felt about getting older (fine, if not for the occasional overheating and the lack of information on perimenopause).

She didn't know that grief felt like the slowest-moving quicksand (what a ridiculous misnomer that word was), pulling me down inch by inch, rib by rib. She didn't know the way it hurt—physically hurt—to think about Spencer, to imagine his last moments, to wonder if I'd even said I loved him that night. She didn't know how there were evenings when I lay down in bed and couldn't recall a single thing I'd done that day.

She didn't know that my head, my heart, my body, were still completely disconnected from one another and I couldn't even remember what it was like to be a whole person.

I imagined Lena's therapy sessions were even less informative. We Parker women didn't talk about our feelings. Not the big ones.

Right now, in this moment, all I could manage was pizza.

It would have to be enough.

"Come visit me on set," Gabe had texted that morning. "We'll have a good time."

A good time. I'd forgotten what that was like.

CHAPTER 2

THEN

THE FIRST TIME I MET SPENCER, I THOUGHT HE WAS SHORT, scrawny, and annoying.

He was my brother's friend, and it was my job as the Very Cool Older Sister to not be impressed with anything—or anyone—Gabe brought home.

The introduction was brief, the two of them quickly escaping into the basement to play video games or hit each other in the arm or burp loudly, whatever it was that boys that age did. I was a year older, and much wiser, so I just stayed upstairs in my room reading.

After that, Spencer just slowly integrated into our lives.

He was at our house. All. The. Time.

Mostly with Gabe, but there were times when he even came over by himself.

"Don't you have your own family?" I asked him one day after he drank the last Yoo-hoo in the fridge.

I had been saving it for when I got the latest Baby-sitters Club book from the library. Which was today.

He wiped away his chocolate mustache.

"No one's home right now," he said.

I knew I was supposed to feel sorry for him, but I was mostly annoyed about the Yoo-hoo.

"Well, Gabe's not home either," I said.

"I know," he said. "Can we hang out?"

"No," I said. "I'm busy."

I expected him to be upset or to cry or pout. He didn't. He just shrugged and went to sit on the front porch with our cat, Big Fat Fuzzy Guy (so named by Gabe).

My bedroom overlooked the front porch, so when I tried to settle in to read—*without* my Yoo-hoo—my eyes couldn't stop wandering to Spencer, who was sitting, drink in one hand, a cat under the other.

After a while it seemed so pathetic that I gave up and went downstairs.

"Just come inside," I said. "We can play, like, cards or something."

My dad had taught me how to play poker, so I ended up teaching Spencer. When Gabe came home an hour later from who knows where, I'd won two dollars off his friend. He thanked me and went downstairs with Gabe to play video games.

At some point, my mom gave him his own key and bought him his own Yoo-hoos and that was that.

CHAPTER 3

NOW

To any casual observer, Lena probably looked like she was having a miserable time—sitting near the crafty table, arms crossed, expression blank—but as her mother, someone who was intimately aware of the subtleties of her moods, the fact that she wasn't on her phone or openly scowling at me was a good sign indeed.

I shifted in my seat, my lower back still smarting from the plane ride over.

Gabe had offered to fly us first class, but I'd declined. His fame and money made a tricky tightrope to walk. I didn't want Lena to take any of it for granted.

Then again, we lived in a house that Gabe had paid for. As did my mom. Then there was the bookstore/craft store, the Cozy, where my mom and I worked, our paychecks covered by Gabe. *And* my car. *And* Lena's extremely robust college fund.

The truth was that first-class tickets from Montana to Philadelphia were nothing compared to what Gabe had al-

ready done for us. And it was all probably a fool's errand—
this haphazard privilege monitoring—but I was pretty sure
that attempting to "succeed" at any aspect of parenting was
a fool's errand.

This time, I'd been rewarded for my effort with a daughter that ignored me completely, while I was seated in front
of a bucking horse, judging from the way I was aggressively
jostled every twenty minutes.

I'd get our tickets changed for the way back. I was too old
for this shit. There was no virtue in suffering for the sake of
suffering. Despite what my mother-in-law's church taught.

After all, this was supposed to be a vacation of sorts.

An escape.

And what could be more unlike my real life—days filled
with stocking yarn, sewing pockets into thrift store dresses,
and making underappreciated dinners—than a week spent
watching my brother film a movie?

It was certainly distracting.

And people who thought you couldn't distract yourself
from grief hadn't yet learned the kind of emotional com-
partmentalization that I excelled at. Sometimes I thought I
should teach a class: Separating from Human Emotion, or
How to Grieve Without All the Mess. Or, How to Put On
a Happy Face So Your Endless, Bond-Deep Sadness Doesn't
Ruin Everyone Else's Day. Or, How to Avoid Thinking
About Your Dead Husband by Teaching Yourself the Lost,
Fairly Useless Art of Mending Socks.

It had taken three weeks to fix one hole on the bottom
of a sock I'd probably gotten from Target, and it looked so
ugly that I ended up putting it back at the bottom of my
drawer where it had been living for the past year.

But I hadn't thought about Spencer the entire time I'd been working on it.

Well.

Only a few times.

And I'd only cried once.

A day.

I was doing fine.

The set was both chaotic and regimented. There were people everywhere and though it seemed like some of them were doing absolutely nothing, everything still managed to get done.

The first time I'd gone to see Gabe working was when he'd gotten his big break, playing James Bond. He'd invited us—my mom, Spencer—before, but Lena had been so young and the last thing I'd wanted was to be the person holding a screaming baby on a multimillion-dollar film set. Instead, we waited until we had a screaming *child* running amok on a multimillion-dollar film set. She'd only ruined one take.

This time she was just sitting over to the side, quietly, ruining nothing but her own general mood. I missed chasing her around. At least it would have given me something to do. As it turned out, being on a film set and having no job or real reason to be there was actually quite boring.

I was starting to think about things. About people. Feelings.

I didn't like that.

Maybe I should have brought the sock to Philadelphia and tried to fix it again.

Instead, I watched the center of this entire production: Ollie.

I wasn't about to tell Gabe, but I was pretty sure the main reason I'd been able to coax Lena to come on this trip was because of Uncle Oliver. He was her favorite person. I wasn't sure if it was his British accent or fondness for weird, expensive gifts or the fact that he wasn't related to her by blood that made him so appealing. It didn't matter. The feelings of love were entirely mutual.

He'd also essentially saved Gabe's life. Well, he and Gabe's ex-wife, Jacinda. They were the ones who called when the drinking got dangerously bad.

Spencer had been alive back then—during that first storm—and we'd weathered it all together.

And then when Spencer died, Ollie had done everything he could to keep the hurricane of press away from our family. He wasn't always successful, but I knew that he'd pulled some strings and done a few interviews he might not have if the distraction hadn't been needed.

That's when we'd learned firsthand that to some members of the media, nothing in Gabe's life was off-limits.

Ollie had tried his best, and I loved him for it.

I liked watching him work. We'd had barely enough time for a greeting and a couple of cheek kisses when we arrived, but there was something very comforting about the way he ran things. Smart. Fast. Efficient.

He knew where everyone was and what they should be doing. It reminded me of when I'd gone to visit Spencer at the hardware store when he was manager. They'd all loved him because he'd been the same—on top of things. Getting shit done.

It had taken a while for me to realize that he'd been depressed underneath the productivity.

I hated to think of the other things I might have missed.

"Those should go to costuming," Ollie said, handing something to a person with a notebook. "We need them by the end of the week." He waved another person over. "Check on Mackenzie, okay?" They were wearing a headset. "If she needs more time, that's fine, we can do a few pickups without her."

Even after all these years, a lot of the terms were still foreign to me. It was like some weird Hollywood Mad Libs where I had to pretend to understand what an "apple box" or "crossing sight lines" meant.

In between giving direction, Ollie caught my eye and gave me a wink.

I smiled at him and watched his gaze shift to my offspring.

"Oi, Lena," he called. "I need your help."

She was on her feet immediately, rushing to his side. He put his arm around her and the two of them huddled in a private conversation that made Lena laugh. Really laugh.

It was the best thing I'd seen in weeks.

Two shadows fell across my lap. I hadn't even noticed Gabe's approach.

"Here she is," he said. "Lauren, this is Ben. Walsh, this is my sister, Lauren."

My mouth dropped open.

A revision to my previous thought was required. The man standing in front of me was possibly the best thing I'd seen in months. Maybe even years.

The magazine shoots and paparazzi photos hardly did him justice. But it was more than just standard movie star gorgeousness. I'd become somewhat accustomed to that.

It was the *zing* I felt. That forward lurch of my heart. A long-forgotten hello.

Chemistry.

If my libido was Sleeping Beauty, she was waking up. Right. Now.

As if my body had finally come online and reconnected to my brain. And both were suddenly screaming for everything I'd denied them over these past three years. Touch. Connection. Intimacy.

Reality.

The feeling was disorienting and thrilling and extremely inconvenient.

I got up carefully from the rickety director's-style chair that I was certain was always one wrong move from flipping me face-first onto the ground. My own knees trembled a bit.

"Hello," I said to Benjamin Walsh once I was upright and steady. Ish.

I held out my hand. He took it between both of his. His palms were warm. A little rough.

Much had been made about his looks—news outlets always finding new and indirect ways to reference his Hawaiian mother, talking about his "exotic" cheekbones and "tanned" skin.

All I could see was his smile. His eyes.

God, his eyes. It wasn't the color of them—brown—but rather the way he looked at me. His attention completely, utterly focused. I felt pinned by his gaze. And I liked it.

I wondered if he felt the same way. Because all I could do was stare at him, unblinking, like I was trying to see into his soul. Which could be seen as either flattering or creepy as hell.

From the ever-growing smile on his face, it seemed that Ben didn't mind the unwavering attention.

"Gabe talks about you all the time," he said. "It's a pleasure to meet you."

His Irish accent—attributed to his Irish father—was, at the moment, barely perceptible.

He was playing an American after all. I assumed he was trying to stay somewhat in character. Gabe had done the reverse of that while playing James Bond. We'd mocked him relentlessly—as family does—when it took months for him to completely drop his English accent. Even now, there were times when he said "water" like he was across the pond.

"Oh no," I said. "*People*'s Sexiest Man Alive. The pleasure is all mine."

Jesus. Rein it in, Parker.

He blushed. It made me smile.

Flirting. I remembered that. It had been fun once.

I'd been fun once.

Ben, on the other hand, looked like he was *lots* of fun. All the time.

Gabe cleared his throat. I'd completely forgotten he was there.

Completely forgotten quite a few things.

Like that my thirteen-year-old daughter would be mortified to watch her mother visibly drool over a man who was definitely *not* her age. The last thing she needed right now was to be reminded that her parent was also a human being with human being urges.

But a glance toward Lena revealed that she was still occupied with Oliver and hadn't noticed the interaction.

Gabe cleared his throat again.

"Walsh has been asking about you," he said.

I didn't appreciate his raised eyebrow or his tone. It was very much a Little Brother eyebrow/tone, one that I hadn't seen in a while but remembered vividly nonetheless. Clearly he was regretting this introduction.

"He's a big foodie," Gabe said.

"An exaggeration," Ben said, his accent slipping through again. "I was merely told that you're quite accomplished in the kitchen."

"I can cook," I said.

"She's very good," Gabe said, almost reluctantly. "Bakes too."

"I can't do either," Ben said. "However, I have been told that I'm quite an accomplished eater."

He made it sound filthy.

I didn't mind at all.

Then again, I had clearly lost all my senses.

I'd heard people talk about twinkly eyes, but I'd never experienced it in real life. Ben's eyes were so twinkly it was almost as if someone had stuffed two stars into his skull.

"If you're hoping for a demonstration while I'm here," I said, "I'm sorry to inform you that I'm on vacation."

That didn't mean I wasn't open to other types of demonstrations. Like how he might look at me while he pinned me to a bed. Or couch. Chair. I wasn't feeling particular about location.

Calm. Down.

It was like I hadn't had sex in three years.

Well. I hadn't had *good* sex in three years.

Ben put a hand to his chest. "I would never presume," he said. "I was only hoping to talk about food with someone who isn't eating lettuce and protein shakes."

Gabe frowned.

"Talk to me in ten years when a normal metabolism finally kicks in," he said.

I gave my brother a briefly sympathetic look. It wasn't his fault that he had the Parker genes, which kept us cozy in the winter, but required extreme maintenance whenever he was on-screen. Keeping his weight movie-ready sometimes required near starvation.

But right now, *Gabe's* deprivation was the least of my worries.

"I would be happy to discuss food with you," I told Ben.

I would be happy to do a lot more with you, I thought.

"Lauren reads cookbooks before bed," Gabe said. "She's obsessed."

Ben put his hands on my shoulders. "Marry me," he said.

I wasn't expecting it. The comment or the touch, which had brought us closer together, my toes practically touching his. It was the surprise of it all that made my arms tense. My reaction was noted immediately, though, and Ben stepped back.

"Hands to yourself, Walsh," Gabe said. "That's my sister."

He was joking—trying to reset the mood—but I bristled.

Because I wasn't just his sister. I was a grown woman. A grown woman who *liked* being touched by Benjamin Walsh.

I was *hungry* for touch.

I couldn't remember the last time I'd been this horny. My tongue was pressed to the roof of my mouth so it wouldn't loll out the side of it like a panting dog.

"Mr. Parker?" A PA interrupted us. "They need you in makeup."

"Okay," Gabe said. "I'll be right there."

He looked at Ben. Ben was looking at me.

"Go," I said to Gabe. "Do your job."

He hesitated. I gave him a shove, probably harder than I should have. But he needed to go.

"Goodbye," I said.

He left, reluctantly, twisting his head back every few steps as if to keep an eye on me. I knew what he was thinking. He wasn't wrong.

But I wasn't a teenager anymore. Despite my hormones roaring to life, I knew how to control them.

I was pretty sure I knew how to control them.

"Must be nice," Ben said once Gabe was out of sight.

"Hmmm?"

"Having siblings," he said.

"It can be," I said. "It can also be extremely annoying."

"I wouldn't know," he said. "Only child."

"Ah," I said.

I looked over at Lena, standing next to Oliver as he showed her something on one of the many screens that surrounded them off to the side of the set. Video village, I think it was called.

Spencer and I had always assumed we'd have another

kid, but Lena just kept getting older, and I kept not getting pregnant, and then Spencer died.

"My daughter too," I said.

Those were the breaks sometimes.

"Is it true?" Ben asked. "That you read cookbooks in bed?"

I was surely imagining the emphasis on *bed*.

"Sometimes," I said.

"What do you prefer?" he asked. "Sweet or savory?"

He was a *good* flirt.

"Savory," I said. "You?"

"Oh, sweet, absolutely," Ben said, accent slipping through. "I have a wicked sweet tooth."

Certainly, Gabe had told him all about me. Who I was. The widow. The tragic widow with her tragic past and her tragic daughter and her tragic life. The widow who needed to be coddled and protected and cared for.

But Ben wasn't looking at me like that.

There was no pity in his gaze. No "poor thing." No sympathetic understanding.

Ben looked at me like he wanted to fuck me.

When I was a kid, the fair would come to town once a year. I would beg and beg and beg to spend the day there, where I used up all my tickets on my favorite ride. The one where they strapped you into a chair, shot you up to the top of a tall, tall tower, and dropped you.

I loved the feeling of leaving my entire body behind for about half a second—leaving my breath, my stomach, my heart—everything up in the air while I hurtled downward. I loved screaming until I was hoarse, delighting in the thrill that was half fear, half triumph.

It felt like that now.

Apparently, Ben's eyes could do more than twinkle. They could undress me. They could seduce me. They could make me feel like I hadn't felt in a long time.

But this was ridiculous. Just because he was looking at me like that didn't mean . . .

"Gabe said you're here for the week," Ben said.

"I am."

"Packed schedule?"

I looked at him. At his mouth, which was curved in a very wonderful, wicked smile.

"I could show you around Philadelphia," he said.

I felt a little breathless. In the best way.

It wasn't as if I hadn't gone on dates since Spencer died. I had. I'd even slept with a few of them. The experience—experiences—had been mostly unremarkable. But I'd expected that because the dates themselves had been wholly unremarkable.

There had been a weird comfort in that—in the reminder of how special things had been between me and Spencer. How irreplaceable he was in every way. I'd assumed that the part of me that *hungered* had died along with Spencer.

This was the first real proof that it hadn't.

Of course, there was that voice in the back of my head reminding me that Benjamin Walsh was an actual real-life movie star who could probably have any woman he wanted. That he was significantly younger than me. That I had no business whatsoever entertaining carnal thoughts about him.

TOTALLY AND COMPLETELY FINE

But if I'd learned one thing in my life, it was that attraction wasn't *that* complicated.

It didn't matter that I was a single mother in my forties and he was a thirty-year-old proudly bisexual heartthrob. It didn't matter that my body was softer and rounder and parts of me hung lower than they once had. That I had wrinkles and gray hairs and arthritis.

None of those things had mattered to Spencer. He'd thought me beautiful and sexy and gorgeous and endlessly desirable.

Years of being with him—being loved like that—had taught me that what mattered was how someone made you feel. That stopping to entertain your own insecurities in the face of desire like this was a waste of time.

Life was short. So fucking short.

There was clearly chemistry here.

It could be that simple sometimes.

Then again.

Lena was back in her seat near crafty. And this time she had her phone out, and she was slouched all the way down. She wasn't looking at me, but somehow, I knew she'd seen what was going on. Her mother behaving in ways unbecoming of a sad, tragic widow.

Reality was a freezing-cold bucket of water over that growling, purring animal in my chest. It hissed and retreated.

What had I been thinking? I wasn't here to fuck a movie star.

"I'm not sure what Gabe's plans are," I said. "But Lena's been going through a tough time." Understatement. "I think she'd be upset if I ditched her to spend time with one of her uncle's co-stars."

I was almost waiting for him to save face and say something like "Oh, how embarrassing, you thought I wanted to spend time with *you*? I was just being polite."

Because I also knew how sensitive men were. Their delicate egos.

"I understand," Ben said.

"I'm sorry," I said instinctively.

"Don't be," he said. "It would have been lovely to take a tour of Philadelphia with a beautiful, interesting woman while talking about pasta and bread, but I completely understand."

I was making the right choice.

"If anything changes," he said, "you have my number."

"I don't actually," I said.

"Well," he said, "let's change that right now."

We exchanged phones and when he handed mine back, he gave me a devastating wink.

My heart went th-thump, th-thump. It purred.

It was nice, but also uncomfortable. Guilty. A part of me didn't like that someone else could make me feel this way. As if it took something away from what I'd had with Spencer.

I wanted it but I didn't.

"Just so you know," Ben said, "I've always wanted to visit Montana."

"Have you?" I asked.

"I have," he said. "I love to travel."

I bet he did.

CHAPTER 4

NOW

GABE HAD RENTED A LITTLE HOUSE ABOUT TWENTY minutes from the set. In the car over, Lena sat in the back, her attention totally focused on her phone, while Gabe and I made sibling small talk.

"How's the store?" he asked.

"Good," I said. "Mom wants to start selling banned books for half off."

"That sounds like her."

"Yep," I said.

"She's doing well?"

"Yep," I said.

Gabe kept looking at me. I wanted to tell him to keep his eyes on the road, but I decided to ignore him instead. Because I knew what he was looking for.

He was looking for signs that I was okay.

That he didn't need to worry.

Everyone treated me—and Lena—like we were un-bearably fragile. Like the mere mention of Spencer, of our life before, of a future without him, would send us into hysterics.

I wasn't sure it wouldn't, but didn't we all deserve a complete emotional collapse once in a while?

Not that I'd know.

We *all* avoided The Conversation. Even me.

And now, after three years, it almost seemed like the time had passed to talk about it. That bringing it up might *actually* cause something, or someone, to destruct.

We'd made it this far without discussing it. What was another twenty, thirty, forty years?

"I'm hungry," Gabe said. "Are you guys hungry?"

Lena said nothing.

"I'm hungry," I said.

"We should probably go to the store," he said. "Ben wasn't wrong about the lettuce and protein shakes."

He was nearing the type of thin that looked better on camera but made him look a little like a bobblehead in real life. Not that I was going to tell him that. I'd save it for the right moment, like a wedding speech or something.

"I thought there weren't going to be any shirtless scenes in this one," I said.

I could see Lena grimacing in the back seat, even though her eyes were still fixated on her phone. It was awkward for all of us, but especially her, knowing that thousands of women (and men) around the world thought her uncle Gabe was, like, totally the hottest thing ever.

"Ollie is still deciding," Gabe said. "Or he's just torturing me for fun."

"I'm going to guess it's mostly for fun," I said, even though it was probably a directive coming from the studio.

They were taking a risk on Gabe this time around, and no doubt they wanted to make sure they got their money's worth.

"Did you tell all your friends what you're doing this week?" Gabe asked the silent back seat passenger.

She didn't look up from her screen.

"Lena," I prompted.

She shrugged.

"I told all *my* friends," I said.

"You don't have any friends," Lena said.

Still no eye contact.

"Ouch," I said. "I have friends."

Silence from the back seat.

"Who is she talking to?" Gabe asked, voice lowered.

"Probably Eve," I said. "Best friend stuff."

"We're not best friends," Lena said. "That's for kids."

"Right," I said. "Sorry."

I liked Eve. She'd appeared in our life last year, her family moving from Eastern Montana to Cooper. She was the sunshiny, show tune–singing, pink-wearing extroverted counterpart to the storm cloud quietly thundering in the back seat. She loved books and puppies and kitties, and she adored Lena.

They were as close as Jessica and I had been at that age. Closer, probably.

"And you?" Gabe asked. "How are you?"

Ah. The indirect version of The Conversation. I could tell he wasn't even sure he should be asking from the way his voice went up after each word, like all of it was a question. "And? You? How? Are? You?"

At least he tried.

"Fine," I said.

Because I knew he didn't really want to know. Didn't want to know that I hated sleeping alone, that I still couldn't drive past the intersection where Spencer had been killed—which was kind of a problem in a town as small as Cooper—and that there were days when showering and eating and generally staying alive felt like too much effort.

That I suspected if someone were to cut me open, they'd find nothing but a cobweb-strewn cavern of emptiness and longing. The kind where if you called out, all you'd hear was echoes.

It had been three years and yet.

I just wanted to be okay again.

I was pretty sure I never would be.

Gabe just hummed and nodded. What else could he do?

I'd done the same when we'd tried to talk about his drinking for all those years. Gabe might have been the professional actor, but everyone in our family was pretty good at pretending like we were just fine. Totally fine. Completely fine.

If my dad's death had been the trial run, well, then Spencer's death was the marathon.

Except I'd be running forever. There was no finish line. Just the constant ache of your muscles and your shortness of breath and the thirst for something you couldn't have and the voice that said "You can't stop."

You can never stop.

Teddy was in the window of the rental when we pulled up. I could see her tail wagging furiously.

The car had just barely halted when Lena leapt from it.

Gabe tossed her the keys as she bolted down the driveway, and she didn't catch them, but didn't seem to care that she fumbled as she snatched them up and got the door open.

"Teddy!" she cried, opening her arms to greet the furry mutt that plowed right into her and began licking her face as if she were made of sausage.

"Well," Gabe said, pulling her bag out of the car, "at least she's glad to see one of us."

CHAPTER 5

THEN

IT GOT HARDER AND HARDER TO PRETEND THAT THINGS were okay when they shaved Dad's head. When he came home with a big, bulky bandage that eventually revealed a long, jagged scar across his skull. That's when everyone knew something was wrong. When people would come up to Mom in the middle of the grocery store, their eyes shining with unshed tears.

"You must be heartbroken," they'd say.

Or: "I can't imagine what this must be like for you."

Or: "How can you bear it?"

Or: "I knew someone who was sick like that, and he's fine. Have faith."

Or: "We'll pray for you."

Or: "He was such a nice man."

He'd still been alive at that point. But it didn't really matter—as far as the town was concerned, he was going to die and therefore was already dead in a way. Easier to get through the mourning process if you did it preemptively, or something like that.

The doctor said that his hair would come back and cover the scar, but Dad didn't live long enough for that to happen.

The funeral was the first time I met Spencer's mother, Diana.

Cooper was a small town, so there were a couple of things I knew about her. She was a churchgoing woman. She wasn't divorced but her husband—Spencer's dad—wasn't around. Details varied when it came to what had happened. Some people said he was a drunk who just took off one night. Or he was a drug addict. Or a gambling addict.

The basic gist was that Diana was a saint and her husband was unreliable and troubled.

Spencer never spoke about him. Never spoke about his family at all.

At least, not to me.

It surprised me how much she cried. I sat in the front row with Jessica, our hands intertwined. I didn't want to cry at all, but I couldn't help it, everything mixing together as it came down, tears, snot, blubbering sobs as some guy in a suit talked about how great my dad had been. How'd they'd had *so much* fun in college and how he was going to miss him *so much*.

I resented him. Resented anyone who thought they knew what it meant to lose my dad. And I hated listening to a woman I'd never met wail and keen in the back row. Even Spencer had looked embarrassed when I caught his eye as we walked out of the funeral home.

"Did she ever meet Dad?" I asked Gabe.

She'd barely been able to get a single sentence out, she'd been wailing so violently. It had scared me a little.

"I don't think so," Gabe said.

"Some people are very emotional," Mom said. "Their hearts are too tender."

I didn't like that explanation—or the crying—but I couldn't explain why.

I just knew that I was angry. All the time. At everyone.

After the funeral, it was as if my father had never existed. No one spoke about him. We never saw that college friend of his again. We didn't get stopped on the street anymore. We just got those sad, poor-you looks as people hurried away from us as if grief were contagious. As if mentioning my father would kill him all over again.

The collective consensus was that it would be better if we all moved on. That the funeral had been the period on the end of that sentence.

That it was our responsibility—to the community, to the world, to ourselves—to be okay now. To just get over it.

I kept waiting for the anger to disappear, to feel that kind of peace that movies and TV and books seemed to tell me would come, but didn't. I waited for the acceptance of my father's death. For it to be real. For it to be done. But that didn't happen. I was still angry. And *that* only seemed to get worse.

CHAPTER 6

NOW

I MADE LENA DO THE DISHES AFTER DINNER. SHE POUTED but put her headphones in and went from ignoring us across the table to ignoring us from the kitchen.

Gabe ran a hand over his face, which bore all the telltale wrinkles of worry. Wrinkles that were considered sexy and stately on a man of his age but horrifying on any woman over twenty-five.

He was taking Lena's sullen behavior in stride, but I knew he was hurt.

I wanted to tell him that it wasn't personal, that it was just hormones and grief and growing up, but honestly, I couldn't even tell at this point. Maybe it *was* personal. When I'd been her age, it had felt personal—the anger that bubbled up out of nowhere, turning me into a spitting, sputtering, boiling cauldron of fury and bad feelings.

And there was the whole non-conversation about Gabe's addiction. Lena and I had never talked about it—

another strike against my winning Mother of the Year—but I could sense the anger there.

Maybe it was cowardly, but that was something I could deal with. I could take it. I'd rather be her punching bag than ask about her feelings. Because it was what was beneath the anger—what I still struggled to cope with—that was the really scary shit that I didn't know how to address. That I still hadn't addressed in myself.

Was there a Wish She Wasn't My Mother of the Year Award? Because I was probably going to medal in that.

"Saw you and Walsh talking," Gabe said.

I looked at him.

His tone and expression were trying way too hard to be casual. I immediately knew what he was trying to suss out and decided not to make it easy for him.

"You literally introduced us," I reminded him. "What was I supposed to do, stare silently at him?"

I would have. Gladly.

"Most women do," he said, sounding a little grouchy.

"Awww." I patted his cheek. "Are you jealous of the handsome new movie star?"

He jerked away. "No," he said. "I'm just . . . I just didn't like the way he was looking at you."

I had liked it a lot. But Gabe really didn't need to know that.

In fact, no one needed to know that.

"He's harmless," I said.

Gabe nodded, but his concerned expression didn't go away. I wanted to roll my eyes.

"He's a child," I said.

I regretted it immediately. Ben was young—I knew

that. Much younger than me. But if one thing was clear, whatever was going on between us was the opposite of childish, and it was a bit condescending and unfair to categorize him that way. Especially since I'd been an equal participant.

I said it because I knew it would make Gabe relax.

And because nothing was going to happen. I'd had a good time flirting with a beautiful man, but that's all it was. A moment outside of reality.

Even if he had given me his phone number.

"He's nice enough," Gabe said.

"But . . ." I prompted, and then immediately wished I'd held my tongue.

"But he's got a bit of a reputation," Gabe said.

For fuck's sake.

"Oh," I said. "A *reputation.*"

He flushed.

One thing I loved about my brother was that he could be a big fucking movie star with women and money being thrown at him from all angles and I could still embarrass him. It made me feel at peace in the world.

Because we both knew that whatever anyone was saying about Ben Walsh had been said about Gabe Parker, albeit ten years earlier.

Not to mention what had been said about me, ten years or so before that.

A *reputation.*

"Is this your way of telling me that he's bi?" I asked. "Because I know."

"Everyone knows," Gabe said.

It was on his Wikipedia page. And mentioned in most

articles about him. Not that I'd read many. Only a dozen or so.

He'd been born in Hawaii, educated in Ireland. Never went to college, but moved around the UK performing at small theatres until some talent scout saw him doing Shakespeare and decided he would be perfect for the BBC's latest teen-aimed adaptation of *Sense and Sensibility*, called *SXS*. He'd instantly become a fan favorite and then did the rounds on *Doctor Who, Coronation Street, Midsomer Murders,* and *EastEnders* before Hollywood finally took notice. Then, much like Gabe, he landed small roles in period films, usually playing soldiers, his roles growing larger and larger until Ollie had swooped in and given him a choice role as Macaulay Connor in his update of *The Philadelphia Story*.

Also, he was bisexual.

And gorgeous.

That was all I knew about him.

"That's not the kind of reputation I'm talking about," Gabe said.

I waited for him to continue, but he took his damn time.

"He's got a bit of a death wish," he finally said.

"What does *that* mean?"

Gabe looked a little flustered. "He just seems like the thrill-seeking type. He's got his motorcycle, of course, but also takes folks skydiving or hang gliding or whatever on the off days, goes to the desert and races cars, that kind of stuff."

"It sounds like he's an adrenaline junkie," I said.

"He's also very popular," he said. "Knows everyone on the crew."

"What a monster," I said. "I can see why you can't stand him."

"That's not what I'm saying."

"Then say what you're saying." I was getting annoyed.

"He's just not . . ." Gabe seemed to search for his words.

I waited but started counting to ten. If I got there and Gabe still hadn't spit it out, I was shutting down the conversation. But the truth was that I was a little curious.

"He's still sowing his oats," he said.

With meaning.

"Are you trying to tell me that he sleeps around?" I asked.

Gabe nodded like he'd just imparted some deep, dark secret instead of something I could have guessed just by looking at Ben.

He was gorgeous, talented, and famous.

Of course he slept around.

"I'm scandalized," I said.

"I'm just telling you what I've heard," Gabe said, sounding very put out.

"Then it *must* be true," I said. "Just like the talk about you and that model, Annaleigh someone?"

There'd been a time when we all felt like the only place we were getting information about Gabe's personal life was from the tabloids. Information he swore was incorrect.

"Munro," Gabe muttered. "And that was just a misunderstanding."

"Right. And that story about you jumping into the pool at that big Oscar party?"

"Exaggeration."

"Of course," I said. "What about that wild night in Paris with Jacinda and her friends?"

Gabe's face was getting redder and redder.

"It wasn't what it looked like," he muttered.

"And the *Broad Sheets* interview?" I asked. "Was the *whole* thing just taken out of context?"

I knew I had him there. Everyone—Spencer included—was convinced that something had happened between Gabe and the woman who had interviewed him all those years ago.

Gabe denied that any unprofessional naughtiness had occurred, but no one believed him.

My point stood.

"I was young and stupid," Gabe said. "The media likes to blow things out of proportion."

"Exactly," I said. Pointedly.

Gabe looked supremely uncomfortable.

"Like you didn't get into trouble at that age," he said to his feet.

"I was married at that age," I reminded him. "My troublemaking days were behind me."

I felt a weird twinge of longing for those days. How wild I'd been. How bold. How unafraid.

Not that I'd gone skydiving or anything like that. I'd just been reckless.

Maybe that was what I'd been craving. Not Ben, not sex, but that feeling. That out-of-control, do-what-I-want, be-what-I-want feeling that I'd had before I learned that nothing in life came without consequences.

"I remember what it was like to be in his position," Gabe said. "It can fuck with your head."

His expression was placid, but I could see the lines of tension around his mouth and eyes. It was more than just warning me away from an on-set horndog. He was worried.

About me, but also kind of about Ben too.

It was sweet.

From what I could tell, Ben was at a very particular point in his life—and career—one that was wholly unique. He was on the cusp of having the kind of fame and money that most people think they want, think will make all their problems go away, but once they have it, don't really know what to do with it.

Most people don't do a good job handling that kind of luck.

Gabe didn't. Hadn't.

Hence why some of those rumors hadn't been rumors at all.

Things were better now, but it had been touch and go for a while. Funny how if someone had asked me who I'd be more likely to bury three years ago, it would have been my brother.

Not funny ha ha, but funny horrible.

"But you're right," he said. "It's pointless to believe rumors."

We sat there. I thought about excusing myself—to go read a book or stare at the wall or sit in the general vicinity of my daughter while pretending she wanted me there—but Gabe cleared his throat.

If he said one more thing about Ben, I was going to punch him in the arm.

"I have a favor to ask," he said, looking over at Lena.

I couldn't understand what kind of favor he could possibly be asking for unless it was to keep my sullen daughter from ruining the vibe of not just the entire movie, but the whole damn city.

"I'm getting tomorrow off," he said. "And I was wondering if I could take Lena for the day? Just the two of us?"

"What?" I asked as if he hadn't been perfectly clear.

"I thought I'd take her to a museum or something," he said.

I looked over at my purse. Where my phone was. Where Ben's number was.

No. I was being ridiculous.

"Just the two of you?" I asked, keeping my voice steady. Casual.

"I know I invited both of you here," Gabe said. "But things have been really strained between me and Lena, and I was hoping that some time together would help."

They'd been close—he and Lena—thick as thieves. After Spencer died, they'd formed a special bond, the kind you have when you've both lost your fathers around the same age.

I was quiet for too long, and Gabe took that silence as a refusal.

"Never mind," he said. "I'm sorry. You guys are here for a vacation and to enjoy yourselves and spend time together. I'm being selfish."

I reached out and put my hand on his.

"Gabe," I said. "I think it's a wonderful idea."

I did.

I also couldn't stop glancing toward my bag. Ben was

probably busy. After I'd turned him down, he probably just asked someone else. To talk about food.

Sowing those oats and all.

"I think Lena would probably love having a day that's just the two of you," I said.

Gabe relaxed. "You think so?"

"Well." I paused. "She might not seem like she's enjoying it, and she might not act as if she is, but maybe in a few years she might casually admit that it wasn't the worst thing she ever experienced."

"I really fucked up, didn't I?"

My poor brother. He had such a big heart but fumbled with it.

"She's a teen girl who misses her dad," I said. "Remember how that was?"

There were times I wished I couldn't.

Gabe winced. "I don't know how Mom put up with us."

We sat in silence, looking through to the kitchen, where Lena was standing with Teddy at her feet, hoping desperately for scraps.

"You'd really be okay with me taking her for the day?" Gabe asked.

"Yes," I said.

I wasn't going to text Ben.

"You'll be okay by yourself?"

Then I thought about his eyes. About how they'd made me feel.

One text couldn't hurt.

"I think I'll manage," I said.

CHAPTER 7

THEN

AFTER DAD DIED, MONEY WAS TIGHT, AND EVERYTHING was so much harder. Mom did her best, but there were plenty of nights when all we had in the house was a box of noodles and some butter. Or weeks with jelly sandwiches for lunch. It was bad enough living without a parent, but being dad-less *and* hungry? All the time? I couldn't handle it.

I set up a secret poker game in the basement. Jessica helped.

I was the dealer, but she played the host—and she took to it like a pro. One night she even showed up wearing a big fake diamond necklace because she said it added an aura of class. We were a formidable team.

It was pay-to-play, and it wasn't long before I started raking in my classmates' allowances and the older kids' paychecks from after-school jobs. I felt less bad about taking money from students whose parents had enough to give them, but in the end, I'd collect my share no matter how the player got their hands on the cash.

Gabe—who could never say no to me—was the bouncer. I was pretty sure that if he'd had to actually enforce anything, he'd turn and run, but his presence ended up being enough to keep my classmates in line. He also liked how Jessica would call him "the muscle." I caught him once flexing and checking himself out in the mirror.

Spencer hadn't liked it at all, but things had gotten tense between him and our family. Between me and him. After the whole thing with his mom—all that weeping and wailing at the funeral of a man she'd never met—we'd started getting letters from her church.

They wanted to plant a tree for him in their garden. They said we could visit it whenever we wanted. They said that the congregation was praying for us and that we were welcome there anytime.

Dad had been an atheist; Mom was a lapsed Protestant. We celebrated Christmas and sometimes Easter, but mostly for the candy and the presents, not the religion.

And we didn't need a tree. We didn't need prayers. We needed to pay off my dad's medical bills. We needed a new roof. A better water heater. A car that didn't break down in the summer. Groceries. Gabe needed new shoes. I needed a haircut. We needed help. *Real* help.

I didn't want to go to Spencer's church with him and his mom, but Gabe was interested. He went one Sunday, but when he came home, he went straight to his room and wouldn't talk about it until I sat on him and demanded he tell me what happened.

I knew he wanted to tell me because he could have easily pushed me off. He was just at the beginning of a growth spurt.

Spencer had taken him to a youth group meeting where Gabe had been told that Dad was in hell because he hadn't believed in god and that unless Gabe made a change in his life, he'd go to hell too.

I was furious.

Gabe refused to tell Mom, and he didn't want to end his friendship with Spencer either.

"It's not his fault," he kept saying. "His family is just like that."

But Gabe was a more forgiving sort than I was.

The next time Spencer came over, I cornered him in the kitchen. He wasn't as big as Gabe, and I knew how to be terrifying. I stabbed my finger into his chest.

"Don't you ever—*ever*—take my brother to see those people again."

He went white and quiet but nodded.

"I just wanted to help," he said. Almost whispering.

"Well, you didn't," I said. "Asshole."

I could see that he wanted to say something else— probably chastise me for my language, which he had done in the past—but he smartly kept his mouth shut. Lately my temper had felt like a caged animal, just looking for someone to come close enough to the bars so I could swipe them with my claws.

We kept our distance from each other after that. Which was good, because I knew for a fact that he wouldn't have approved of the super-secret basement poker game, or the complete lack of guilt I felt taking money from some of our shittier classmates.

I told myself I didn't care when he stopped coming over. When Gabe would leave to meet him instead of the two of them hanging out in the basement, which I'd commandeered. All of a sudden, after years of spending afternoons at the house, he was just gone.

I told myself I didn't miss him.

I told myself that I was right, and he was wrong.

I told myself forgiveness was overrated.

And then it was easy to stay mad at him when one of his church buddies tattled about the poker game. After he lost most of his savings by being an arrogant asshole who couldn't play poker but wanted to look like a big man in front of our peers. Who had been near tears when I told him I wasn't giving the money back.

I didn't feel guilty.

Not at all.

And I wasn't surprised when the little shithead told his parents about the poker game, who then told the church leadership, who then told the whole fucking town.

That's when everyone found out what I'd been doing.

That I wasn't the sad, sweet, mournful daughter that they'd expected me to be.

That I was, in fact, trouble.

CHAPTER 8

NOW

"Is THERE ANYTHING IN PARTICULAR YOU'D LIKE TO DO?" Ben asked.

He'd just picked me up and we were still parked in his rental car outside of Gabe's place.

My brother and Lena had left about fifteen minutes earlier. I'd ignored the heavy, dramatic sighs that Lena had made all morning. It had been like being stalked by an elderly pug. I felt bad for Gabe, but then again, he'd *literally* asked for it.

I'd applied deodorant at least four times. Changed my bra twice. Put my hair up. Then down. Then up again. And now down. I'd waited for Ben and paced the length of the guest room, with Teddy at my heels, wondering what the hell I had done.

I'd scheduled a sex date.

Ben looked incredible, wearing exactly what I expected a daredevil type to wear, head-to-toe black with scuffed boots and a silver ring on his thumb. I couldn't see it clearly, but I was pretty sure I spied a necklace or two, a hint of chest hair peeking out from his unbuttoned Henley.

His car smelled brand-new, as if he'd just picked it up. I was a little disappointed—I'd expected a motorcycle. Not that I'd ever been on a motorcycle, and truthfully it freaked me out a bit, but it would have been sexy.

The *whole* Ben Walsh experience.

But I could be content with whatever I got.

That was the hope, at least.

"There's plenty of sightseeing," Ben said. "Lots of great museums, galleries, and historical monuments. Whatever you'd like to do."

I thought about making an excuse. About telling him that unfortunately I couldn't spend the day with him. That I had a headache. Or cramps. Or a bum knee that was acting up.

I thought about all the reasons this was a bad idea.

I thought about Spencer.

I thought about myself.

"I think we should have sex," I said.

Ben didn't move. He didn't even blink.

For a moment I thought he might not have heard me.

I kept talking.

"I mean, I figured that you would be interested, because yesterday, it seemed that way, and I'm attracted to you because you're gorgeous and you like food. Also, I was tested a few months ago and it all came back negative, and I haven't been with anyone else since. But this doesn't have to be some big deal, because I live in Montana and you live . . . somewhere else and this is just a vacation and a onetime thing. I just thought . . . we should have sex . . ."

I trailed off weakly, knowing that I probably sounded like an absolute lunatic.

I put my head in my hands. "I'll see myself out."

"Lauren," Ben said.

I looked at him.

"I would very much like to have sex with you," he said.

This time I was the one who didn't blink.

"I'm very attracted to you," he said. "And I was tested last month and it's all negative as well."

"Oh," I said. "That's great!"

I sounded like I was congratulating him on getting straight A's.

"So where do you want it?" Ben asked. "Front seat or back?"

I stared.

"I, uh . . ."

Then I saw the smile he was struggling to hide.

"Sorry," he said. "Couldn't help myself."

I let out a breath. Teasing was good.

"Or we could go to my place," he said. "It has a bed."

I glanced toward the rear of the car.

"I don't know," I said. "It looks cozy back there."

Ben unbuckled his seatbelt. "Whatever the lady wants," he said, with a dramatic sigh.

I laughed and put my hand on his arm. "A bed sounds nice," I said.

He looked at where I was touching him. Bare hand to bare arm. Skin to skin. I'd done it without thought, but now I could feel the heat from his skin, and the goose bumps rising on my own.

Ben's eyes met mine. Those fucking eyes. The lust I saw there made me feel like I could lift a car over my head.

I didn't think.

I just kissed him.

His reaction was instantaneous—as if he'd been waiting for it. He cupped my face with his hands and kissed me like he'd been lost at sea for months. Teeth. Tongue. Lips. It was messy and hot and bruising and perfect.

But before things could get really good, Ben pulled away, his forehead pressed against mine.

"I'm starting to rethink the back seat," he said.

"Me too," I said.

We'd already steamed up the windows.

"Can you wait ten minutes?" he asked.

"Can you?"

I gave his lap a meaningful look. He laughed.

"Buckle up," he said.

HE MADE IT TO the rental in seven minutes, his hand on my thigh the entire time.

I kept taking deep breaths, my heart racing, my brain as fogged as the windows had been. This was happening.

We pulled into the driveway, and he pulled me into the house.

I was against the door before I could blink.

He kissed me, and his hands went to my top. I closed my eyes and tried to feel everything. Tried not to think. He felt *so* good. His mouth moved downward to my throat as his fingers made quick work of my shirt. It was unbuttoned halfway down my stomach when I caught my breath.

And unfortunately started thinking again.

"I have to keep my phone nearby," I said. "You know, just in case. I wouldn't want to be unavailable if something happens to Lena or Gabe needs me. I mean, they don't even technically know where I am—I'm sure Gabe thinks I'm just hanging out at his place or reading in the backyard or something, so I just need to make sure that if they have to reach me, they can."

Ben had stopped halfway through my babbling and was leaning back with his hands on my hips, giving me a look that was unnervingly fond, like I reminded him of a lost kitten or something.

"How about a drink?" he asked.

"I'm sorry," I said. "I don't mean to be this way, it's just—"

He held up a hand to stop me. I could see how calloused his fingers were, and I wanted to feel that on my breasts.

"Let me get you some water," he said.

"Okay," I said.

He disappeared in what I assumed to be the direction of the kitchen, while I moved out of the entryway. There was a small living room, and I sank down onto his couch, all my feelings of bravado leaving me. I was now just a spineless, limp bag of well-moisturized skin and freshly blown-out hair.

My shirt was still open to my waist.

I buttoned it up.

Like Gabe, he'd elected to rent a house rather than stay at a hotel, but unlike Gabe's—which had all the signs of a single man living there—there wasn't much to look at in Ben's place.

At least, not much that was *his*.

The place was furnished like the typical Airbnb—minimal white or gray furniture, with Ikea pillows strewn about. There was a *Live, Laugh, Love* decal on the wall by the door, which only made the place feel more impersonal, since it stood out among the lack of additional décor.

The couch was nice, at least. I half wondered if I could just disappear into the cushions. One of the few signs of life in the house was on the coffee table. A mirrored tray with glass jars on the far end—the whole thing looked like it had been lifted out of an Instagram ad—and closest to me was a pile of scripts.

The newest pages for *The Philadelphia Story* were on top, and I lifted them to find a few bound projects with titles like *What Is a Man* and *A Lonely Man All on His Own* and . . .

I froze as I looked at the final script on the bottom of the pile.

Untitled James Bond.

"I probably shouldn't have left that out," Ben said.

I dropped the scripts back into place.

"I didn't see anything," I said.

He came over and handed me a glass of water before sitting down.

"You didn't?" he asked.

"Nope," I said.

We sat there, drinking our water.

I couldn't help myself.

"You're going to be the next James Bond?" I asked.

He grinned. "So much for not seeing anything."

"Sorry," I said. "I'm nosy."

Ben pushed aside the top scripts, revealing the one I'd been looking at. We both stared at it, as if we were expecting it to contribute to the conversation.

"It's not a done deal," Ben said. "But they're interested."

"That's great," I said. "Congrats."

"Thanks."

"Is it a good script?" I asked.

"It's not bad. The money, on the other hand"—he let out a low whistle—"is very, very good."

I was surprised. Looking around his rental—and at him—it didn't seem like Ben was someone who was focused on a big payday.

Then again, I didn't know him.

"I've heard that," I said.

I thought of Gabe. The money had been life-changing. For him. For us.

But it hadn't come without major complications.

He'd gone from someone who looked vaguely familiar to the average person to being mobbed by paparazzi and fans whenever he tried to go out for coffee or groceries.

He'd had a few people follow him into the bathroom.

Once Hollywood turned its spotlight on you, there wasn't much that could be done about privacy. Whether it was worth it I didn't know. I'd never asked my brother.

"They don't care about . . ." I trailed off, not knowing exactly how to ask a question that really wasn't my business to ask.

"Care about what?"

"Nothing," I said. "I was just thinking of the last time they were casting Bond."

I saw him make the connection.

Even though it was common knowledge, Ben hadn't said anything to *me* about his sexuality. It must be weird having strangers know that kind of information about your personal life.

He didn't seem bothered, though.

"As far as I can tell they don't care that I'm bi," Ben said. "They haven't mentioned it."

I didn't say anything.

"It's a different director. Different team. Things have changed since—" Ben paused. "Since the Ollie of it all."

It had taken a while for the whole story to be told, but the role had been offered originally to Ollie, until they realized he didn't intend to stay in the closet. That's how Gabe had gotten the gig. One that plenty of people still thought he hadn't deserved.

"I guess they have," I said.

It hadn't changed much in Cooper. Not outwardly, at least. Unlike the military, we still had a strong, unofficial "don't ask, don't tell" policy in our town. Then again, Gabe always joked that Montana was about five years behind the national average of cultural progress. At least.

Ben might not be sure if he was going to get the role, but I was. He was perfect. More than Gabe had been.

I loved my brother, but he'd been an unexpected—and controversial—choice. Ben wasn't. He had that subtle mix of sophistication and danger, which had been reflected in his past roles.

"How many movies?" I asked.

Gabe had gotten locked into three immediately—and then fired from the last one for, well, lots of reasons. Only some of which I knew he regretted.

"At least two," he said. "Probably four."

"That's a long stretch of work," I said.

"Without a doubt. I'd be on set for the next five or six years of my life," he said. "But it would be worth it."

He stretched his arm out along the back of the couch, close enough that his forearm brushed my neck.

"I'm sure I don't have to tell you that this is all top secret," he said.

"I'm very good at keeping secrets," I said.

He gave me a wicked grin.

"Me too," he said.

I took a drink and let myself sink further into the couch. It felt good. Just like it felt good to have Ben draw gentle, swirling patterns along the curve of my shoulder.

But I was scared. Nervous.

Ben sat there, still and casual, like he'd never even heard of nervousness, let alone experienced it.

I directed my attention to the other item on the table. The tray with a variety of circular glasses that had chrome toppers.

"What's this?"

"A new unisex cologne that wants me as their spokesperson," Ben said. "They sent me their stuff to sample."

"And how is it?" I asked.

Ben put his drink down on the table and pulled the tray closer.

"Want to give it a try?"

I nodded, placing my drink next to his.

"There are four different options," he said. "They're supposed to represent the elements—earth, wind, fire, and water."

I raised an eyebrow, and he shrugged.

"I'm just the messenger," he said.

"Potential messenger," I said.

He smiled at that. "Apparently you can wear them alone or layered together."

We both looked at the tray in front of us.

"Want to try fire?" Ben asked.

I shivered. "Sure," I said.

I reached for the bottles, but he got there first.

"It's an oil-based cologne," he said. "You can drop it directly onto your skin, or onto your fingers to press it into the desired spot."

The top popped off to reveal an elegant glass dropper. I watched as Ben let several drops of the perfume fall onto his fingers.

"May I?" he asked.

It wasn't until he gestured to my hand that I understood. I gave it to him.

"The best place for perfume is on the inside of the wrist." He pressed his fingers to mine, his touch warm as he made gentle circles on the sensitive spot there.

I felt the moisture briefly before it sank into my skin, the scent rising upward. It had a smoky element, like a smoldering campfire on a summer night, with a hint of jasmine.

"It's also good to put some behind the ear," Ben said, using his other hand to push my hair off my shoulder, giving him access to my neck.

I tilted my head, exposing myself to him, as my consent.

He drew a small circle there too, near where my earring dangled. The feel of his fingers—a little rough, warm—against my skin was even more intoxicating than the scent.

"There's one other place where they recommend you put perfume. May I?" he asked.

"Mm–hmm," I said.

This time it was his thumb that he anointed with oil. I closed my eyes, and he pressed it into the hollow of my throat, that circular indent between my clavicles. A spot I never knew could feel so many sensations. I imagined that I could feel the whorl of his thumbprint, each delicate line—that he was leaving his mark along with the perfume.

"They say it smells different in each spot," Ben said.

He lifted my hand, tickling my wrist with the feel of his breath. His inhale was deep, indulgent. Then he moved to my neck, his nose just barely nuzzling the side of my throat. My knees trembled. I leaned even closer toward him, the room hot, the tension thick.

"I think fire suits you," Ben said.

His eyes met mine, lips curled into a seductive, satisfied smile. For a fleeting moment, I wondered how many others he'd seduced in the exact same way.

In the next moment, I realized it didn't matter. I didn't care.

All I needed was him. Right now. Right here.

There was such freedom in that. In caring only about this moment—not the past, not the future. Everything contained in the present.

Ben's gaze dropped down to the third spot where he'd

pressed the perfume. He smiled as he toyed with one of the buttons I'd redone.

"We can go slow," he said.

"Yes," I said.

He lowered his head, his hair brushing against my lips as his mouth all but whispered against my skin. When he reached the spot in question—the dent he'd painted with fire—he inhaled deeply. I let my head fall back, eyes closed.

"Lauren," he said.

The slightest tinge of his accent came through at the end, Lau-ron instead of Lau-ren. I all but fainted from the stimuli—sound, touch, smell.

I was ready for taste again.

He curled a finger under my chin, lifting my face toward his.

Compared to the car and the door, this was the most chaste of kisses and yet it was the one that sent sparks through me. It had been a long time since I'd been kissed like this. With intention, but patience. As if he could kiss me forever.

My palms rested against his chest. His hand moved to my hair.

I leaned into his touch and his mouth kissed down my throat.

Oh.

Oh.

Oh.

I was vibrating with need.

No. Wait.

That was my phone.

It was in my pocket, but it was clear that Ben had felt it from the way he paused.

"Ignore it," I said.

He kissed the side of my neck. I tightened my grip on his shoulders.

My phone went off again.

"I think you might want to get that," Ben said.

He was right.

"She's locked herself in the bathroom," Gabe said. "We're at a museum and she was in there for, like, half an hour, and I started to freak out, so I went in and she's in the stall and she won't come out."

I dropped my head into my hand.

"What? Why?"

I couldn't look at Ben, and yet I could still feel his lips on my skin.

"She got her period?" Gabe's voice was hushed. "I think it's the first time."

Fuck.

Poor kid.

"Okay," I said, guilt filling me up. I didn't know for sure, but it seemed likely, and the not knowing only made the guilt sharper.

"She won't leave," Gabe said. "And the stupid machine here is out of pads *and* tampons and when I asked, all I got was a bunch of weird looks. I'd go get some, but I don't want to leave her alone here and she refuses to leave." He paused, let out a breath. "I'm sorry. Can you come meet us?"

"Of course," I said.

"I hope I didn't ruin your day," he said.

I looked over at Ben, leaning against the couch, looking concerned but otherwise unbothered by the interruption.

I bit back a sigh.

"It's okay," I said. "I'll be there soon."

CHAPTER 9

THEN

WE WERE ALL LONG, TANNED LEGS AND STICKY FINGERS, passing the bag of M&M's between us as the fan whirled aggressively from the foot of the bed.

"Why do they make them different colors if they all taste the same?" Jessica asked, holding a melting candy between her fingers, and squinting at it.

"I'm so bored," I said as a response.

"Me too," she said.

We were also *so* high, the two of us, but lately it didn't give me the same numbness I'd grown to expect—to crave. Instead, more and more it made me feel twitchy, like a windup doll that kept malfunctioning.

I was pretty sure my mom knew exactly what Jessica and I were getting up to in my room these days. She wasn't stupid and the dinky little floor fan didn't do much to clear the air. But she never said anything.

"Let's go to the pool," Jessica said.

"Yeah," I said.

But we didn't move. That was the summer routine. Jessica came over, we got high, ate shitty candy until our teeth ached, complained that we were bored, ignored each other's suggestions of ways to alleviate said boredom, and eventually parted around dinnertime.

We were halfway into July.

"We should go to the movies," I said.

"Yeah," Jessica said.

She flipped over onto her stomach and groaned.

"I feel sick," she said.

"Yeah," I said.

"I have to pee," she said.

"Yeah," I said.

The bed shifted as she got up. I stared into the fan. I might have fallen asleep, or just totally zoned out, but when I came back to reality, the sun was starting to set, and Jessica still hadn't returned.

I went searching for her, catching the sound of her laugh as I descended the stairs. She wasn't in the kitchen or the living room.

"Hey," she said as I came down into the basement.

I never went into the basement.

Us Parkers kept to ourselves these days. During the day, I took the top floor, my mom took the ground floor, and Gabe hid out in the basement with Spencer, who had re-integrated into our lives. They'd dusted off Gabe's old games and set them back up on the TV that I could sometimes hear them smacking on the side to get it to work.

Occasionally we'd run into one another in the kitchen or the bathroom, but for the most part we were three people living three different lives.

Jessica was sitting on the couch between Gabe and Spencer playing some sort of game that involved a lot of clackety buttons and two people hitting each other on-screen until blood spurted out and one of them died. Or something.

I could tell from the expression on Gabe's face that he was not pleased about this new development.

Spencer was neutral as always. I wasn't sure the last time I'd seen him express any kind of emotion—maybe Dad's funeral, when he'd been silently crying next to his wailing mother. He reminded me sometimes of my grandmother's dog, Nugget, who we suspected had been dropped on his head a few times as a puppy and was mostly content to sit in his bed in the kitchen staring at everyone with a blank look in his eyes. Not unhappy, but not happy either. Just . . . there.

"Hey," Jessica said when she noticed me standing at the bottom of the basement stairs.

"Hey," I said, but what I really meant was "What are you doing down here?"

"This is fun," she said, pointing at the screen.

Her eyes were red, pupils dilated.

"Yeah?" I asked, not actually caring.

Jessica was lost in the game.

Gabe shot me a glare. Spencer said nothing. Did nothing.

"He's cute," Jessica said, when I finally managed to drag her away and we were walking back to her house, the summer night cooling around us, the smell of lilacs in the air.

I turned up my lip.

"Gross," I said. "That's my brother."

"Not Gabe," she said. "Though, he is kind of cute too."

"Spencer?" I asked. "Really?"

Jessica blushed a little at that. "He *is,*" she said.

"Okay," I said.

I didn't really see it, but then again, I hadn't really been looking. Why would I, when there were older, cuter, more experienced guys around? *That's* what I was interested in. I didn't need a guy who was "cute." I needed a guy who was hot. Who made me feel all squirmy and excited and eager.

"He's nice too," Jessica said.

Another thing I didn't care about. *Nice* was meaningless.

"Okay," I said.

Jessica shrugged. "I mean, he's no Mikey Garrison."

Now we were talking.

"No, he's not," I said.

Mikey was on the baseball team. He was tall and broad and looked really squeezable in those tight white pants. He was lifeguarding that summer, and looked just as good in his red shorts.

And I was more than ready to leave little-kid things behind in the basement.

CHAPTER 10

NOW

I ARRIVED AT THE MUSEUM WITH PADS, TAMPONS, AN extra set of pants, and underwear. Ben dropped me off out front and I watched him drive away.

I was a weird combination of disappointed and relieved. The further away I got from the situation on the couch, the more I realized how insane the whole thing would have been. How reckless. Wild.

I hadn't been that person in a long time.

I power walked to the museum bathroom, bag in one hand, the other tracing my lips. As if I could hold the feeling of his mouth on my skin forever. As if he'd left a mark.

Lena's discomfort, which quickly morphed into anger, was all-consuming, so even if I wanted to think about Ben, it was Lena and that keen sting of embarrassment that was now fixed at the center of my attention.

It was better that way.

———

"HEY." I CAME INTO the guest room where she was lying on the bed on her stomach, looking at her phone.

She'd barely said a full sentence since snatching the bag of sanitary products and pants from under the bathroom door. When she came out, her jeans crumpled in the plastic CVS bag, she didn't look at me or Gabe. Her eyes were red, her jaw set.

It was like looking at a portrait of myself, age ten through eighteen.

We'd come back to Gabe's rental, where she'd immediately gone into the shower and stayed there until the bathroom resembled a rainforest in summer.

"How are you feeling?" I asked.

She was wrapped in a big, fluffy robe that Gabe had clearly stolen from some fancy hotel. It was comically large on her, which only made her seem younger.

Like a little me, and not like me at all.

I hadn't even realized how quickly time was moving.

Like a spinning ballerina, I'd been keeping my eyes on one fixed point while the rest of my life blurred around me. I didn't think about the things that would change. The things that had to change.

Still no response from Lena, who was doing her best to act like I wasn't there, even though the stiffness of her shoulders and the way she wasn't even pretending to swipe through stuff on her phone indicated she was painfully aware of my presence.

"How does your stomach feel?" I asked.

I tried to remember what it had been like the first time I'd gotten my period, but I honestly couldn't. Like losing my virginity, it had been unremarkable. Unmemorable. All these supposedly life-changing events—forgotten. Or maybe it was that society tended to put more value on the way a woman's body changed versus anything else about them.

But if it was something that could be forgotten, then maybe Lena would forget all of this too.

Then again, I was pretty sure I hadn't gotten my first period in the middle of a museum trip with my famous uncle during a visit to his film set.

"Do you have cramps?" I asked.

The look Lena gave me was of such disdain that it nearly gave *me* cramps.

"I'm. Fine," she said.

"If you need anything . . ."

She turned her head—her entire body—away from me. I could take a hint. She didn't need *anything* from me.

"How is she?" Gabe asked when I came out of the room.

He looked so concerned.

I wanted to tell him that this was the unfortunate reality of being a person with a uterus—pain and blood and humiliation—every month now. That this was hardly the worst thing my daughter's body—and the society witnessing it—would inflict upon her.

That life would just continue to get harder and harder.

"She'll be fine," I said, even as I shuddered internally. "Eventually. I give it twenty years or so."

Gabe sat down on the couch and put his head in his hands.

"I'm sorry," he said.

"Stop it," I said. "You didn't do anything."

"Exactly," he said. "I just fucking froze. I couldn't even handle it by myself—I had to call you and have you fix the problem."

"It's honestly okay that you didn't know what to do in this situation," I said.

He looked at me with those big, sad actor eyes of his. Somewhere in the distance, Sarah McLachlan was singing.

"I'm starting to worry that I don't know what to do in any situation," he said. "That when it comes to a moment of crisis, I just . . ." He waved his hands. "I just can't get it together."

I knew this was about more than just today.

Then again, "I just can't get it together" could have been the Parker family motto at this point.

"You can't even trust me to take Lena for an afternoon. What kind of person can't watch their niece for an afternoon?"

"These were unusual circumstances," I said. "And you did exactly the right thing."

He snorted. "Yeah, called an adult."

"You're an adult," I said.

He looked at me. "I'm pathetic. Forty years old and what?"

"And what?" I rolled my eyes. "You're a fucking movie star, Gabe."

"Failed movie star."

The pity party was getting to be a little too much. Besides, he wasn't the biggest fuckup in the room. That was me.

"You're doing great. You're doing your best."

He sighed. "Yeah," he said. "But what if that isn't good enough?"

I was pretty sure this had to do with his sobriety, but maybe something more.

"It's good enough for me," I said.

It wasn't the answer Gabe was looking for, but he didn't say any more and leaned his head back against the couch cushions.

"Did I totally ruin your day?" he asked. "What were you doing when I called?"

"Uh," I said. "Nothing much. Don't worry about it."

My neck tingled.

I gave myself a little shake. *Move on, Parker.*

"Up until the . . . incident . . . how was the museum?" I asked.

"Good," Gabe said. "I think. I don't know. She wasn't really speaking to me."

"Join the club," I said.

There had been a time when she couldn't get enough of him. Whenever he'd visit, she'd demand a hug and then would hang there, refusing to let go. Gabe would play along, hands on his hips, pretending she wasn't doing an impression of an oversize necktie while he asked everyone around him if they knew where Lena was. She'd giggle the whole time, squealing with joy when he finally "realized" she was there.

And when she'd been really little, she'd all but lived in my lap. Couldn't get close enough. Head against my chest, fingers playing with my hair or my necklace or earrings. Just constantly touching, exploring.

I'd known back then that those times were precious and fleeting. It's what they warned all moms. I just hadn't realized that when she outgrew that need, she'd also move completely out of arm's reach. That when she stopped wanting it—stopped needing it—that was the time when I would miss it the most.

"I hate it," Gabe said.

"Yeah, me too," I said.

Gabe glanced over toward the guest room door, which I'd closed behind me.

"Is she . . . will she . . ." He couldn't seem to put it into words.

"I've been told this won't last forever," I said.

I wasn't naïve enough to think that things would ever go back to the way they were before.

The problem was that I still couldn't help hoping that they would. That fixed point I kept staring at. That lie my heart just couldn't seem to shake.

Stupid, stupid, stupid.

"We're all doing our best," I said.

Hollow words. And was I really? Was I doing my best when it came to Lena?

Gabe nodded, but the guilt on his face mirrored the way I felt. All. The. Fucking. Time.

"Yeah," he said.

I didn't think he believed me. That was fine. I wasn't sure *I* believed me.

We sat there.

"Wanna watch some Star Trek?" he asked.

"Sure," I said.

He'd become obsessed with rewatching old episodes of *Next Generation*. It had been something he and Dad had done together.

It wasn't like I forgot that loss. It wasn't like it hurt any less.

But it was a throbbing bruise, while Spencer's death was a slash across my ribs. Sometimes it felt like I was quietly bleeding out.

We were all just doing our best.

Gabe leaned forward, reaching for the remote. Stopped. Sniffed. Sniffed again.

"Is that a new perfume?" he asked.

Fire suits you, Ben had said.

"Uh," I said. "Yes?"

"It's nice," Gabe said.

"Thanks," I said, even though I was pretty sure whatever fire had sparked that afternoon was dormant once again.

CHAPTER 11

THEN

I'D EXPECTED IT TO HURT. THAT'S WHAT EVERYONE—movies, books, gossip—told me would happen when I had sex for the first time. That there would be a barrier that would tell the guy that I was a virgin, and then he'd have to break through it with some big, intense thrust that would make me cry out. I expected blood and pain. I expected to feel different afterward.

There wasn't and I didn't.

It wasn't much of anything, really. It felt strange, sure, to have someone else's body part inside of me, but I'd used a vibrator before, and it wasn't halfway as nice as that.

Still, I wanted to make Pete feel like he was doing a good job, so I moaned and groaned and dug my nails into his back and said "Yes, oh yes, that's it" even though it really wasn't it at all.

Afterward we lay on his bed, both covered in sweat. His sweat. His skin was flushed, and his hair stuck to his temples, and he looked kind of sweet and cute, his face all relaxed like that. And I thought to myself that even though it hadn't really been good, it hadn't been bad and that meant that it could get better. He had seemed to enjoy himself, at least.

Then he rolled to his side.

"You were kind of loud," he said.

I didn't sleep with him again.

It was bad enough that the experience had been average—at best—but to be criticized for something I was doing to inflate *his* ego?

No thanks, Pete.

I made sure to tell Jessica so she could avoid him too. We shared all our escapades with each other, though I seemed to grade them far more harshly than she did. Even if she didn't come, she always found some excuse for why it hadn't been the guy's fault.

I refused to believe the clitoris was *that* hard to find. *I* could find it. It wasn't the Lost City of Atlantis or the Shroud of Turin. It was right. There.

After Pete, I slept with one of his teammates. Both as a bit of revenge, knowing that he'd hear about it, and also because the gossip on the street was that Matt was actually good at sex.

He should have been my first.

Because he *was* good at sex. Boring as hell before and after, but extremely, extremely good with his hands and his mouth. I didn't have to fake anything with him, and he didn't complain once about how much noise I made.

By senior year, I'd seen quite a few dicks.

Not as many as the fine people of Cooper assumed, but enough to be able to form opinions and make comparisons. They were fascinating, in their own way, something extraordinary about the way they could transform, soft to hard, unobtrusive to centrally featured.

I hadn't seen much of Pete's, both of us rushing toward the finish line without much warm-up. Matt gave me more of a chance to explore. Examine. He was my first blow job, and I discovered that I loved the power it gave me. The next guy, Kyle, was somewhat of a letdown, being that he knew plenty about what *he* wanted, but seemed to think that handling my body was akin to operating heavy machinery and he'd never gotten his license.

I'd had high hopes for Mikey Garrison. He had a big dick. That wasn't so much of a surprise, since his baseball pants were pretty snug, but he seemed to think that just being in possession of a penis of that size made him great in bed.

He wasn't. Barely a four out of ten, and that's if I was being generous.

I didn't realize it until later, but there were some real benefits with a smaller dick.

Because as good as Mikey looked in his tight white baseball pants, he sure as hell didn't know what to do with the equipment he had in there. A lot of loud grunting, sloppy thrusting, and a quick finish.

He'd wanted to do it again, but I'd declined. He'd gotten mad. Called me a slut.

I thought I didn't care.

That's when he started running his mouth.

And I realized how stupid I'd been. Stupid in thinking that I could just go around doing whatever I pleased with my body.

By the time I realized that it was too late.

Jessica was really the canary in the coal mine.

She'd started making herself scarce. There were excuses—she had a test, and then some after-school thing, and then her mom wanted her to go to church. That should have been my first warning that something was different. Because Jessica's mom had *always* wanted her to go to church.

Jessica and I both had daddy issues. We'd joke about it sometimes—that my issue was I didn't have a dad anymore, and hers was that she had two and hated both of them.

Not that I could blame her—I'd met her bio dad once or twice and he more than lived up to the deadbeat dad stereotype, swanning in and out of her life whenever he needed something. Totally aimless. Pathetic.

Her stepdad was the opposite—a former military guy who'd never heard of the concept of leisure, let alone experienced it himself. He was regimented and strict, and both Jessica and I were pretty sure the main reason he'd married her mom was because it guaranteed he'd get three home-cooked meals a day and clean underwear.

At first, Jessica told me he was the reason she was going to church regularly again.

"It's just easier than fighting with him all the time," she said.

I started seeing her less and less. There was a youth group that held meetings on Tuesdays and Thursdays after school. I knew about it because Spencer had been trying anew to get me and Gabe to go with him. He said things were different now—that they would only accuse us of going to hell after they got to know us a little better.

I wondered if Jessica and Spencer sat next to each other

at church. If sometimes she offered to share her prayer book with him or if she "forgot" hers and had to share his.

Now whenever I saw her, it was like watching a photograph fade. All the detail, all the specificity, all the Jessica-ness, seemed to get duller and duller.

She was slipping away, but there wasn't anything I could do about it.

When the rumors started circulating, I knew we were done. Because it was easy to tell where most of the stories were coming from—exaggerations peppered with just enough truth to sell it. Including details that I knew Jessica had taken from her own experiences.

I was the shield, and she wielded it well. It wasn't hard to convince people.

The whole town already knew that I was trouble. First the poker game and now sleeping around. Those poor horny boys—how were they supposed to say no?

No one cared that I was just as horny as them. That it sometimes felt like my entire body was vibrating from the inside out and I just needed to feel something—*someone*—or I was going to start running around town screaming. That I was so lonely and sad and lost and the only things that made that disappear were boys and weed, and even then, it was only a temporary relief.

It didn't matter.

No one judged the guys, of course. No one questioned why Jessica knew all these details. No one remembered how wild we'd been together.

She walked away—born again.

I bore the brunt of it, having to listen to Mikey "slut"-cough under his breath every time I walked by. He cornered me once in the hallway and called me the town bicycle in front of the rest of the baseball team. You would have thought he was Chris Farley from the way they laughed.

"Looking for the next rider?" he asked, thrusting his hips toward his hand.

I knew he expected me to run. To cry. To cower.

I stood my ground. Leaned into one hip, arms crossed as I gave him a slow, unflattering once-over.

"Maybe," I said. "Can you recommend anyone that lasts longer than five seconds?"

There was some choking laughter from the group.

"Fuck you," Mikey said.

"Not if you begged me," I said. "Oh, wait, you did."

His ears turned red at that because he had. But he pretended that I hadn't said anything, turning back to his group of lackeys instead.

"You'll want to double-bag it with this one," he said. "Who knows where she's been."

It shouldn't have hurt. I didn't care what Mikey Garrison and his big, useless penis thought. I didn't care what his friends thought.

But past all of them, I saw Gabe. And Spencer.

They'd heard everything.

I never forgot the look on Spencer's face.

He pitied me.

And that was what hurt the most.

CHAPTER 12

NOW

I WAS STARING AT BEN, AND I WASN'T BEING VERY SUBTLE. Gabe and Lena had left for crafty a few minutes ago—the actress playing Tracy had paid for a fancy local fro-yo truck—so I had a few moments to indulge myself.

I told myself that if I couldn't touch, then I might as well look.

Not that it would be possible to ignore him. For whatever reason, the scene they were shooting required Ben to get in and out of a white-tiled swimming pool multiple times, water sluicing off his movie-ready muscles.

He'd taken off his ring and his necklaces. There were some patches on his skin that looked slightly off-color—his chest, shoulder, side, and arm—and it took me a while to realize that it was makeup, probably to cover up tattoos.

"See something you like?"

I jumped. I hadn't even heard Ollie approach. He dropped into the chair next to mine, and I pretended I hadn't been ogling one of his actors.

"Shouldn't you be directing?" I asked.

He waved a hand. "Lindsay's got it," he said.

Lindsay was the assistant director, and from the look of it, she did seem to have it all under control.

"She's my retirement plan," Ollie said. "I expect her to take over Hollywood in the next five or so years, after which I will be shamelessly leveraging any gratitude, guilt, or sense of obligation that I've accrued during this time."

"Sounds foolproof," I said.

"I know how to spot talent," he said.

My gaze had wandered back to Ben, and vice versa. The smile he sent my way was so hot it could have given me a sunburn.

"Lauren," Ollie said.

"Hmmm?"

"Eye fuck each other any harder and you're going to get the entire crew pregnant."

I smacked Ollie in the arm to distract from the blush I felt creeping up my face. Busted. I still tried to play it off.

"You cast him for a reason," I said. "He's attractive."

"He certainly is," Ollie said.

"I'm just imagining that I'm your audience," I said.

"Oh, is *that* what you're imagining?"

He winked and I let out a sigh of acceptance.

"Okay, he's gorgeous and I'm very attracted to him."

Ollie's grin only grew wider.

"But it's nothing," I said.

"Oh, sure," Ollie said. "Nothing."

"I'm leaving tomorrow," I said. "It's nothing."

"Hmmm."

"What?"

Ollie shrugged. "I just remember hearing a few rumors about a younger, braver Lauren."

"Gabe gossips like a housewife," I said.

Ollie looked like he was going to say something else, but before he could, we were joined by Lena and Gabe, both armed with fro-yo.

"Got you a swirl," Gabe said, handing me one.

"And for me?" Ollie asked.

Gabe gave him a look. "Shouldn't you be directing?"

I lifted a hand, all *what did I just say?*

"I assure you both that I know how to run a film set," Ollie said, standing. "And this is why Lena is my favorite Parker."

Lena didn't exactly beam at the compliment, but the corners of her mouth lifted slightly, which was basically the same thing.

"I was thinking . . ." Ollie said.

I noticed he'd positioned himself between me and Ben. As if I was incapable of containing my lusty stares in the presence of my brother and child.

Then again, I could vaguely see a PA dumping a bucket of water over Ben's head and was grateful that I didn't have a full view of the way Ben's swim trunks clung to his hips and thighs and . . .

"What do you think, Lauren?" Gabe nudged me.

I hadn't even heard the question. I was truly pathetic.

"Sounds great," I said.

"Great," Gabe said.

"We can go out to dinner afterward," Ollie said. "A nice, *long* dinner."

"Is there any other kind with you?" Gabe asked.

Ollie ignored him. "Why don't you find a nice place for us to go, Lena?" he suggested. "Expensive. Exclusive. I'm sure your uncle would be happy to treat us to a five-course something."

The gleam in Lena's eyes told me that she was going to do everything she could to make a significant dent in Gabe's credit card. With her phone out, she headed toward video village.

"No seafood platters!" Gabe called out, before shooting Ollie a look. "Bastard."

"You're a movie star, love," Ollie said with a wave of his hand. "You can afford it."

Gabe scowled and followed Lena.

"Dinner?" I asked, wondering if that was all I'd agreed to.

"I invited you all to watch some dailies," Ollie said. "It's not always the best idea to show your actors uncut footage, but I thought it would be nice for Lena to see some of the process."

We both looked over at my daughter and my brother, who were now standing next to each other. I hadn't realized how similar their body language was until I saw them with their arms crossed, each leaning on one leg, their hips at almost the exact same angle.

"She's a great kid," Ollie said.

It made my heart warm to know that other people could see past Lena's tough exterior to the soft interior. And Ollie had been around long enough to know exactly why she'd had to develop such a thick skin.

"I hope she's having fun," I said.

"I think she is," Ollie said. "She's been nothing but an angel to me."

"It's the accent," I said.

He threw back his head and laughed.

"You Americans," he said. "All someone has to do is roll their R's or silence their H's and you go weak in the knees."

"You're not wrong."

"Ben's got a lovely accent," Ollie said, without a drop of subtlety. "Hard to top that growly, sexy Irish lilt."

I didn't take the bait—instead deliberately *not* looking toward the set. Ollie had made his point.

"And yet, you made him get rid of it for the movie," I said.

"Of course." Ollie winked at me. "I had to give Gabe a fighting chance against him."

I laughed.

"He's a good man," Ollie said.

"Gabe? Yeah, he's all right."

"I was talking about Ben."

I looked at him. He was meddling.

It was a bad idea.

The last thing I needed was someone else's approval about the whole Ben thing. Which was nothing. Because I *was* leaving tomorrow.

"I'm sure he's lovely," I said. "Despite his reputation."

Ollie laughed. "Gabe told you? Now that's the pot calling the kettle black."

I rolled my eyes.

"I know all about how popular and charming and *dangerous* Ben is," I said. "And good for him."

"Good for all of us," Ollie said. "He's going to be a massive star."

"I have no doubt."

I thought about James Bond. Massive was probably an understatement.

"I'm quite certain this movie will get him a lot of attention," Ollie said. "His life is going to be different after this."

"Probably very chaotic and busy," I said.

"Things do change very quickly."

He was being annoyingly vague and pointed at the same time.

"If you're trying to say something, just say it."

"I promised myself that I wouldn't meddle in the love lives of others."

I snorted at that. "Since when?"

"Last night," he said. "But I've decided to make an exception."

Ollie looked at Gabe and Lena.

"I'll be showing them footage for about an hour and then, of course, dinner," he said. "You are more than welcome to come. Or . . ." His gaze shifted to Ben. "Or I could tell them that you felt like heading back to the rental."

I didn't understand.

"Do I *want* to go back to the rental?"

Ollie shrugged. "You could. Or you could find something *else* to do for a few hours. If you felt like being brave."

It took me a moment, but then realization sunk in, and I turned to find Ollie wearing an impish grin.

"Oliver Matthias," I said. "Are you trying to *dare* me into a one-night stand?"

His expression didn't change as he examined his nails.

"I'm merely making a suggestion," he said.

"Sure," I said.

He leaned over and gave me a kiss on the cheek before getting up.

"I would just hate for you to miss an opportunity to have a good time," he said. "Or, if that reputation of his is true, several good times in succession."

My entire body went hot. Ben did look like he could provide exactly that. Probably just through extended eye contact, and maybe a few words murmured in that famed accent of his.

The way he'd kissed me . . .

"You can see the movie when it hits theaters," Ollie said.

I hadn't thought I'd get another chance, and here was one being handed to me on a silver platter. This time, when I looked over at Ben, he glanced back, and our eyes caught. The spark caught too.

I couldn't look away. And it didn't seem like Ben could either. He grinned at me.

"He'll be done in about twenty," Ollie said. "His trailer is the one at the end of the second row."

"Great," I said.

"Have fun," Ollie said, and I could hear him laughing as he walked away.

CHAPTER 13

THEN

"I DON'T THINK IT'S A GOOD IDEA," GABE SAID.

He was standing in the doorway of my bedroom—outside the threshold, because he wasn't stupid—rocking back and forth on his ratty old sneakers.

He was always outgrowing his shoes these days.

"I don't know what you're talking about," I said.

I knew what he was talking about.

Gabe made that tooth-sucking sound that I should have found extremely annoying, but it was something our dad had done. It gave me that hurt-nostalgic feeling, like for this tiny, brief moment Dad was there and real and familiar and wonderful.

But he wasn't. He was dead. Had been for years now. All the people who told me that I would get over it, or that things happened for a reason, or that time would heal this deep, endless gaping hole inside of me were total fucking liars.

"Go away," I said.

"Not until you promise to leave Spencer alone."

I laughed at him. "Fuck off," I said, and spun my desk chair away from him.

If we were younger, Gabe would have stomped his foot. He would have stuck out his bottom lip, his entire face contorting into an obscenely exaggerated expression of sadness, and then he might have even started crying.

But we were teenagers now and didn't cry. Didn't pout. Didn't stomp our feet.

"He's my friend," Gabe said.

"He's my friend too," I said, pretending to look at my book.

"Everyone thinks you're going to hurt him," Gabe said.

I turned back. Slowly. Menacingly.

Gabe took a step back.

"*Everyone?*" I asked. "Everyone *who*?"

"You know," he said.

It was kind of sweet, what Gabe was doing. Not for me, of course, but for Spencer. Gabe was trying to protect his best friend. From the town harlot. Who just happened to live across the hall.

"Aren't there other guys?" Gabe asked.

Of course there were. That was the problem. There *had* been other guys. Too many guys. I'd gone beyond the so-cially approved limit of the number of boys a seventeen-year-old girl was allowed to date and now I was expected to just stop. Stop going out. Stop flirting. Stop having fun. And definitely stop having sex.

Life was short. I could be dead tomorrow.

It wasn't my fault that all of a sudden Gabe's annoying friend, who only yesterday had been slurping Yoo-hoo and playing video games, had grown several inches and a whole lot of muscle after spending a summer doing construction.

And had ingratiated himself back into our household just like old times.

Jessica had been right about one thing. Spencer was hot. That wasn't *my* doing.

And sure, I had taken to wearing some really low-rise jeans and "forgetting" to wear my bra whenever he came over—which was often now—but it wasn't as if he hadn't seen me in my swimsuit every summer since we were kids.

I couldn't stop him from looking.

And it wasn't like *I'd* started going to church to get his attention. When I'd heard that Spencer had gently, kindly turned Jessica down after she'd been going to his church for almost six months, I hadn't been proud of the vindication I'd felt.

But we weren't friends anymore.

Jessica abandoned me for Spencer. And god. Unfortunately, only one of them was interested in return.

That was fine. It wasn't like I had anything to say to her. Unless it was "told you so."

"Just stay away from him, okay?" Gabe asked.

I rolled my eyes at him.

It wasn't my fault that the other night, when I'd been alone in the kitchen, Spencer had come up from the basement, where the guys were playing video games or watching porn or whatever. It wasn't my fault that it had been hot, and I'd been standing in front of the fridge in a thin white T-shirt trying to cool off. And it definitely hadn't been my fault that Spencer had smelled like grass and clean hair, or that his arm had brushed my side when he reached past me to get a can of pop.

If anything, I was just an innocent bystander.

But still.

Nothing had happened.

Nothing besides a few more accidental bumps and brushes against each other.

And it wasn't like there'd be anything more than that. Spencer was the Good Churchgoing Boy. I was the dangerous man-eating succubus slut.

It would never happen.

"Go away," I told Gabe. "I mean it."

"But—"

"*Now*," I said.

I was gratified that he jumped before scurrying off. It made me feel powerful and in control. Which was a lot better than feeling like the entire world—my brother included—thought I was the biggest slut that ever slutted.

CHAPTER 14

NOW

I STOOD OUTSIDE OF THE TRAILER DOOR—THE ONE with Ben's name on it—with that free-fall feeling in my stomach, though it was mixed with a little queasiness, like I'd eaten too much funnel cake. My hands were clammy. My armpits damp. I felt nervous and anxious and not especially sexy, but then I thought about the way Ben had been looking at me.

I thought about how I likely wouldn't get another chance.

I thought about what I wanted.

I knocked—a quick one, two, three—and waited.

When the door swung open, there he was, smiling down at me. His hair was wet. His eyes were . . . everything.

"Hello," he said.

"Hi," I said.

He extended a hand toward me, and I took it, allowing myself to be pulled up the steep steps to the trailer.

He shut the door behind me, leaning back on it. He was wearing the same shirt he'd worn to pick me up the other day—or another identical one—and a pair of sweatpants. All black. His feet were bare.

The makeup was gone, and I could see a tattoo on his arm—it looked like . . .

"Is that a harp?" I asked.

He pushed his sleeve up to reveal the whole thing.

"Symbol of Irish independence," he said. "All changed, changed utterly: A terrible beauty is born."

I stared.

"That's a quote from Yeats," he said. "Fran's favorite."

Of course. He was just reciting poetry. Who was this man?

And who was Fran?

I wanted to know, but also, did I?

Instead, I moved closer to him, lifting a curious hand. He angled his shoulder toward me, allowing me to touch.

"It's beautiful," I said, tracing the strings of the instrument.

"Do you have any?" Ben asked.

I shook my head. "I don't like needles," I said.

"It's not so bad," he said.

"That's what everyone says. And they're always wrong."

Ben rolled down his sleeve.

"I've been told it's nothing compared to childbirth."

I laughed. "Still not selling me on it."

Ben smiled, and I turned away, looking at his space.

I'd visited Gabe on various sets and was able to witness how his trailers got progressively larger and fancier as his name moved higher up on the call sheet. When we'd gone to see his current one it was decked out with all sorts of creature comforts—mostly comforts for the actual creature who accompanied him. But Teddy's items notwithstanding, Gabe's trailer felt like *his,* the way his rental house felt like his.

Likewise, Ben's trailer felt like his rental.

It was a decent size, but it seemed even larger because it was so empty. It was extremely clean and very sparse. The only sign of life was the various photos tacked up along the kitchen cabinets and fridge.

I took a tour while Ben stood aside, leaning against the wall, patient and gorgeous.

There was a photo of him in what looked like a parachute or skydiving gear, standing on the ground, hair windblown, grin as big as the sky. Another of him in the passenger seat of a race car, throwing the camera a thumbs-up. And, like a true Hawaiian, there was a picture of him on the beach, wet suit unzipped to his waist, standing next to a surfboard and three other surfers.

They were all in focus, with perfect lighting and depth of field. iPhone photos.

Then there was the sprinkling of older photos on the fridge—ones that were blurry with a distant, waterlogged look—mostly of a young woman with long black hair. She had Ben's smile. From her clothes and general style, it was clear most were from before Ben—and I—were even born. There was one of her in a wedding dress, a simple courthouse-style sheath where the slightest curve of her belly was visible. There was a hand on her shoulder, but the picture had been ripped in half, so the hand belonged to no one.

Beneath it was the same woman holding a baby. Ben.

He was crying, but she looked happy, her arms wrapped around him, keeping him close to her chest like she was afraid he might fall from her grip.

My hand reached out toward that one, but Ben cleared his throat before I could connect with the shiny surface.

I jerked back.

"Can I get you something?" he asked. "Water?"

I shook my head and took the hint, stepping away from the photos. Away from the kitchenette.

I directed my attention elsewhere.

On the table was a bike helmet, next to a large wrench.

I looked at it and then at him, eyebrow raised.

He picked up the wrench, testing the weight in his hand, as if he'd forgotten.

"The shower was leaky," he said.

"Aren't you supposed to call someone about that?"

He shrugged. "Just needed to borrow some tools," he said. "Now I have to remember to give this back to Amira tomorrow."

I didn't think he could be more attractive to me, but between quoting Yeats and admitting he was handy around the house, I could barely keep my head above the rising desire I felt. Then I added the memory of him on set today—water sliding down his neck, his chest, his stomach . . .

I went under.

"I don't know why you're giving me that look," Ben said. "But let me tell you, I like it."

"Just thinking about some things," I said.

"Oh yeah?" He came over and put his hands on my hips. I loved the way his palms felt—warm and sturdy. "Anything you'd like to share with the class?"

I looked up at him. He twinkled down at me.

"Just how good you look when you're all wet," I said.

It seemed I had only two speeds with Ben. Uncontrollable babbling or aggressive come-ons. The latter was much better for the task at hand.

His hands slid upward, notching into the curve of my body just below my breasts. His thumbs came around to stroke my ribs, which was not a spot I'd thought of as sensitive. But it seemed that Ben knew exactly where I needed to be touched.

"That's funny," he said. "Because I was just wondering how quickly I could make *you* all wet."

My breath left me. His eyes were right there, and they were so intense. So beautiful. Focused.

I leaned toward him so I could whisper in his ear.

"Let's find out," I said.

He turned his head, his lips meeting mine.

It was as if the time between now and our last kiss had been nothing more than a tick of the clock. I melted into him, and his arms were around me, corseting my torso with heat.

My purse—and my phone—were somewhere out of reach.

I told myself it was okay. That I could have this moment. That I could disappear into my own needs—into myself—for a little while. That I was allowed it.

I was so focused on his kiss that I hadn't even noticed him walking backward. I let out a muffled squeak against his lips as I was pulled down, straddling his lap as he leaned back against the kitchenette bench.

I sent a word of thanks to my earlier self who had decided to wear a dress as I sunk down onto his lap. I also spared some praise for whoever was the inventor of sweatpants. They had just become my favorite type of pants.

Ben let out a groan, his mouth against my throat. I slid my hands over his shoulders, tracing the tattoo once more before I reached for the hem of his shirt.

He had another tattoo on his pec. This one was far simpler—a clean-lined heart with *Mom* in the center. I traced it.

I saw goose bumps rise on his skin.

"I got it when I was thirteen," he said. "Forged my mom's signature."

"Was she mad when she found out?"

"She cried; she loved it so much."

I wanted to know more, but Ben stopped any further questions I might have had with a kiss. His mouth was hot and wet, the kiss sloppy but in the best way, his hands moving upward.

I stopped thinking about anything but what his reaction would be once he reached the top of my thighs.

He went completely still, and then lifted his head, eyes gleaming.

"Lauren, Lauren, Lauren," he said, almost like a song in his accent. "How long have you been walking around without your pants?"

I'd slipped off my underwear before coming to the trailer, but I wasn't going to tell him that. Let him believe I was the kind of woman who went around bare-assed.

I wanted him to touch me between my thighs, but his hands went back around my hips instead, fingers digging into my ass as he pulled me forward. I choked back a gasp as his cock slid along me right where I needed it.

With my hands on his shoulders, I repeated the movement, this time his hips thrusting up to meet me.

"Fucking hell," he said, fingers now fumbling with the buttons on my dress.

The bra was the prettiest one I owned. I don't know what had inspired me to bring it to Philadelphia, but I thanked my lucky stars that I had. The black lace cupped me perfectly, my cleavage just about to spill over.

Ben stared at my breasts like he'd been given a gift.

I liked that look.

"I've been thinking about these gorgeous tits all week," he said, pressing his mouth between them.

I sighed.

"I kept imagining how you'd sound when I touched you," Ben said, voice in my ear, hips rocking against mine. "How you'd feel against my cock."

I couldn't speak, I could only moan.

"I want to taste you," he said. "Here." His hand coming around to the side of my breast, his thumb stroking me there.

"Yes," I said.

"And here," he said, his fingers going lower, and I lifted my hips up so he could cup me, fingers thick and warm and perfect.

Beneath my palm, I could feel the thrum of his heartbeat.

"God, you're beautiful," Ben murmured.

The look in his eyes was almost like reverence. I held his face and kissed him, my hair falling down around us, Ben's fingers fumbling with the clasp of my bra. I felt it unhook, then Ben's hands smoothed up over my shoulders and pushed the remaining fabric away.

He lifted my breasts together so he could bury his face in the valley there.

"I love the way you smell," he said. "Like cinnamon. Butter. Sugar."

I felt him take a breath, his chest expanding beneath my hands.

He ran a tongue across my cleavage. "Delicious."

I pulled his mouth up to mine.

He hummed, sliding a finger inside of me. I untied the drawstring of his pants, reaching in so I could stroke him. His eyes closed, head back.

I wanted this so badly. Wanted to feel. To forget.

"It seems like you spend a lot of time on your bike," I murmured against his lips.

If he was surprised by the non sequitur, he didn't look it.

I felt wild and free and out of control. That bravado overloaded every sane thought in my head. I was stupid with lust.

I didn't care about anything but this.

I freed his cock and positioned myself above it.

"But I'm about to give you the ride of your life."

CHAPTER 15

THEN

WITH FINALS APPROACHING, SPENCER WAS BACK TO his once-common routine of coming to our house every day after school. Only, this time it was him and me walking back, sitting at the kitchen counter, heads bent together studying for math tests. It wasn't until we'd been doing it for a few weeks that I even bothered to ask where Gabe was.

"Practice," Spencer said.

"For what?"

"He joined the football team," he said.

Spencer hadn't been the only one to fill out. Gabe had grown several inches and packed on enough muscle that the football coach had stopped him in the hallway and asked him to try out. Apparently, he'd been on the team for months.

"Huh," I said.

I wondered if Mom knew.

She'd probably be thrilled. A football star in the family.

"He's not that good," Spencer said. "But he doesn't really have to be."

True. Central wasn't really known for its football team. As much as I hated to admit it, Mikey was the school's star athlete—and everyone talked about how he was probably going to go to the minors and then, of course, he'd be in the majors. Because everything always went right for Mikey Garrison.

He and Jessica were engaged. Or pre-engaged. Or something. All I knew was that he'd given her a ring and she waved it around wherever she went. Once in the bathroom, I overheard her calling it a "promise ring," saying it represented her and Mikey's decision to stay "pure" before marriage, and I had to put my entire fist in my mouth to keep from laughing.

"Do you want to go over last week's pop quiz?" Spencer asked.

"No," I said.

"Great," he said, and pushed my test toward me.

He'd marked it up even more extensively than our teacher had, only his corrections weren't in *failure* red, and they actually explained what I'd done wrong.

"I'm not going to pass," I said.

"Yes, you are," he said, his attention focused on the work in front of him.

His knee pressed up against mine as we sat perched on stools, leaning over the counter. We each had our own textbook, but for whatever reason, I could never remember to bring mine down from my room, so we always leaned over the same copy when we worked. Our foreheads were close enough to touch.

If I wanted to.

But I'd sworn off guys. Swapped them out for other activities. Ones that wouldn't get me into trouble. Baking. Knitting.

Anything to keep my hands occupied.

I'd made a dozen scarves. Perfected my brownie mix. Baked more cookies than I could count. Masturbated until my clitoris was numb.

Until I was numb.

I was fine. Totally fine.

I didn't care—or even notice—how strong Spencer's thigh felt against mine. His hand, drumming along the side of the textbook, that wide, square palm and those impeccably tidy nails. Or the way his eyes kept dropping to my mouth. And then to my boobs. Or the way he smelled, which was all fresh and lemony and just so damn good.

I really didn't notice his hair. How it was long enough to brush against the collar of his shirt and looked so soft and touchable that I thought about it alone in my room at night, imagining my fingers threaded through it and my nose buried atop his head, just inhaling him.

I certainly wasn't indulging in that fantasy now. I wasn't imagining sliding my arms around his neck and lifting myself into his lap before bringing his mouth to mine.

He was probably a terrible kisser.

Definitely.

I didn't care.

"You're staring," Spencer said.

I was. This time *I* was the one staring at *his* mouth.

I flipped my hair back. "Yeah, so what?" I challenged,

standing up and pushing back from the counter. From the fridge, I got a can of pop. Opened it. Drank.

Watching him the entire time. And he watched me.

"I'm not afraid of you," he said, a small quirk to his lips.

I put my arm around his shoulder like I'd imagined doing. Leaned close enough that my mouth touched his ear. That his hair brushed against my lips. Soft. So fucking soft.

"You should be," I whispered.

He shivered, but instead of pulling away, he turned.

Just turned his entire body toward me, trapping himself between me and the counter. Standing up, we were about the same height, so with him sitting, I towered over him. In control.

"Lauren," Spencer said.

He put his hands on my hips.

"What are you doing?" I asked.

"You know what I'm doing," he said.

"Yeah, well," I said, pretending bravery even though my throat was dry. "If you're making a move, you're going to have to try a little harder than that."

"Yeah?"

"Yeah."

I tried to move back, just a little, but he held me there. It felt good, the way his hands came around my hips, meeting at the base of my spine. His palms were warm. His breath was on my chin.

"I like you," he said.

The sincerity in his eyes unnerved me.

"You like everyone," I said.

He shook his head. "Not like this."

Those hands of his pulled me closer. I went willingly and my arms did go around his neck. My fingers into his hair. He let out a soft sigh and pressed his cheek against my jaw. It was more intimate than half the things I'd done with other guys.

"Spencer . . ." I tried, but he lifted his head to look at me again.

And instead of using my lips to voice the rejection I knew I should give him, I used that mouth of mine to kiss him.

He had no idea what he was doing. That was immediately clear. His mouth was hard and eager on mine, but when I put my hands on his face, giving just a little pressure, he reacted immediately and softened his touch. His kiss.

I opened my mouth for him, and when our tongues touched, I felt electricity like I'd never experienced before. In that moment, kissing Spencer against our kitchen counter, teaching him how I needed to be touched, having him respond in kind, I realized that I felt good for the first time in a long time. That I was okay.

And more than that, I felt safe.

CHAPTER 16

NOW

"YOU SCARE ME SOMETIMES," ALLYSON SAID, LOOKING at my shelves.

I ignored her, unfolding the dress she'd brought me. Not that it mattered, she didn't need a response to keep going.

"This is the sign of someone in emotional peril," she said.

"Do you want pockets or not?" I asked, examining the side seams.

"It's color coded," she said.

"I like being organized," I said.

"There's being organized and then there's this." Allyson waved a hand at my craft wall.

She might have had a point. The whole thing was Pinterest-perfect, every box labeled (including the one with the label maker in it) with everything in its right place. It wasn't that I cared that much about organization. It was just that sometimes, when I couldn't sleep at night, I'd come down to the basement and find ways to keep myself busy. Distracted.

There were lots of nights I couldn't sleep.

The bed was just too empty. I missed Spencer's snoring, and the way he'd sometimes mumbled when he dreamed. How he'd sleep through thunderstorms but always woke up the second Lena cried as a baby.

I'd come downstairs, bleary and cotton-mouthed, to find him bouncing her around in the kitchen, singing made-up songs to her.

Now, every time I came downstairs in the middle of the night, there was no one there. Organizing was an escape. If I couldn't figure out anything else in my life, at least I knew where the glue gun was. And the Bundt pans. And the duster thing we used to clean off the top of the fans.

"Please tell me you haven't sorted your buttons by size," Allyson said, answering herself as she pulled open a drawer labeled *buttons*. "Oh my god. It's sorted by color as well."

I'd done that around midnight a week or so ago. There was something extremely satisfying about the sound that buttons made when they were dropped into their proper place. How it felt to slide your hand through a box of them, lifting and letting them fall through your fingers. Not that I was going to tell Allyson that. I didn't need to provide any more kindling for this fire.

Maybe she was right to be worried, but we didn't have time for that now.

"I thought you were going to pick some fabric," I said. "It's over there."

"I know," Allyson said, finally making her way to the other side of the wall. "It's very clearly labeled."

She pulled out a box labeled *fabric scraps for pockets* and let out a dramatic gasp. I knew what she was looking at. A jumble of fabric pieces without any discernible organization.

"Shut up," I said. "I haven't gotten around to that one."

"There's hope for you yet," she said.

I rolled my eyes. "Just pick some fabric," I said.

As she dug through the bin, I began taking out the side seams on the pretty blue dress she'd found at the charity council shop last week.

"Here." Allyson put down two different plaid pieces. "How about this?"

"Mismatched pockets," I said. "How daring."

"You know me," she said. "I love making a statement. Quietly. Invisibly."

I could have easily done the pockets with plain muslin, but there was always something about having a little secret tucked into your clothes.

"Lay your hand here," I said.

I'd folded each piece of fabric and stacked them on top of each other. Pockets like these weren't too complicated— all you needed was a basic teardrop shape that I could easily eyeball once I had the sizing right.

Allyson's hands were petite, but I gave her some extra room anyway. I couldn't remember a time when I'd wished a pocket was smaller. Once I'd traced the shape with washable ink, I began cutting them out.

"You know the whole lack of pockets thing is because of sexism," Allyson said.

She'd perched herself on the edge of my sewing table.

"I know," I said.

She'd told me this before. Multiple times.

"Pockets are important," she said. "They're a symbol of freedom."

"I know," I said, thinking of Ben's harp tattoo.

"It's like with high heels and wire bras and all that stuff," she said. "All the ways that fashion limits and restricts us."

"I know," I said, thinking of how Ben stared at my tits in my black bra.

"And don't get me started on makeup," Allyson said.

I looked up from the fabric I was pinning to the dress's seams.

"You're wearing lipstick," I reminded her.

"I know!" she said.

I laughed.

Allyson had moved to Cooper about two years ago from the Bay Area. I couldn't imagine why anyone would have willingly left such a place, and as it turned out with Allyson, it wasn't entirely willingly.

"I could actually afford a house here," she'd told me. "Good thing I moved when I did, because you know it's going to be impossible in a few years."

She was only one of many out-of-towners who had come to Montana looking for a cheaper, simpler life. All the while driving up the prices of said life. Luckily, Cooper was still too small of a town for most people.

It wouldn't last, though.

Nothing did.

Allyson wasn't here because she was looking for something.

She was here because of her ex.

"He'd never come to Montana in a thousand years," she'd said. "He'd be lost without Trader Joe's."

I knew all about Trader Joe's—Gabe was also obsessed with it. It seemed like a nice enough store, but we had Costco, which had everything, including but not limited to motor oil and muffins.

Cooper wasn't a big town, but it had everything I needed.

Mostly.

"You need to get out more," Allyson said.

She was once again looking at the wall.

"I just got back from Philadelphia," I reminded her.

"That was months ago," she said.

"It hasn't been months," I said.

She gave me a look.

"Has it?" I asked.

Time seemed to both speed past me and slow down to a painful crawl. It was hard enough for me to remember Lena's schedule, let alone my own. When was the last time I'd gotten a haircut? I had no idea.

Probably before Philadelphia.

Months ago.

Two months. Three?

"Have you heard from him?"

I sighed.

"You could always call him," Allyson said.

She didn't have to clarify who she was talking about.

I'd been surprised when Ben texted me. The sex had been incredible, but based on Gabe's and Ollie's comments, I'd assumed that was part and parcel for Ben. That he did what most men in his situation would do—fuck and fuck off.

Instead, he'd sent flirty, sexy texts. Little reminders of what we'd done in his trailer in Philadelphia. Comments about how much he missed my "magnificent tits" and "gorgeous arse." I'd responded in kind, shocking myself a little with the way I talked about his cock—"perfect" and "talented" had been some of the descriptors.

He praised me for my "fuckable mouth."

I'd been surprised by how much I'd liked hearing that. How much *his* mouth turned me on. New things were being learned.

Maybe I *had* delivered on the promise of being the best ride of his life.

One day, he changed it up and instead of asking what I was wearing, he asked what it was like in Montana at that exact moment. I'd taken a picture of the snow from the window at the front of the store and sent it to him.

He never sent me pictures of where he was, but then again, I never asked. I let him take the lead, figuring that this was all temporary, that he was just bored during breaks or projects or whatever he was doing now. That eventually he'd stop texting. That eventually this whole thing would fade into a really, really wonderful memory that could keep me warm in the winter of my years.

He always wanted to know what was happening in Cooper. He'd text: *If I was visiting, what would we do?*

I told him about the fair that still came to town in the summers, about the 4-H competitions and rodeos in the spring. There was the influx of bird-watchers that came with the yearly migration, and people that came to ski and snowboard. I told him about hiking Cooper's Peak, how you'd get to the top and there'd still be ice from the winter, but everyone would be in shorts and short sleeves.

One night, while I was telling him about the local hot springs, my phone started vibrating in my hand.

A FaceTime from Ben.

I screamed and threw my phone across the room.

It was probably an overreaction, but I left the phone where it was until it stopped buzzing.

The next time he texted—the following day—he didn't make any mention of the attempted call. I allowed myself to assume it had been a mistake.

Things continued as before.

He kept texting, and I kept responding, but there was a part of me—the smarter, wiser part—that knew it couldn't continue like this. It needed to stop.

I told myself it was better this way. That maybe I was acting as some sort of crutch for him. That he needed to go talk to other women. Or men. Someone who was within a motorcycle's radius.

Someone who wasn't a single mom with some serious emotional repression.

What we'd shared in his trailer had been a moment.

One that I'd moved on from.

That I *would* move on from.

"We text. There's no reason to call him," I said.

Allyson gaped at me. "No reason?" She put her hands on the table in front of me and leaned down to look me in the eye. "How about the fact that he's gorgeous and sexy and thinks the same of you?"

"I'm starting to see the downside in sharing this information with you," I said.

I didn't mean it. When I'd returned from Philadelphia, I had been dying to tell someone what had happened. Allyson had been more than eager to listen, her eyes growing bigger and bigger with each new detail I recounted.

I even shared my motorcycle-riding comment and we'd both giggled at how cheesy and ridiculous and kind of perfect it had been. A part of me still couldn't believe I'd said it. And then done it.

Allyson had been surprised by my initial boldness. But then again, she hadn't lived here when I was a teenager. She didn't know how I'd once been penalized for such brash behavior.

A part of myself that had been under lock and key since then.

It had been nice to let it out. If only for a few hours.

"It was a onetime thing," I said. "We established that from the beginning."

Or I'd word-vomited it *at* him, and he hadn't disagreed.

And despite the regular text messages, he'd never mentioned anything about seeing me again.

Theoretical conversations about what we'd do if he were in Cooper didn't count.

"I'm still thinking of stealing your phone and calling him for you," she said.

I hadn't told her that the lack of communication was coming from my end. Because I knew how she'd react.

Mainly, she'd be horrified and disappointed and probably *would* steal my phone.

I shuddered.

It was better this way.

"How was last night's date?" I asked, not so subtly changing the subject.

"Ugh." She flopped onto the couch I'd shoved against one of the basement walls.

This space had been Spencer's once. He'd had his tools and projects in piles—organized chaos. It had taken a long time for me to clear it out—not just because of the amount of stuff but because I hadn't wanted to.

There was still a closet upstairs packed with his things—all the items I couldn't bear to get rid of. I'd shoved it all in there and locked it away. A metaphor for other things, no doubt.

I fiddled with the scarf around my neck. I'd made it for Spencer ages ago—it was one of the first things I'd completed, one of the first things I'd given him—and I hadn't realized that he'd kept it until I found it on his side of the closet three years ago.

Cried over that for a couple of days. No big deal. Grief stuff.

Running my fingers over it, I could feel the mistakes—it wasn't my best work, I'd been a beginner—but he'd loved it. Those first few years he'd wear it every day during the fall and winter. Eventually, it left the rotation when he was gifted nicer scarves as my knitting got better, and I would complain whenever I saw him wear it.

"You're making it look like I can't make you a decent scarf," I'd tell him.

"You're nuts," he'd respond.

I thought he'd thrown it out, but I should have known better. Of course he'd kept it. And now *I* was the one who couldn't take it off. Even inside.

I wrapped it one more time around my neck to keep it out of the way.

"The picture on the app was outdated," Allyson said. "By about fifteen years."

I winced as I threaded the sewing machine.

One of the many things Allyson and I had bonded over was the horrific lack of decent men within a fifty-mile radius of Cooper. Apparently, it was just as bad in San Francisco, except there were more opportunities to be disappointed.

At least Allyson kept trying, while I'd had the app deleted for months now.

I had been reconsidering it before leaving for Philadelphia.

Because there were things I missed. Connection. Touch. Affection.

I thought that my encounter with Ben would have quenched that desire, but it hadn't. If anything, it had only fed what was becoming a quickly growing need.

Apparently, I was lonely.

Who would have guessed?

"He didn't ask me a single question," Allyson said. "But I now know all his favorite movies, TV shows, and bands. He thinks Joni Mitchell is overrated, by the way."

"What a prize," I said.

"And yet, still the best date I've been on since I got here," she said. "At least he didn't throw a tantrum because the waitress brought the wrong salad dressing or expect me to blow him behind the restaurant because he'd paid for dinner."

I'd gone to Philadelphia looking for a vacation. I hadn't expected Ben and our chemistry and the first good time I'd had in a long while, but at the end of the day, it had served the same purpose as the trip. It had been an escape.

But those were always temporary.

Still, I'd hoped the double dopamine hit of successful flirting and orgasms in Philadelphia would have tided me over for a while. No need to reinstall any apps.

And yet.

"Maybe I should try dating women," Allyson said.

"Are you attracted to women?"

She was silent a moment. "I mean, I think Rachel Weisz is gorgeous."

"Everyone thinks Rachel Weisz is gorgeous," I said.

"I guess I haven't really thought about it," she said. "I'm not against it. But wouldn't that be ironic? Leaving the center of gay life to come out *here*? This part of the country isn't exactly known for its love of rainbows and pride parades."

She wasn't wrong. We didn't have a pride parade in Cooper. We didn't have a gay bar.

The queerest thing we did was an annual wood-chopping competition, but I was pretty sure that didn't really count.

"It would just be a novelty to go out with someone who was nice to me."

"I'll take you on a date," I said. "How about next week?"

Allyson perked up. I was almost done with her pockets.

"Movie and dinner?"

"If Lena can hang out with my mom or Gabe, we can do the whole nine yards," I said. "I'll even let you pick the movie."

"See?" Allyson said. "Women. They're nice."

"If I buy you popcorn, I will expect you to put out," I said.

"If you buy me popcorn, trust me, I will," she said.

CHAPTER 17

THEN

I HAD PLENTY OF EXCUSES FOR WHY I WASN'T LEAVING Cooper after graduation. Some of them were half true, like that I didn't have the money. I'd been working at the grocery store for a while—and could have easily found a job anywhere else in the state doing the same thing. I could even afford a few months' rent from the way I'd been saving—it would just be rough for a bit.

The other excuses were laughably false, like that I was concerned about leaving my mom. In actuality, she probably would have helped me pack.

My feelings about Cooper at that point were mostly ambivalent. There were times I loved living there, like the days when the skies were clear and big and gorgeous, and the entire place smelled of lilacs.

Then there were days I hated it—when it felt like the town seemed to be closing in around me, and there was nowhere to hide. Those were the days I dreamed of a life where I could be someone different. Someone new.

Not that I knew who I wanted to be.

The real reason I didn't leave was because of Spencer. He had one more year of high school, and I didn't want to be away from him. I didn't want to be by myself in a new town. I didn't want to be alone.

I stayed and worked at the grocery store and saw Spencer all the time. He had dinner at the house every week, and though things were awkward between me and Gabe—both of us trying to navigate having different kinds of relationships with the same person—mostly it was okay. Mom was happy to see Spencer, and if she was surprised about the romantic development between me and him, she never said a word.

And it was kind of nice because Mikey had gone off to some college in Tennessee that had scouted him for their baseball team, and Jessica had gone with him. I was certain it wasn't a coincidence that their absence begat less gossip and interest in my sex life.

There was a certain irony in that, because contrary to my reputation as a wanton whore, Spencer and I hadn't had sex. Still.

He wanted to wait.

I'd almost broken up with him when he told me that.

Because it wasn't just about getting off—I could do that on my own—it was about the other things. The little familiarities that you learned when you were naked in front of someone. The secrets you couldn't hide from each other when your bodies were fused. When you came together and came apart.

There was something there. Something important.

To me, at least.

With the guys I'd been with, sex had been a moment when I could see them clearly. It's not like I knew them on a fundamental level or anything like that, but I knew something about them. Something I couldn't discover any other way.

I wanted to know Spencer that way. More than I'd wanted to know those other guys.

Thankfully we came to a compromise, one that mostly came down to semantics.

Spencer defined sex in the biblical way. Penis. Vagina. Penetration.

He wasn't ready. And I discovered that I was completely, totally fine with that.

Because I tended to define sex in the broader way. Mouth on breasts? Sex. Hands over underwear? Sex. Rubbing against each other fully clothed until we both came? Sex.

We had fun. Gasping and laughing and being silly and also very, very serious. I was grateful for the experience I had. One of us needed to know what we were doing, and the thing about Spencer was that he was the best kind of student. Focused, curious, and hell-bent on getting a good grade.

He was a straight-A student.

My body was a math equation he was intent on solving. Which he did. Over and over and over again.

I didn't need his definition of sex. I wanted it, sure, I craved it, but I didn't need it. I was satisfied.

Because I realized, with Spencer, what I really wanted. What I had been desiring above all else. What I needed.

Intimacy.

I'd thought I could get that closeness through physically being with someone. Spencer showed me that it was more than that.

Graduation came, and both Gabe and Spencer got scholarships to Jeannette Rankin College, which was a two-hour drive from Cooper. Gabe's was for football, and Spencer's was for academics. There was a running joke that the two of them together made one decent student-athlete.

They were going to room together their first year, when they had to stay on campus. I wanted to go with them, but apartments were hard to find in September, and we decided that it would be better if I waited until the next year when we could get an apartment together.

I'd never told Spencer that he was the reason I'd stayed behind in Cooper, so I knew I didn't have any right to ask him to do the same, but it still hurt.

And I was jealous, so deeply jealous, of him and Gabe going off to have a normal college experience—something I hadn't really wanted until I realized how left out it made me feel.

I didn't tell Spencer that either.

Because his mother was already giving him plenty of guilt about leaving. Didn't he understand that she would be ALL ALONE? That she would have NO ONE? That she'd done so much for him and now he was ABANDONING her?

He promised he'd come back every weekend.

"What about your dad?" I asked him once.

I'd been curious about it forever—not sure what to believe when it came to the rumors about Spencer Sr.

"I don't know," he said. "I remember him a little from

when I was a kid, but then he wasn't there anymore. I asked my mom about it once and it really upset her—she didn't understand why I wanted to know about a man who had left us. She cried for a week—she thought she wasn't good enough for me alone, which of course she is."

I couldn't stand his mother.

Spencer saw her as a perfect angel who loved him more than life itself. I saw her as a manipulative self-serving martyr who'd only be happy if her son lived with her forever.

It made sense to me now why Spencer had kept coming back to our house. It wasn't just Gabe. It was all of us. It was my dad.

We never really spoke about it, but that was when I realized that Spencer had felt that loss too. That we had that shared experience. That connection.

It made me feel closer to him. And I didn't want him to leave.

But I wasn't going to be his mother. I wasn't going to make him feel like he had to choose. He was the only person I knew who really loved school. Loved learning. College was going to be the place where he really blossomed.

Spencer being Spencer, he did exactly as he promised. Every Friday night he was back. He spent Saturday with me, went to church with his mom on Sunday, and then headed back to school. Occasionally Gabe would join him, but that stopped after he was cast in the college's upcoming production of *Cyrano de Bergerac* and started spending his weekends in rehearsals.

"I thought he was there to play football?" I asked Spencer when he told me the news.

"He is," he said. "But I guess it's the offseason?"

Neither of us really knew anything about football. Not that we knew much more about theatre either, but I was way more interested in going to see Gabe acting than trekking out there to watch him play a game I didn't understand or care about.

"He said he did it to meet girls," Spencer said.

I rolled my eyes. "Between that and football, how many girls does he need?" I asked.

Spencer shrugged. "I think he likes the attention. And he can drink more when he doesn't have to do drills and stuff."

It was the first time he'd mentioned Gabe's drinking.

I'd noticed, of course. Before leaving for college, Gabe always seemed to have a beer in his hand. I knew it wasn't that hard to get a six-pack in Cooper, even if you were underage, and I imagined it was even easier in a college town.

"Bet there's a lot of partying," I said.

We were hanging out in the basement. It seemed so small now—the video-game console sitting dusty in the corner, the ring-stained coffee table, the couch that squeaked literally any time you shifted. Which was the main reason we were sitting and talking instead of making out.

"Yeah," he said.

His hand was playing with the edge of my sleeve. I'd begun mending my own clothes. Last week this shirt had a hole in the shoulder and the sleeve. Now all that was visible of my handiwork was a loose thread that Spencer was tugging at.

I slapped his hand away. "Don't unravel it," I said. "Are you going to these parties with Gabe?"

I didn't want to be jealous.

But I was.

"Sometimes," Spencer said. "But they're mostly on the weekends."

He sat forward. The couch squealed its unhappiness.

"My mom is having surgery," he said.

I rarely saw Diana, but my animosity for her was clearly mutual. She referred to me as "that girl" to other people—I'd overheard her once in the grocery store before she knew I worked there. But even if I wasn't her biggest fan, I didn't wish harm on her.

"Is she okay?"

"It's her knees," Spencer said. "They've been bothering her for a while, and she's decided to get surgery on both of them."

"Isn't that kind of a big deal?" I asked.

"The surgery is pretty straightforward," he said. "But it's a long recovery. She's going to need help."

I eyed him, pretty sure I could tell where this was going and not liking it at all.

"I think I'm going to take some time off school," he said. "Just a semester, so I can be there for her after the surgery."

"You're in the middle of a semester," I said. "She can't wait until May?"

He shook his head, but I knew he hadn't asked. Hadn't pushed. Diana had said she needed him, and Spencer was going to abandon everything to help her.

"You can't drop out of school," I said.

"I'm not dropping out," he said. "It's just for a semester."

It wasn't, of course. Diana's knees were still bothering her by the following fall, and when Gabe went back for his sophomore year, he went alone.

CHAPTER 18

NOW

I'D SUBMITTED LENA TO A CRUEL ARRAY OF TORTURES OVER the years, but apparently, the worst of them all was forcing her to be seen in public with me while we went shopping for a new backpack.

"My old one is fine," she kept saying.

"It has a hole the size of my fist," I said. "How can you carry anything in it?"

"Backpacks are for kids," she said.

I considered reminding her that she was, technically, still a kid, but I also wanted to make it through the next hour in one piece, so I said nothing. It was my best parenting tactic.

I'd promised her that she could go to the movies with Eve afterward, which was the only thing that seemed to make her smile these days.

We went to the walking mall, and while Lena decided between two nearly identical green backpacks (for someone who didn't need one, she had very strong opinions about which one to get), I thought about Ben.

I didn't do it on purpose, but I found myself imagining the kind of shopping trip I'd drag him on if he were here. All the places I'd told him about. There was Birds and Beasleys, of course, the local hot spot for birders and nature lovers alike. They had a little parakeet named Button that was basically a town mascot, though we didn't talk about the fact that the current Button was actually the third in a line of identical birds, carrying on a noble tradition.

I'd take him to the Finnish Line, one of the few non-chain coffee places in town. They had incredible hot chocolate and fun Finnish treats, like Shrove buns and munkki, a delicious type of donut. I wasn't a coffee drinker, but Spencer had liked getting their traditional kaffeost, which involved dipping cheese into a light roast. I had a feeling Ben would be excited to try it.

He'd probably be up for anything I suggested.

Eventually, a green backpack was reluctantly chosen, and I was about to offer to buy Lena a hot chocolate when we were spotted by my mother-in-law. She was standing outside with Jessica, selling desserts under a banner that had their church's name on it.

Lena's shoulders tensed up to her ears as we walked toward them.

"You just have to say hello," I told her.

I knew I probably should have been trying harder to encourage a relationship, but I honestly couldn't blame Lena for wanting to avoid her grandmother. If Cooper—

and Montana in general—was about five years behind the times, then Diana was a good thirty to forty.

She'd lost her goddamn mind when Spencer had told her that he wanted to take *my* last name. Which, to be fair, was pretty progressive of him, but she also had some extremely outdated views on just about everything regarding gender roles and sexuality.

I couldn't prove it, but I had long suspected that she'd been behind quite a few of the rumors that had been spread about me.

I hadn't slept with the *entire* baseball team.

Just three members of it.

We reached the table, and Diana immediately pulled Lena to her and pressed her against her chest, forcing my ever-growing daughter to hunch down. I was certain it was uncomfortable, for several reasons.

"Grandma . . ." Lena said, trying to wriggle out of her tight embrace.

For such a tiny woman she was strong as hell.

"Don't I get a hug?" I asked.

Diana glared at me but released Lena.

I never got a hug.

"Look at you." Diana was now holding Lena's face in her hands, pushing her hair back from her face.

Lena's discomfort radiated off her like a bird in distress.

"Such a pretty girl," Diana said. "If only you'd get your hair out of your face."

Lena shot me a glance.

"How are you, Diana?" I asked.

My mother-in-law finally released Lena, who took several large steps away.

"I'm as good as can be expected," Diana said.

She glanced over at Jessica, who had been busying herself with the bake sale goods. Sometimes it seemed impossible that we'd ever been friends.

"I'd feel much better if I could see my granddaughter more often," Diana said.

Lena looked down at her feet.

"That's my fault," I said. "I'm very strict about Lena's free time."

That was a lie, but Diana had probably stopped listening after I said it was my fault.

"Spencer always made sure I got to see Lena," Diana said, more to Jessica than to me.

I felt a twinge of pity.

Lena was the last living reminder of Spencer that Diana had. And she had been devastated by his death—unable to leave her house for a month. The church had taken care of her, and I was grateful for that, because I had been in no shape to tend to anyone else's needs but mine and Lena's.

It was an ungenerous thought, but there were times I got the sense that Diana felt like she was the only one who'd lost Spencer. That her grief was greater than anyone else's.

Her church had done exactly what they'd done when my dad had died. Offered prayers and invitations to services but nothing that we could use.

I minded it less this time around because we had other people taking care of us, but I had nearly lost it when I found out that they'd planted a tree in Spencer's honor—without my permission or knowledge—in the back garden. They'd even held a celebration to unveil it.

Diana brought Lena. She'd told me they were just going shopping.

Whoever had been in charge of it, however, did a terrible job, because the tree died within a year. Last I heard, Diana had been given the shriveled-up trunk—barely wider than a pencil—so that she could bury it in her backyard. Instead, she put it on her mantel alongside all the pictures she had of Spencer.

Sometimes it was hard to stay mad at her.

Sometimes.

"The youth group is going to be volunteering to clean up the gully this spring," Jessica said. "Maybe Lena could join them."

Diana's eyes lit up. "What a lovely idea," she said. "What do you think, Lena?"

Lena was still staring at her shoes, and she was doing some sort of toe-in, toe-out movement that had her unable to answer.

"Lena!" Eve, ever our saving grace, appeared.

Diana's lips puckered.

"Hey, Mrs. P!" she said. "Mrs. Garrison! Mrs. Lennard!"

Her timing was impeccable.

"How are you doing, Eve?" I asked.

"So good!" she said. "Lena, did you see that we have all of our classes together this semester?"

Lena's entire face lit up like she'd swallowed a lightbulb.

"Cool," she said, which was about as much enthusiasm as I could expect from her in this situation with so many adults around.

I caught her eye, and she gave me a furtive look.

Pulling out my phone, I made a sound of surprise.

"You guys are going to be late for the movie," I said.

They weren't.

"You'd better hurry along," I said. "I'll see you afterward."

"Thanks, Mrs. P!" Eve said.

"Thanks, Mom."

The two of them walked off, Eve's arm looped through Lena's.

I glanced over at Jessica, wondering if she was thinking what I was thinking. Because that had been us. Once upon a time. Truly inseparable.

But she wasn't even looking.

"They seem to spend a lot of time together," Diana said.

"They're friends," I said.

"Friends are one thing," Diana said. "But how is Lena going to get a boyfriend if she's not more social?"

"Isn't she too young to date?"

That had always been her rule. No dating until eighteen. Not that it mattered what Diana's rules were pertaining to *my* child, but I was still surprised she was suddenly eager for my thirteen-year-old to have a boyfriend.

Diana frowned. "I just think she needs to be spending more time with other kids."

Which meant that Diana wanted Lena to spend time with the *right* kind of kids.

"The church youth group is great for that kind of socializing," Jessica said.

"She would love it," Diana said.

I knew for a fact she wouldn't. I knew because I'd asked her, and she'd said no.

"She's always welcome," Jessica said. "I think it would do her good."

Diana looked at Jessica like she wished *she* were her daughter-in-law. It wasn't the first time I'd seen that look. Or had this conversation.

"This looks delicious," I said, changing the subject by focusing on food.

Another lie. The cookies were store-bought, the cake looked stale, and someone had brought brownies with frosting. I hated brownies with frosting. As far as I was concerned, if you needed it, then your brownies weren't good enough.

"Have some," Diana said, handing me a paper towel with a brownie on it.

I took it.

"Maybe don't eat it all at once," Jessica said.

She gave me a once-over. I knew she was trying to imply that I looked fat or fat*ter,* but I already knew that I didn't look like I had in high school, and I didn't care.

Apparently, Jessica cared.

If I were a nicer person, I might have felt sorry for her. But who cared about high school anymore?

We *were* older. Fatter. Grayer. Those were just the facts. That was what happened when people aged.

I knew better than anyone what a gift that was.

Spencer would never get older. Fatter. Grayer.

Even though I hated brownies with frosting, I ate the entire thing. It burned my teeth and made me feel sick, but I relished the horrified disgust in Jessica's eyes as she watched. If Lena were still standing here, she probably would have died from embarrassment.

Bad enough that I'd forced her to be in public with me, but now I was standing in the middle of town with cheap chocolate frosting smeared on my cheek.

Diana handed me a napkin.

"Don't make a mess," she said.

CHAPTER 19

THEN

I MOVED INTO AN APARTMENT OF MY OWN AT THE END of spring. The snow was melting into an awful slush that soaked my pant legs as I transferred bedding from my car to my tiny basement unit right off Nickle Junction. It was barely insulated, and my upstairs neighbors were apparently tap dancers or bowling ball enthusiasts from the noise they made, but I didn't care.

I'd raided the local secondhand stores for dishware and curtains. Stocked my pantry—which was merely a cabinet with a broken hinge—with dented cans and label-less tins I got for half price at work. My coffee table was a piece of wood stacked on a couple of cement blocks that Gabe had piled into the basement for reasons unknown. I had two chairs. My couch was patched with duct tape, mismatched fabric, and hope. I held my breath every time I sat on it.

The apartment was hot in the summer and cold in the winter.

On its best days, it smelled like garlic; on its worst, feet.

But it was mine.

I'd wanted Spencer to move in with me, but unfortunately Diana was recovering from yet another surgery where she needed her son to be available to her at all times.

"I'm just worried she'll fall and hurt herself," he said.

She'd had a mole removed from her arm.

I didn't argue. There wasn't any point. If I'd learned anything about Spencer it was that when he was ready, he was ready. Not a second before.

At least he was only a few blocks away. And there was something undeniably pleasurable about having a place that I didn't have to share with anyone. I could do anything I wanted. It was delicious and terrifying at the same time.

Spencer was my first official guest. He brought an air freshener plug-in wrapped up in a bow and pizza from work. King Cheese had taken him back when he dropped out of college, though he'd also started working at the hardware store on the weekends. We ate at the coffee table, sitting on the floor.

"I keep expecting to hear my mom down the hall," I said. "It's so quiet."

From upstairs came a crash and the sound of something rolling across the floor.

Spencer laughed. "Quiet?"

"Different kind of quiet," I said.

He nodded. "It's nice," he said, looking around. "We could paint it, you know?"

"I'm thinking pink," I said. I wasn't, but I could if I wanted to.

I could do *anything*. Within the confines of my lease.

"I can get you a deal on that," he said.

We finished the pizza, did the dishes—all two of them—and carefully, cautiously sat down on the couch. It didn't collapse immediately, which I took as a good sign.

"What now?" I asked, thinking we'd make out.

Maybe touch each other. Maybe I'd give Spencer a blow job. He'd liked that last time, and I'd liked the way he'd come undone. It was sexy and intimate, and he was so beautiful that sometimes it made my heart hurt.

"Maybe you should show me your bedroom," Spencer said.

He was looking at the floor, his cheeks red.

"You saw my bedroom," I said.

"I know," he said. "But . . . we're alone."

"Oh," I said. "Okay."

We'd never really done anything on a bed before. Some kissing in my room when we first got together, but that had always seemed so precarious, so most of our experimenting had happened in the back seat of Spencer's car. Not the most comfortable place.

I took his hand and led him to the bedroom, both of us stopping in the doorway.

My bed wasn't big. It wasn't fancy, though I'd taken some pride in making it this morning and even fluffed the pillows to give it a magazine-y look.

Spencer turned toward me, taking my hands in his. We were smushed together in the doorway. On the threshold.

"I'm ready," he said.

It took a moment for me to understand what he was saying.

"Really?"

He nodded.

"I thought you wanted to wait," I said, not knowing why I wasn't just pulling him into the bedroom and tossing him onto the bed.

I guess I had matured somewhat.

"I'm done waiting," he said. He took my face in his hands. His eyes were focused, clear. Direct. "I want to be with you."

I swallowed.

"I want to be with you too," I said.

I'd never been more sure of anything in my life.

"I have condoms," he said.

"I do too," I said. "And other stuff."

His eyebrows went up. "Other stuff?"

This time I was the one who blushed. "Just, like, lube and that kind of thing."

We took out our supplies and sat on the edge of the bed together. Spencer's hand was on my knee, mine on top of his.

"I'm nervous," he said.

"Me too," I said,

We were both whispering.

"*You're* nervous?" he asked.

I bristled at that a little. "Yeah. I'm allowed to be nervous."

He smiled. "I know. It's just, I didn't expect that. It's nice."

I softened. "Yeah?"

"Yeah," he said. "Though, I'm glad that one of us knows what we're doing."

I kissed him. He kissed me back.

We both knew how to do that.

We kissed and kissed and kissed.

I took off his shirt. He took off mine. Then my pants. Then his pants. Then my bra. Then my underwear. Then his.

We were naked and alone in my apartment.

I was ready. But Spencer hesitated, the two of us kneeling on the bed, facing each other, not a thing between us.

"Here," I said. "Let me show you."

CHAPTER 20

NOW

THE WOMAN FROM THE INTERVIEW WAS TALLER THAN I'D expected.

"Hi, I'm Lauren, Gabe's sister," I said.

"Chani," she said.

She had a good handshake. My dad had always been big on handshakes. He'd taught all of us—me, Gabe, and Spencer—the trick to one. Grip firmly, shake once, and let go. No limp wrists. No knuckle busting. Just a good, solid shake.

My dad would have liked her on that merit alone. Spencer too.

Then again, neither of them had been especially hard to impress.

I thought about when I'd met Ben. Taking my hand with both of his had been a nice touch. A little more personal than the average handshake, but I'd liked it.

"This is Lena," I said.

"Hey," Lena barely managed, her attention purposefully focused elsewhere.

The timing was bad. Gabe had texted us to say that he was coming back to Cooper with a guest in tow. Technically two guests, as Ollie was in town as well. Unfortunately for Lena, he was not the one joining us for dinner tonight. Instead, it was Chani.

The woman who'd written the article about Gabe all those years ago. The one my mom was convinced he was halfway in love with. The one who he insisted had nothing to do with why he rushed off and married Jacinda immediately after the interview was published.

The rumor that hadn't been a rumor at all.

When Lena learned who he'd brought back to Cooper, she'd muttered something about Uncle Gabe not being the best judge of women.

Now, as she played with Teddy in the bookstore, ignoring Chani, I looked at her—this awkward, in-between girl—and saw both who she'd been as a child and who she'd be as an adult. It was weird. Good-weird. But sad-weird too because I knew that Spencer would have delighted in every stage, even the difficult ones.

I knew—intimately enough—that being a teenager without the dad you adored was kind of the worst thing ever, but she would have been swept up in the riptide of hormones and acne and crushes and utter loathing of adults no matter what. Would it have been more bearable for her if her dad were here? Or just more bearable for me?

The answer was obvious—yes, of course, to both.

If Spencer were here, would she still be as sullen and taciturn and completely emotionally closed off? If her dad were here, would Lena give him the same cold shoulder she gave me? Or would their relationship have withstood the ravages of teen years? They'd had a special bond—their own way of communicating. He always knew how to make her smile.

He'd been her favorite parent.

It wasn't fair, but it was true.

I had my own strengths.

I could turn a mishmash of ingredients into a meal, scraps of fabric into a pillow, and a skein of yarn into a hat. If it was tactile and a little bit fidgety, that's where I excelled. There was something about the attention it required that really appealed to me. How the world could narrow into a single, simple point of concentration, everything else going blurry.

It was harder for something to hurt you when it wasn't even in focus.

Gabe hadn't given us much time to prepare. He'd texted yesterday saying that he'd be back in Cooper and was bringing a guest and could we take care of Teddy and then also host dinner the following night?

Little brothers. They had no respect for schedules. Timing. Planning.

Instead of telling him that, of course, I made a lasagna and homemade garlic bread. Dessert. All ready to go. Gabe could be an inconsiderate idiot sometimes, but he took care of us in his way.

Besides, making things? I could do that.

Focus narrowed, attention centered. Everything else a blur.

"She seems nice," Mom said once the three of us were

in the car heading back to the house. "Don't you think, Lena?"

There was barely a shrug from the back seat.

"You need to be polite," I told her. "Chani is our guest."

She rolled her eyes. I'd had enough.

"Lena!"

"What?" she snapped back.

I turned completely around in my seat.

"Do not give me that tone," I said. "I don't care what kind of mood you're in today."

Sometimes life sucked. We still had to be polite to guests.

"You will be kind and courteous to your uncle's friend while she is visiting," I said.

"She's not his friend," Lena grumbled. "She's a reporter."

To Lena, the word was basically synonymous with "soul-sucking monster." I couldn't really blame her—the press had been shitty and relentless after Spencer's death, during Gabe's time in rehab.

But I also knew that Chani wasn't just some reporter that Gabe had brought to Montana.

"They're friends," I said. "And you will behave yourself."

I knew she wanted to keep arguing. I could see it in the way she set her jaw, the scrunched-up set of her eyebrows.

"Let's just get through dinner," Mom said.

"How long do you think she's in town for?" I asked.

My mom looked over at me, eyebrows raised.

"From the look on Gabe's face?" she said. "I think he's hoping forever."

DINNER WAS PAINFULLY AWKWARD.

Or maybe just according to me, because I kept cringing at Lena's behavior—which had *not* improved—and hoping that Chani wasn't judging us too harshly. Gabe was running interference to the best of his abilities, making himself the butt of jokes when possible and gently teasing everyone else. His newly grown beard was helpful fodder.

It was clear that my mom was right—that he was fully and completely smitten with this woman. I couldn't remember the last time I'd seen him like this. Even when he'd been with Jacinda—who I adored—their relationship had always been more of a transactional friends-with-benefits thing.

We Parkers had never really understood the point of it, but we had considered Jacinda family nonetheless. Still did.

"They're married but not in love?" Spencer had asked me many, many times.

"He's *your* friend," I'd respond.

That's how it had been with us and Gabe. When I thought he was being ridiculous, he was "Spencer's friend." When Spencer thought that, he was "your brother." And then when Lena joined the mix, we also got to call him "Lena's uncle" as a way to excuse what we couldn't understand.

"I don't get it," Spencer had said.

"Yeah, well, it's a Hollywood thing, I think," I'd say, as if I had a clue.

I watched Lena stab her lasagna—which thankfully had

turned out very well—and made a furtive wish that we could get through this dinner without bloodshed.

That wish was quickly dashed.

"I know who you are," Lena said suddenly.

"Lena," Gabe warned before I could.

"What?" she snapped.

I thought about taking her by the arm and dragging her out of the dining room before she could say anything else. Instead, I glared at her. She ignored me. Ignored all of us, her focus fixed on Chani, who remained frozen, silverware in hand.

"You're the reporter," Lena accused.

Chani put her fork down.

"I am," she said. Her voice was calm. Steady.

"I read the article," Lena said.

The one that had gone viral. The one that made Mom ask about Chani in the first place. That had Spencer placing bets on what had happened.

The one where Gabe denied anything had.

The one where no one had told the truth, apparently.

"What did you think of it?" Chani asked.

"Lena," I warned, knowing that her response was not going to be flattering.

"It's fine," Chani said. "Gabe didn't like it either."

I gave my brother a look. I was pretty sure Mom gave him the same one.

"That's not true," he said, but he sank down a little in his seat.

"Trust me," Chani said. "I've heard far worse."

I was a coward but let Chani handle it. Which she did. With grace.

"You can't hurt my feelings," she continued. "And it's okay if you didn't like it."

Her directness seemed to throw Lena off.

"It wasn't terrible," she said. "Just, like, whatever, okay?"

She pushed her chair back so hard that it fell to the floor, and then she was gone—heading upstairs on heavy feet—before anyone could say anything.

I took a deep breath, preparing to apologize.

"I'm sorry," Chani said.

I liked her. Or maybe I was just grateful that I wasn't being noticeably judged for the shitty behavior of my kid.

My phone buzzed. It was rude to look but I'd do anything to ignore the tension at the table.

It was Ben.

I can't believe you've never mentioned you have something called a Testicle Festival, he'd written. *I'm hurt and insulted.*

I bit my lip to keep from smiling.

He was talking about the Rocky Mountain Oyster Festival that used to happen every year in August. It hadn't been in Montana for a few years, but it was still talked about, usually with the moniker Testicle Festival or Testy Fest.

I'd never gone.

I'm sure Ben would have.

When I looked up from my phone, I saw that Gabe was frowning at me.

There was no possible way he could have known who was texting me, and yet . . .

"Again?" he asked.

I'd made the mistake of telling him Ben had texted me after our trip to Philadelphia. Gabe then jumped to the conclusion that Ben was harassing me and taking advantage of my cooking knowledge.

It was somewhat humiliating that my brother was convinced that the only reason a handsome man like Ben would be contacting me would be food related.

And although, technically, he *was* texting me about food at this exact moment, I hadn't corrected Gabe then.

I'd hoped he'd forgotten.

Apparently not.

"It's fine," I said, putting my phone away.

I'd respond later.

"I'll tell him to stop," Gabe said.

I knew he was trying to be helpful in his stupid little brother way, but it was time to make it clear that this was none of his fucking business.

"I don't . . . mind," I said.

Gabe crossed his arms. *Great.*

"I can handle this," I said. "I am older than you, remember?"

"And he's younger than you," Gabe said. "Younger than me. Probably younger than Chani."

I didn't need the reminder. Also, who the fuck cared? We were both adults. And most importantly, it was no one's goddamn business. Especially not my brother's.

"Who is this?" Chani asked.

"Ben Walsh," I said.

I was not going to be embarrassed.

And I was extremely gratified at her response. Not shock, necessarily, but definitely some awe.

"He's . . ." she said.

"A decent actor," Gabe said.

His arms were still crossed.

"Very handsome," Chani said. "Like, painfully handsome. The kind of handsome where you can't even look at him directly without feeling a little lightheaded."

I couldn't help but laugh. Not just at her description—which was one hundred percent accurate—but also at Gabe's reaction.

He crossed his arms even tighter. I was reminded of little-kid Gabe, annoyed whenever someone else got a slice of cake first.

"I'm *right* here," he said.

It was official. I liked Chani. I liked her a lot.

"You're very handsome too," my mom said.

"So, Ben Walsh . . . ?" Chani prompted.

I liked Chani way more than Gabe at the moment, because at least she didn't seem to have any judgment on my age and Ben's age and his fame and my . . . whatever. Because Gabe would just not. Shut. Up.

"He's been sniffing around Lauren ever since she came to visit the *Philadelphia Story* set," he said.

That was enough. I'd had enough.

"Sniffing around?" I asked. "I'm a person, not a lost steak. Don't be a macho asshole."

At least Gabe looked a little guilty at that.

Not that it stopped him from talking.

"Sorry," he said, not sorry at all. "It's just—"

"You don't like him, I know." I sighed. "You've made that perfectly clear."

Before he could say any more, I pushed back from the table.

"Excuse me," I said. "I'm going to go check on Lena."

I could see my mom giving Gabe a look as I left.

Poor Chani. We were really giving her a front-row seat to the Parker family dysfunction. She'd have to really like Gabe in order to stick around.

But I was pretty sure she did.

There was no accounting for taste.

CHAPTER 21

THEN

"WHEN WE WIN THE LOTTERY," SPENCER SAID, "I'M going to buy one of those big stone mansions over on Lloyd Street."

"You'd have to win the lottery to pay the heating bill on it," I said. "I heard it costs more than the mortgage during the winter."

We were eating dinner—spaghetti and meatballs because it was the kind of meal that we could stretch over a couple of days, putting the extra grocery money into the house fund.

"That's not how the game goes," Spencer chided me.

He had dark circles under his eyes from working the late-night shift at King Cheese and then the early shift at the hardware store. But the overtime money was good, and each check brought us closer and closer to our goal.

Spencer's goal.

He wanted to buy a house with the kind of intense focus and desire that had once been reserved mostly for me.

There were moments when I was jealous of this new devotion.

It was all he thought about. All he talked about. Sometimes, he confessed, he had dreams about it. And I wanted to move out of our crappy apartment—the place that had once felt like adulthood and freedom—which now seemed to be getting smaller with every passing month. But I didn't need a house, I just needed more space.

I was still working at the grocery store and took on as many extra shifts as I could, but I'd gotten tired of seeing all that money go into a savings account. There were so many things we could have used, things we needed but went without.

"When we win the lottery," I said, "I'll buy that electric blanket back."

Spencer's mouth paused in the middle of chewing to curve into a frown.

"What?" I demanded, even though I knew exactly what.

We'd been fighting over that damn blanket for weeks now. I'd seen it in the window of a store downtown and, knowing that we had another cold winter coming and a heater that barely worked and cost too much to run, bought it and brought it home.

"I told you we couldn't afford it," Spencer said.

"It was forty dollars," I said. "We can afford it."

We'd had this argument dozens of times over our short married life. About a whole number of things. An electric blanket. New curtains. A bedside table that hadn't been found on the side of the road.

There was saving money and there was being ridiculous.

Spencer thought we were the former, while I knew he was the latter.

"It will go on sale," he said.

"Yeah, after the worst of winter has passed," I said.

"We have to think of the house," he told me.

That's what he always said.

"What if I don't want to?"

The look he gave me was sheer confusion and bewilderment.

"What if I don't want to think about a stupid house all the time?" I asked. "What if I want to think about myself? What if I want to spend our money on an electric blanket so I can be warm in the winter, and buy a new swimsuit in the summer because my old one is starting to sag? What if I want to go out to dinner once in a while instead of figuring out all our meals from the half-off can section of the store?"

I'd felt this way for a while now but didn't know how to say it. Didn't know how to tell Spencer that the house mattered to him a lot more than it mattered to me, and if I had the choice, I'd spend our money on a nicer apartment and a night at the movies. *With* popcorn.

I wanted to enjoy life, not wait for it to begin.

And now that I'd started, it all came pouring out. How much I hated our place, how I hated how tired he was all the time, how we barely saw each other between shifts, how I was worried that we would never be able to buy a house and we'd just be stuck in this basement forever, freezing and miserable.

He listened silently until I was done. Then he stood and walked out of the apartment.

"Fuck!" I said to the empty kitchen.

We never fought. We argued occasionally over small things, like who had left hair in the drain (me) and who needed to do the dishes every night (him), but it never came from a place of real anger.

I hadn't realized, until that moment, exactly how angry I was. How resentment about our finances was festering deep inside of me. How I felt left out of our plans for the future because they centered completely around Spencer's needs.

It was hours before he returned. I had cleaned up dinner and paced the apartment dozens of times. I thought about calling Diana to see if he was there, but if he wasn't, I didn't want to give her the satisfaction of knowing anything was wrong, and if he was there, well, I honestly didn't want to know.

A few months ago, Gabe had come home for a visit, staying with our mom. She still hadn't retired—the mortgage on her place would be too much if she left at this point. We went out for dinner almost every night he was in town, on him. He'd looked thin and unhappy and reeked of the beer he was constantly drinking. He kept blaming it on Los Angeles—the city was grinding him down, but he was fine, so stop bugging him.

If he were still here, I'd know exactly where to find Spencer. The two of them would be doing a loop around Central's football field, talking the way they always had. I was pretty sure Spencer never spoke to me the way he talked to Gabe.

It was dark when I heard him come home. I was in the bedroom, in bed, trying to read a cookbook I'd gotten from the library when I heard the squeak of the hinge and then the scrape of the door against the linoleum where it bottomed out every single time.

I'd gone from angry to worried and back to angry, which is why I didn't get up out of bed. I listened to the shuffling in the other room and waited. He finally appeared in the doorway. He had a bag in his hand. I recognized the label on the side as he handed it to me.

I tore it open to find the electric blanket and hugged it to my chest. It was soft and even though it wasn't plugged in, I swore it warmed me immediately.

"I'm sorry," Spencer said, sitting down on the bed.

"I'm sorry too," I said, still cradling my precious gift.

"I just want us to have a home."

I looked over at him.

"We don't need a house for that," I said. "*You're* home."

I could tell that meant a lot to him—after all, I wasn't one for being too sentimental or mushy with my feelings. It was probably the most romantic-adjacent thing I'd ever said to him, besides "I love you."

He reached a hand across the bed, and I took it.

"We don't have to stop saving," I said. "Just . . . just not everything, okay?"

"Okay," he said. "Okay."

"Come here," I said, pulling back the covers so he could climb in.

"Wait," he said, and came over to my side of the bed.

I didn't understand what he was doing until he untangled the cord from the electric blanket and plugged it into the wall.

"Crank it," he said.

I did, and snuggled up next to him, slept better than I had in months.

CHAPTER 22

NOW

I T WAS THE THIRD TIME THAT WEEK. THREE *DIFFERENT* couples.

"Out, out, out." I shooed the two teenagers from the corner stacks. "You'll have to find somewhere else to do that."

Both of their faces were bright red, but the store was basically empty, so they were able to scurry off without too much attention. I didn't want them doing . . . whatever they were doing . . . *here,* but that didn't mean I was going to shame them for it.

"I swear, there's something in the water," I said.

Allyson was at the counter, eating half my lunch, flipping through one of the books that I needed to shelve.

"I thought you brought your own food," I said.

"I did." She pointed to some Tupperware. "But you're a much better cook than I am."

"Good thing I made extra," I said.

"It's like you knew," she said.

I rolled my eyes, but fondly. She wasn't wrong, and this wasn't the first time this had happened.

"More face sucking in the stacks?"

"It's like someone's written something on the bathroom door at the high school," I said. "For a good time, go to the third bookshelf in the back of the Cozy."

"It is pretty secluded back there," Allyson said.

I gave her a look.

"Not that I have anyone to suck face with," she said, only a little bitterly.

I patted her hand. "One day your prince will come," I said. "And you will once again suck face."

"Gross," Lena said.

I hadn't heard her come in. She was followed by Gabe and Chani—it was clear that she had been walking as far in front of them as possible.

"That's right," Allyson said. "It is gross. Until you're eighteen."

"Eve's books are in the back," I said, knowing exactly what she was here for.

She went into the office.

"More problems in the stacks?" Gabe asked.

"The stacks?" Chani asked.

"Calling it that just makes it sound more legit," I said. "It is literally just that corner of the store where people are hiding and making out—I need to move the bookshelves around so it's not so secluded."

"Teenagers will be teenagers," Gabe said.

"Is that what you were doing at that age?" Chani asked him.

She said it innocently, but if I'd learned anything about

her in the brief time she'd been here, it was that she knew how to keep my brother on his toes.

I could see the struggle on Gabe's face—wanting to brag about all the girls he'd hooked up with (especially after he'd joined the football team) but also knowing that it probably wasn't what his current girlfriend wanted to hear.

"I did okay," he mumbled, eyes down at the floor.

"I was never popular with the guys in high school," Allyson said with a sigh. "I didn't see a penis until college."

Chani and I laughed at that, while Gabe just looked even more uncomfortable.

"I can't count the number of penises I saw before I even went to college," Chani said. "Jewish summer camp is the horniest place on earth."

Gabe opened his mouth to say something but then seemed to think better of it.

"How old were you?" I asked.

She thought about it. "Sixteen? Fifteen?"

I glanced back at the office door, hoping that Lena hadn't heard any of this. Then I lowered my voice.

"Lena's probably too young for the sex talk, right?"

Gabe looked horrified. Chani amused. Allyson thoughtful.

"I don't remember when my parents told me," Allyson said. "I'm sure they taught me about it at my Berkeley Montessori elementary school."

"Elementary school?" I echoed.

There was no way we'd had sex ed in elementary school.

"It was dinner conversation," Chani said. At Gabe's look, she continued: "Liberal Jew, remember? There's no such thing as an inappropriate topic with my family."

"I'll take that as a warning," Gabe said.

"Don't worry." She patted him on the arm. "I don't think they'll ask you anything too personal. At least not at the *first* dinner. After that, you might want to think about how you're going to answer blunt questions about your finances and what it's like doing nude scenes."

I stifled a laugh at my brother's shell-shocked look.

Chani winked at me and went to check out some books.

"She's joking, right?" Gabe asked.

"Sure," I said.

He disappeared after her, probably hoping for confirmation that it was, in fact, a joke.

"What about you?" Allyson asked. "When did you have the sex talk?"

I thought about it. "Never," I said. "I don't think I've ever spoken about sex with my mother."

"Really?"

"I'm just lucky that I wasn't taught that sex was sinful and dirty," I said, thinking about Spencer. "Just that it was dangerous and bad."

"Isn't that basically the same thing?"

I shrugged. "One involves god judging you, the other involves everyone else judging you."

"I think I'd prefer god," Allyson said, going back to her book.

I chewed my bottom lip.

"I should probably talk to Lena about sex, right?"

"Probably." Allyson didn't even look up.

"I probably should have done it already."

At my tone, Allyson's attention focused back on me.

"Hey," she said. "You're doing your best."

I snorted. People needed to stop saying that.

Even if it was true.

"I'll talk to her," I said with conviction.

"Great," Allyson said.

Lena came out of the office, a pile of books in her arms, an annoyed expression on her face.

"One of the books isn't there," she said. "The new Mona Morris."

"Are you sure?"

"Yeah," she said. "I looked everywhere."

I put my hand to my head, realizing. "Sorry," I said. "I think I shelved it."

Lena's look told me she was not impressed.

"It's just in the fiction section at the end," I said.

She let out the loudest, most aggrieved sigh I'd ever heard and trudged off to get her friend's book.

"That kid really has it rough," Allyson said.

"She thinks so," I said.

"EW! GROSS!"

Lena came tearing out from around the corner, her face red and scrunched with disgust, hands balled into tight little fists.

I was about to ask what was going on when Gabe and Chani emerged from behind her. Their sheepish expressions, and the way both of their shirts were now untucked, made it clear exactly what they'd been doing.

"You're kidding me," I said. "You literally live upstairs!"

"I'm scarred for life," Lena said, rubbing her eyes as if she'd been blinded.

"We were just, we weren't—" Gabe tried but I stopped him.

Because they *were,* and they *would.*

"You're coming in this weekend and moving those shelves," I told him. "The stacks are closed for business."

THERE WAS SOMETHING IN the air. I would have chalked it up to the weather, but we'd been surrounded by the same lousy gray sludge for weeks now. Maybe it was making people feel like entering an extended hibernation, getting all warm and snuggly with someone else, but whatever it was, I hated it.

As it turned out, the Cozy make-out corner was just the tip of the iceberg.

I couldn't go anywhere without seeing people in love. There was the couple all but mauling each other in the freezer section of the market. The double date at the movies, all four of them talking and giggling and the pairs holding hands and being disgustingly cute. At the dog park, a couple was sitting with their legs and arms wrapped around each other—even their pet seemed to be fed up with it, sitting at their feet with its ball, looking annoyed. There had even been a proposal outside the shop, and the entire block had heard the squeals of joy.

"I can't take it anymore," I said.

"You know my solution," Allyson said.

I was giving her a ride home after she'd taken her car to the shop. We'd had to wait because the guy at the desk had been making cutesy kissing noises to whoever was on the other end of the phone.

There was something in the water. Not *my* water, un-fortunately.

"I can help you set up a profile," Allyson continued. "And we'd probably need to take some new pictures, but I have an iPhone, so we can just get a bunch in portrait mode."

"It just seems like so much work," I said.

"Uh, yeah," she said. "Dating *is* work."

"Didn't it used to be fun?"

Not that I'd really *dated* before Spencer. I'd had fun, though.

"Dating hasn't been fun since the internet was invented," Allyson said.

"The last time I tried, I couldn't even get past a first date with anyone," I said.

"You only went on three dates!" Allyson said. "Before I moved here, I'd go on three dates a week!"

"You did not."

"Didn't I?"

I truly couldn't tell if she was joking, but I did know that Allyson went on far more dates than I did.

"It's a numbers game," she said. "Unfortunately, the numbers are not in our favor here."

That was true—it was hard enough to find a decent gynecologist in or around Cooper; finding men equally acquainted or skilled with vaginas was nearly impossible.

"You just have to take a few more risks," Allyson said. "Try widening your parameters."

I sighed.

"Or not," Allyson said.

"No, you're right," I said.

"Do you even *want* to be in a relationship?" she asked. "Or get remarried?"

"Those are two different things," I said. "And I don't know."

I couldn't imagine ever getting married again. Ever finding room in my home—or my heart—for someone who wasn't Spencer.

But I wanted . . . something.

"If you're looking for a good time, I think you can find that," Allyson said. "Maybe."

I thought about Ben and wondered if he was any good at phone sex. Which was dumb. *Of course* he was good at phone sex. He was great at sexting, and I was pretty sure hearing anything in his accent would get me off, but I hadn't heard from him since he'd asked about the testicle festival.

It had only been a day or so, but he was usually quick to respond. I'd taken to putting my phone in a drawer at work and deep in my purse every other time to keep from checking it nonstop.

I'd been expecting our conversations to end.

I told myself it was ridiculous to be disappointed.

"I just want to spend time with someone I like," I said. "Someone nice and kind and funny and smart and—"

"You're asking for too much," Allyson said.

We'd pulled up in front of her house, and as Allyson unbuckled her seatbelt, she faced me.

"Look, I'd love to tell you that there are available men out there like that," she said. "But I can't. If there are, I haven't found them, and sadly, right now, the bar is in hell, and most guys don't even bother to try to meet it."

"This is depressing," I said.

"No shit."

We sat there.

"I'm lonely," I said.

It was startlingly honest. I scared myself a little by saying it out loud. But it was the truth.

"Me too," she said. "There are times I even miss my ex and he's an asshole who cheated on me."

I wanted to cry.

There was so much I missed about Spencer—things I'd taken for granted. What it was like having someone who knew what kind of toothpaste you preferred. Who knew what would cheer you up on a shitty day. Who knew exactly where you liked to be touched.

Someone who knew *you*.

"It sucks," Allyson said. "Missing someone you actually hate."

"You'll always have me," I said.

Allyson took my hand. "Keep trying," she said. "Don't give up so easily."

As if any of this were easy.

"I'll think about it," I said.

CHAPTER 23

NOW

I WAS CLEANING OUT THE OVEN WHEN I HEARD LENA come home. I stood as she came into the kitchen, followed by Eve. My hands were covered in grease.

"Ew, Mom," Lena said.

"Glad to see you too," I said. "Hi, Eve."

"Hi, Mrs. P!"

Everything about Eve was an exclamation point.

"What are you girls up to?" I asked, washing my hands in the sink.

"Homework," Lena said, making it clear that she didn't want me asking any more questions.

I was certain she'd only come into the kitchen to scrounge for something to snack on.

"There are some blondies in the freezer," I said.

Lena didn't move.

I knew it was because of the pizza dough that was shoved way in the back. The last time she'd gone looking for something—ice pops or ice cream—she'd started sobbing uncontrollably at the sight of it—of Spencer's hand-writing listing the date it had been made. Forever ago.

Now she avoided the freezer as much as possible.

I opened the bottom drawer and pulled out the bag of blondies. I avoided looking at the pizza dough as well.

"Here you go," I said.

"Thanks, Mrs. P!" Eve said, taking them from me, and unwrapping them.

She knew the drill—thirty seconds in the microwave and they'd be just as gooey and fresh as when I pulled them from the oven.

"Milk?" I asked but pulled it out before they could re-spond.

Because of course milk.

"You guys want to do your homework in here?" I asked.

Lena shook her head, but it was too late.

"Okay!" Eve said. "Can we play music?"

"Sure," I said.

I was playing dirty, and I knew it. I also didn't care. If blondies and blasting show tunes was the way I spent more time with my daughter, I'd offer them always.

The girls put their books on the counter. Health.

Fuck.

I'd told myself I'd have the sex talk with Lena, but I hadn't. It definitely wasn't because I kept thinking about Ben and how his texts had abruptly stopped. We'd been having fun, hadn't we? It didn't matter, though.

I certainly wasn't obsessing about how he'd finally moved on and was probably spending his time with some sweet new thing. It had barely been a week, but I knew how these things were in Hollywood. I kept telling myself it was for the best and had managed to keep myself from looking at our text log to see where it had gone wrong. My self-control astonished me.

After all, there was a first time for everything.

Things had been busy and complicated lately. My brain had been scrambled up in a dozen different things that needed doing. That was my excuse in regard to the sex ed conversation. Plus, I was pretty sure my brain kept pushing it out of memory's reach because it was a conversation I really, really didn't want to have.

"What are you guys learning about?" I asked.

Maybe they were getting all they needed from school.

Lena grimaced, and I looked at Eve.

"Just stuff!" she said.

"Sex ed stuff?" I asked.

"Mom!" Lena looked horrified.

"Sorry, sorry," I said. "I was just curious if they're teaching you about all that."

All that.

"I mean sex," I said.

I should have rehearsed or written something down, but that had never been my style. I was not a measure twice, cut once kind of person. I was a measure maybe, swear twice, cut again. And again. And again.

Lena both blushed and blanched at the same time—two round spots of red across her cheeks, standing out against the rest of her pale skin. I was a little surprised that she didn't completely bolt from the room. I was a little surprised *I* didn't bolt from the room.

Eve, on the other hand, looked interested.

Something I hadn't thought about.

I cleared my throat.

"Eve, this is probably a conversation you should have with your mother," I said.

"She won't mind," she said. "She's from Portland."

I had no idea how that was relevant.

Then again, I didn't know how this conversation was supposed to go. I'd learned most of the basics of sex from erotic magazines that had always been stashed in a tree trunk in the overgrown park near our house.

They hadn't been especially accurate. After that, I'd just learned from experience.

Too much experience as some people in our town might have said.

People who had too much time on their hands.

"Sex," I started again.

Lena recoiled. Eve leaned forward.

"Is natural," I said.

"Ew," Lena said.

Even though this was probably the one time when Spencer's presence would have made things worse—thanks mostly to the purity culture shit that he'd struggled his whole life to deal with—I still couldn't help wishing that he were here.

At least to just hold my hand.

I missed holding his hand.

I took a deep breath.

"We should have talked about this earlier," I said.

Lena's face wrinkled into an expression of total disgust.

"It's important that we talk about it," I said.

"Whatever," Lena said. "I already know about the birds and the bees."

"No," I said. "We're not going to talk about it like that. No euphemisms. Real words. Penis. Vagina. Vulva."

I was half worried that Lena was going to fall off her chair. Her back was as straight as a knitting needle, and it seemed like she was holding her breath.

At least I had her complete attention.

Eve's as well.

"I'm sure you have all talked about sex," I said. "Or that you've seen things. Online. Or in the movies, or whatever. But I want you to know that there is a big difference between what our society is willing to show you and what sex actually is."

Lena relaxed—just the tiniest bit—and I could tell there was some genuine interest crouched behind her usual teenage nihilism. Good. I could work with that.

"What have they taught you in school?" I asked, that guilt bobbing back to the surface. Because that was something I *should* know.

She shrugged. "Just, like, don't do it."

I was pretty sure that was the equivalent of my school-mandated sex ed as well. Extremely *not* helpful.

"And the chewing gum thing," Eve said.

"The chewing gum thing?"

"Like, how you're a piece of gum and no one wants an already-chewed-up piece of gum." Lena's cheeks were bright red. "Or whatever."

I closed my eyes. For. Fuck's. Sake.

"Okay," I said. "That. That is absolute bullshit."

Both girls looked stunned at my language.

"Sorry," I said. "But you are not a piece of gum. You are not a piece of anything. You're a person."

I was so mad, I wanted to scream. Weren't things supposed to be better for kids now? Wasn't there more information available to them? *Real* information?

"Okay," I said. "I think we need to start from the beginning. What do you know about your vagina?"

CHAPTER 24

THEN

My BLADDER FELT LIKE IT WAS CONSTANTLY BEING stepped on, everything from my ankles to my neck was swollen, my heartburn was out of control, and I couldn't tie—or untie—my shoes. I was so tired of being pregnant.

It didn't help that Spencer—who'd never done well in moments of heightened emotion—thought that the most helpful thing he could do was to never. Leave. Me. Alone.

"Do you want a glass of water?"

"Are you hungry? Craving anything?"

"Maybe you should put your feet up."

"Should you be lifting that?"

It was sweet at first and then, after a while, I wanted to smother him in his sleep just so I could get some peace and quiet. Because even at night, when I was trying to sleep, I'd hear him whisper: "Do you need another pillow?"

"I can't take it anymore," I told Gabe.

He was somewhere in the UK filming a World War II

movie. Apparently, he had the perfect look for a soldier during that era. One that tended to appear in the first fifteen minutes, bright-eyed and eager, only to be shot dramatically and cinematically for someone else's character development. We'd seen a lot of movies where a "dead" Gabe was lying in someone's arms while they cried over him and gave their Oscar-reel speech about life and death and how it wasn't fair to lose someone so young.

I watched these movies, and Gabe did a great job, but it sometimes felt like the people who were making them only had a passing relationship with death. That they didn't really know what it was like.

These roles had become Gabe's bread and butter. He made good money, but I could sense that he was getting tired of playing the same part over and over again.

"There's no telling what I'll do if he wakes me up in the middle of a nap to ask if I want another blanket," I said. "Help."

I rarely asked for help. It was a Parker family trait for sure—don't let anyone know you're struggling—but I'd reached the end of my patience. It was, however, a testament to my growth as a human being that it took a lot longer to reach that point than it had in the past. Apparently, impending motherhood *did* change a person.

Or maybe I just didn't want to go to prison for murdering my husband when he was just asking if I needed more water, while I was in the middle of drinking water.

"What can I do?" Gabe asked.

"I don't know," I said. "Can't he come visit you, or something?"

"You're due in a month," he said.

"I. Don't. Care," I said. "Get him out of the state or neither of us will make it that long, and this baby will be an orphan, and you'll have to take care of it. How will a BabyBjörn look strapped to your historically accurate uniform?"

It took a lot of convincing, but I managed to get Spencer to go to Scotland for a week to see Gabe. I made it seem like Gabe needed him more, but I could tell that Spencer knew I was desperate for a break. That was the only reason he didn't argue with me in the end and made me promise to call him *immediately* if I felt any signs of labor.

I didn't feel a thing, and the week he was gone was one of the most blissfully peaceful times of my pregnancy. I lay on the couch after my shifts at the grocery store with a bowl of ice cream balanced on my enormous stomach, watching movies on TCM.

When Spencer came back, I was happy to see him, even though I expected the mother-henning to continue. Instead, he was quiet and aloof, which was unusual for him in the most normal of times, but after several months of his constant circling around me, trying to figure out what I needed, the change was startling.

He wouldn't tell me what was wrong. I called Gabe and he denied that anything had happened on the trip. It was clear both of them were lying.

"Tell me what happened, or I'll go make myself a sandwich entirely out of cold cuts," I said to Spencer when I had become well and truly fed up with the weird behavior.

That's when I found out that the casual drinking Gabe had started in high school, and continued through college, was no longer quite so casual.

"He hides it well," Spencer told me. "He doesn't drink when he's working, but the minute he's off the clock? It's like he can't help himself. One drink and then another and then another."

He was mad at me for dragging the secret out of him, but I was glad I'd done it. Even if I had no idea what to do.

"Did you talk to him about it?"

Spencer gave me a look.

"I tried," he said. "But you know how Gabe is."

I nodded. It was how we all were. Something's only a problem if you make it one. No doubt, Gabe felt his drinking was fine, and that *Spencer* was the issue.

"He's probably stressed," I said. "He's been disappointed with the work he's been getting, so it's probably a coping mechanism."

"I don't like it," Spencer said. "He's clearly lonely, constantly going from place to place, traveling to another country for every new role, but he won't admit that there's a problem. He keeps saying it's under control."

"Maybe it is," I said. "I mean, you were just there for a week. He probably wanted an excuse to go have fun with you."

"You didn't see him, Lauren," Spencer said. "He doesn't need an excuse to get plastered."

I could hear the concern in his voice. I knew he was probably right, but what could we do about it? Gabe was an adult. On his way to maybe becoming a famous actor.

We knew nothing about his life and what he had to do to make it through the day.

At least, that's what Gabe told me when I spoke to him next. I'd never heard him so angry. He actually hung up on me. We didn't speak again until Lena was born.

CHAPTER 25

NOW

REINSTALLED A FEW DATING APPS. ALLYSON TOOK SOME
new pictures, and I set my filters wider—both in age and
distance. This was Montana, we were used to traveling to
get what we wanted and needed. At least this search pre-
sented me with a few decent options.

I even had a date scheduled.

"Tell me everything about him," Allyson said as we
headed into the restaurant for dinner.

Lena was over at my mom's. I'd asked Gabe because I
knew he wanted to spend more time with her, but he already had plans—plans that I hoped did not involve making out with his girlfriend in the corner of my shop.

At least the overall lovefest in Cooper had calmed down
a bit. I'd only had to chase one other couple out of the
stacks that week.

I still needed to move those bookshelves, though.

"His name is Carl," I told Allyson, but had to stop as our
waitress approached. "Hey, Annie."

She was a member of one of our book clubs—a regular at the shop.

"Hey, Mrs. P.," she said. "Have you heard anything about when the new Miranda Eddy book is coming out?"

"I'm not supposed to say anything," I said, "but they should be arriving at the store this weekend. But you know we can't put them on the shelves until release day."

Her excitement deflated quickly.

"Of course, if you want to come and help me unbox them, I can't really keep you from reading a few pages while you're at it," I said.

"Really?" she asked.

I tapped my nose. "You didn't hear it from me."

She grinned and took our orders. As she left, the hostess walked a pair of familiar faces past our table.

"Hey, Monica," I said as they stopped to say hello. "Jerry. How's Pickles?"

Pickles was their cat.

"A handful," Monica said. "She disappears for weeks on end and Jerry here is convinced she's gone to the great cat tree in the sky."

"Then she shows up yesterday morning meowing for food like she's always been there," Jerry said. "Like we hadn't been worried sick."

"You know cats," I said.

"I do indeed," Monica said.

They headed to their table.

"I could go weeks in San Francisco without running into a single person I knew," Allyson said. "And I lived there my entire adult life."

"How does this still surprise you?" I asked. "This is small-town life in a nutshell—everyone knows you and your business."

"Seriously," Allyson said.

Wherever I went, I knew someone, and they knew me. Knew about my dead husband and my famous brother. Just the way I knew about Russell Conway's DUIs and the time that Marissa Hamlin won a lifetime supply of ranch dressing from a contest back in '94—it had been big news at the time. We were all too involved in one another's business.

My mom had once said that hot gossip was cheaper than firewood.

It was currency. Connection.

In Philadelphia, I'd been no one. Not a single person there had known about the time I'd upended an entire display of canned green beans while I was stacking them for the Thanksgiving rush. No one knew about the dress I'd worn to graduation—some thrift store find that I'd washed, shrunk to a nearly indecent size, and worn anyway. And there were no whispers about how sad my life was. How lonely I must be. How alone.

Philadelphia had been glorious.

But it had been temporary.

Everything about it had been temporary.

It had been weeks since I'd last heard from Ben.

It was fine. I was over it.

Completely over it.

Hence, the dating apps.

"Okay, tell me about Carl," Allyson said.

I gave her the basics, stopping only for her to interject

her opinions—he was about five years older ("his dick is probably still in decent shape"), he was divorced ("the big test is how he talks about his ex-wife"), and he lived an hour or so away ("he gets one shot to prove he's worth the mileage").

"What should I wear?" I asked.

Allyson thought for a moment. "You have that red dress," she said. "Makes your boobs look incredible."

"My boobs are incredible," I said.

"That's true and also fuck you," she said, before looking down at her own chest. "Don't listen to her, girls. Some men like them small."

I laughed. "I think men just like them in general," I said.

"You also have a great ass," she said.

"You're too kind," I said.

"Now say something nice about my ass," she said.

But before I could bestow any compliments, our nachos arrived.

I hadn't gotten a chance to eat lunch, so I was starving. I practically hoovered up my first bite, and immediately reached for the next.

"No drinking," Allyson said. "On your date."

"Obviously," I said. "I'm going to be driving to meet him."

"Don't shave your legs."

"I'm not going to sleep with him," I said.

"Sure," she said. "I've totally said that to myself at the beginning of several dates."

"I guess I just have better self-control," I said.

Allyson rolled her eyes at me, laughing when half of my nachos ended up on my shirt—cheese everywhere.

"Such control," she said. "Such grace."

"Shut up." I reached for her napkin and dabbed at my shirt. It was going to leave a stain.

I turned away from the table to wave Annie over for another napkin, but both I and my arm froze before I could.

Gabe had just walked into the restaurant talking to Ollie.

"You have cheese on your chin," Allyson said, trying to help me clean myself up.

With Ben Walsh right behind them.

"Fuck me," I said.

"It's not that bad," Allyson said, still looking at my shirt.

"Oh, yes it is," I said.

She finally glanced up and did a literal double take.

"Holy shit," she said. "Is that—"

"Yes," I said.

Ben Walsh was in Montana.

Ben Walsh was in Montana.

Maybe I was dreaming. He *had* been in my dreams after all. But not like this. Not in a busy restaurant with half the town gawking at the trio of movie stars. And Allyson had seen him too—he was really here.

The crowd parted to let him through.

His eyes were on me the whole time.

Why hadn't he texted?

"Hey, nachos," Gabe said, helping himself.

"Ladies," Ollie said, ever the gentleman.

I had barely looked at them.

"Hello," Ben said.

"Hi," I said.

"You've got something on your face," he said.

"It's cheese," Allyson said.

I all but slapped my chin to get it off.

"Hello," Ben said, holding out a hand to Allyson. "I'm Ben."

"Oh, I know," she said.

I kicked her under the table, but Ben just grinned as if he wasn't surprised at all that I'd told people about him. Smug bastard probably expected it.

Why hadn't he texted?

"It's good to see you, Lauren," he said.

"What are you doing here?" I asked.

It was rude, but I was too stunned to be anything but.

This didn't feel real. I thought about pinching myself to make sure it wasn't a weird, fucked-up dream, but then a tiny voice in the back of my head piped up, hoping it wasn't.

Which was ridiculous, of course. I'd just set up a date with a man of an appropriate age, who lived within driving distance, and wasn't about to be the next James Bond. A date that had long-term potential.

Ben did not.

Ben wasn't even supposed to be here.

"We're getting dinner," Gabe said, sliding into our booth.

I glared at him, but he didn't notice.

"Do you mind if we join you?" Ollie asked.

Allyson had already moved over to let Gabe in and made even more space for Ollie. Ben remained standing, looking down at me.

"Is this seat taken?" Ben asked.

His accent was back. God, it was delicious.

I let him in.

He looked annoyingly good. Head–to–toe black again. I was pretty sure he was wearing the same boots I'd seen him wearing in Philadelphia.

"How have you been?" he asked. "How's the store?"

"Oh right," Gabe said. "You guys have been talking."

He said it with a *tone*. I glared at him.

"Just a few texts," I said. "A while ago."

I looked at Ben. He looked confused.

What would I have done if I knew he was coming?

Probably shaved my legs.

His own leg was pressed up against my unshaven one.

"What are you doing here?" I asked him, lowering my voice to a whisper, as if the three people across the table wouldn't hear me.

Of course they did.

"I told you I had plans tonight," Gabe said, sounding indignant as he ate more of our nachos. As if I'd been talk-ing to him.

Somehow, he didn't get any food on his chin, despite the beard he'd been growing.

I rubbed my face, hoping the cheese was gone.

"It was just supposed to be me and Ollie, but Ben sur-prised us," Gabe said. "We thought he'd arrive tomorrow."

I looked over at my brother.

"Tomorrow?"

He was not providing me with *any* answers. Then again, this was the same brother who had married Jacinda without telling anyone, and then more recently sprung Chani on us with a few hours' notice.

I reminded myself to throttle him later. And teach him how to use a calendar app.

"He's here for the theatre," Ollie said, providing me with much-needed information. "I'm directing these two in *Rosencrantz and Guildenstern Are Dead* for the theatre's premiere production."

"Oh," I said.

That explained *why* Ben was here, and yet . . .

I looked at him. He grinned at me. I felt flustered—and not in a good way.

He put his hand on my thigh.

"Excuse me," I said. "I need the bathroom."

I wiggled my way out of the booth and headed immediately to the bathroom where I locked myself in a stall and put my head between my knees.

What. Was. Happening?

There was a knock on the door.

"I know you're in there," Allyson said.

I unlocked the door and pushed it open. She was standing with her hands on her hips, as if *I'd* done something wrong.

"What?" I demanded.

"There's no Carl, is there?" she asked. "There's no date. You were just fucking with me."

"Allyson—"

"You can't just spring your hot movie star hookup on someone like that," she continued. "That's so not fair. I haven't plucked my eyebrows this week!"

"Allyson." I came out of the stall and grabbed her shoulders. "I didn't know."

"What?"

"I. Didn't. Know."

She was silent as I went to the mirror.

My reflection was that of a woman in shock. With unwashed hair. Why, oh why hadn't I washed my hair today? For a brief moment, I thought about dunking my head in the sink, but I was pretty sure that was a bad idea.

"You didn't know?" Allyson asked, finally seeming to understand what was happening.

"He sprung *himself* on me," I said.

Allyson pressed her lips together as we both heard how that sounded.

"Don't you dare laugh," I said.

She mimed buttoning her mouth closed.

"Oh my god," I said. "What am I going to do?"

I pressed my palm to my forehead.

"Just an idea," Allyson said. "But we could return to the table and have dinner with him. Them."

I stared at her.

"Or not," she said.

"I can't go back out there," I said.

"Sure you can."

"No," I said. "I can't."

I felt hot, my heart racing. I knew it was a ridiculous reaction to what was happening, but I couldn't help it.

Just as I had started to fully accept that my Philadelphia fling had fizzled out, the man himself showed up. In my town. My small town. Where everyone loved to talk.

No doubt gossip was already spreading about his presence. Most people were used to Gabe, somewhat accustomed to Ollie, but Ben? That was a lot of Hollywood for
Cooper to handle.

I really didn't want to get caught in that spotlight.

Life had just started to feel normal. Well, as normal as
one could expect. The store was doing well. Lena and I
were communicating better than we had before. Gabe was
sober and working and in love.

I did not need this right now.

Allyson regarded me for a moment and then seemed to
realize that I was serious about not returning to the table.
She shifted into problem-solving mode. It calmed me. If I
was the queen of organization, Allyson was the titan of getting shit done.

"Okay," she said. "If you really want me to, I'll tell them
you felt sick, and you'll slip out the alleyway exit at the end
of the hall."

It was cowardly and pathetic, but I nodded anyway.

"What about you?"

Allyson gave me a look. "Stuck at dinner with three
gorgeous men? I'll be fine."

There was one problem. I didn't have my purse.

"I'll go get it for you," Allyson said.

She was a good friend.

But when we opened the door to the bathroom, Ben
was standing there.

"I'm gonna, uh, go get . . . um . . ." Allyson mumbled
something and then she was gone.

Coward.

Not that I blamed her. I wanted to run too.

"Hello," Ben said.

"You're in Montana," I said, cutting right to the chase.

"I told you I always wanted to visit," he said.

He looked so good. I tried not to focus on that.

"You could have said something."

Ben tilted his head, like he was a confused puppy.

I was probably being dramatic but the whole thing felt like it was out of a movie. Not in a good way.

"I did text," he said.

"It's been a while," I said.

His brow furrowed.

"Maybe I thought I'd surprise you."

"I hate surprises," I said.

Which was true. I was the kind of person who liked knowing the endings of movies before I watched them— just in case the dog died or something. I hated April Fools' Day, which to me was just an endless parade of mean surprises. And everyone in my life knew better than to throw me a surprise party.

Of course, Ben didn't know that.

Because he didn't really know anything about me. Except that he liked my tits and ass.

"Huh," he said. Like it was no big deal.

He had an earring. A little gold hoop in his right lobe. I hadn't noticed that in Philadelphia. It was sexy. His hair was longer too. That was also sexy.

Not that it mattered.

It didn't.

"I gotta go," I said, turning toward the exit.

He caught me by the arm. And oh, it felt good. Stupid good.

It's a damn hand, I told myself. *Get it together.*

"I'm sorry," he said. "Let me make it up to you?"

The look in his eyes indicated exactly how he wanted to make it up to me.

I was momentarily tempted, and that was exactly the problem.

"Are you insane?" I hissed. "We're in a restaurant. In my hometown. My brother is in the next room."

He laughed. "I was thinking we'd go somewhere and *talk,* but I kind of like this exhibitionist side of you."

Terrifyingly, so did I.

I needed to get out of there.

I shrugged his arm off and headed away from the dining room toward the exit. It didn't matter that I didn't have my purse. Allyson would bring it to me tomorrow—and that was one good thing about small towns, I could walk home, and my back door wasn't locked.

The cold air reminded me that I'd also had a jacket inside, but it didn't matter. It had been a mild winter. I could walk fast. I could run.

"Lauren, wait. Let me explain."

Ben had followed me out into the alley. I turned on him, anger rising.

"Let you explain?" I fumed. "I haven't heard from you in forever, and you just show up making jokes about having sex in a restaurant?"

"Technically, *you* made the suggestion," he said.

I narrowed my eyes at him, and he held up his hands in surrender.

"I realize now that I should have texted about coming," he said. "But I thought . . ."

"What?"

He shook his head. "*You* never responded to *me,*" he said. "Days ago."

I sputtered. "Yes, I did!"

There was that head tilt again. This time it wasn't confused, though. It was condescending.

"Okay," he said. "My mistake."

I glared at him, but somewhere in the back of my mind, doubt was starting to root. *He'd* left *my* last text unanswered.

Hadn't he?

The last few weeks felt like a blur.

"What are you *really* doing here?" I asked.

"The play," he said. "Gabe asked a while ago. I thought you knew."

I shook my head.

"I *did* keep asking about Cooper."

That's why he'd been asking those questions?

It had been a game. Hadn't it?

From the look on Ben's face—disappointed and surprised—clearly not.

"It's not for long," he said. "Just a short run to get the theatre started. You'll barely know I'm here."

That seemed completely unlikely.

"How long are you here?"

"Not sure," Ben said. "At least a month. Probably two."

My jaw dropped.

"Two months?"

"Maybe," he said, taking one step back as if he could tell I was starting to get manic. "I really thought you knew."

I couldn't understand how he was so casual about all of this. Then I remembered. He was a thirty-year-old actor who lived out of a suitcase. He was casual about *everything*.

And that was the problem.

"This is not going to work," I said, pinching the bridge of my nose between my fingers.

"What—"

I held up a hand, silencing him. "I'm not talking to you," I said.

My mind was spinning. Everything was spinning. I leaned up against the cold brick wall in the alley, my eyes shut as I tried to make sense of the farce that was currently occurring around me.

Ben was here. In Cooper.

"Philadelphia was a onetime thing," I said. "And I don't have time for whatever this is. I have a date."

"A date?"

"I'm forty-one, Ben, and you're *not*. Our lives are completely different. You're just starting out and I'm, I'm basically done with all the things you still need to do. I don't even know if I want to get married again—or have someone else in my house. I never should have listened to Ollie, and I never should have gone to your trailer. I shouldn't have gone to Philadelphia in the first place."

"Lauren?" Ben asked, his voice tentative.

"Why are you doing this to me?" I asked. Still not really talking to him.

"I was just going to the bathroom," he said.

I opened my eyes.

Ben was looking at me like I was the crazy one.

"I can't do this," I said.

"Okay," Ben said. "Can you let me know what *this* is so we're both on the same page?"

"I'm not having sex with you," I said.

"Right," he said.

"Not in the restaurant, not out here in the alley, and not at your place."

Once again, the head tilt. I tried not to be charmed by it.

"You can't just show up here," I said, as if repeating it would make it make sense to him. "I live here. My family is here. My friends. And people talk. They talk a lot."

Ben nodded, and it finally seemed like it was all sinking in.

"As far as anyone knows, you are someone working with my brother," I said. "*We* do not have a relationship. *We* are basically strangers."

"I wouldn't say—"

"Basically. Strangers," I repeated. "No one can know what happened between us."

"Why not?"

I was speechless for a moment. "Why not? Why not? Did you not hear me before?"

"I thought you weren't talking to me."

I barely stifled a growl.

"Okay," he said, clearly sensing I was at the end of my rope. "I don't understand, but I'll be a stranger, if that's what you want."

"It is what I want," I said.

"If you say so."

"Stop that," I said.

I should have stepped back.

Because we were done here. I'd made my point—I'd made it very clear.

I moved toward him instead.

"Lauren," he said.

God. The way he said my name.

And his eyes.

They twinkled at me.

The moment I kissed him, I forgot every reason why I shouldn't. His reaction didn't help. His arms went around me, and I melted, my body molding against his. I thought I'd been ravenous before, but now I was desperate. Out of my mind with need. I wanted him—my hands going to his belt, his going to my shirt. The two of us mauling each other like drunk teenagers at homecoming. But better. So much better.

He was such a good kisser. And his hands . . .

They moved down to my ass, and all I wanted was to be hoisted up against the brick wall of the alley and reminded of exactly how talented and perfect his cock was. I could feel it hard against my stomach.

It would have been so easy to just . . .

I shoved him back, stopping the kiss abruptly as I realized exactly what I was doing. Exactly what I was thinking about doing.

Both of us were breathing heavily. It was cold out, but I only felt the heat from Ben's body. I wanted to unbutton his shirt and crawl inside.

What was wrong with me?

"We should talk," Ben said, his face flushed. "I feel like there's been some confusion."

His eyes were warm.

I shook my head.

"This is not . . . I can't . . ."

He reached for me, but I stepped back and, like a coward, ran away.

CHAPTER 26

NOW

ALLYSON BROUGHT MY PURSE AND JACKET TO THE STORE the next day.

"I'm going to need you to tell me everything," she said.

Immediately, I fished my phone out of my bag.

I didn't look at Allyson.

"You were the one who spent the evening with them. I think you have more to share than me," I said. Deflecting.

"Oh please," she said. "You think I didn't observe how Ben came back to the table with his shirt collar all fucked up as if someone had been gripping it with her horny, denialist hands?"

As I glanced up, I could feel the color drain from my face.

"Don't worry," she said. "Gabe didn't notice."

"Thank god," I said.

I was scrolling through my phone, looking for the text thread I'd been trying to ignore.

"Ollie, on the other hand," Allyson said. "He was shooting me knowing looks for the rest of the meal. Which he paid for, by the way. Such a sweetheart." She tilted her head. "You're sure he's not interested in women?"

"Completely sure," I said. "And Ben . . . did he . . . ?"

"He didn't say anything," Allyson said. "Though he did look a little bit like he'd been run over by a truck."

I found Ben's number.

Read the last text.

Fuck.

I groaned and put my head down on the counter.

"I'm a bad person," I said.

Because I was.

Allyson patted me on the shoulder. "No, you're not," she said.

"No," I said. "I am."

Ben had been right. *I'd* been the one to stop texting.

Our last exchange had been about the Testy Fest. I could have sworn I'd responded, but I hadn't. Things had just been so chaotic, and I'd been trying not to think about him, and in the process . . .

I'd left him hanging. After he'd texted me about testicles. Then reamed *him* out for his lack of communication.

Oh god.

"You have to tell me what happened in that alley," Allyson said.

"We kissed," I said.

Maybe this was for the best.

"Obviously," she said. "Who kissed who?"

"I kissed him," I admitted, forehead still on the wood counter, phone in my hand.

It would have ended eventually—our conversations— I was just the one to stop them. Accidentally.

Subconsciously?

I felt dizzy.

"Good for you," Allyson said. She sounded surprised and proud at the same time.

"No." I lifted my head. "Not good. Crazy. Bad. Insane."

Confusion skated over her face.

"How is kissing a gorgeous man in an alley a bad thing? Especially since you already know he wants you and he's good in bed." She paused. "He *was* good in bed, right? You weren't lying about that?"

"I might have underplayed his strengths there," I said.

Allyson's mouth dropped open. "You said you had two orgasms with him."

"It was three," I said.

What was I doing? Shut up, I told myself.

She hit me in the arm. "I hate you," she said.

"I know."

We stood there, my hands braced on the counter, hers on her hips.

Ben thought I'd given him the brush-off.

"Let me get this straight," Allyson said. "Ben has the hots for you. He's fantastic in bed. He's *here*. What exactly is the problem?"

"It's not reasonable," I said.

"Reasonable?" Allyson's voice went up with each syllable. "Who the fuck cares about reasonable?"

"Shhh," I told her.

The store was empty.

"I don't understand," she said. "Explain it to me like I'm a child."

"*He's* the child," I said. "He's thirty years old."

"So?"

"None of this is real."

"I think the alley at Susannah's Steak House would dis-agree," she said. "Besides, you didn't have a problem with his age in Philadelphia."

"Philadelphia is not Cooper," I said.

"No shit."

I rolled my eyes. "You said it yourself last night. Every-one here knows me. There are no secrets in a town like this."

"And Ben needs to be a secret?"

"You don't get it," I said. "You don't know what it's like to have people watching you constantly and judging you."

"I didn't think you cared," she said.

"It's not about me," I said. "It's about Lena—whatever I do affects her and this *thing* with Ben would not be a good idea."

I thought about all the ways people had talked about me. How small it had made me feel.

"People would have thoughts. And they wouldn't be subtle about them." I closed my eyes. "Jesus. If my mother-in-law found out . . ."

"I'd imagine she'd be happy you found someone."

I laughed without any humor. "You don't know Diana," I said. "And Ben is not *someone*. He was a good time, noth-ing else."

A throat cleared behind me, and I didn't have to turn to know that it was Ben. Of course it was. Because my life was a never-ending trainwreck, currently of my own mak-ing.

Well. If there had been any chance of salvaging this—of

apologizing for unintentionally ghosting him and shoving him aside last night—I'd killed it right there.

I turned toward him, telling myself it was for the best.

It was something I had to repeat when I was facing him.

Because he was so damn kissable.

He was a complication that I didn't have time for.

But god, was he one gorgeous complication.

I wondered if he had any clothes that weren't black. Or another pair of shoes. He was wearing the same boots he'd worn that first night in Philadelphia, as well as last night in the restaurant. He had a leather jacket and bike helmet under one arm, and his hair looked stupidly good for someone who should have had helmet hair.

"I'm gonna go," Allyson said.

"She seems to do that a lot," Ben said once she was gone.

"I didn't mean for you to hear that," I said.

"Guess that answers *that* question," he said.

"I—"

He held up a hand. "I was hoping to talk to you, but I do actually need some books."

"You wanted to talk?" My voice was small.

Ben shrugged. "Don't worry about it," he said. "I should have taken the hint." He let out a toneless laugh. "Note to self, talking about testicles is not the best way to flirt."

"You were flirting?"

I felt stupid saying it out loud. Of course he'd been flirting.

I'd been flirting right back.

"I thought—"

"It's fine," he said. "And like I said, you'll barely notice I'm here."

"I don't think that's possible," I said.

He let out a breath like I was being ridiculous. And I was.

"I'll keep out of your way," he said. "I'm sure I'll be distracted by the show anyways. It's not a big deal."

He wasn't looking at me—his attention was focused on the bookshelves.

"Things are just complicated," I said. "Lena—"

"Believe it or not," he said, "I get it."

I felt lower than a squashed worm.

"Where's the nonfiction section?" he asked.

"Over there." I pointed.

I followed him.

"Living in a town like this—"

"I come from a small town too," he said, examining book titles. "And I went to boarding school. I know what it's like to live in a community where everyone knows one another. Where everyone knows your secrets."

He picked up a book. Put it down.

"You're protecting your daughter," he said. "It's one of the things I like about you. How you always put her first."

The compliment warmed me. Even though I disagreed with the sentiment.

"You were right," I said. "About the text messages."

He shrugged.

"I really thought I'd texted you back," I said.

"Don't worry about it," he said. "We were just a one-time thing, right?"

He hadn't made eye contact since he'd appeared in the shop.

"I thought with the whole James Bond thing that this was for the best," I said.

A wry smile twisted his lips.

"Right," he said. "The whole James Bond thing."

"Did something happen?"

I had no right to ask, but Ben answered anyway.

"No," he said. "Which is exactly the issue."

"Oh," I said.

"Yeah," he said, finally looking up at me.

All I saw in his eyes was disappointment.

"I'm sorry."

"Don't worry about it," Ben said. "My agent said it's still a possibility, but I think she was just trying to protect my feelings."

At least there was someone out there looking out for him.

"You have a nice agent."

He lifted a shoulder. "You can blame her for my presence here. She always said I should get back into live theatre. And now that my schedule's opened up for the time being, I decided to take Ollie up on his offer. He thought the show would be good for me."

"Ollie does know how to spot talent," I said.

Ben flipped through a book. Stopped. Read a few lines. Stuck the paperback under his arm.

"At least it will be a distraction," he said. "I could use that."

Ouch.

"I really am sorry," I said.

He paused and leaned into one hip.

"Me too," he said. "I should have told you that I was coming."

"I don't like surprises," I said, repeating what I'd told him last night.

"I guess I thought you might be glad to see me."

"I was," I said.

He gave me a piercing stare.

"If that's how you look when you're happy, I'd hate to see how you act when you're upset."

"I *really* don't like surprises."

"Noted," he said.

He pulled another book from the shelf.

"Don't stress about me being here," he said. "I'll keep my distance."

Why did it hurt to hear that? It was what I wanted.

Right?

"And I'm good at keeping secrets," he said. "No one will know what happened between us in Philadelphia."

"I told Allyson," I said, not knowing why.

He managed a wry grin. "I gathered that," he said. "She seems nice."

Was he going to go after Allyson next? Was it any of my business?

"She is nice," I said. "She won't say anything either."

Another shrug. "I don't care," he said. "I know what people say about me. That I sleep around. I learned a while ago that it doesn't matter—that if enough people tell the same kind of stories about you, it becomes the truth. You need a thick skin to be in this industry."

He grabbed one more book.

"I'll get these," he said.

We walked back to the counter, and I rang him up. He'd bought *Zen and the Art of Motorcycle Maintenance, Tom Stoppard: A Life,* and *Cowgirl Up! A History of Rodeo Women.*

"Thinking of taking up rodeo?" I asked, still trying to fix what I'd broken. "It's pretty dangerous—easy to get hurt."

Ben looked at me.

"I've gotten hurt before," he said. "You get used to it."

He took his books and left.

CHAPTER 27

THEN

I HAD NO INTEREST IN BEING A HERO WHEN IT CAME TO childbirth. Whatever drugs they offered, I took. And when they said that a C-section would probably be best, I was quick to agree. It was major surgery, sure, but at least it wouldn't rip my vagina apart. Maybe I'd save that for the next kid. If we had one. Though when they put the epidural needle in my back, I realized I wasn't even sure if I wanted *this* one.

I told that to Spencer and he informed me that, unfortunately, it was a little too late. I also told him that all of this was his fault, but he didn't seem to mind. He didn't seem to mind anything, not when I was squeezing his hand so hard that his fingers turned white, or when I shouted that I hated him and he was never touching me ever again.

"You're doing great," he kept saying.

"Fuck you!" I screamed back.

The nurses thought it was hilarious. I didn't find the

humor in it until at least six months later. Even then I didn't think it was *that* funny.

Lena was not a beautiful baby. She was a wrinkly-old-man baby, like a raisin. She was completely bald and tiny, which seemed impossible because she'd felt enormous inside of me. She had fingernails. I marveled over those most of all. Fingernails. On a baby. Who knew?

Apparently everyone, but I hadn't read many parenting books. There were surely going to be some surprises.

We were lucky—Lena arrived just as Gabe's movie was wrapping up, so he was able to come home to meet her while I was still in the hospital.

He wasn't drunk, but he was hungover.

"She's adorable," he said, leaning over us.

He smelled like stale whiskey and unclean armpits. I told myself it was because he'd just gotten off a plane. That he would come back the next day showered and bright-eyed.

"She's a prune baby," I said. "Have you seen her fingernails?"

"Wow," he said.

"Yeah," I said.

We both stared at Lena with a quiet kind of awe.

"You made that," he said.

"Can you believe it?"

"Nope," he said, but he looked proud.

Happy.

"Can I hold her?" he asked.

I hesitated. But only for a minute.

"Mind her head," I told him as I passed her over.

There was something so special about watching other

people holding her. Everyone gazed at Lena with such marvelous wonder that it made my heart swell. Because yes. I *had* made that.

"We're gonna be best friends," Gabe said, tickling under her chin with a finger.

Lena reached out and grabbed it. Held tight.

"I think that's a binding agreement," I said.

The next day he was sober. He stayed that way for the entire visit.

It didn't last.

CHAPTER 28

NOW

I WAS MAKING BROWNIES—*WITHOUT* FROSTING—WHEN Gabe and Ollie walked into the kitchen.

"Excuse me," I said. "Did you forget how to use a doorbell?"

As a response, Gabe stuck his finger into the bowl of batter before shoving it into his mouth.

"That's disgusting," I said. "Please tell me you washed your hands."

Gabe gave me a look as if I'd wounded him terribly.

"You know," I said, "you could have warned me that you'd hired Ben to do the play."

"I thought he would have told you," he said. "You know, during all that *texting* you were doing."

I threw a dish towel at him.

"He didn't say anything?" Ollie asked.

I hoped Gabe didn't pick up on his knowing look.

Luckily, my brother was busy molesting my brownie mix.

"It's no big deal," I said. "It just would have been nice to know."

Ollie gave me a sympathetic smile.

"Sorry about that," he said.

"It's not your fault."

"Hey," Gabe said, clearly having ignored the last few exchanges between me and Ollie. "Can we use your dining room table?"

"My dining room table?" I repeated.

"Lauren, darling," Ollie said, "we are at your mercy."

I rolled my eyes at the drama.

"Don't you already have a table at your apartment?" I asked Gabe.

"We just need to spread out," he said. "And you have more space."

"Spread out?"

"Theatre things," Gabe said. "Come on, it's not like you're currently using it."

"You know Mom is at the store," I said. "You could use hers."

"Yeah, but there aren't any brownies at hers," Gabe said, giving me that sad little brother look, which was a bit harder to pull off with the beard. "And I promised Ollie."

"Fine," I said, waving a hand. "You might as well stay for dinner then."

The grin on Gabe's face indicated that he'd been hoping for that as well. In fact, that might have been the plan all along.

"Chani too?" he asked.

"Sure," I said, adding chocolate chips to the mixing bowl.

I'd decided to play around with the recipe today. Spencer had always said there was no need to improve on perfection, but I liked experimenting. And tonight I had three more guinea pigs to feed in addition to the one I lived with.

"Thank you," Ollie said.

"*You're* welcome," I said, before turning back to my brother. "How did you even know I was making brownies?"

Gabe swiped another finger of batter and neatly avoided my attempt to swat him with my dish towel.

"You're always baking something," he said.

I rolled my eyes as they disappeared into the dining room.

As soon as the brownies were in the oven, I started on dinner. I'd been planning on making a casserole anyway, so there would be plenty of food, but I also doubled the amount I usually made for salad and took some frozen rolls out to thaw.

All the while I kept replaying the disastrous interaction I'd had with Ben the day before. My stomach felt sour just thinking about how unkind I'd been. How much I wished I could take back my words.

But a part of me knew it was for the best. Considering how I'd jumped him the first moment we'd been alone, being an absolute asshole was probably the best way to keep it from happening again. The last thing I needed was a too-young, too-charming, too-gorgeous man tempting me with his smile and those damn eyes of his. And the last thing he needed was a skittish, scared widow with an unhealthy organizational coping mechanism.

Whatever had happened between us in Philadelphia was

going to stay in Philadelphia. And in the alley of the restaurant.

The brownies were barely out of the oven when Gabe poked his head back into the kitchen.

"They're too hot," I said as he eyed dessert.

"No such thing," he said, coming toward them.

"You're going to have to wait," I said, trying to push him away.

He resisted and put his arm around my shoulders.

"Lauren, my wonderful, sweet, caring, perfect sister."

I gave him a look.

"What do you want?" I asked. "I already gave you use of my table."

"It's just a tiny favor," he said.

"Plus brownies and a homemade dinner."

"Please, please, please," he said.

I sucked in a breath. "What is it?"

"Come with me," he said.

I allowed him to steer me into my own dining room, which was now an absolute mess—papers completely covering the surface of the table.

"You're going to have to clean this up before we eat," I said.

Jesus. When had I started sounding like such a nag?

"Is this what it's going to look like?"

I was looking at a rendering of the inside of the theatre—brand-new seats, a refurbished stage, all while keeping the old-fashioned feel of the place. I still didn't really understand why Gabe had decided to buy a run-down theatre in Cooper, but from the looks of my dining room, he and Ollie had big ideas.

"That's what we're hoping," Ollie said. "There's still a lot to do, but it should be done in time for the opening."

"Chani's already reached out to her contacts," Gabe said. "I think we'll get a lot of press."

I'd only heard bits and pieces about their plans for the theatre.

"I'm pretty sure that both your names and Ben's will be enough of a draw," I said. "You could probably leave the theatre as it is and still sell out."

"For the first show, sure," Ollie said. "But we're thinking long-term."

That was the part I wasn't exactly clear on. What *were* they expecting long-term?

"Do you have an idea for the next show?" I asked.

Gabe and Ollie looked at each other.

"Not exactly," Gabe said. "We're working on it."

That didn't sound like a particularly solid business plan.

Then again, it wasn't as if I was a genius at running the Cozy. It just happened to be the closest bookstore in a fifty-mile radius, so we did pretty well. Not great, but good enough. And we also had a wealthy sponsor to keep us in the black during slow months. Which we'd had quite a few of in the early days of the shop. If we hadn't had Gabe's financing, we probably would have closed after the first year.

But his money and privilege afforded us a second chance and we'd used it to figure out how to make the most of our local patrons while also building a decent online following. At least my mom had. She was the driving force behind any of the Cozy's success. She was devoted. Focused. I loved the store, but it never felt like mine, even with its crafts section.

The store had been kept afloat by our good fortunes. By Gabe's good fortunes.

It seemed likely, between his and Ollie's finances, they'd probably be able to do something similar with the theatre.

Though I was sure that wasn't the goal.

"We want to offer the space to the local high schools," Gabe said. "The theatre program is lousy here and they just have a worn-down auditorium to use."

"Okay," I said, still not sure how that was going to make them any money.

"We want to run acting classes, as well as produce shows with local performers," Ollie said. "The big headlining stars will be an occasional bonus, when we can get them."

"You're not trying to bring Hollywood or Broadway to Cooper?" I asked, feeling slightly relieved.

"Absolutely not," Gabe said.

I'd gotten a taste of what it was like to be spotlight-adjacent whenever we'd visit him in L.A. or go to a red carpet event with him. It was a bunch of people taking your picture and shouting at you. It was terrifying and overwhelming. I didn't want that coming here.

The town could only take so many visitors at once.

And they were already squirrelly on newcomers. It had taken Allyson months to convince people she wasn't here to turn Cooper into the new San Francisco.

"I'm taking a break from Hollywood," Gabe said. "Why would I want to transplant it next door?"

That was the first I'd heard about him taking a break from film. Was it on purpose or something he'd been forced into?

I thought about Ben.

Why *hadn't* he gotten the Bond role? He was perfect for it.

"There are other things in my life worth my attention these days," Gabe said.

That was probably the real objective behind the theatre—an opportunity for Gabe to stay in Cooper. To spend more time with family. With Lena. Without going insane from boredom.

Raising a theatre from the dead would certainly keep him occupied.

"How does Chani feel about this?" I asked.

"She's . . . adjusting," he said. "I'm not giving up my place in L.A., so we can go back whenever we need to, but I think we're both looking forward to being away from the paparazzi."

"Until you invite them all here for the opening," I said.

"Until then," Gabe agreed.

It had been a circus when Gabe came home for Spencer's funeral. A horrible, fucked-up circus.

I didn't want that near my kid again.

"Sounds like a plan," I said.

"As long as we can get the production up and running," Ollie said.

I caught the way they looked at each other, and it made me nervous.

"Look at this," Gabe said, his hands still on my shoulders.

In front of me was a pile of sketches. I picked them up and began flipping through them. They were simple but beautifully done—a few different versions of figures that looked vaguely like Gabe and Ben in a variety of outfits.

"Are these going to be the costumes for the show?" I asked.

Ollie leaned over and plucked two images—one of Gabe and one of Ben—out of the pile and put them in front of me.

"We're hoping so," he said.

"They look great," I said. "Very . . . hobo chic."

Because they were. Both costumes were suits in various states of disrepair, patched elbows and knees, ragged hems, and sleeves half torn off. Each of them had a broken-down hat and shoes with their toes sticking out.

I found myself staring at the one for Ben. Whoever the artist was had done a very good job capturing his essence.

God, he was gorgeous.

I remembered that I was a cruel and fickle bitch who didn't deserve to look at a sketch of him.

I put the drawings down.

"You like them?" Ollie asked.

"They're good designs," I said. "Who's making them?"

There was silence.

"No," I said, finally realizing what this was all about.

"You don't even know what we're asking," Gabe said.

I put my hands on my hips.

"You're asking me to make the costumes for the show."

Gabe exchanged more looks with Ollie.

"Yeah," Gabe said. "That is what we're asking."

"And that's why the answer is no," I said.

It was Ollie's turn to try, and he did so by pulling out a chair and gesturing for me to sit.

"Lauren, darling," he said, "we all know how good you are with a sewing machine."

"Whatever bullshit Gabe has been telling you about my skills is clearly a lie," I said. "I can make pockets and hem pants."

"You made that ladybug costume for Lena," Gabe said.

"That was years ago. And it was mostly felt and a glue gun."

I had been pretty proud of it—she'd looked downright adorable with her little pipe cleaner antennas.

"It was beautiful," he said.

"It was," Ollie said. "I've seen pictures."

"You're both delusional," I said. "I'm not a seamstress."

"We're not expecting you to make two suits from scratch," Ollie said. "But we thought you could help deconstruct ones we buy."

I examined the sketches again.

"And maybe add a few details," Gabe said.

"What are those few details exactly?"

"Just some knitwear," he said.

"Just *some* knitwear?" I shook my head. "Do you know how long it takes to knit something? There's a reason that knitters rarely take commissions. It's time-consuming and expensive and *never* appreciated."

"Money isn't a problem," Gabe said. "And we appreciate you."

"Why don't you hire a professional seamstress?"

Another wordless conversation.

"We tried," Gabe finally said. "No one's available to come here and get it done in the time we need."

I doubted they'd looked far before settling on this brilliant plan. I squeezed my eyes shut, already knowing how this was going to end, but wanting to delay the inevitable as long as possible.

"Let me guess," I said. "I'm your only option."

"Kind of," Gabe said.

This time, when I looked at the sketches, I did so from a construction mindset. The truth was that they weren't wrong about the necessary skill level. If they had suits, I could make them look like they were falling apart. I could probably knit a scarf and a pair of fingerless gloves that would be perfect for one of the characters.

I could picture it easily.

"Dammit," I said.

CHAPTER 29

NOW

"YOUR MOM IS GOING TO MAKE THE COSTUMES FOR the play," Gabe told Lena, who was picking at her casserole.

She looked at me, and I nodded. She shrugged.

Things had only gotten frostier between her and Gabe since Chani had moved into his apartment. As far as Lena was concerned, there wasn't a single member of the press that could be trusted.

"It's going to be spectacular," Ollie said. "You should stop by the theatre next week, Lena. We're going to be installing the stage lights."

"Okay," she said, still staring at her plate.

"Maybe you could come watch a rehearsal sometime," Gabe said.

Lena ignored him.

His face fell.

"We might need some volunteer ushers," Ollie said. "Do you think you and your friends would be interested?"

"Maybe," Lena said.

I saw Chani pat Gabe's arm as his frown deepened.

"Isn't Eve a big fan of *SXS*?" Ollie asked.

That was the show that had first thrust Ben into the spotlight—a sexy, modern BBC retelling of *Sense and Sensibility* where he'd played the charming and rakish John Willoughby. It had been so popular that even teenagers in the States had become obsessed. Eve included.

"Yeah," Lena said.

"We can introduce her to Ben," Gabe offered.

Still no response. At least Gabe wasn't giving up. I shot him an encouraging smile across the table.

"Hollywood certainly loves stealing actors from the UK," Chani said.

"Only the best ones," Ollie said with a toss of his head.

"Of course," Chani said, keeping her smile in check. "I mean, he's no Mr. Darcy."

Ollie had played Darcy back in the day.

"Darcy versus Bond," he said. "Who's more iconic?"

"Darcy," Lena and Chani said simultaneously.

"Thank you very much," Gabe said, but he didn't seem upset.

Bond had been complicated for him.

"I suppose you think I did you a favor," Gabe said. "Since Bond is such a crap role."

Ollie laughed. "It's not a crap role," he said. "And I would have been amazing, but you were the right choice."

Gabe rolled his eyes.

"Things would be different if they cast it now," he said.

Clearly Ben hadn't confided in Gabe about the possibility of getting the role.

"*Everything* is different now," Ollie said. "You don't even have to come out—people are just *out*. Like Ben—it's always been part of his bio."

Lena's eyes focused on Ollie.

"He's gay?" she asked.

It was the first real interest she'd shown all night.

"He's bi," Ollie said. "Another thing that people didn't talk about when I was starting out. You were either straight or you were gay, and there was no question which one was preferred."

"We're old," Gabe said.

"Speak for yourself," Ollie said. "I'm still fresh as a daisy."

Lena and I were left alone as the guests cleared the table. Her face was scrunched in a frown, her shoulders tight and tucked in toward each other. I took pity on her.

"Want me to bring a brownie to your room?" I asked.

The relief was immediate.

"Is that okay?" she asked.

I nodded. "I know this is hard for you," I said. "But you might want to give her a chance."

We both knew I was talking about Chani. Lena's lip curled.

"She's important to your uncle Gabe," I said.

That did nothing to deflate the sneer.

"He's trying," I said.

"Can I go now?"

I sighed. "Sure," I said. "I'll bring the brownie up in a bit."

GABE WAS AT THE foot of the stairs when I came back down post–brownie delivery.

"Ollie and Chani are finishing the dishes," he said.

I raised an eyebrow. "You're not helping?"

"I helped," he said. "I took out the trash and put the leftovers away."

He sounded so indignant that I gave him a pat on the arm.

"Thank you for that," I said.

"Is Teddy up there?" Gabe asked, looking up toward the second floor where Lena's door was shut.

"Want me to go get her?" I asked, knowing the two of them were probably sprawled out on her bed, Lena scratching Teddy's stomach.

Gabe shook his head. "Naw, it's okay if she spends the night here."

"She does like that," I said.

"She's barely talking to me."

"She's a dog, Gabe. If she talked at all, I'd be concerned."

"Ha," he said. "You know what I mean."

He rubbed a hand over his face, and it made him look so tired. He had a bit of gray in his beard. We were both older than Dad had been when he died.

"The whole Chani thing caught her off guard," I said. "She'll get over it."

"Will she?"

"I hope so," I said. "But maybe think twice before you two start making out in my store."

"Yeah," Gabe said, rubbing the back of his neck, looking only a little embarrassed. "Whoops."

We hadn't really talked about Chani. About everything that was happening.

"How are you doing with all"—I gestured, hoping to illustrate what I was trying to say—"this?"

"Good," he said. "I'm . . . happy?"

"Is that a question?"

"I love her," he said.

I was a little taken aback by the straightforward honesty of that statement. How Gabe could just *say* it.

I thought about the way I'd felt about Spencer those first few years of marriage. How it didn't even compare to how I felt the longer we were together. After we had Lena. It was like I hadn't even known what love really was.

How could Gabe know?

Then again, he and Spencer had always held their hearts out first.

"She seems nice," I said.

I hadn't gotten much one-on-one time with her.

"She is," he said. "And really smart. Like, way smarter than me."

I hit him on the arm.

"Come on," I said. "You're smart."

"Maybe," he said. "Smart enough to know that I don't want to fuck it up."

"You won't," I said.

I tapped my fingernails on the banister. I couldn't remember the last time we'd spoken this way to each other. Honestly. Openly. It was nice. Strange, but nice.

"It's hard," Gabe said.

"What is? Love?"

"Yeah."

"Duh," I said.

We both laughed.

"Are *you* happy?" he asked.

"I've got Lena. I've got Mom. I've got you."

This was my life. And right now, it was good enough.

I was happy enough.

"I was thinking," Gabe said, attention focused on his hands, "that I should take Lena on a trip. It might be a nice way for Lena and Chani to get to know each other."

"It might not be a very fun trip," I said.

I felt like a terrible mother saying that.

"Did you have a bad time when you came to Philadelphia?" Gabe asked.

"Uh. No?"

I was not going to think about Ben.

I was not going to think about Ben *more*.

"I'm going to New York," Gabe said. "And I remember her having fun when we went last time."

"Well, yeah," I said. "She got to sit front row at *The Lion King,* eat street nuts until she puked, and ride around in carriages through Central Park."

"We could do all those things again."

"She was eight," I reminded him.

"Okay, we can do other things," he said. "A friend of mine is directing his first Broadway show. I could take her to see that."

"That's very generous," I said, still feeling hesitant.

"She could bring her friend," Gabe said. "Eve, right?"

"That's *too* generous," I said, but he shook his head.

"I want to spend time with her." He looked down at the floor. "Things have been . . . tense between us. For a long time now, even before Chani. I just feel like I need to do something about it."

He was trying, and I loved him for it. And he asked me for so little.

"I'll think about it, okay?"

"Yeah, okay," he said, giving me a smile.

"We should have taken bets," I said, wanting to lighten the mood a little.

"About?"

"You and Chani," I said.

Spencer probably would have won. He'd been Team Chani from day one.

"Shut up," Gabe said, but he was laughing.

CHAPTER 30

THEN

I T SEEMED FOR A WHILE THAT GABE WAS GOING TO BE stuck in the literal trenches for his entire career. That his résumé would read Dead Soldier 3, Wounded Soldier 4, Dying Soldier 2, Ghost of Soldier, and so on and so forth until he got too old and then he'd be Dead General 3, Dying Veteran 4, etc.

He told us that he was thinking about quitting.

We'd moved into the new house only a week ago. I still couldn't believe it was ours—I would go around at night when I couldn't sleep, touching the walls, the windows, the doorknobs—needing to convince myself over and over again that it was real.

Spencer had never been so happy. After all the work and saving we'd done, he'd finally accomplished the thing he'd wanted so deeply. We had a home. A daughter and a home and we were really, truly adults now.

It didn't always feel that way, but sometimes it did.

Gabe was staying with us. He'd offered to help Spencer fix a few of the more immediate things, like the steps on the back porch—because we had a back porch! And a yard!—and the wonky shelves in the upstairs closet. We'd all agreed that manual labor for a bed and warm meal was a pretty good trade-off.

I was getting better at cooking. I had a real kitchen with a properly functioning stove and an island where I could chop things while Lena's baby chair was clipped on to it. She loved watching me—her chubby hands reaching out to help. I'd usually give her a wooden spoon, which she stuck in her mouth and gummed for hours.

Things were still in boxes and there was an entire room that Spencer had urged us to stay out of because it needed so much work, but I was deeply in love with the house. I didn't love it as much as Spencer, of course, but it was pretty close.

Part of me had never imagined that it would actually happen.

But it had, and we'd never again have to live in an apartment where our landlord ignored us and the rats didn't. We were the landlords now. And the rats? Well, I just hoped they'd stay in the basement most of the time.

I could sense some envy in Gabe. It was most evident when we sat down for dinner every night. I'd catch him looking at me and Spencer, holding hands across the table, with an expression on his face that took me a while to recognize.

Even though he wasn't getting the roles he wanted, he was still working steadily, still getting paid good money. He lived in Los Angeles where it was sunny all the time. Where there was a beach he could go to whenever he wanted—even though he insisted that no one in L.A. actually went to the beach.

I never imagined he'd be jealous of *my* life.

"It's good being home," he said one night when we had Mom over for dinner. "Maybe I'll just stay."

"That would be nice," Mom said.

But we all knew that wasn't going to happen. He'd barely given Cooper a backward look when he left. He'd complained nonstop about how small-minded everyone was, how all anyone ever did was gossip. And he wasn't wrong. His exploits, as it were, had become a popular topic of conversation—not usually flattering.

People claimed that he'd "gone Hollywood."

I didn't know what it meant, exactly, but it clearly wasn't good.

A part of me was secretly glad that *Gabe* was now the Parker everyone gossiped about. Lena never had to know. As far as Cooper was concerned, I was reformed, married with a baby, while my brother was off galivanting through Hollywood.

He'd be miserable if he stayed here. Wouldn't he?

"What would you even *do* here?" I asked.

"I don't know," Gabe said. "Maybe I could get a job at McKinley's with Spencer." He looked at my husband hopefully.

Spencer, who had a forkful of macaroni halfway to his mouth, froze.

"Uh," he said. "Yeah. Sure."

"You're not going to work at a hardware store," I said.

"Why not?" Gabe asked.

I gave Lena some smushed peas.

"I think it's a lovely idea," Mom said.

"Thank you," Gabe said. "At least *someone* is excited for me to stick around." He leaned toward Lena. "You too, I bet."

She gurgled at him.

"I could babysit," he said, sitting up. "You guys could go on dates or something and Lena and I can bond." He gave her tummy a little poke. "It would be great."

She stared up at him with her big eyes, marveling at her uncle and his big, bright smile.

Spencer and I exchanged a look.

Gabe would not be babysitting. Because Gabe was drinking again.

I DIDN'T SAY I told you so when Gabe got sick of Cooper after a month and decided that he was going to go back to Hollywood. The opportunity to continue being a dead World War II soldier was clearly more appealing to him than sitting around our small town hanging out with his baby niece.

There were times I wondered what it would be like to switch places. To get a chance to live outside of Cooper, outside of Montana.

But we had our house and work and a kid. We'd put down roots. We weren't going anywhere.

The trip ended with a huge blowout fight between Gabe and Spencer. The kind of fight they never had—angry and vicious—about the thing they'd been arguing about for years: Gabe's drinking.

Gabe insisted it wasn't a problem. Spencer disagreed.

Gabe told him he was being a fucking mother hen. Spencer said that if he kept this up, he wasn't going to be allowed to be alone with Lena.

Gabe told him that Lena was his niece, and no one was going to keep him away from her. Spencer said over my dead body.

"I tried," he told me after Gabe flew back to Los Angeles. "He's in denial."

"It doesn't help that he's such a functional drunk," I said.

I'd finally seen it firsthand. The daily act of it—how he drank from the time he got up until the time he went to bed. And it wasn't like he was a mean drunk. He didn't yell, didn't throw things, didn't even really get in trouble.

When he drank, he kind of just disappeared into himself. His eyes were flat, his mouth loose in a grin that he couldn't seem to control, and he bumped into things a lot. Most people would have considered him pleasant to be around. People who didn't know him. Or people who didn't care.

I had a feeling that described most of who he knew in Los Angeles.

None of us felt good about him going back to that.

Maybe I didn't want to trade places with him.

"I think it's pretty common over there for people to drink that way," Spencer said. "Maybe he should have stayed here."

"He would have gone insane," I said. "Working at the hardware store? What kind of life is that?"

I hadn't realized what I'd said until Spencer's silence had me looking up from Lena, whose hair I had been brushing.

He was staring at the floor looking sadder than I'd seen him in a long time.

"I'm sorry," I said immediately. "I didn't mean—"

"It's okay," he said. "At least I'm the manager, right?"

"You're a great manager," I said.

Which was true. Everyone loved Spencer. He was even-tempered and fair and kind. His employees adored him, his bosses trusted him.

He took Lena's hand, her small fingers curling around his calloused one.

"I never should have dropped out of school," he said quietly, almost to himself.

I hadn't realized he still thought about it.

Hadn't realized he regretted it.

Because he'd never said anything. Never complained. Never wished for anything besides the house.

I didn't know how to respond because I largely blamed his mother for his short-lived college career, but I knew better than to bring her up now. That was one thing about Spencer and his overwhelming kindness—he never considered that someone wouldn't have his best interests at heart. Especially his mother.

"Maybe when Lena's a little older, I'll go back to work—and I'll get a better job—and you can go back to school," I said. "Or maybe take some evening classes. Or online ones."

"Sure," Spencer said, but we both knew how unlikely that was.

The house was wonderful, and I loved it, but it was a lot of money—all these hidden costs we hadn't planned on. It had been more than we expected.

"When we win the lottery," he said.

"Maybe Gabe will make it big, and all our problems will go away," I joked.

Spencer smiled at that. "Sounds like a foolproof plan. What could go wrong?"

CHAPTER 31

NOW

I KNEW THE DATE WAS A BAD IDEA ALMOST AS SOON AS I got out of the car.

Carl was waiting outside for me, and I had one brief moment of relief when it was clear that the photo on the site was accurate. However, the problems started when I tried to open the door for him.

I'd been slightly ahead of him, so I reached for the handle, only to have him reach past me and yank it out of my hand.

"Allow me," he said.

It made for an awkward sort of do-si-do as I tried to move under his arm to get through the door.

"I'm an old-fashioned kind of guy," he said as we waited for the hostess. "My mama raised me to have good manners."

I nodded, but refusing to let someone else hold the door for you—especially if it was your date and she was currently already doing that—seemed less like an old-fashioned thing and more like a chest-beating, pissing contest thing.

We were less than five minutes into the date, and I was already exhausted.

I'd told my family that I was going to meet a friend. No one asked any follow-up questions, which I supposed I should have been offended about but was for the best.

I hadn't seen Ben since the incident at the bookstore. He'd kept his word and kept out of my way. I should have been relieved. Instead, I felt hurt.

I wanted to see him.

I didn't know what I wanted.

I did know that I didn't want to be thinking about one man while on a date with another. No matter how unequally matched the two were.

At least the restaurant was nice.

"We'll have a bottle of the house red," Carl said when the waitress arrived.

"Oh," I said. "I'm not drinking tonight."

Carl frowned. "Come on," he said. "It's a Friday night, don't you want to loosen up a little?"

"I have a long drive home," I said. "And I don't like red wine."

My date flushed, and the waitress bit her lip as if she was holding back a smile.

"Just iced tea for me," I said.

"Do you still want the bottle?" the waitress asked.

Carl glared at her.

"That was embarrassing," he said the moment she walked away.

I shrugged, continuing to peruse the menu.

"Is the steak good here?" I asked.

He didn't say anything, and when I glanced up, I found Carl—face red—staring at me.

"I'm sorry I embarrassed you," I said.

"You didn't embarrass *me*," he said.

"Okay," I said.

Maybe Carl was just nervous, and his coping mechanism was to be an enormous asshole.

It seemed unlikely, but I'd driven an hour and a half to get here, and I wanted a steak.

"So, Carl," I said. "You mentioned in your profile that you're originally from Texas."

I half expected him to cross his arms and continue pouting, but he didn't.

"That's right," he said. "Great state, Texas."

"That's what I've heard," I said. "I've never been."

"You have to go," he said, sour expression dropping away to reveal genuine interest. "Best barbecue you'll ever have."

Okay, now we were getting somewhere.

"What makes it so good?" I asked.

That set him on a five-minute soliloquy about the types of rub they used in Texas, and how the meat was well sourced, and how even the worst Texas barbecue was still better than most places in the country.

"And the spices?" He grinned at me. "They're amazing."

"Do you know what they use?"

"Paprika, I think," he said. "But then again, everyone has their own 'secret recipe.' It's considered bad taste to pry."

I laughed.

"It's probably from their grandma," I said. "That's where the best recipes come from."

"No question," Carl said. "No one could top my grand-mother's chili. She won first prize anytime she entered it in a contest."

"Let me guess," I teased. "She used paprika?"

"Precisely," he said.

Things had gotten off to a bad start, but a guy who could talk about food was a guy I wanted to be talking to.

"Spencer—my husband—used to think that it was rude to add salt to his food, so he spent most of his life assuming that food was always bland."

Carl's smile fell.

"Your husband?"

I'd put in my profile that I was a widow, but maybe he'd forgotten.

"He died three years ago," I said.

"I see," Carl said.

Awkwardness settled around us and I didn't completely understand why. We'd been having a good time.

When the waitress returned, things went from weird to worse.

Carl apparently had a thing about ordering food for people.

"We'll have the Cobb salad and stuffed mushrooms," he said.

"I don't like mushrooms," I said. "And I'll have the steak and a Caesar salad."

We were making the waitress extremely uncomfortable.

"I'm sorry," I said, even though I wasn't sure what I was

apologizing for. "I just really don't like mushrooms. They kind of taste like tires to me."

A clever response might have been "How do you know what tires taste like?" but Carl just stared down at the table, like his cutlery was the most interesting thing he'd ever seen.

The silence just got more and more tense.

"Is something wrong?" I finally asked.

"Why would anything be wrong?" he asked.

But he wasn't looking at me. And there was a nasty bite to his words.

"Clearly you're upset," I said.

"I just expected that you'd be over him by now," Carl said.

I didn't understand what he was talking about.

"Your ex-husband," Carl clarified.

"Excuse me?" I asked. "Over him?"

"You said it yourself that it's been three years."

I couldn't believe what I was hearing. Luckily Carl didn't need me to respond, he was fine to just keep on talking.

"I'm sorry for your loss and all that," he said.

And all that.

The waitress returned with our food, which was good because I was about half a second away from stabbing Carl in the hand with my fork. It was a real sharp one too— sturdy. I could have caused some damage.

At least the steak was good. I had a piece of it in my mouth when he continued his unwelcome monologue as if he'd never stopped.

"It sounds like you're new to this whole dating thing, so

I'll give you some advice. Don't talk about your ex," he said. "Makes it seem like you're still obsessed with him."

I took a deep breath.

"I hate to tell you this, but I'll always be 'obsessed' with him," I said. "He's the father of my child. And he's not my ex, he's my dead husband. There's a difference."

Carl sighed as if I'd just confirmed his worst suspicions.

"I get it," he said. "You're one of those."

The next piece of steak didn't make it to my mouth.

"One of those?" I asked.

"Someone who can't let go of the past."

"Excuse me?"

Carl gave me a look that was so condescending and paternalistic that I thought about stabbing my fork into both his hands. Maybe even his crotch.

"You're going to have to move on," he said. "No one likes to be second fiddle to a dead guy. It's unattractive."

I put down my napkin.

"You know what," I said, "you're absolutely right."

Our waitress returned with the wine bottle, about to offer Carl another glass. But she backed off the moment she saw our expressions.

I stood.

"I'd hate to force you to spend the rest of this meal across from someone you find so unattractive," I said.

"You're not leaving," Carl said.

"Sure am," I said.

"Oh, come on," he said. "Don't be that way."

"Unfortunately for all of us," I said, "this is the only way I know how to be."

CHAPTER 32

NOW

THE PLAN WAS TO DRIVE STRAIGHT HOME.

But it would be empty—with Lena sleeping over at Eve's tonight. And for whatever reason, the thought of going back to an empty house made me unbearably sad.

That lonely feeling.

It wasn't as if I hadn't felt it since Spencer died.

But this loneliness was different. It wasn't as sharp—more like a bruise that I'd just discovered and couldn't stop prodding.

Maybe it was because I'd gone into this date with hope. Not an abundance of it, but more than I'd had in the past. I knew it was because I'd allowed myself to be hopeful.

I wasn't going to find the kind of love I'd had with Spencer. That was okay.

But I needed something.

I'd felt that way for a while but couldn't really put my finger on it—*what* I needed. There was just this general wistfulness that had settled in my heart next to the longing.

The affair with Ben had made me realize what I needed. That I was hungry for affection and touch and the simple presence of someone I could depend on.

It was exhausting going through this life alone.

I had Lena, of course, but she had her own life, her own grief that was separate from mine. My job was to be her mother, *her* support.

Sometimes I felt angry at Spencer. It was irrational, it was ridiculous, but when things were hard, I blamed him for going down *that* road *that* night. As if he didn't take that route every week. As if he hadn't been driving these roads since before he got his license. As if Montana wasn't known for shitty, drunk driving.

It wasn't Spencer's fault he was dead. It wasn't mine either, though that didn't alleviate the guilt I felt every time I thought about that night. Unable to remember if I'd even said goodbye. If I'd said that I loved him.

I didn't want to go home.

Instead, I just drove around downtown Cooper—which took about five minutes—and parked outside of the Cozy.

Maybe I'd go in and organize the yarn wall again.

The streets were quiet, and I could see the lights on over the shop in Gabe's apartment. I could have easily texted to see if he and Chani would be up for a visit, but I didn't. I was happy for my brother, I really was, but the last thing I needed right now was to spend time with a couple that was deliriously in love.

I had taken out my shop keys, thinking that I could also probably do some work on the office—things were getting kind of messy in there—when movement caught my eye.

At the other end of the long, empty block, someone was walking in the opposite direction.

I didn't know how, but I knew it was Ben. Something about the way he moved, that loose-limbed ease. Or maybe it was the bike helmet under his arm. I couldn't see from this distance, but I was also pretty sure he was wearing the same boots he always wore.

I'd been horrible to him.

The smart thing would have been to text him or even call him—he was too far away for me to shout, and the wind would have stolen my words anyway.

Instead, I followed him.

Like a creep.

Just as I was beginning to catch up to him—taking the longest strides I could without risking slipping on the few patches of black ice that refused to melt—he turned a corner.

I thought I'd lost him, but when I got around that same corner, I saw him heading into a building. It was a small apartment complex, and I waited outside until the light came on in one of the windows on the second floor.

It was easy to figure out which place was his.

I spared a moment to chide myself for my insanity before I pushed it out of my mind and knocked on the door.

Ben was wearing his boots, black pants, and nothing else. Well, nothing except the necklaces gleaming from his thicket of chest hair. One had a circle charm; the other was just a simple chain.

"Lauren?"

"Hi," I said.

"I feel like I should be surprised that you're here," he said. "But strangely I'm not."

"I saw you on the street," I said.

"And you followed me."

I nodded.

"That's a very normal thing to do," he said.

He was leaning up against the doorframe, arms crossed, looking like an absolute dreamboat. I forced my eyes to stop wandering down to his bare chest.

I didn't have the right.

Technically I didn't really have the right to be there in the first place, but . . .

"I was going to go to the store," I said.

He pulled out his phone and looked at the time. It was almost ten o'clock.

"I'm pretty sure you're not going to be getting much foot traffic at this time of night."

"I wanted to apologize," I said. "Again."

"You really don't have to."

He didn't close the door, but he didn't welcome me inside either.

"Could I come in?" I asked.

"Aren't you worried someone will see you?"

The question had a touch of bitterness, but I deserved it. Because the truth was that I *was* worried. Not a lot—this was a quiet building, and it didn't seem like anyone was around—but it was still risky.

I was here anyway.

I was starting to wonder if my impulse control was deteriorating with age.

Ben didn't wait for a response, just stepped aside and let me in.

Just like in Philadelphia and in his trailer, the space was neat but mostly empty. There were the familiar items— pictures on the fridge, his bike helmet on the table, and another wrench?

Ben followed my eyeline.

"Leaky shower?" I asked.

"Wobbly bed frame," he said. "Borrowed some tools from my landlord. Nice lady."

"Mrs. Hopkins?" I asked.

He nodded.

"Don't take her up on her offer to do your laundry," I said. "She still does that by hand."

"Good to know," Ben said.

The place was a studio apartment, so I could see said wobbly bed over in the corner. It was neatly made, the books he'd bought from the Cozy stacked on a nearby table.

"So," he said.

He gave me a once-over.

"That's a nice outfit."

"I was on a date," I said, regretting it immediately.

"Oh?" Ben lifted an eyebrow. "How'd that go?"

He was asking a rhetorical question and we both knew it.

"I said some awful things to you," I said.

"Technically you said them to Allyson, but continue," he said, with a gesture of his hand.

"I *am* sorry," I said.

"For what exactly?" he asked. "For what you said or the fact that I heard it?"

"Both?"

He laughed. "A politician's answer if I've ever heard one."

I let out a sigh. "You don't have to forgive me," I said. "I just wanted to make sure that *you* knew that *I* knew I was wrong."

"It's not a matter of forgiveness," Ben said, arms crossed, leaning against the dresser. "I'm not one to hold grudges, especially over something we all have."

He stood and came toward me. Close. Closer.

"Which is?" I asked.

"A wayward tongue," he said.

Of course he made "tongue" sound filthy.

I should have left or apologized more. Instead:

"Do you own any other shoes?" I asked.

We both looked down at his feet.

"You don't like my boots?" he asked. "They were quite expensive."

They didn't look that way. They were scuffed and well-worn all around.

"I think you were ripped off," I said.

Why couldn't I shut up and leave?

Ben laughed. It was such a good laugh.

"I bought them when I booked *SXS*," he said. "They've been around for a while."

"And you haven't thought to replace them?"

He lifted a foot, examining the shoe.

"And lose all the hard work I put into breaking them

in?" he asked, looking at the other boot. "They're supposed to last a lifetime. Hence the initial expense."

"Oh," I said.

"I don't really need that many shoes," he said. "And I travel light."

"Sure," I said.

"These are actually one of the most expensive things I own," he said.

That surprised me, but then I remembered his comment about how much money he'd make playing James Bond.

"Saving your pennies?" I asked.

"Something like that," he said.

I wanted to know more.

"Though I suppose they could use a polish," he said.

He had his hands in his pockets and just stood there. Didn't ask me to leave. Just looked at me.

"What about your motorcycle?" I asked. "Wasn't that expensive?"

"Lillian?"

I blinked.

"You named your motorcycle Lillian?"

"After Lillian La France," he said. "She was a stunt rider in the twenties. Also known as The Girl Who Flirts with Death."

"Oh," I said.

"You've found me out," Ben said. "I like expensive shoes and bikes. Though I nearly backed out of buying Lillian when I had to write the final check."

"Is Ollie not paying you enough?"

"For the play?" Ben asked. "Not nearly enough, but I don't do theatre for the money."

"Just movies?"

Ben shrugged.

"Your agent doesn't mind you not making money on this show?"

"Naw," Ben said. "In fact, I'm pretty sure that Fran thinks I should be spending more of my money instead of saving it. She was the one who pushed me to buy Lillian. Said I needed something for myself."

"Fran is your agent?"

If I was remembering correctly, she was also the woman who he'd gotten the harp tattoo for. Or because of.

"Since the beginning," Ben said. "Though she keeps trying to fire me."

"Fire you? Why?"

Ben leaned back against the wall. We were still just standing there in the middle of his apartment.

"She thinks I need better representation," he said. "Says I've outgrown her."

I was confused—I'd never heard of an agent who wanted to off-load a successful client. Then again, Hollywood in general confused me.

"Have you outgrown her?"

"I don't want another agent," Ben said, sounding slightly petulant. "I trust Fran, and that's more than I can say for most people in this industry. She might not have the clout and connections of other agents, but I know she'd never fuck me over."

I nodded as if I understood.

I understood loyalty, of course. And trust.

It just seemed out of place in Hollywood.

I wondered if she was the reason he hadn't gotten the James Bond role.

"How did you meet her?"

"Christmas break," he said. "I was sixteen."

I blinked. "Sixteen?"

"The guy I was dating at the time, Danny, knew I hated going back to the islands over the holidays, so he invited me to stay with his family in Dublin. After that, I just ended up spending every break with them. Fran is his mom."

My eyes shifted over to the photos on the fridge. I couldn't see them clearly, but I spotted enough of one to recognize it—the one with the woman and the baby. Ben and his mom, I assumed.

I just wasn't sure why he'd display a picture of someone he wanted to avoid over the holidays.

"And she became your agent," I said.

"Her clients do print work—advertisements mostly—but she knew I needed to make money. Especially after graduation," he said. "She'd seen that I could act, school plays and things, so she'd look around for actual roles. I got my first big job because of her—some small movie that was filming in Ballinrobe. It was enough for me to move out of their guest room and to London."

"I didn't know," I said.

"Yeah, well." Ben lifted a shoulder. "You didn't ask."

"What happened after you moved to London?" I asked, shifting on my feet.

Ben gave me a look, and then crossed the room, pulling out a chair for me. I sat, but he continued to stand.

I let out an unintentional moan as I settled into the chair. My toes had been killing me. Allyson *was* right. Heels were a torture device.

"You can take them off," Ben said.

There was a twinkle in his eye. He was talking about my shoes, but his gaze drifted down to my dress.

"London?" I prompted, slipping my heels off and trying not to moan again at how it felt. I couldn't imagine how I was going to get them back on when I had to leave.

Which would be soon.

Soonish.

Ben leaned back against the kitchen counter, arms crossed.

"More job opportunities, but more competition," he said. "I'd do plays whenever I could, waited tables, busked if I had to." He scratched his neck. "Spent a lot of time on couches during that time—and Fran called in a lot of favors."

"Then *SXS*," I said.

"An overnight sensation," he said. "And it only took five years of eating ramen, sleeping on lumpy futons, and landing bit parts to get there."

Gabe had been called an overnight sensation too.

"I'm sorry about Bond," I said.

Ben waved a hand. "It would have been nice," he said. "But I've been rejected before."

He gave me a look.

"Wha—I didn't—that wasn't a rejection," I said, even though that was patently untrue.

It just made me feel bad to think about it that way. It also made me seem insane. Because who rejected a man like Ben? A woman with too many issues to count.

"It wasn't you. It was me," I said.

"That's what they all say."

"I—"

"It's okay," Ben said. "Missing out on Bond *was* rough. It would have been nice to get that paycheck . . . But I'll get over it."

"What are you saving for?" I asked. "A house?"

"Not exactly," he said. "It's more about repaying a debt."

"To who?"

Ben didn't say anything, and it was clear we'd reached the end of that topic of conversation. It was the perfect time to excuse myself and limp home.

"What happened to Danny?" I asked. "Isn't it awkward that you still work with his mom?"

"We're still friends," he said. "Went to his wedding last year, in fact. Pablo's a good guy. Stays in one place. Stable. Reliable. That kind of thing."

I nodded.

"Is that when you bought Lillian?" I asked. "When you booked *SXS*?"

"Lillian was my big splurge when I booked my first job back in the States. When I figured I'd be here for a while." He gave me a once-over. "I'd offer to take you on a ride, but I don't think you're dressed for it."

His eyes lingered on my tits. They *did* look spectacular in this dress.

I shifted in my seat. He took a step toward me.

"I should go," I said.

I didn't want to go.

"Mm-hmm," Ben said.

And then he was kneeling in front of me, his hands on the legs of the chair.

"It's late," I said.

It didn't feel late. And I certainly wasn't tired.

"You know what?" he said.

He wasn't touching me, but I felt his fingers all over my body. I wanted to close my eyes and sink into the sensation.

"I'm pretty sure you didn't come to my apartment at ten o'clock at night to talk about my bike. Or my boots. Or my career."

"I came to apologize," I said.

"Which you already did," he said.

"I just—I felt really bad about what I said."

Ben shook his head, tsking slowly.

"I think you're here for a completely different reason," he said.

I swallowed hard.

"I think that you were on that date," Ben said. "That you were having dinner with some guy—some boring, perfectly fine, completely average guy."

"He was a jerk," I said.

In fact, I'd completely forgotten about Carl. Had that date really been tonight?

Ben laughed, his hands moving inward, thumbs brushing the sides of my legs.

"You were with this guy, and you were thinking about something else."

I wanted him to touch me. I wanted him to touch me so badly.

"You're right," I said. "I was thinking about dessert."

Ben's grin was wolfish as he shook his head.

"Lauren, Lauren, Lauren," he said. "We both know what you really want for dessert."

This was the perfect opportunity to leave. To tell him once again that I was sorry, and that actually I hadn't been thinking about him, I'd been thinking about the steak I'd been eating and the general nature of loneliness, but . . .

"Maybe," I said.

My stomach flipped like a flapjack as his fingers traced the curve of my thighs. I sucked in a breath.

"Maybe?" Ben asked.

His voice.

God, it warmed me like whiskey.

"Maybe," I said.

He didn't say anything, and I opened my eyes. He was standing.

"Well," he said. "I guess that's that."

I was stunned. He was stepping away?

But he'd been touching me. About to touch me.

I was confused. Hurt.

I rose, my knees trembling.

"It was nice seeing you, Lauren," Ben said.

Suddenly it was clear.

"Yeah," I said. "Nice seeing you."

I was being punished. For what I'd said. Done.

Wincing, I forced my feet back into my heels and started the long hobble toward the door. As I reached it, I turned back to him.

"Sorry again," I said.

I took a deep breath and turned the knob.

But just as I had pulled the door open, it was slammed shut. I looked up to find Ben's hand flat on the wood.

I turned and found his eyes.

They were hungry. Eager. Hot.

"Tell me that you've been thinking about me," he said. "The way I've been thinking about you."

I remembered the last time he'd pressed me up against a door.

"Tell me that you've been thinking about kissing me. Touching me."

My breathing was shallow, my pulse racing.

"Tell me you've been thinking of what I might do to these tits and that arse. The curve of your hip. The back of your neck. The inside of your knees," he said. "All the places I could touch you to make you scream."

I clenched my teeth together, feeling as if I might fall apart right then and there.

"Tell me."

I looked up at him. Met his gaze.

"You know I have."

"I want to hear it," he said, voice nearly a growl.

I wanted him to touch me. To kiss me. To fuck me.

"I've been thinking about you, Ben," I said.

His smile made my toes curl.

And I was eager to discover what he would do to the rest of me.

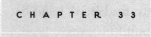

CHAPTER 33

THEN

WHEN GABE BECAME FAMOUS EVERYTHING CHANGED very quickly.

Lena was just about to turn three when the James Bond rumors started swirling around, and we first got a sense of what it would mean to Gabe's career. To his life. To our lives.

Suddenly Gabe's face was everywhere. Online, in magazines—popular enough that even our town, five years behind every trend, was aware of every movement, arc, and climb of Gabe's rising star.

He'd just finished a movie with an actor named Oliver Matthias, and it seemed that they were becoming off-screen friends as well.

For the first time, I saw Spencer get jealous. Truly jealous.

"It's always Ollie this and Ollie that," he said. "Has he not met other people in Hollywood?"

"You're still his best friend," I told him, which of course made him even more indignant.

"That's not what this is about," he said.

"Sure," I said.

I could barely hide my smile whenever the topic came up.

As fast as Gabe's life changed, ours did too.

Suddenly there was all this money. So much money.

And Gabe had no idea what to do with it.

One morning I came downstairs to find Spencer hanging up the phone, looking stunned.

"What's wrong?" I asked.

"Gabe paid off our mortgage," he said.

"What?"

"He—"

I reached past him and grabbed the phone.

"What did you do?" I demanded when Gabe answered.

"This is a weird way to say thank you," he said. "You and Spencer really need to work on that."

"You paid off our mortgage?"

"Is this phone broken? I just gave Spencer all the details."

"You're going to tell me," I said.

He did. It wasn't just our mortgage. He'd paid off our mom's as well.

"Oh, and I started a college fund for Lena," he said.

"How long are you expecting her to be in school for?" I'd asked when he told me the eye-watering amount he was putting aside.

"I always thought it would be nice to have a doctor in the family," he said.

"You don't need to do this," I told him. "We're fine. We're doing fine."

"Consider it back rent," he said. "From when I stayed with you."

"You were here for a month."

"It's about the monthly rate here in Los Angeles," he said. "Don't worry. I want to."

It was hard to tell how Spencer felt about it. For the rest of the week, he was quiet and kept to himself more than usual.

"We did kind of wish for this," I told him one night after we'd put Lena to bed.

We were sitting in the living room. Of a house that we now owned free and clear.

"We wanted to win the lottery too," he said. "But I never expected it would happen."

"Are you upset that it did?" I asked.

He was silent and I could see that mind of his spinning.

"It would be pretty dumb if I was," he said.

"Since when has that stopped you?" I teased.

It got a smile out of him. A small one, but a smile.

"It's just a lot," he said. "We won't ever be able to pay him back."

"I don't think he'd accept it if we could," I said.

Spencer nodded. And then he took my hand.

"I would have found a way to pay the house off," he said.

"I know," I said.

"I had a plan."

"I know," I said.

"Okay," he said once he seemed convinced that I understood what he was saying.

And I did. This wasn't a gift we could turn down—we

didn't want to—but Spencer's sense of self—his worth—
had taken a hit in the process. We were out of debt, but it
took him a while to recover.

He would dodge Gabe's calls, pretend he wasn't home
when I answered the phone, feign forgetfulness at not answering his messages.

"Just give him time," I told Gabe.

"I don't get it," he said.

Then he bought us the store.

"No," I told him when he showed us the plans.

"Why not?" he asked. "Mom doesn't want to teach
anymore; you don't do anything all day—"

"Hey!"

"Cooper needs a bookstore."

"I hope you're saving some of this money for yourself,"
I said.

"Lauren," he said, "you have no idea."

When it was announced that Gabe was officially going
to be the next Bond—and the first American to play the
role—things went bonkers. He told us that he'd become a
hot commodity for the paparazzi, that he was recognized
constantly, and that he got stares everywhere he went.

"Are you sure it isn't because you have an abnormally
large head?" I asked him.

Someone had to keep him humble.

"Hilarious," he said.

"Are you coming home for the holidays?" I asked him.

If he was still drinking, I couldn't tell.

Spencer was sure he was. But things were still tense between them. The store had been a lot for Spencer to swal-
low.

"I'm going to try," Gabe said. "We start filming in the New Year, but I have this one interview I have to do in L.A. before I get time off."

"Don't say anything stupid."

"Great advice," he said. "I'd planned to exclusively say stupid things."

Unfortunately, when he arrived in Montana a few days later, it seemed that he'd done exactly that. When I tried to ask him how the interview went, he refused to say anything about it.

And Spencer was right. Gabe was still drinking.

If anything, his drinking had gotten worse.

"Maybe his best friend *Oliver* can get him to stop," Spencer said after Gabe finished off a six-pack and parked himself in front of the Christmas tree.

There was so much bitterness in Spencer's voice.

I'd never really understood when people said how ruinous money could be, but I saw it now. There was a gulf forming between Gabe and Spencer, and neither of them wanted to admit that anything was wrong.

I didn't say anything. I knew I couldn't get Spencer to talk to Gabe before he was ready, and I wasn't sure anyone could get Gabe to stop. He had that Parker stubbornness, and as far as he saw it, nothing was wrong with his drinking.

"It's nothing compared to what other people do," he'd said that evening after his fourth beer. "Stop nagging me."

He'd crawled under the tree like we'd done as kids and fallen asleep. Or passed out. I couldn't tell.

Tucked against his side was the puppy he'd just gotten.

She didn't have a name yet; Gabe had said he was thinking about calling her Teddy.

Spencer was in the kitchen washing dishes. He'd been avoiding Gabe since he arrived in town.

I watched the rise and fall of my brother's chest, his face slack and peaceful, lit by Christmas lights, and worried. It felt like Gabe was a runaway train and all we could do was watch and hope he didn't crash and burn.

CHAPTER 34

NOW

LENA HAD PILED THE CART HIGH WITH THINGS I KNEW she didn't need. This was supposed to be a trip to get supplies for New York, but I said nothing as she threw a fuzzy, fat lobster Squishmallow right alongside boxes of razors and tampons. A simple, tasteful sheet set with tiny blue dots chosen with just as much certainty as a robe with a pair of bunny ears on it.

I didn't say anything, because I knew that there was no point in mentioning the obvious juxtaposition between the two types of things she wanted, a visual of that sweet, tentative bridge between childhood and adulthood.

Things had been good between us. I wasn't going to ruin that by saying something stupid.

Or doing something stupid.

Something *else* stupid.

It wasn't kind, but I'd been avoiding Ben since our last . . . encounter. I just didn't know what to say to him.

"I appreciate all the orgasms, but that's about all I can

handle, and would you mind so terribly if I used your body at my own convenience for the kind of mind-clearing sex that I'm evidently in desperate need of? Kthanksbye."

It was a shame they didn't have Hallmark cards for occasions like this.

We turned the corner and all but ran into Jessica and her two daughters, my mother-in-law right behind them. It seemed she went everywhere with them these days. Maybe Diana had finally gotten the daughter-in-law and granddaughters she'd always wanted.

She still greeted Lena with the same smothering affection she always did.

"You look more like your father every day," she said. "Don't you think, Jessica?"

Jessica tilted her head. "A spitting image."

"Lucky girl," Diana said.

Yes. Good thing she didn't take after her mother, the bridge troll.

My brain immediately flashed back to Ben's hot voice in my ear murmuring how good I was. How gorgeous. How sexy. All while fucking me down deep into his mattress.

Now was *not* the time.

I rolled the shopping cart over my foot. It was just enough pain to force me to stop thinking about Ben.

Jessica's daughters were polite and greeted Lena.

"Hey," one of them said, waving awkwardly.

There was something comforting about how self-conscious they were, despite being a year or two older than Lena.

"Hey," Lena said.

"Why don't you girls go pick out something for church on Sunday," Jessica said.

Her two daughters looked at her.

"I thought we were getting Tums for Dad."

"Heartburn?" I asked, trying for sympathy.

But both Jessica and I knew that Mikey's chest could literally be in flames and I wouldn't care.

"Are you coming?" one of her daughters asked. "To church?"

Lena shook her head.

"Oh," the other one said. "Well. The youth group is fun, if you ever want to join."

"Thanks," Lena said.

"We'll see you later, Diana," Jessica said, before turning to give me a brief nod. "Lauren."

I briefly nodded back. "Jessica."

It was only after they left that I noticed that Lena had one hand in the basket, fingers squeezing the Squishmallow. Hard.

"We should go," I said.

But Diana had never been one to take a hint.

"Did you know your dad used to go to our church with Mrs. Garrison?" she asked. "He *loved* it."

Lena looked at me. Had I told her about that? I must have, but then again, by the time Lena was born, Spencer had extracted himself from most of his religious background.

I couldn't tell what she was thinking. And she didn't say anything until we got back to the house. I'd just turned off the car when Lena turned to me.

"Is that true?"

I didn't know what she was talking about until she continued.

"What Grandma said. About Dad going to church?"

"He did when he was younger," I said.

"Did he go a lot?"

"Uh, sometimes," I said.

"Sometimes?"

"He used to go every week," I said, feeling extremely uncomfortable.

"Every week?" Lena's eyes were huge.

"He was in the youth group," I said.

It was like I'd just told her that her father was a werewolf.

"He was in the youth group," she repeated.

"Yeah," I said.

Lena looked at the house. She was very purposefully not looking at me.

"So, he believed that stuff," she said. "Like, in the Bible."

Lena and I had talked—at length—about what Spencer's mom believed. That she could argue all day that she was just "old-fashioned," but that didn't change the fact that she believed that everyone except the attendees of her church was going straight to hell when they died.

We hadn't talked about what Spencer believed.

I hadn't even thought to.

I figured that Lena knew.

But how could she?

She'd been ten when he died. There were so many things he hadn't had a chance to talk with her about, so many discussions they'd never get an opportunity to have.

"Your dad was different when he was your age," I said.

Lena's arms were crossed.

"He was religious," I said. "But he changed."

"Religious how?" she asked.

I thought about the time he'd taken Gabe to church after our dad had died. How he'd believed—truly believed— what his mother believed. That my dad had gone to hell. That we were going to hell.

How he'd wanted to help.

That had never changed.

But other things had.

"He believed a lot of the things your grandma believed," I said. "But he didn't know any other way."

Lena nodded.

"What about ghosts?" she asked. "Did he believe in those?"

I hadn't been expecting that one.

"Uh," I said. "I don't know."

She looked at me like I'd slapped her. For whatever reason, this answer seemed to upset her more than learning her dad had been a regular member of a youth group.

"You don't know?"

"I'm sorry, honey," I said. "I don't."

"What about reincarnation?" she asked. "Or, like, heaven, or something?"

It hit me with startling clarity. Lena wanted to know what Spencer believed would happen after someone died.

I couldn't remember talking about that with Spencer. About what we believed happened after. We'd been to- gether for so long that there were things I didn't even think to ask. Why was that? It wasn't as if we didn't have experi- ence with death and loss. We just didn't talk about it. Part of me thought that Spencer likely still held tightly to what he'd grown up with. That he believed in heaven and maybe even hell.

But I wasn't sure.

It was clear that wasn't what Lena had been looking for.

And I couldn't give it to her.

Without a word, she got out of the car. I followed her, ordered pizza, and didn't talk about church or ghosts or death.

CHAPTER 35

NOW

IT WAS EARLY WHEN THEY LEFT FOR NEW YORK—JUST shy of five A.M. None of us had wanted to get out of bed.

"Have fun," I said to Lena.

She grunted at me. It was quiet at the airport, just a few sleepy travelers getting in line to go through security. I watched her fiddle with her scarf before I realized that it was mine. Well, the one I'd made for Spencer. Lena must have taken it from my closet.

Her eyes followed mine.

"Is that okay?" she asked.

"Of course," I said, biting the inside of my cheek so I wouldn't cry.

It looked good on her.

"Do you think I brought enough?" Eve asked, sounding worried as she pulled graphic novels out of her carry-on.

She'd slept over, and I was pretty sure they'd both stayed up late deciding which ones to pack. It had been the main topic of conversation over dinner.

"I think you'll be okay," I said.

It looked like the bag was ninety percent books.

"We can always buy more," Gabe said.

"Don't spoil them," I said.

"Books don't count," he said. "They're educational."

I wanted to argue with him, but he wasn't exactly wrong. He was going to spend money on them, it might as well be on books.

"There are lots of great bookstores we can visit," Chani said. "I know some people."

Eve beamed at her, and even Lena managed a small smile. Progress.

Over the intercom came the announcement that their plane was ready to start boarding.

"Ready?" Gabe asked.

"Yeah!" Eve said, while Lena merely shrugged.

I got hugs from everyone. Lena's was short and perfunctory, but I pulled her back before she could escape. This was the longest we would be apart since Spencer died.

"Love you," I said, squeezing her tight.

I half expected her to wiggle out of my grasp wearing an "ugh, Mom" face, but I was pleasantly surprised to feel her hug me back. Quick, but tight.

"Have fun," I said.

"Yeah, okay," she said. And then, quietly, "Love you too."

I bit my lip. I was not going to cry over that rare admission here in the airport. Besides, if I did, Lena would never come back from New York.

Instead, I drove home listening to a playlist that Spencer had made me a few years ago. All of his favorite songs. He'd always had eclectic taste, while I was much more into the Top 40 hits. He'd tease me nonstop about my love of the Goo Goo Dolls and Michelle Branch, while I'd make fun of him for being into a band called Toad the Wet Sprocket.

A Pearl Jam song came on. Eddie Vedder singing about someone with a motorbike and unkempt clothes.

I thought about Ben.

I stopped by the Finnish Line on my way to the store and was greeted enthusiastically by the owner.

"A free treat for you," Johanna said, waving her hands at me. "Anything you want."

I knew I was a frequent customer, but her reaction still seemed over the top. But was I going to say no to a baked item? Not a chance.

"What about that one?" I pointed at the lower shelf in the glass case. "Laskiaispulla?"

I was surely butchering the pronunciation, but Johanna just beamed at me as she put the pastry—which looked like the Finnish cousin of the cream puff—into a to-go bag.

"Thank you," I said.

"Thank *you*!" she said. "You've brought us one of our newest, hungriest customers."

I'd been looking into the bag at the delicious treat and glanced up at her with confusion.

"I have?"

"Oh yes," she said. "That nice young man who works with your brother. Benjamin."

Ben. Of course she was talking about Ben.

"He says it's his goal to try everything on the menu while he's here," Johanna said. "He's got a very big appetite. He'll probably end up trying everything three times!"

I could practically see hearts bursting in her eyes.

"And he loves our coffee," she said. "Says it's the best he's ever had."

"He's traveled a lot," I said. "He would know."

"That's what he said!"

"I'm glad he came in."

"I've told him he needs to go to Finland next—everything always tastes better after a sauna there."

A wistful look came over Johanna's face. I knew she'd been wanting to go back and visit her family, but ever since Starbucks moved in, her business had been suffering.

"I'm pretty sure *everything* is better after a sauna," I said.

She smiled, dimples showing. "This is true," she said.

"Thank you for the treat," I said. "Can I get another for my mother? But put this one on my tab."

Teddy lifted her head as I came into the shop. She was curled up in her favorite leather chair, the one right by the door, where she could get the maximum amount of pets from customers. There were some people who came in just to say hi to her—we'd hear the bell above the door jangle, then a happy "Hi, Teddy!" and then another jingle as they left.

"We should charge," I'd suggested once and had been met with absolute horror from everyone, as if I'd said we should send Teddy out to panhandle.

Mom was behind the desk, checking things off one of her many lists. I kept telling her that she didn't need to print everything out, but she insisted that she liked doing things her way, and that if I didn't like it, I could talk to her boss.

Which was her.

She was the boss.

I dropped the Finnish Line bag on the counter.

"Ooooh." She reached for it, peering in.

"Laskiaispulla," I said, probably still saying it wrong.

"Gesundheit," Mom said.

"Ha."

"What's the occasion?" she asked, pulling the treat out of the bag.

Powdered sugar settled across her list as she took a bite.

"No reason," I said, picking up my own.

I turned it in my hand, wondering what the best way was to eat it without getting sugar or cream everywhere. In the end, I figured it was going to happen anyway, so I just shoved it into my mouth and took a huge bite.

Cream got all over my fingers, sugar all over my mouth.

"And to think, Gabe was the messy eater when you were kids," Mom said as she handed me a napkin.

"Mmph," I said.

"Speaking of Gabe," Mom said, looking back down at her lists, "a friend of his stopped in this morning looking for you."

I had the laskiaispulla halfway in my mouth when she said it. I unwittingly sucked in a breath, and powdered sugar, which went right into my throat. I coughed out a white puff of air.

"Are you okay?" she asked.

"Fine," I croaked.

Powdered sugar was hell on the airway.

"A friend of Gabe's?" I asked, as if I didn't know who she was talking about.

"I think he said his name was Ben?" Mom said. "He's

doing a play with Gabe and Ollie. Said he was here in town for a few months. Guess he's staying at Mrs. Hopkins's apartments. Seemed like a lovely young man."

One who apparently told strangers every little detail about his life.

"Do you know him?" Mom asked, looking up at me when I didn't say anything.

"Um," I said. "Kind of. He likes baked goods."

"Ah," Mom said as if that explained everything.

"I'm going to do inventory in the craft section," I said.

"Do you think you can do some deliveries later on?" she asked. "Just two and they're close by."

"Sure," I said.

I passed by the stacks on my way to the craft wall, stopping briefly to make sure that no one was back there doing inappropriate things in front of the books. I kept meaning to rearrange the shelves, but they were too heavy for me to move on my own, and I wasn't going to ask Mom and risk her throwing out her back or something. I'd just have to ask Gabe when he got back from New York.

"Deliveries?" I asked a few hours later when I'd inventoried all I could inventory.

Mom pulled the two orders from under the counter with a rubber band around each of them, holding the receipt to the top of the books.

"Why don't you take the rest of the day off?" she asked. "You know it's our slowest time."

"Trying to get rid of me?"

She rolled her eyes. "The first one goes to Rosemary at Birds and Beasleys," she said, pointing at the books. "The other is going to Melanie at Pump Up the Boys."

It was a straight shot down the street to Birds and Beasleys. Instead of a bell, their door chirped whenever someone came into the store.

Rosemary's daughter, Brynne, was behind the counter.

"Book delivery," I said, holding out the paperback.

"Thanks, Lauren," she said, taking it from me. "Mom has been waiting for this one. You know how she is with Paulette Benton books."

"I do, and we are grateful for her steady patronage," I said.

Paulette Benton's cozy mysteries were a big seller for us.

"How's Button?" I asked, turning to peer into the big wire cage.

"She's doing great," Brynne said. "Mom thinks she's in love."

"Oh really?" I asked. "Is there going to be a Mr. Button joining her soon?"

Brynne laughed. "Sadly, it's not a bird that she's in love with."

I made some little clicking bird noises toward Button, who ignored them.

"I think it's really that my mom is in love," Brynne said. "There's this guy who's been coming in several times a week."

I closed my eyes briefly—already knowing where this was headed.

"He works with Gabe, I think," Brynne said.

"Ben," I muttered.

"Yeah," she said. "Mom loves him. He's been buying up her birder equipment and birdhouses. We've had to place a new order with Milton."

Milton was the seventy-year-old former shop teacher that made birdhouses out of reclaimed wood. They were beautiful, and we had one, but so did everyone else in town. Milton's latest had been sitting on the shelf at Birds and Beasleys for a while—his craftsmanship was so good that no one ever needed a replacement.

"That's great," I said.

"He's wonderful," Rosemary said—she'd just emerged from the back room. "Said he's going to send all his friends Milton's birdhouses. Even has us shipping them to Ireland!"

No doubt Fran, Danny, and Pablo were all about to get their very own birdhouses. Possibly two.

"And the birding equipment?"

"He says he's always wanted to give it a try," she said. "Bought the top-of-the-line binoculars and all our birder maps and guides."

Somehow, none of this surprised me.

"Such a nice young man," Rosemary said, a dreamy look in her eyes.

Brynne gave me a look that clearly said "See, I told you so."

Pump Up the Boys was on the other side of the walking mall, but since I was on my way home, I ended up driving there. The little gym was never too busy, which made it a perfect job for Melanie, who seemed to spend most of her time at reception reading through our romance collection. Cozy mysteries came in second to that powerhouse of sales. Kept our lights on for the most part.

"Oh my god, thank you," Melanie said when she saw me arrive.

She reached her hands out, fingers wiggling.

"Didn't you just order a stack of books last week?" I asked.

"So?"

I smiled and gave her the paperback.

"I've heard really good things about this one," she said.

"That's what you say about all of them."

"And it's always correct."

She had already cracked the spine, her attention focused on the page in front of her.

"I guess I'll see you next week," I said.

"Oh, wait!" Melanie said, head bouncing up. "I wanted to thank you."

"For?"

"Your recommendation."

I searched my brain, trying to figure out what she was talking about. Had I recommended a book to her lately? Some yarn? A needlepoint kit?

"It's always so empty in here," she said. "It's nice having someone stop by once in a while."

"Uh, sure," I said.

"He said you told him about us," Melanie said, her thumb gesturing behind her.

I knew what I was going to see before I saw it.

And I still wasn't prepared.

Ben was in the gym—alone—wearing a pair of boxing gloves and going at the punching bag like it had personally insulted him.

"Oh," I said.

"Yeah," Melanie said, now standing to stare at Ben with me. "It makes coming to work a lot more fun."

This was truly ridiculous.

His back was to us, so he had no idea he was getting ogled, but I didn't think he would mind. Apparently, he was making it a point to become the favorite of every single local business in town.

I couldn't escape him.

"Excuse me," I said to Melanie.

I pushed the door to the main gym open. It smelled like antiseptic and sweat.

I watched Ben. He moved to a rhythm that seemed to be in his head. One-two, one-two, one-two. Left-right. Left-right. Each punch hit the bag with a solid thwack. Sweat was gathered at the back of his neck, making his hair stick to his skin.

I remembered the last time I'd seen him exerting this much energy. He'd been on top, his hips moving with the same driving rhythm, my legs around his waist.

"Lauren?"

I'd been so lost in the memory that I hadn't even noticed him notice me.

"What are you doing?" I asked.

He tilted his head. "I'm working out. What are you doing?"

"Not that," I said. "Your handshake tour of Cooper. Why does everyone in town know you?"

He pulled off one of his gloves and picked up a water bottle. Took a long drink. I didn't watch his throat as he swallowed deeply.

I didn't watch for too long.

"I'm just being friendly," he said after he'd drawn the back of his hand over his mouth.

"There's being friendly, and there's running for mayor," I said.

He looked at me and there was a small shake of his head.

"What?" I demanded.

"You sound jealous," he said.

"No, I don't."

He lifted his hands—one still wearing a boxing glove. "Okay," he said.

"It doesn't matter to me," I said. "I got a free pastry so it's fine."

"Johanna is great, isn't she?" he asked. "She was telling me about her nephew and how he's working with huskies so he can race them."

I gave him a look.

"What?"

"I just don't understand what you're doing," I said. "You're only here for a couple of months."

"And I'm not allowed to be friendly?"

We were going in circles.

"Whatever," I said, and turned to leave.

"Just because you're avoiding me doesn't mean I'm going to pretend I'm not here," he said.

I stopped in my tracks and whirled back around.

"I'm not avoiding you!"

An absolute, bald-faced lie. Ben didn't even dignify it with a response. He was taking off his other glove instead and unraveling the fabric wrapped around his fingers and palm.

"I like people," he said. "I like talking to them. Getting to know them."

"Yeah, I heard you were very popular," I said.

I regretted it the minute I said it. Because it wasn't just the unkind regurgitation of gossip he'd already said was overblown, but it was also the most jealous thing I could have said.

Ben glanced up at me.

"Sorry," I said.

He just shook his head. "I don't understand what you want, Lauren."

I bit my lip. *I* didn't know what I wanted.

"You're bold and direct in Philadelphia. Fun and sexy while we're texting. Then, suddenly, you stop responding. Then, the next time I see you, you're kissing me and then shoving me away," he said. "You tell me this is all too complicated, then you come to my place after a date looking like a goddamn fantasy and fuck me like you've thought of nothing else for days."

My face flushed.

"Yeah, I'm only here for a few months," Ben said. "But I'm not going to hide away in my apartment just because my presence confuses you."

I opened my mouth. Didn't have anything to say. Closed it.

"I feel like I've made myself pretty clear," he said. "You know what I want. Give me a call when you accept that you want the same thing."

CHAPTER 36

NOW

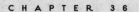

I PRACTICALLY RIPPED THE DOOR OPEN WHEN I HEARD Allyson's knock. We'd made plans for dinner and ever since my conversation with Ben yesterday, I'd been dying to talk to her. Preferably over cocktails.

It seemed the universe had other plans for me—ones that did not involve the girls' night that I'd been desperate for.

"Don't be mad" was the first thing that she said to me.

Which was pretty much a guarantee that I would be.

"Why?" I asked, trying to peer around her.

I should have known something was up, she usually honked at me from the street.

"I didn't plan it," she said. "But . . ."

"But what?"

I finally managed to move her to the side. There was a man in her car.

"That better be for you," I said.

"Ugh, no," she said. "That's my cousin. I totally forgot that he was coming to visit this week."

"We can reschedule dinner," I said. "It's fine."

But Allyson was biting her lip. A sure sign that it wasn't fine.

"What?" I demanded.

"We don't have to cancel our plans," she said. "Why don't we all go out?"

"I'm sure you two have plenty to catch up on," I said. "I don't really feel like being a third wheel tonight."

And I definitely didn't want to dish about all this Ben *stuff* around a stranger.

"I was actually hoping *I'd* be the third wheel," Allyson said.

I realized what she was doing.

"No," I said.

"Oh, come on," she said. "Peter is a good person—kind, funny, generous. My favorite cousin, in fact."

"Allyson," I warned.

"What?" she asked. "The apps weren't working for you, so why not try this? Someone who has already been vetted. Someone who's not obsessed with holding doors and ordering food for you."

I didn't need this right now.

"What's the harm in giving him a chance?"

I also knew that Allyson wouldn't let it go. And that the path of least resistance was . . . I looked again at Cousin Peter.

It wasn't easy to get a gauge on him through the car window, but I could see enough to note that he was handsome. He wore glasses. As far as I could tell, he was dressed well—unless, of course, he was wearing cargo shorts and flip-flops with his button-up shirt.

He waved. I sighed.

"Fine," I said. "But let me go put some lipstick on."

I SUPPOSED I SHOULD have been grateful that I wasn't home alone. It had taken me forever to fall asleep last night, and when I did, I'd been plagued with nightmares where I was hiking somewhere that looked familiar but wasn't, and I could see Lena up ahead of me, but every time I tried to call to her, no sound came out.

"Did you hear the news?"

Unsurprisingly, the moment we walked into the restaurant, I was spotted by someone I knew and waved over to their table. This time it was Mrs. Carmelo, who had been my elementary school teacher. It would have been rude not to say hello.

I braced myself for another person to gush about what a nice young man Ben was, and how he'd Hallmark-movied his way into the heart of this town.

"Jackie's pregnant!" she said. Jackie was her daughter who lived in Bozeman.

There was no way this had anything to do with Ben. I relaxed a little.

"That's wonderful," I said. "Congratulations."

"We were starting to get worried," Mrs. Carmelo said.

"Sure," I said.

She gave me a sympathetic look. "It's probably too late

for you," she said. "Though, I've heard of miracles happening. Of course, you'll need a man first." She glanced behind me. "He looks nice."

"Lena and I are doing great," I said. "Lovely seeing you."

"Oh, and I met this nice young man at the library the other day," Mrs. Carmelo said. "A friend of yours and your brother's?"

I bit my tongue, and just nodded before excusing myself.

I headed back toward the table but was stopped once more. This time by the hostess, who was also a member of one of the store's book clubs.

"Do you know if Heather is going to be there tomorrow?" Kelly asked.

There had been some sort of falling-out between the two of them. I really hadn't wanted to get in the middle of it, but sometimes it was unavoidable. They'd been glaring at each other and not speaking during book club for a few weeks now.

"I don't know," I said. "But I hope you'll come anyways." Kelly made a face, but then sighed. "I probably will."

"Good," I said. "See you then."

"I also invited someone new," Kelly said. "I guess he's in town doing something with Mr. Parker?"

Was there anyone in town that Ben *hadn't* charmed?

I was finally able to get to the table only for Allyson to excuse herself the moment I arrived.

"I'll be right back," she said. "You two get to know each other."

Peter and I watched her go.

"What's the chance that she's leaving out the back?" I asked.

He laughed. "Hopefully low, since she's our ride."

I smiled. "I'm sure we could get you back to your hotel."

I hoped that hadn't sounded suggestive.

"I'm actually staying with Allyson," he said. "She insisted."

He was a nice-looking man. The glasses suited him, and he was wearing a pair of dark, well-fitted jeans that looked good with his blue button-up. It was the kind of thing that Spencer would have worn on a date. The kind of thing that most men wore in Cooper when they put some effort into it.

"She's a good friend," I said.

"She is," he said.

"Did you grow up together?"

He shook his head. "Not exactly. I was in New Mexico, and she was in the Bay Area, but our parents—our dads are brothers—used to go on these weeklong fishing trips, and we'd usually get thrown together because we were around the same age and flying one of us out for the summer was cheaper than camp."

"You must be hating this weather if you're from New Mexico," I said. "Not the best time to visit Montana, I'm afraid."

"It's nice," he said. "We don't get snow, though it can get pretty cold at night. It is a desert after all."

"That's what people say."

He smiled at me.

"Allyson said you own a bookstore."

"We sell books and crafts," I said. "I mostly do the craft part."

"What kind of crafts?"

"All sorts of things," I said. "There's needlework and quilting and sewing and drawing and watercolors and jewelry making. Pretty much any kind of craft you're interested in, we have something for it, or if we don't, we know where to get it and we can order it. We have lots of relationships with small businesses across Montana, and we try to support them instead of buying things from big-box stores, you know?"

I was rambling, but Peter was a good listener—his attention focused solely on me.

Unfortunately, I couldn't say the same. Because just as I'd caught my breath after explaining the main difference between knitting and crochet—the first involved two needles, the other just one—I found myself completely distracted.

"You've got to be kidding me," I said.

"Is everything okay?" Peter asked.

"What a surprise," Ollie said, coming over to our table.

"*Such* a surprise," Ben said.

This was ridiculous.

"Ben insisted we come here," Ollie said.

"It had been a recommendation," he said. "Though I can't remember who mentioned to me that Juniper's had the best burgers in town."

Me. I'd mentioned that to him.

"You're Ben Walsh, aren't you?" Peter asked, since I rudely hadn't made introductions. "And Oliver Matthias?"

"Sorry," I said. "They're friends of my brother."

"Gabe Parker, right?" Peter asked.

I nodded, but Peter had already returned his focus to Ben and Ollie.

"I'm a big BBC fan," he said.

"Nice to meet you," Ollie said, and the three men exchanged handshakes.

"Why don't you join us?" Peter suggested.

"I wouldn't want to interrupt your lovely evening together," Ben said, giving me a look.

It clearly said "So much for never dating again."

"This is a surprise," Allyson said, returning to the table.

"That's one way to put it," I muttered to myself.

Everyone ignored me.

"Darling." Ollie gave her a kiss on the cheek. "Wonderful to see you again."

"We were just meeting Lauren's date," Ben said.

"Oh, I'm not her date," Peter said.

A little too quickly.

"This is my cousin," Allyson said, throwing me a sympathetic glance. "He's visiting from New Mexico."

"*Love* New Mexico," Ollie said.

He took the seat next to Peter, across from me, while Ben pulled up a chair and set it right next to mine. The table was a four-top so it was a bit snug. I didn't say anything. Ben's calf brushed up against mine, and I thought about pulling away, but I didn't do anything either.

I tried not to think about how I'd left him that night after my disastrous date. How he'd been in bed, arms behind his head, watching me as I re-dressed. The smug grin on his face had been annoying but well-earned. I'd been pinned to the mattress and thoroughly fucked.

I could still hear his voice in my ear, breathy and filthy.

"I could lose myself in this cunt."

"Your tits will be the death of me."

"I want to run my tongue all over your gorgeous arse."

I gulped down a glass of water.

"I'm feeling a bit starstruck," Peter said. "You're both so talented."

"That's quite kind," Ollie said.

"I must have seen *Tommy Jacks* half a dozen times in the theaters," he said to Ollie, before turning to Ben. "And I was obsessed with *SXS,* even though I know I'm not its target audience."

"Cheers, mate," Ben said.

Now Peter was the one who was flushed, and it became even more clear that, excellent listening skills and impeccable manners notwithstanding, I wasn't the person he wanted to be out to dinner with.

Under the table, I felt Ben's knee press against mine.

I glanced over at him, and from his self-satisfied smile, I could tell that he'd come to the same conclusion about Peter that I had.

We all ordered burgers.

"Have you heard from Gabe and the girls?" Ollie asked.

I shook my head. "You know how he is with communication."

"The worst?" Ollie asked.

"I don't expect to hear much while they're gone."

"Allyson mentioned that they're in New York?" Peter asked.

"Have you ever been?" Ollie asked.

Peter had been wearing a permanent blush, one that only seemed to deepen anytime Ollie talked to him or looked at him. It was cute.

"I've always wanted to go," Peter said.

"Next to London, it's the most magical city in the world," Ollie said.

"Excuse me," I said. "Is Cooper not magical enough for you?"

Ollie leaned back. "I must admit," he said. "The place is growing on me."

He gave Peter a wink.

I knew Ollie was married, but I also knew that their relationship was an open one. If Peter played his cards right, he might be going home with Mr. Darcy at the end of the evening.

"What about you?" Ollie asked, his question now directed at Ben. "What do you think of Cooper?"

I wanted to scoff at Ollie's ridiculous attempt at subtlety, but with Ben's eyes on me, I forgot basically everything except what it had felt like to have his mouth on my calf. His breath on my inner thigh. His tongue . . .

"I think very highly of it," Ben said. "I've been having a great time exploring all it has to offer."

This time, when he put his hand on my knee, I didn't jump up from the table and run to the bathroom. I parted my legs instead, allowing his fingers to curl in and downward.

I'd lost my mind.

"That exploration won't take long," Allyson said. "I remember for the first week I was here, I was convinced there was another part of town that they were just hiding from me. That it couldn't possibly be this small."

"Reminds me of boarding school," Ben said. "Everyone doesn't exactly know each other, but we all know *of* each other."

"Exactly," Allyson said.

"You went to boarding school?" Peter asked.

"In Ireland," Ben said. "Started at fourteen."

"Did you like it?" Allyson asked.

"Not at first," Ben said. "It was a . . . complicated time in my life. But my father insisted. He'd wanted me to go from the get-go, but my mom pushed for me to stay home."

I'd never heard him mention his father before.

"I hated being away from the island," Ben said, before clarifying to Peter, "*another* island—I was born in Maui. But I found the theatre program at school and some friends, and after that, I never wanted to leave."

He took a drink of water.

"Ironically my father didn't like that," he said, with a shrug. "Then again, I could never do anything right according to him."

"My father was like that too," Peter said.

"What? Uncle Charlie?" Allyson asked. "I thought you guys got along great."

"We did," Peter said. "Until we didn't."

An awkward silence fell over the table.

"Was it an all-boys school?" Allyson asked, the question directed toward Ben.

"It was indeed," he said.

"Did anything naughty happen?" she asked.

"Allyson," I scolded.

"What?" She looked affronted. "My ex went to an all-boys school. He always denied that there was any fooling around, but I didn't believe him. Because we all know stuff happens at all-girls schools."

"I think that's just in the movies," I said.

"Nope," Ben said. "She's right. At least about my school. Lots of naughtiness."

"Go on," Allyson said, leaning forward, her chin on her palm.

Ben grinned at her. "What would you like to hear about first? The skinny-dipping or the pillow fights?"

THE NIGHT GREW LONG, and the restaurant began emptying out.

Ben had told us about meeting Danny ("We both auditioned for the role of Peter in *Peter Pan*. I got the lead—he got to be Wendy"), about his first Christmas in Ireland ("I was the first one to jump off the Forty Foot, and it was before they could warn me how fucking cold it was"), and about the time he'd gotten caught making out with the captain of the soccer team ("Straight guys never know how to kiss, but it sure is fun to teach them").

He was a good storyteller—gesticulating and pulling faces—and he made everyone laugh. And I wasn't sure the rest of the group noticed, but every time a question went back to his family—the father who had sent him to boarding school, and the mother who had fought it—Ben neatly deflected. It seemed practiced.

It made me insanely curious.

"You'd never drank before?" Allyson asked.

Ben had just confessed he'd had his first pint at the age of eighteen.

"What did you think?" Ollie asked.

"That Guinness tastes like chocolate," he said. "And I could understand why the Irish are known for their drinking."

The table laughed. I realized he'd only had water all night. Was he sober, like Gabe?

"My first drink was a Smirnoff Ice," Allyson said.

Everyone at the table visibly shuddered.

"Hey," she said. "I was a teenager. You take what you can get."

"I stole whiskey from my dad's liquor cabinet," Ollie said. "A cigar too. I'd never been so sick in my entire life."

"You went all in," I said.

"Sure did," Ollie said. "What about you? Lauren? Peter? First drinking stories."

"Mine's boring," Peter said. "Flat beer from a keg in someone's basement."

"Mine was beer too," I said, but didn't elaborate.

Because it had been a beer stolen from one of Gabe's ever-present six-packs, and I'd never fessed up to taking it, even though he accused me of it for months after.

"I was never a big drinker," I said.

"Me neither," Ben said.

He smiled at me.

With each passing moment it became harder and harder to remember why the whole Ben thing was a bad idea. Why I needed to stay away from him when all I wanted to do was crawl into his lap and thread my fingers through his hair. When I wanted to give his necklaces a tug, pulling his lips to mine, feeling the cool steel of his ring against my hip.

Ben's hand was back on my leg. He squeezed gently.

I tried not to sigh audibly.

Across the table, Allyson yawned. Loudly.

"I am exhausted," she said.

An actress she was not, though Juniper's was getting emptier and emptier by the moment.

"Are you ready to go back to your place?" Peter asked, about to rise from his chair, but Allyson put a hand on his shoulder.

"Why don't you stay out?" she said. "I'm sure Ollie could give you a ride home."

"I'd love to," Ollie said, taking Peter's arm and pulling him back into his seat.

Peter's face was bright red.

"Are you sure?" he asked.

"Absolutely," Allyson said, before turning to look at me. "You'll get the check, right? Let me know what I owe you?"

What *she* owed *me*.

Ha.

I imagined it hadn't been easy to be the odd man out during this hormonally charged meal, but she left the table with a smile. There was a long pause.

I ate one of the remaining french fries even though they were cold.

Ben cleared his throat.

"You know," Ollie said, "I have a great bottle of wine at my hotel."

"I love wine," Peter said.

"Great," Ollie said.

They both got up as if it had been choreographed.

"Have a good night," Ben said, draping an arm over the back of my chair.

"We will," Ollie said.

They left. And then there were two.

"I can drive you home," Ben said.

"I can walk," I said.

"Or you can let me drive you home."

"Okay."

I ate another fry. Ben played with my hair, his hand out of sight. I didn't stop him, even though I knew I should. This whole thing felt dangerous. The restaurant was mostly empty, but now, without the others to provide the illusion of a group outing, it was just Ben and me at our table. If we stayed too long, people would begin to talk.

It should have made me nervous. Instead, it just made me hotter.

What was wrong with me?

"I thought about what you said this afternoon," Ben said. "You really only have yourself to blame."

I almost choked on my fry. "Excuse me?"

"You were the one who raved about Juniper's," he said. "And told me about the gym, and Birds and Beasleys, and the Panhandler—"

"You've been to the Panhandler too?" I asked.

It was an all-purpose store at the far end of the walking mall that mostly specialized in cooking and baking supplies.

He nodded. "Talked to the owner for a while about whether or not raisins belong in cookies. He was pro. I was against."

"You talked to Rich about cookies?" I asked.

"Nice guy," he said.

"Is there anyone in town you don't know?"

He shrugged. "There are a few people I'm hoping to get to know better."

I narrowed my eyes at him.

"I'm talking about you," he said.

"Yes, I gathered that," I said, and sighed. "What do you want to know?"

"Don't look so excited," he said. "I'm just curious."

"*You're* curious?" I echoed. "I barely know anything about *you*."

"Ask," he said.

"What about your mother?"

He leaned back in his seat.

"What about her?"

"You don't talk about her," I said, knowing I was digging into something very personal.

"She died," he said. "When I was fourteen."

"Oh," I said. "I'm sorry."

"Thank you," he said.

"Fourteen," I said. "Isn't that when—"

"My father sent me to boarding school?" Ben took a sip of water. "Yep. Right after the funeral."

I gaped. "What?"

"They had a complicated relationship," he said. "What about your mother? Your father?"

"I work with my mom at the store," I said. "She used to teach high school English."

"Was she ever your teacher?"

I shook my head. "Cooper is small, but not so small that it doesn't have two high schools. We were at Central. She taught at West Cooper."

"And your dad?"

"He died when I was eleven," I said. "I'm sure Gabe has mentioned it."

Ben nodded. "It might have come up. What was he like?"

"My dad? He was great. Funny, in a silly way. Always could get my mom to laugh even if she was annoyed with him. Worked really hard—everyone at his job came to the funeral, even the people in HR. Stray cats would follow him home—we had a bunch of them over the years. Peaches, Wabbit, Darryl Strawberry, Big Fat Fuzzy Guy, Spoon," I said. "He basically adopted Spencer too."

I bit my lip. I hadn't meant to bring him up. Even though I knew Carl had been an absolute asshole, I still couldn't help the twinge of self-consciousness I felt at mentioning Spencer.

"Do you still spend Christmas with Danny and his family?" I asked.

Now I was the one who wanted to change the subject.

"When I can," he said. "But it can be complicated because Fran is my employee, or colleague, or something.

Makes it feel kind of weird to act like we're family, though she insists it's fine."

"Maybe you *should* fire her," I said. "That way it doesn't have to be weird."

"Have *you* been talking to Fran?" he asked.

"She sounds smart," I said.

"She is," Ben said. "But now that thing with Bond—"

He abruptly stopped himself.

"Did something change with Bond?" I asked.

"Why don't I get the check?" Ben suggested.

Had he gotten an offer? Been put back in the running? Whatever it was, he didn't want to tell me.

"Okay," I said.

He went up to the hostess's podium, and I wiped my hands on my jeans. They were sweaty and cold. I ate another fry, and then pushed the plate away and went to meet Ben at the front of the restaurant.

The parking lot was empty except for one vehicle.

"Is this Gabe's truck?" I asked.

"He's letting me borrow it while he's out of town," Ben said.

"Ollie didn't want a ride on Lillian?" I asked.

Like half the things I said to Ben, it was far more suggestive than I'd intended.

"Lillian's not his type."

"Pity," I said.

"If you're interested," he said, "all you need to do is ask."

"I'm good."

But the thought of wrapping my arms around Ben, his machine vibrating beneath us, was becoming more and more appealing. And I was running out of reasons why it was a bad idea. Why all of this was a bad idea.

"Open offer," he said.

I stared at my feet.

"Got any more hot dates planned?" he asked.

"That wasn't a date," I said.

"Of course not," he said.

I gave him a look.

"I'm done with dating," I said.

"That's too bad. I personally thought your last one ended very nicely."

"It won't happen again," I said.

"By that do you mean have incredible sex that you flee from the moment you've come?" Ben asked.

My face burned hot, but he wasn't wrong.

I glanced around quickly, worried someone had heard. He noticed.

"We're in a parking lot," he said. "No one is here."

He was right.

"You have to be careful," I said.

"I'm very careful," he said. "And I'm pretty sure *I'm* not the one sneaking off to a strange man's apartment or molesting said man during dinner."

My mouth dropped open. "Your hands were on *me*."

He grinned.

"You're the worst," I said.

"You still like me," he said.

"I don't like you at all."

"Liar."

It was cold and I pulled my jacket tighter around me.

There was no reason for me to be standing there—if I'd started walking home when we left the restaurant, I would have been back already.

To an empty house.

"Come on," Ben said. "Let's go for a drive."

CHAPTER 37

NOW

I DIDN'T EVEN KNOW WHAT KIND OF MUSIC HE LIKED to listen to.

As it turned out, he had the local country music station playing as we pulled out of the parking lot and headed toward the edge of town.

"Didn't take you for a country boy," I said.

"When in Rome," he said. "And I like all types of music."

"What about Joni Mitchell?" I asked, thinking about one of Allyson's disastrous dates.

"What's not to love?" he asked.

"Correct answer. You're going to take a left up here."

"Where are we going again?" he asked.

"I haven't told you," I said. "Another left at the stop sign and then a right just after the fence."

"I thought you hated surprises," Ben said as he followed my instructions.

"It's not a surprise for me," I said. "And I figured *you* liked them."

He grinned at that, just barely visible in the dark. We were far from streetlights and window-lined neighborhoods.

I didn't tell him that the actual surprise was that I'd agreed to go with him in the first place. I should have been home. Alone. In bed.

I was getting tired of *shoulds*.

"You can park here," I said.

He did and shut off the pickup. All we had was the light from the moon, which was round and full and bright above.

"*Now* are you going to tell me where we are?"

"The Ridge," I said.

"That actually means nothing to me."

I smiled. "It's the make-out spot in town."

"I see," Ben said. He undid his seatbelt, then without missing a beat, undid mine.

He leaned forward, but I put my hand on his chest.

"We should talk."

"You brought me to the local make-out spot to *talk*?" Ben asked. "I'm getting dizzy from all the mixed signals you're sending."

He leaned back against his seat.

"But I'm happy to talk," he said. "In fact, I'm pretty sure you like it when I talk too."

I knew what he was referring to. He was *very* mouthy in bed. And I did like it.

"That's exactly what we need to talk about."

Ben waited for me to continue.

"I like you, but—"

"I like you too," Ben said.

Those fucking eyes of his.

"It's complicated," I said, feeling like a broken record.

"It doesn't have to be," he said.

I held back a snort. "Sure," I said.

"Go on a date with me," he said.

"What?"

"A date." Ben gave me a grin. "You know, those things you go on with other men and then shag me after."

"I don't—"

"Dinner," he said. "That's all I'm asking."

"You make it sound so simple," I said.

"And you make it sound so complex," he said. "I like you. You like me. I really like having sex with you, and I'm pretty sure you enjoy yourself as well."

The mother of all understatements.

"You're only here for a few months," I said.

"And?" he asked. "There is this thing called a telephone. You can communicate with it—in multiple ways."

"I know how to use a phone," I said.

"Do you?"

"Touché," I said.

He shifted in his seat, fully facing me.

"A date," he said. "And maybe we'll go to my place afterward. And maybe we'll go on another date. And another. And then maybe I'll have to leave."

"And then?"

"And then we figure it out," he said. "I'm actually quite good at problem-solving."

I had a sneaking suspicion that Ben could talk me into

nearly anything if he kept looking at me like that. He made my reservations melt away, and it suddenly seemed silly that I wasn't willing to give it a try.

He was asking for a date.

I'd gone out with far worse men already, why not give Ben a chance?

Because he was going to leave.

At least I'd have good sex until he left. Eventually another role, another offer would come along, and he'd have to go. And I'd have to stay.

But there was the part of me—that small, quiet voice in the back of my head—that whispered: *What if he didn't leave? What if it worked out?*

That voice was an idiot, obviously.

He had a life—a career—that would take him away from Cooper. From this.

Ben was smiling at me.

"Okay," I said.

There was a long pause.

"Okay?"

I nodded. "A date." I held up a finger. "One date."

"One date," he said. "At a time."

We sat there in the car.

"Does this count?" I asked.

He laughed. "Fuck no," he said. "Maybe if we were teenagers, but we're adults. I'm going to take you to dinner."

"Not in Cooper," I said.

He didn't actually roll his eyes, but it was implied.

"Fine," he said. "We can go to dinner somewhere else."

"Thank you," I said.

"I *can* be a gentleman," he said.

I sighed. He was being so patient with me. I was being a dick.

"I'm sorry," I said.

He leaned his head back against the seat and looked over at me.

"It's okay," he said. "I get it."

"Small towns," I said.

"Small towns," he agreed. "Love 'em and hate 'em."

"Do you miss yours?" I asked.

Ben turned his gaze forward. "There are things I miss about it," he said.

"The beach?" I asked. "Never-ending sunshine?"

"I miss my mom's house," he said. "It had been her parents', so she'd grown up there too—all these generations of Akinas—that was her maiden name—in one place. It was a tiny thing, barely two bedrooms, but it held a lot of memories."

"What happened to it?"

Ben made a face.

"My father."

I didn't understand.

"He's a developer," Ben said. "When mom died, the house went to him. They never divorced, but never really lived together either. He keeps threatening to tear it down and build something bigger and then sell it. He'd get a lot for it—beachfront property, you know."

"But he hasn't sold it yet?"

"We made a deal," he said, and held up his hand, his

thumb and finger measuring about an inch. "And I'm this close to fulfilling my end of it."

I wanted to know more, but Ben shifted in his seat.

"Tell me about Spencer," he said.

I blinked. "What? Why?"

I hated hearing Carl's voice in the back of my head.

"Because he's important to you," Ben said.

The use of present tense was what got me.

Without warning, tears began flooding my eyes. I put my face into my hands and sobbed.

Ben said nothing, he just rubbed my back, soft, slow circles between my shoulder blades.

I couldn't remember the last time I'd lost control of my emotions like that. When they'd completely taken over.

"I'm sorry," I said, once I'd gotten ahold of myself.

"Why?" he asked. "You miss him."

I nodded. "But it's been three years," I said. "I realize I should be over it. Over him."

Fucking Carl. He'd really gotten under my skin.

"I don't think you ever get over someone who died," Ben said. "I don't even think you get over grief. You go through it."

I sniffed.

"My mother died sixteen years ago," he said. "I miss her every day. I hope I always do."

"It doesn't make you sad?"

"Of course it does," he said. "But why is sad such a bad thing? It's normal, right?"

"What if you're mad?" I asked, thinking about how I'd felt after my dad died.

"I think that's normal too," he said.

He tapped his fingers against the steering wheel.

"I lied before," he said. "About that pint of Guinness being my first drink."

I tilted my head.

"The night before my mom's funeral, I drank an entire bottle of wine. Because I was mad. Mad at my mom, my father, everyone, everything," he said. "The next day I was so sick that I couldn't stop throwing up. Could barely stand upright during the memorial." He gave me a wry smile. "My father was furious and refused to speak to me. It was the only good thing that came from that."

"I'm sorry," I said.

"Yeah," he said. "Me too."

It was dark outside, and I could see the stars from the windows of the car. That was one thing about Cooper that I never stopped loving—its sky at night. How small it made me feel. How insignificant and at the same time miraculous we all were.

"Why don't I drive you home?" Ben asked.

"Okay," I said.

The house was dark and quiet, just one light on in the living room. Mom had probably dropped Teddy off a few hours ago—I was watching her tonight.

I didn't want to go inside.

I turned to Ben, about to ask if we could go to his place, when his hand came up, cupping my cheek, thumb against my jaw.

"Good night, Lauren," he said.

The kiss he gave me was unlike any of the others. It

was brief and sweet. Like the kind of kiss that you might share on a first date. I closed my eyes, leaning into it, but he pulled back before things could get any more interesting.

"Good night," I said, got out of the car, and went inside.

CHAPTER 38

THEN

THE MORE FAMOUS GABE GOT, THE LESS CONNECTED WE were. He was constantly on the move—going from set to set, project to project. We saw more of him in the tabloids than in person. He even got married in Vegas and we found out about it via *People* magazine. Mom was pretty pissed about that. Even after Gabe said it was more a mutual arrangement than actual love.

"What does that even mean?" she would ask me.

I could only shrug. Gabe now seemed to operate in a different world than we did—different rules, different expectations. It was better not to ask too many questions.

There wasn't any big moment of forgiveness, but things between Gabe and Spencer eventually settled back to how they had been before. Whenever I asked Spencer what had happened, if Gabe had apologized or he had apologized, I always got some vague nonanswer.

"We dealt with it."

"It wasn't really a big deal."

"I'm over it, and he is too."

We all just pretended nothing had happened.

The store turned out to be the best gift Gabe could have given us.

Most of us.

Mom loved putting her expertise and years of English-teacher experience into effect without the firm hand of the school board telling her what she could or could not teach.

I enjoyed the routine of it all—expectations neatly lined up, lists of tasks to be done—it made me feel in control of my life for the first time in a while. I never had to go work at the grocery store again, never had to bring home armfuls of bent, discounted cans that no one else would buy. I made my own schedule and learned a whole bunch of new skills I'd never been given a chance to develop. I had time to work on things I loved: knitting and baking. The early access to new cookbooks was a major bonus.

We'd all assumed that once he got used to the idea—once Gabe and he had made up—Spencer would manage the Cozy. That it would be something we'd all do together.

Instead, he continued working at the hardware store, even though I could tell he was exhausted and bored by it all.

But when I asked him why he didn't want to switch, his answer nearly broke my heart.

"It would just be the same thing in a different location," he said. "It's all the same."

I could tell he was depressed, but he wouldn't admit it. Not to me, not to himself.

Yes, he loved me, and he loved Lena, and he was always

present with her, but at night, when we'd crawl into bed, I'd have my cookbook to read and I'd turn to him, halfway through a recipe, and find that he was just sitting there, staring out into nothingness.

"I'm fine," he always said. "Everything is fine."

Gabe brought Jacinda to Cooper for Lena's birthday. It was the first time we'd met her, and she was beautiful and refined and initially intimidating. But after a day or so, the two of us bonded over our preference for tea over coffee and our shared interest in fiber arts (her as a consumer, me as a creator).

Lena was showered with gifts.

"She doesn't need all this stuff," I told Gabe.

He shrugged. "What else am I going to spend my money on?"

"I hope you're saving some of it," I said. "Instead of blowing it on Legos."

He looked good, though, and he didn't touch a drop of alcohol the entire time he was visiting. If nothing else, that helped to endear Jacinda to my mother, since she seemed to be at least part of the reason Gabe was able to stay sober.

Not that anyone mentioned his drinking.

The best part was that he and Spencer started going on their long walks again. Spencer took time off, and every morning they'd set out and wouldn't return until lunchtime. And just like when they were kids, when I asked where they were going, Spencer would just say "around."

He was happy.

It was a nice visit and none of us wanted it to end.

Gabe, of course, had gotten us "goodbye gifts."

"That's not a thing," I told him.

"I'm making it a thing," he said.

"We don't need anything else."

He'd already bought us a new TV, a new TV stand, a swing for the backyard, and a new set of towels for the guest room (though I was pretty sure that was for his and Jacinda's benefit), and had taken us out to dinner almost every night.

"I am a decent cook," I'd remind him.

"And I'm not," he'd say. "So let me do this for you guys, okay?"

I wanted to tell him that his presence was enough. That all we wanted was to see him and spend time with him. But part of me wondered if he'd believe me.

"One more gift," Gabe said. "This one's for Spencer."

The person who would never admit to wanting anything. The person who was utterly impossible to shop for.

The gift was a slim envelope. A check.

"This is too much," Spencer said when he opened it. "We don't need more money."

"That's a scholarship," Gabe said. "So you can go back to school. Get your degree."

There had never been a more perfect gift.

Spencer didn't cry, but he did stare at the check for a very long time and then gave Gabe a hug. I heard a muffled *thank you* and *I love you*.

I knew this was going to change his life.

The next day, Spencer called the hardware store and quit.

CHAPTER 39

NOW

I DREAMED ABOUT SPENCER THAT NIGHT. IT STARTED AS one of those nonsense dreams—I always seemed to be without pants, and wandering some weird mall that felt familiar but wasn't. For whatever reason, I really needed to find a certain stand that served those Chinese egg yolk pastries that I'd had once when I'd gone to visit Gabe in L.A. for a premiere. Instead, I kept finding saltwater taffy sellers, but all they had was cinnamon-flavored taffy. Every time one of the vendors would offer me a sample, Spencer would take it, as if he'd been with me the whole time. He kept saying "This is good, Lauren, you should try it," and I'd try it, and it wouldn't be right, and I would get mad at him because they weren't the pastries I wanted. Right before I woke up, I remembered him saying "Fine, if you don't want it, then I'll just give it to the fish."

I woke up wondering who or what the fish was.

It was a disorienting dream—and I even tried getting back into it by scooching deeper down into bed, under the covers, but I needed caffeine, and Teddy needed break-fast.

Though I didn't see Teddy at the foot of the bed, where she usually was in the morning. Apparently, she'd gotten tired of waiting for me and had decided to start her day.

I could take the hint.

I'd probably never have that dream again, and never know what the fuck the point of the fish was.

I went downstairs and screamed when I entered the kitchen.

Gabe put his finger in his ear, twisted, and winced. "Jesus Christ, Lauren," he said.

He was sitting at the kitchen island with Chani.

"What are you doing here?" I asked, my heart pounding from the surprise.

They should have been in New York. The plan had been that they'd return on Sunday night—I was supposed to pick them up at the airport. It was Saturday morning.

I noticed Lena sitting there. Her face—her entire being—looked like a volcano on the cusp of eruption.

"What happened?" I asked, suddenly terrified. "Is everyone okay? Where's Eve?"

"She's fine," Chani said quickly. "We already dropped her off. Everyone is fine."

"I sent you a text," Gabe said.

"You did?"

But there were no missed texts on my phone.

"Shit," Gabe said. "I *meant* to send you a text."

Chani shot him a look, and he gave me an apologetic glance.

"Sorry," he said.

We were going to have a talk about communication, but at the moment, I didn't care about that.

"What is going on? Why are you home so soon?" I looked at Lena, but she was glaring at the countertop. "Lena? Did something happen?"

Gabe crossed his arms. "Lena, do you want to tell your mom why we came back this early?"

There was no response.

"Lena!" Gabe barked.

Chani and I both jumped. Gabe never raised his voice. Especially not at Lena.

But the person in question didn't startle. Instead, she slowly, dangerously fixed her eyes on her uncle. I wasn't proud of myself, but I took a step back at her murderous expression.

"Fuck. You," she said to Gabe.

"Lena!" I was shocked. I had never—ever—heard her speak to someone that way, especially not her uncle. "What is going on?"

"Ask him." Lena raised a hand, an accusatory finger pointed at Gabe. "Ask him why he's a hypocrite."

"It's not the same thing at all. I'm an adult," Gabe said, but his face was white. "You are thirteen years old. It's actually illegal for you to drink."

"You were drinking?" My head was spinning.

"She raided the minibar at the hotel," Gabe said. "She and Eve were as drunk as skunks. I can't tell who's the worse influence, but I think we all need to rethink this friendship."

"We had to tell Eve's parents," Chani said, her voice quiet.

I didn't know what to say. Gabe was crossing a line in making any kind of rules pertaining to my kid, but he was also clearly upset and worried.

"I don't understand what's going on," Gabe said. "This isn't like you at all."

"Shut up! Shut up! Shut up!" Lena screamed, pushing back from the counter.

"Lena!"

"You don't know me at all," she said.

She focused on Gabe, her gaze lethal.

"It was one night." Lena's eyes were tearful. "But you. You were drunk. All. The. Time. Birthdays. Holidays."

Chani's hand was at her mouth, her eyes wide. Gabe looked like he wanted to throw up.

I wasn't sure anyone had ever spoken to him like this.

"Dad's funeral!" Lena's voice cracked and the tears came. "You were drunk at his *funeral.*"

"Lena," I tried again, but all she had were eyes—and words—for Gabe.

"And Eve is not my *best* friend," she said. "She's my *girlfriend.* My girlfriend! Because I like girls." Her face was wet. "But you don't care. You're too busy with your movies and *your* girlfriends, and your drinking, to care about me. To care about any of us."

It was as if all the air had dissipated from the room. All the color from our faces as well.

"I wish you'd just go away," Lena said to Gabe, and with that, she was gone, feet pounding up the stairs, the door slam shaking the entire house.

WE TRIED TO NOT listen, but the problem with the house was that it echoed.

And Lena wasn't trying to keep her voice down.

I sat in the kitchen with Chani, the two of us pretending to drink tea, when in reality we were listening to my thirteen-year-old daughter drag my forty-year-old brother to hell.

In fairness, he'd asked for it.

He'd asked for it by following her up the stairs after her tearful, shocking departure, knocking on the door, and saying he wanted to talk.

It had started quiet, with the low rumble of his voice.

"I've got some cookies," I'd said to Chani.

"Okay," she'd said.

They were chocolate chip oatmeal.

No raisins because Ben was right. Raisins didn't belong in cookies.

"They're good," Chani had said.

"Thanks," I'd said.

We sat there, with our tea and cookies, and I realized it was the first time Chani and I had been alone, just the two of us.

"How was the rest of the trip?" I asked. It seemed like a safe enough topic.

Unless Lena had broken something in the Met or burned down a tree in Central Park. I braced myself.

"It was good," Chani said, one hand resting on top of the other. "Nice." Her cheeks were a bit pink.

"The show was good?"

"It was."

"How does Gabe know the director again?"

"He did the choreography for the first Bond movie," Chani said.

"Ah."

"We had drinks with him afterward."

"That sounds nice," I said.

"I mean, Gabe had water," she said. "He's been really careful about his sobriety."

"I'm glad," I said.

"Being here has been good for him," Chani said. "Being around family."

"How is it for you? I know we're a lot."

Chani gave her cup a wry smile. "It's taking some adjustments. Awkward family dynamics I'm used to," she said. "I'm less accustomed to being the only Jew in a fifty-mile radius. Gabe does his best to help me feel at home, but his Yiddish is atrocious."

We shared a smile.

I understood what it was like to feel out of place. What it felt like when you were outgrowing the world you'd always known.

Cooper had never felt so small before.

"We're glad you're here," I said.

"Thank you."

There was a long silence. My tea was too hot to drink, so I just blew on it continuously to give myself something to do.

I imagined Spencer here right now. He would have been asking a billion questions about the article Chani had written: What happened that weekend? Did she actually sneak out of Gabe's house before he woke up? Had she really never seen a Bond movie before?

Was it true that Gabe had said that *I* was his best friend?

We'd teased him about that for months, but I was pretty sure that Spencer had been slightly hurt by that.

"It's better press," I'd kept telling him. "Makes him sound all sweet and down-to-earth."

Guys could be so sensitive sometimes.

Chani tucked her hair behind her ears. She had a ring on her left ring finger. It looked like a lizard or a dragon or something. I was pretty sure she hadn't been wearing it before New York.

Gabe, you sneaky bastard, I thought. *Did you propose?*

I was happy for him. For them.

But sad too.

Lonely.

I shook those feelings away.

Now wasn't the time to be thinking about myself.

"For the record?" I tilted my head toward Chani. "Spencer was always convinced that there had been something between you and Gabe. He would have been so smug when you showed up."

That made her laugh.

"We weren't very subtle," she said.

"No," I said. "Not at all."

She shook her head with an embarrassed smile.

One that faded as the voices from upstairs amplified.

Or rather, one voice.

"You could have died!" Lena screamed, and the frayed

pain in her voice made me want to storm into her bedroom and sweep her up in my arms.

But I didn't, because I knew this was something she had to say to Gabe and something he had to hear.

Chani and I exchanged a look, but neither of us moved. We both sipped our tea instead.

We'd all been so careful with him about his addiction—first while he was in the midst of it, afraid we'd just make it worse, and then afterward, when we were worried we'd push him back into it.

No one had spoken to him the way that Lena was speaking to him now, and even though a part of me wanted to protect my little brother from what was already a devastating attack from someone who he loved deeply and someone he had hurt equally deeply, it wasn't my place.

"I needed you and you weren't there." Lena's voice was all cracking and lilting and horrible and beautiful. "You cared more about a stupid fucking drink than you did about me."

We were going to have to have a conversation about her language. It was not what I wanted to hear from her, but it was also the kind of language she needed to use in this moment. That she deserved to use.

Teddy—who was lying under the counter—let out a long, drawn-out groan.

"I know, buddy," Chani said, reaching down to pet her. "We'll go soon."

"They might be up there a while," I said to Chani. "Maybe it would be good to get Teddy home."

"Are you sure?"

"It also might be good for Gabe and me to talk after . . ." I searched for the right words. "After he's been reduced to a pile of ash."

Chani managed a laugh. "She's a good kid."

"Yeah," I said. "That's what I keep telling myself."

"Thanks. Thanks for the tea and cookies," she said, leashing Teddy.

I waited alone.

When Gabe finally came downstairs, I had more hot water going and a cup with a tea bag ready for him. He sat at the counter, his face pale, his eyes red. It looked as if all the life had been leeched out of him, which was exactly how it felt when a thirteen-year-old tore you a new one. Especially if you knew you deserved it.

I made him a cup of tea and set it in front of him. We both stared at it, the thin line of steam trailing from the rim so beautiful and elegant that it seemed out of place. He drank it, and even though I knew it was too hot, he didn't wince once. Didn't even pause to absorb the pain he was probably feeling. He just drank it. Just took it.

"She hates me," he finally said.

"It's not a chronic condition," I said.

He managed a choked laugh, but halfway through, there were tears rolling down his cheeks. It broke my heart. I couldn't remember the last time I'd seen him cry. It had been a while.

Apparently we were all crying at the drop of a hat now.

He pushed the tears roughly aside.

"I'm so sorry, Lauren," he said. "What the fuck was I thinking?"

I didn't know exactly what he was talking about, but I was pretty sure it had to do with the worst accusation I'd heard Lena levy at him: being drunk at Spencer's funeral.

I'd noticed, but I'd hoped that she was too young—that she didn't even really understand what Gabe's bloodshot eyes and occasional slurring meant.

It was a stupid assumption.

"You weren't," I told him. "You were in the midst of the worst part of your addiction."

"It's not an excuse."

"I know," I said. "It's just reality."

Gabe put his head in his hands.

"I'm a monster," he said.

"Stop it," I said, even though I'd said the same to myself.

"I can't believe how selfish I was—how selfish I am," he said.

"Gabe," I said. "Stop."

He looked up at me, his eyes red and pained.

"I miss him so much," he said.

Dad. Spencer.

"I know," I said. "I miss him too."

Gabe nodded, but it was a tight, taut movement, as if he wasn't sure he was allowed to make it. As if he wasn't allowed to feel what he was feeling.

"It's not the same, though, is it?" He sounded miserable. "We were friends. But you and he were . . . you guys were . . ."

I stopped him.

"That's not how this works. There's not a limited amount of grief and you need to make sure I get the right ratio of pain. It's something we all share. Something we *should* share."

We hadn't.

That needed to change.

It terrified me. The wave of emotions I'd been holding back.

I was worried it would pull me under. That I'd never find the surface again.

Then I thought about what Ben had said. You don't get over grief—you get through it.

We could get through this.

Gabe looked up at the ceiling and let out a breath.

"It's not fair," he said.

"No, it's not," I said, but I sensed that he meant it in more than just the general sense of the word.

He looked over at me.

"Can I tell you something horrible?" he asked.

"Of course," I said.

Gabe closed his eyes.

"It should have been me," he said.

I was speechless for a moment. Not surprised, really, because I'd had the same thought—not about Gabe, but about myself. I'd just never said it out loud and my heart filled with tenderness and love that Gabe had. He was brave.

Braver than me.

"You should have been the one driving down Main Street that night?" I asked lightly.

"You know what I mean," he said.

"I know," I said. "But I also know that there's no way it could have been you."

He rubbed the back of his neck.

"Not like that," he said. "But I'd been drinking so much

at that point. Why didn't that kill me? Why do I get to be here and he's not? He was a good person. A good husband. A good father."

His voice was raw. Rough.

It hurt to hear the pain, and I had to blink back tears.

"Can I tell you something horrible?" I asked.

"Please," he said.

"I can't remember if I told Spencer I loved him the night he died," I said.

I'd never told anyone that before. My deepest shame. My regret.

"He was going out to run errands and I was at the kitchen counter looking at my phone or something, and he said I love you, and I can't remember if I said it back."

I felt a small sort of relief in saying it out loud.

"He knew," Gabe said. "Of course he knew."

I took his hand. "You're not a monster. You're a good person."

He wouldn't look at me.

"I'm an addict," he said.

I nodded. "And a good person."

He was holding tight to my hand, and I didn't know if he even realized it.

"If we were different people, maybe I could say something about our journeys and our place in this world and a greater purpose, but I think you'd think it was just as much bullshit as I do," I said. "I don't know why Spencer is dead and you're here. There's no reason to it. No greater purpose, no lesson to be learned. There's *nothing* good about his death. But I am glad that you're here."

A tear slid down his cheek.

"I'm glad I'm here too," he said.

He wrapped an arm around me, and I leaned into him. In some ways, he felt so much like Dad these days, and if I *were* someone who believed in a greater purpose maybe I'd allow myself to think that was the reason he was still here. But I didn't believe that, so I just let myself be held.

CHAPTER 40

NOW

THE DOOR WAS CLOSED, AND I KNOCKED, BUT WHEN there was no answer, I opened it anyway.

Lena was lying on the bed, facing away from me, draped over her comforter like dirty laundry. She didn't look up when I entered, not even when I sat down on the edge of the mattress.

"Lena," I said.

"I'm sorry," she said, still looking at the floor, her words half muffled by the arms she had folded under her chin.

"For what exactly?" I asked.

"Drinking," she said. "It was gross anyways, and I never want to do it again."

I certainly hoped that was the case since addiction was often hereditary. But that was a conversation for another time.

"I'm glad to hear it," I said.

I traced the patterns on her bedspread. Little stars intermingled with swirls of color. It wasn't the one we'd bought on a recent Target run. This was an old one. I could feel its well-earned softness, the kind that only came from generations of washing.

"You and Eve," I said. "How long?"

Lena shrugged. "We're not really into labels."

It was the most thirteen-year-old thing to say, and I almost laughed. But I didn't.

"Right," I said, seriously. "Of course."

We were both silent.

"We might have to reconsider sleepovers now," I said.

Did we? I wasn't sure of the rules.

"Okay," Lena said, and then looked at me. "You don't mind?"

"Mind what?"

"The whole"—she extracted an arm to give it a generalized wave—"you know, liking girls thing?"

"Of course not," I said. "I love you. No exceptions."

I hadn't realized she needed my approval, but of course she did.

"Honey," I said, "I think Eve is great. And I think you're the best—at least, in between the times when you're drinking in hotel rooms and slamming doors and yelling at your uncle."

Lena winced.

"But I will always love you—even in those moments. I love you no matter what," I said. "All of you."

"Thanks, Mom," she said.

"Though, we will have to revise those sex ed lessons," I told her. "Do you know what a dental dam is?"

"Mo-om," Lena groaned, burying her face in her hands. "Gross."

I smiled and missed Spencer terribly.

CHAPTER 41

THEN

THE COURSE CATALOG WAS OPEN ON THE TABLE, TWO heads bent over it.

"What do you think?" Spencer asked. "The Basics of Evolution or Introduction to Ecology?"

Lena, who was standing on a chair next to him, peered seriously at the pages and pages of tiny words in front of her. Then, she pointed.

"Of course," Spencer said. "The Origin and History of Life on Earth. Good call."

"Please don't tell me you're letting a five-year-old choose your college schedule," I said.

I was making brownies for an upcoming bake sale, and the house smelled of chocolate and butter.

"She's almost six, and so far she hasn't steered me wrong," he said.

"More!" Lena declared, watching me add chocolate chips.

"She is very opinionated," I said. And added more chocolate chips.

"More!" she said.

"How many classes are you going to try to take this semester?" I asked.

"Three, I think," he said. "Maybe four."

"Four?" I raised my eyebrows at him. "I thought that was too much last time?"

The money that Gabe had given Spencer—which we dubbed Spencer's Super Special Scholarship of Serious Schooling—had been a lifesaver. I'd never know how long Spencer would have been willing to keep working at the hardware store, or how long he would have denied his depression, but I didn't have to.

He was happy. Happier than I'd seen him in years.

Even when he took on too much schoolwork and had to stay up late studying for back-to-back tests, even when he told me that sometimes he felt like an old man next to his fellow students, even when he failed his very first class—Intro to Physics—his good mood didn't budge.

"Guess I'm rusty," he'd said when his report card had arrived. "I'll just have to take it again."

We'd still posted it on the fridge, right next to Lena's latest crayon masterpiece.

"I hope Spencer's college fund is just as big as Lena's," I told Gabe the next time I spoke to him. "Because I'm pretty sure if you want one of them to become a doctor, it's probably going to be Spencer. He'd be thrilled at the thought of an extra decade in school."

"Great," Gabe had said. "They can start a joint practice together. Parker and Daughter."

I liked the sound of that.

I didn't like the sound of ice cubes clinking in a glass on

the other end of the phone. Gabe insisted it was nothing, but I knew he wasn't over there sipping on lemonade. Jacinda had confirmed as much when I'd spoken to her last week.

"He doesn't think it's a problem," she'd said.

"What do you think?"

"It doesn't matter what I think," she said. "Until he real-izes what he's doing and wants to make a change, there's nothing any of us can do."

I hated feeling so helpless.

"What should we have for dinner?" I asked.

"I can make pizza," Spencer said.

"Pizza! Pizza! Pizza!" Lena cheered.

"Is there any dough in the freezer?" I asked.

"Mmm?" Spencer's attention had returned to the course catalog. "I wonder if I should take American Art this se-mester."

"Too many classes," I warned him.

He gave me a sheepish look. "It's just so hard to choose—and who knows if this class will be recurring."

"You're the one who made me promise to hold you back if you started going overboard."

"I know," Spencer said. "And I should listen to you—and myself—but I don't know. I think I'm going to sign up for it."

I sighed but I wasn't really annoyed. Because even when he was stressed about school and balancing too many courses, he was still the same Spencer. Kind. Patient. Loving.

He never lost his temper with Lena, never yelled at her. On the rare occasions he got frustrated to the point of an-noyance, he always—always—apologized to her. It was something I struggled with, so I was grateful that Lena had one parent that knew how to connect with her.

I watched them at the table, licking the brownie bowl and getting it all over the course catalog, their shirts, and most of Lena's chin.

"You two are a mess," I told them, coming around with a wet dish towel.

Lena squirmed as I wiped off her face, but Spencer just beamed up at me as I dabbed at the chocolate stain on his collar.

"You're my favorite wife," he said.

I rolled my eyes at him. "You just like the brownies," I said.

"They are good brownies."

I tossed the dish towel at him. It landed neatly on his head, like a too-small ghost costume, and Lena started hiccupping with laughter.

"What's so funny?" Spencer asked, pretending that nothing was wrong. He had his hands on his hips as he looked around, his face still covered with the towel. "Where did Lena go?"

"I'm here, Daddy!" she said.

"I can hear her," he said. "But I just can't see her."

"Daddy!" She waved her arms, and when that didn't work, she pulled the towel off him.

"Oh, there you are!" Spencer said.

He had such a great smile.

"I was worried I'd lost you," he said to Lena.

She shook her head. "You're silly, Daddy."

"I know." He pulled her into his lap and tickled her. "I know."

CHAPTER 42

NOW

"I FEEL LIKE A SPY," BEN SAID AS WE PULLED OUT OF the parking lot.

"You're definitely dressed like one," I said, glancing down at his outfit.

"I'll have you know these are my cleanest blacks," he said. "And I shined my boots. Just for you."

I had noticed that.

Of course, it was one of the last things I'd noticed since he'd shown up to our meeting spot on his motorcycle. Nothing could have prepared me for how fucking hot it was to watch Ben swing his leg over the bike, pull his helmet off, and run his hand through his hair.

My mouth had gone entirely dry.

My underwear? Wet.

"Another surprise?" Ben asked when I wouldn't tell him the restaurant we were going to. Or the town.

He didn't seem to mind.

Lena had decided to spend the night at my mom's but had actually considered taking Gabe up on his invitation, which was more than she might have done when he first arrived in Cooper with Chani. In the end, it had come down to who was guaranteed to have the best snacks. No one could beat Elizabeth Parker in that department.

"Just keep playing the long game," I'd told Gabe.

No one even asked where I was going, but I'd concocted an entire excuse anyway—that I was out with Allyson and didn't know when we'd get back.

"You owe me," Allyson had said. "Because now I have to sit at home, in the dark, and pretend I'm not there."

"No one is going to be driving by your house," I told her.

"You don't know that!" she said. "All I'm asking is for you to have the best night you can."

I'd given her a look.

"Okay, and to share all the sexy, dirty details when you get back."

"It's just dinner."

"Sure," she'd said.

She almost seemed more excited than I was for my date. Almost.

"We're going to a restaurant," I told Ben. "Just about an hour away."

"Wow," he said. "You *really* don't want to be seen."

I shifted in my seat. He wasn't wrong, but it didn't feel great hearing it out loud. Especially since he'd been so understanding about . . . everything.

I still couldn't believe I'd started crying in front of him.

It was so embarrassing. I'd thought about talking to my therapist about it, but then I'd have to tell her about Ben and that would be a whole other conversation that I didn't have time for.

We were still working through my slutty teen years.

"It's just easier this way," I said. "Less chance for folks to gossip."

"You look great," he said.

I'd put in some effort tonight—a dress and heels and lipstick. I'd even shaved past my knees and made sure to pluck those astonishingly long nipple hairs that always seemed to appear out of nowhere.

"Thank you," I said. "And I do like the black."

Ben looked down at himself, his leather jacket slung over his knees.

"I'm basically color-blind," he said. "Or, as Danny would say, fashion-blind. I can't be trusted to pair clothes with the right patterns."

I tried to imagine Ben in a bright plaid or checked shirt. It made me smile. He'd look gorgeous, of course, but I couldn't deny that his style fit him.

"What about your jewelry?" I asked.

I'd been dying to know about them ever since I noticed he always wore the same two necklaces and signet-looking ring.

"My mom's," Ben said, pulling his necklaces from inside his shirt. "She wore this chain every day. I think it used to have a charm on it or something, but she could never remember what it was or how she'd lost it."

"Did she have a bad memory?"

"Something like that," Ben said. "The other necklace is

a hibiscus blossom—or one that was pressed into a mold. My mom loved flowers, and the hibiscus was her favorite."

It was clear that Ben's mother meant a lot to him.

"The ring was a gift from Fran," he said. "Her grandfather's, I think. The Celtic cross—I'm not religious, but I like having a piece of Ireland that has nothing to do with my father."

"And the harp," I said, remembering his tattoo.

"When I showed it to Fran for the first time, she cried," Ben said. "I'd love one day to get a tattoo that didn't make someone break into tears."

He was joking.

"I always thought that when I went back to Maui for my mother's house, I'd go full traditional and get a kākau—where they use bone and ink to apply it."

I winced.

"That sounds far more painful than your average tattoo," I said.

"And still, apparently less painful than childbirth," he said.

"Is that the barometer you measure all pain by?"

He shrugged with a smile.

"What was your mother's name?" I asked.

"Leilani," he said.

"Leilani Akina," I said.

There was silence. When I glanced over at him, I found him staring at me with a look I'd never seen before. Something like wonder.

"What?" I asked, feeling self-conscious.

"Nothing," he said. "It's just been a long time since someone has spoken my mother's name out loud."

"Your father doesn't call her Leilani?"

Ben snorted. "He doesn't call her anything. If it wasn't for me, he'd be happy to pretend she never existed."

"What? Why?"

"She embarrassed him," Ben said.

I had a billion other questions.

"Have you ever been to Maui?" Ben asked.

I shook my head. "Where would you take me?"

He lit up at the question.

"Okay, so the best way to start your day in Hawaii is always in the ocean," he said. "I'd get you up early—"

"I already hate this," I said.

He ignored me. "We'd grab some surfboards."

"I don't surf."

"And hit the waves for a few hours."

"Hours?"

"You've never been surfing?"

I shook my head. "Montana isn't exactly known for its sick waves."

Ben laughed.

"It was like therapy for me," he said. "Before, you know, I started actual therapy."

The highway was empty, just us and the road, heading far out of town.

"It's not even about riding the waves. Not always. Sometimes, it's just about going out past the swell and sitting there on my board, nothing but the sea and the sky."

"What about sharks?" I asked.

He laughed. "Rare, but they're around."

"Don't you worry about a *Jaws*-like situation?"

"Part of the risk," he said. "But worth it for the reward."

"You seem to like taking risks," I said.

"You make it sound like a dirty word."

I gave him a sideways glance. *I* wasn't the one with the mouth.

Ben grinned. "Jump out of *one* airplane and people think you're some sort of daredevil. Jump out of six . . ."

"Six?"

"Maybe seven. Eight? I lost count. It's kind of addictive."

"*I've* never jumped out of an airplane."

"You'd love it," he said.

"Would I?"

"I've got a feeling you're a secret thrill seeker," he said.

"That's a joke," I said. "I've barely left Cooper, let alone jumped out of an airplane."

"Say the word and I can have us diving from a plane in twelve hours," he said.

"I'll keep that in mind," I said, knowing that if I wanted to, he would absolutely make it happen.

"There's just something about it," he said. "Jumping out of planes, racing cars, surfing with sharks, it's peaceful."

"*Peaceful?*"

He looked over at me. "I know," he said. "It sounds bloody crazy, but those are the times when your mind lets go. You can't think, you can't worry, you can't do anything but breathe and be alive. You're completely in the moment—where everything just narrows into one clear goal."

"Staying alive?" I asked dryly.

He laughed.

The truth was I knew exactly what he was talking about.

My crafting wasn't nearly as dangerous as his hobbies, but they seemed to provide the same comfort. The same focused distraction—something I struggled to find in the rest of my life.

The car was quiet for several miles; the only sound was the radio turned down low.

"That's a lovely jumper you're wearing."

"Thank you," I said. "I made it."

"Course you did," he said. "I heard you're making some additions to the costumes."

I'd had to measure him earlier that day, and it had done nothing to calm my nervous anticipation for this evening. Strangely it wasn't the inseam that had given me the most issues—it was wrapping the measuring tape around his chest, trying not to bury my face in it.

"A scarf for you and a pair of fingerless gloves for Gabe. Nothing too major."

"I bet they'll look great," he said.

"They aren't supposed to," I said. "I have to make them imperfect, since it all needs to look moth-eaten and worn."

I was surprised by how much fun I was having with the process. Learning how to age and deconstruct fabric in a way that looked realistic. It wasn't as easy as one might assume. But I was enjoying the challenge, even if I hadn't started working on the scarf I was supposed to be making for Ben.

"Allyson told me about your craft room."

"And what did she say?"

"That it was like a serial killer's lair," he said. "If serial killers were really into fiber arts."

"Ha," I said. "She should talk—her basement looks like

a legitimate murder took place there. And she won't let me organize it."

"You two seem close," he said. "Did you grow up together?"

I shook my head. "She moved to Cooper fairly recently. It's a new friendship, but a good one."

"Did she know Spencer?" Ben asked.

I froze, wondering if I was going to start weeping again.

"No," I said, tentatively. "He'd already died."

So far, so good.

"You and Spencer grew up together, right?" Ben asked.

I nodded. "He was friends with Gabe first," I said. "They were the same age."

"Should I make the obvious joke about how you prefer younger men?"

I laughed.

"*He* was only a year younger," I said. "How old are you? Twenty-two? Twenty?"

"Sadly, I'm the ripe old age of thirty," Ben said. "Are you disappointed?"

"*So* disappointed," I said.

CHAPTER 43

NOW

APPARENTLY DATING *COULD* BE FUN.

We probably ordered far too much food, but Ben wanted to try everything the waitress had recommended. They had a five-minute conversation about the catfish, and I witnessed firsthand the spell that Ben had cast over the population of Cooper.

He was kind and curious and interested. Asked questions. Laughed at jokes. Looked into your eyes when he spoke to you. Remembered names. His so-called charm, I realized, was basically just good communication skills. Which unfortunately was a novelty among men these days.

"Exactly how many hearts have you broken?" I asked when the waitress—Suzanne—left with our orders.

"Not a one," Ben said.

"I don't believe that for a second," I said.

He shrugged. "I've never been the one to end a relationship," he said. "The heart that breaks is usually mine."

I snorted.

Ben leaned back and counted off with his fingers. "Danny wanted to date other people. Martina thought I was a sellout for taking the *SXS* job instead of staying in theatre. Keenan didn't like the distance. Eric cheated. Safiyyah realized she was not in fact bisexual, but actually a lesbian. Pedro also didn't like the distance, and my last relationship was about a year ago, and they cheated as well."

I blinked.

"And how many hearts have *you* broken, Lauren Parker?" Ben asked.

Thankfully I was saved from answering that question by our drinks arriving. Mocktails for both of us.

"Someone thought you were a sellout for taking *SXS*?" I asked.

Ben smiled. "How did I know that's the one you were going to want details on?" he asked. "Martina is an actor's actor. At least, that's how she'd describe herself. We met doing a ramshackle production of *A Doll's House*. She was Nora. I was the porter."

I didn't know much about the play but I could infer that Ben's part had not been a prominent one.

"She was the experienced actress, I was the fresh-faced newbie," Ben said. "She took me under her wing."

"And then some," I teased.

He winked. "I always did have a thing for older women," he said.

"Here I was, thinking I was special."

Ben reached across the table and took my hand.

"You *are* special, Lauren," he said. The honesty and seriousness of his tone surprised me.

We pulled apart as our appetizers arrived—fresh corn fritters with homemade huckleberry sauce.

"So," I said. "Martina. Would I know her from anything?"

"Naw." Ben shook his head. "She's a strictly theatre kind of person. The kind that thinks that TV and movies are where talent goes to die."

"Ouch," I said. "Guessing she didn't like it when you started getting movie roles?"

"You'd be right," he said. "Booking *SXS* was kind of the death knell of that relationship. She thought I was a traitor."

"That's pretty harsh," I said.

"She's an intense person," he said. "We talk now and then."

"Does she still think you're a traitor?"

"Absolutely," Ben said with a smile. "But she watches everything I do. And sends me notes."

"You're kidding."

He shook his head, a big smile on his face. "It's her version of an olive branch."

"I would think she'd want you to do well," I said.

"She does. I think she was jealous when I got the offer, though she'd never admit it," Ben said. "Told me that it was my looks that got me work, not my talent."

At the look on my face—I was frowning—Ben shook his head.

"It's fine," he said. "It's a hard business. Competitive. Brutal. I'm sure Gabe has told you how wearing it can be on your self-esteem."

"I don't know how he does it," I said.

"It's a delicate mix of ego, stupidity, and a love of attention that gets people into it," Ben said. "But once I found it, I never wanted to do anything else."

He took a drink. I watched him—he looked gorgeous in the candlelight.

"What about you?" he asked.

"I would rather get that tattoo you were talking about than have to stand in front of a bunch of people and entertain them."

Ben laughed.

"What about in high school?"

"Hated public speaking even more," I said.

"I mean, what were you like back then," he said, looking at me with a discerning gaze. "I'm trying to imagine you in high school."

"What do you think I was like?"

He considered this.

"Quiet," he said. "Thoughtful. Spent most of your time in the library reading sexy novels."

I laughed and choked a little on my drink.

"Am I close?" Ben asked.

"Not at all," I said.

"Tell me."

"I was a pretty big stoner," I said.

"No way," he said.

I nodded. "Spent most of my teen years high out of my mind."

"I bet you're hilarious when you're high," Ben said. "I tend to get very quiet and sleepy."

"I get hungry and bored," I said. "It was one of the reasons I got into baking."

"Okay, so you weren't reading sexy novels in the library," Ben said. "What else did you do in high school?"

"I slept around a lot," I said.

He laughed, clearly thinking I was joking. At my expression he stopped, a new appreciation appearing in his eyes.

"You slept around a lot," he repeated.

I shrugged as if it wasn't a big deal. And it wasn't. I didn't feel the shame I used to feel when I thought about who I'd been.

If anything, I found myself missing her more and more these days.

"You're not the only one with a reputation," I said. "I sowed quite a few wild oats when I was younger."

"Every time I think I've figured you out, you surprise me."

I wondered what else about me surprised him.

"I've got layers," I said. "Like an artichoke."

"Isn't it supposed to be like an onion?"

I shrugged. "Who peels an onion like that? You chop it. An artichoke, though, you have to get through a bunch of spikey leaves to reach the delicious center. And then you dip it in butter." I sighed. "Mmmm, butter."

"Always salted," Ben said.

"*Always,*" I said.

"If I've learned anything about cooking it's that."

"The golden rule."

"What about after high school?" Ben popped a cherry tomato into his mouth. "Did you sleep around in college too?"

"Never went," I said. "Spencer dropped out after his

first year, and we got married pretty young. He worked at the hardware store, and I worked at the supermarket."

"Until the Cozy."

"Until the Cozy," I said. "Gabe also paid for Spencer to go back to school, which he'd always wanted to do."

"What about you?" Ben asked. "Did you ever want to go back to school?"

"I wasn't a great student," I said. "I pretty much only graduated because Spencer tutored me in math."

"Yet you taught yourself how to cook and knit," Ben said. "You clearly like to learn."

I'd never thought about it that way.

"Have you ever thought about living outside of Cooper?"

Had we? Thinking back on it, I probably just assumed we'd always stay in Cooper.

"It was never really part of the conversation, especially after we had Lena," I said. "And Spencer would have never moved too far from his mother."

Ben tapped his pec, where I knew his *Mom* tattoo was.

"Mama's boys," he said. "I know a little about that."

I smiled into my glass.

"What about cooking school?" he asked. "How did you learn?"

"My cooking school was the library," I said. "And lots and lots of mistakes."

"A self-taught chef." Ben leaned back. "That's quite impressive."

I shrugged. "You've never tasted my food," I said. "For all you know, I'm terrible."

"I don't think there's a single thing you could be terrible at," Ben said.

His tone was suggestive. His eyes too.

I was about to make a suggestive comment of my own, when the sound of glass breaking startled both of us.

I turned to find that one of the servers had dropped an entire bottle onto the floor, where it shattered, and the smell of sweet white wine filled the restaurant. The waitress was mortified, and almost looked like she was going to start crying.

"Poor girl," I said, before glancing back at Ben.

He was pale.

"Are you okay?" I asked.

He didn't respond, just waved Suzanne over. I could see the tension in his jaw, like he was grinding his back teeth together.

"I am so sorry about that," our waitress said.

"Do you think we could be moved to another table?" Ben asked. "At the other side of the restaurant?"

"Of course," she said, and gestured to an empty spot along the wall.

We picked up our drinks and moved. The smell of wine was far less intense over here, and I saw Ben relax. A little.

"Are you okay?" I asked again when our food was placed in front of us.

For someone who had been so eager to hear about the quality of the catfish, he hadn't even picked up his fork. He still looked stricken, the color not yet fully returned to his face.

"Sorry," he said, blinking.

"You must really hate white wine," I said.

It was meant to be a joke, but Ben pressed his lips together, wariness in his gaze.

"I really do," he said.

I waited, wondering if he was going to say more, but he didn't.

We ate. The meal was quiet, but not awkward. I wanted to know what was going through his head, but I didn't mind the silence.

It wasn't until the dessert menu was brought over that Ben spoke.

"I'm sorry," he said. "It's just . . ." He shook his head and offered a self-deprecating smile. "Remember how I told you I drank an entire bottle of wine the night before my mother's funeral?"

I nodded.

"It was white wine," he said.

"Makes sense that you can't stand the stuff," I said. "I ate a bad tuna melt once and it took me years to try one again."

"It's not just that," Ben said. He took a deep breath, let it out. "The reason I had that white wine in the first place was because that's what my mother drank."

"Oh," I said.

"Yeah," he said, rubbing the back of his neck. "She'd averaged about a bottle a day—our pantry was full of the stuff."

"I'm sorry," I said. "I know a little something about what it's like to love an addict."

Ben nodded. "I admire Gabe," he said. "It's no small feat that he's been sober for as long as he has. My mother could only handle it for a week or so, and then she'd be back at the liquor store. There wouldn't be any money to fix the

AC or get me a new pair of pants, but there was always enough for another bottle."

"Makes sense why you don't drink," I said.

He lifted his mocktail in a faux salute. "I take risks, but not like that."

Then he gave his head a shake, and picked up the dessert menu.

"I think we've gotten the addiction talk out of the way. Why don't you tell me about some of your high school sexual escapades, and don't leave out any details."

He smiled at me. I smiled back.

CHAPTER 44

NOW

WE ORDERED A CHOCOLATE CHILI TART.

"Can you make *this*?" Ben asked after taking a blissful-sounding bite.

It *was* good.

"I'd just have to find the right recipe," I said. "However, I do know how to make an excellent pavlova from memory."

"A pavlova? Like one of those things with bells and dogs?"

I could tell he was purposely playing dumb.

"That's Pavlovian," I said. "A pavlova is very different. And very delicious."

"Tell me more," Ben said.

I walked him through the process of what had been one of Spencer's favorite desserts.

"Yes," Ben said when I'd finished. "I want that."

Afterward, as we walked out of the restaurant, Ben

reached out and took my hand, threading his fingers through mine. I looked down at our entwined hands.

"Too much?" he asked.

"No," I said. "Not too much."

I looked up at the beautiful night sky.

"The sky here is so big," I said. "But everything beneath it feels so small."

Ben chuckled.

"What?" I asked.

"Now I can tell you were a stoner in high school," he said. "Because that's the most high thought I've heard in a long time."

I smiled. I didn't bother telling him that he was the reason I was completely sober but felt intoxicated. There was no need to give his ego any more of a boost.

Ben told me about the play on the way back to Cooper.

"I'm glad I took Gabe up on his offer," he said. "I didn't realize how much I missed the theatre until we started rehearsing."

"It seems like you're having a good time," I said.

"It's fun," he said. "Gabe is a great scene partner, and I love working with Ollie again. Not all actors are good directors, but he's fantastic. Knows exactly how to tell you that you're not getting it right without sounding like an arsehole."

"That sounds like Ollie," I said.

We drove on.

"Can I ask you something personal?"

"Sure," Ben said.

"How have you been able to keep your mom's death and

alcoholism out of the picture?" I asked. "Gabe had people digging deep into his past when he became famous—it seemed like nothing was off-limits, but I don't remember reading anything about your family."

"It's classic misdirection," Ben said. "With my bisexuality as a shield."

"How does that work?"

"If given the choice, the press would prefer to talk about sex more than anything else," Ben said. "And I don't care, so I can dangle that carrot in front of them whenever it seems like they might start digging."

"I can't believe that's worked," I said.

"Me either, to be honest," he said. "But I also know it won't last. If this Bond thing goes—"

He stopped.

"Shit," he said.

"Bond thing? Does that mean you're back in the running?"

"Maybe," he said.

I reached over and slapped him on the arm.

"Oh my god," I said. "Congratulations."

"Ouch, thanks," he said. "There are still about a billion more hoops they want me to jump through before they give me the part, but Fran says it looks good."

"That's amazing," I said. "You must be thrilled."

"I am," he said, but he didn't quite look it. "Or I would be if I believed it—I don't think it will sink in until I get the actual contract. Maybe not even until I get the first check. That's what will make it real."

"Life-changing money," I said, knowing from experience.

"You have no idea," he said, as we pulled into the parking lot.

I turned off the car. We sat there.

That's when I realized I really didn't want the date to end.

Oh boy. I was in trouble.

I glanced over at Ben who was tapping his fingers along his knee in rhythm with the song on the radio.

Maybe trouble wasn't such a bad thing.

Maybe it was okay to be scared.

"Do you ever think about what you'd do if you didn't work at the Cozy?" Ben asked, indicating that we were done talking about Bond.

I shook my head. "My options are pretty limited."

"Or limitless," he said. "You *could* go back to school."

"I'm more focused on getting Lena through school," I said.

"Then what?"

"Then . . ." I thought about it. "Then I can figure out what I want."

We were both lingering.

"This was nice," I said.

Ben grinned at me. "I'd love to say I told you so, but I'll be a gentleman."

I rolled my eyes at him.

"Will Lena be waiting up for you?"

I shook my head. "She's at her grandmother's tonight, though she'd usually be over at Eve's."

"The two of them are a hoot," he said.

I wasn't sure if he knew they were a couple.

"They truly are," I said. "Thick as thieves."

"Two of a kind."

"Two peas in a pod."

"Like a pair of socks."

"Socks?" I laughed.

I was pretty sure he knew they were together. Mainly because he wasn't looking me in the eye.

"I'm glad they have each other," I said. "It's hard enough standing out in a small town—at least they can do it together. As a couple."

He let out a gust of air.

"You know?"

I smiled. "I know. They told you?"

"The other day at the theatre," he said.

They'd been helping out there after school. Apparently, they'd already started angling to get paid for what I'm sure Gabe had assumed would be volunteer work. I wouldn't have been surprised if they formed their own two-person union and managed to get health insurance as well.

Eve was that kind of kid, and Lena was that much in love with her.

It made me so happy to see them together.

"They talked to Ollie, but he thought I'd be a better resource," Ben said. "Since I'm a child myself."

"Ha," I said. "Just don't encourage them to jump out of airplanes."

"Not until they're eighteen at least," he said.

"No. Airplanes," I said.

He lifted his hands. "Fine. But how do you feel about paragliding?"

"No," I said. "Nothing resembling flight."

He laughed.

"I do have to tell you something," I said.

He glanced over, looking concerned.

"For someone who is a professional actor, you're a terrible liar."

"Thank you," he said. "I hate lying."

"Isn't that what acting is?"

"Is that what you think?"

I shrugged.

"Acting is about telling the truth," Ben said, and I could see him warming to the topic. Something he clearly cared about—had thought about. "But you do it through someone else. Someone else's words, someone else's character. You get to inhabit a new world, and you can bring people along with you. But it's all about connection—you are reaching out, to show them something new about themselves. About others. About the world around them. It's a chance to be open and vulnerable. To practice empathy. Lying is about being closed off. Putting up distance and walls and deception."

"Oh," I said.

We got out of the car.

I'd never thought about it that way.

"Sorry," he said. "I tend to get a little preachy when it comes to that stuff."

"You care about your work," I said.

"I do."

"You'll make a great James Bond," I said.

He held up a hand, fingers crossed.

"What about you?" he asked.

"I don't think I'd be a very good James Bond," I said.

He smiled. "I mean, what do you get preachy about?"

"Salt," I said. "It needs to be in everything."

A gust of wind blew through the parking lot. I shivered, and Ben draped his leather jacket over my shoulders. It was time for me to go home. Time to say goodnight.

"Early morning tomorrow?" he asked.

I shrugged. "Just the usual—unpacking books, setting up supplies, reorganizing the office. There's also this broken step in the back of the Cozy that I need to put a sign on so no one else trips on it. We've had a few close calls."

"It probably has a loose screw or nail," he said.

"Probably," I said. "I keep meaning to call someone."

Ben lifted his eyebrow.

"What?" I asked.

"Do you have a hammer? Screwdriver?"

"Of course," I said.

It seemed probable that there was one of those somewhere in the store.

"Then I can fix that step," he said.

"Oh," I said.

He moved closer to me. Brushed hair away from my face.

"Let me fix your step, Lauren," he said.

"Okay," I said.

CHAPTER 45

NOW

IT TURNED OUT THAT WE DID NOT HAVE A SCREWDRIVER or a hammer.

"Well, shit," I said.

"If you can get one tomorrow, I can come by and fix it," Ben said, pushing up from the crouch he'd been in. "It won't take much. Just a screw or two."

I looked at him. He looked at me, eyes twinkling in the dim light.

We were both waiting for the other to pick up that dropped innuendo.

It wasn't going to be me.

"Maybe you could give me a tour," he said. "I've always wanted to wander around a bookshop after hours."

We were painfully transparent, but it was also kind of fun, so I just kept playing along.

I'd only turned the lights on near the office, so I led him to the other side of the store, mostly in shadow.

"This is the crafts section," I said.

I'd lowered my voice to a whisper. Even though I knew there was no way for the upstairs tenants—Gabe and Chani—to hear me, it still felt right.

"This is pretty," Ben said, also in a whisper.

He was running his fingers over a skein of yarn, and I was imagining him running his fingers over me.

I moved a little closer to him.

"We have everything you need if you decide you want to take up knitting," I said.

He glanced back at me, grin flashing in the dark.

"I might take you up on that," he said. "If you'll be the one teaching me."

"I'm not a very good teacher," I said.

"Mmm." Ben turned to face me. "I don't think that's true."

He put his hands on my hips.

"You've taught me lots of things."

"Oh?"

He lowered his head, dropping a kiss on my neck.

"You've taught me what a pavlova is," he said.

Another kiss, this time below my ear.

"You've taught me that cookbooks are best read before bed," he said. "Especially the sweet ones."

This kiss landed on my jaw, light as could be.

"You've taught me that you're the kind of woman who goes after what she wants," he said, and stepped back.

I looked at him, gorgeous in the shadows, his expression eager, his stance patient.

He wanted me to make the next move.

"There's another place in the store I should show you," I said.

He lifted an eyebrow, and I crooked a finger at him.

He followed.

"This is nice," he said.

"These are the stacks," I said. "It's become quite the make-out spot lately."

"Oh really?"

I smiled at him. "It's completely hidden from view," I said. "No one can see us."

"Hmmm," he said, and walked toward me.

I moved back until I hit one of the bookshelves. He was crowding me, but in the best possible way.

"I have a confession to make," he said.

His voice was low, whispered.

"I've always had this fantasy about being in a library after hours."

"This is a bookstore," I said.

"I'm aware," he said. "But I'm sure you can use your imagination. I know I can."

He moved his hands from my hips to my wrists, gently pushing them back.

"You might want to hold on to something," he said.

I gripped the shelves as he dropped to his knees.

His fingers were on my legs, pushing the hem of my dress upward.

"We might get caught," I managed.

"Oh, I know," Ben said, grinning up at me. "I have a feeling that's part of *your* fantasy."

I could barely breathe, let alone speak. If it hadn't been a fantasy before, it certainly was *now*. Maybe I *was* a bit of a thrill seeker. Maybe I'd always been one.

"I—I—"

"Shhh," Ben said. "You don't need to say anything, except yes."

He kissed the top of my thigh, and my head fell back against the shelf.

"Yes," I said.

CHAPTER 46

NOW

"YOU ARE GLOWING," CHANI SAID.

I'd stopped by the theatre to drop off the fingerless gloves and tell Ollie that I wasn't going to be able to finish the scarf in time—expecting that I'd just see him and head back to the store. Instead, I arrived and found my whole family hanging out in the theatre. Lena and Eve were on the stage talking to Ben, my mom was unpacking lunches, and Gabe was following Chani like a lost puppy.

"Yeah," Gabe said. "You look really happy, Lauren. What's up?"

I knew I was smiling like a lunatic. I'd seen myself in the mirror that morning.

I couldn't help it. Last night had been amazing. Ben had been amazing.

All of it had been amazing. More than I ever could have expected. It almost didn't feel real.

Gabe lowered his voice, leaning toward me. "Are you drunk? High?"

I slapped his arm. "No!"

"She's allowed to be happy," Chani said.

"I guess," Gabe said, but he didn't stop staring at me suspiciously.

"I'm not drunk."

"Sure," he said.

I rolled my eyes at him. "Can you go get your director? I have to talk to him."

"He's backstage—you really want me to shlep all the way back there?" Gabe asked, and then looked immediately at Chani with an eager expression.

"That's very good," she said, patting him on the arm. "And the proper use of shlep."

"Don't do too much kvetching while I'm gone," he said.

"Okay, Rabbi Parker," I said.

Chani and I exchanged grins as he hustled off.

"His Yiddish *is* improving," she said.

She seemed happy.

"So." She turned to me. "What is it?"

"What's what?"

"The thing that's giving you that glow because . . ." she trailed off.

I was only half paying attention because I'd just caught Ben's eye. He winked. Thankfully the girls had gone over to my mother. My face got hot, and then I realized Chani was still standing there, watching me.

"What?"

"Oh, nothing," she said, biting her lip as if to hold back a laugh.

The way her eyes darted between me and Ben made it clear that she knew exactly why I was grinning.

"It's not what you think," I said, even though it was exactly what she was thinking.

She lifted her hands. "None of my business," she said.

"A sentence that's never been uttered in this town," I said.

"If you're happy, that's all that matters," she said.

If only it were that simple.

Ben came off the stage and toward me.

"Hi," he said.

"Hi," I said.

"Bye," said Chani.

Ben and I just stood there, grinning goofily at each other.

"I really enjoyed last night," he said.

His voice was low, which was good, because I suspected this theatre had great acoustics.

"Me too."

"I'd love to take you out again," he said.

"Okay."

"Yeah?"

"Yeah."

He had his hands in his pockets, his Celtic signet ring glinting from his thumb, which was hooked into his belt loop.

"I know you're an expert cook," he said. "But apparently, there's this place in Carvey where they teach you how to make soup dumplings. I was thinking we could do that."

"I'd like that," I said. "I've never made soup dumplings before. I don't think I've ever had soup dumplings before."

Ben put a hand to his stomach and leaned back dramatically.

"Then we *have* to go," he said. "You haven't lived until you've slurped broth from a fresh dumpling."

How did he make everything sound so dirty?

"Mom!"

I jumped at Lena's voice.

She was stalking toward me, Eve on her heels, Spencer's scarf flying behind her. It was going to be too warm to be wearing that soon.

I took a step back from Ben.

"What's up?" I asked.

"Can Eve come over for dinner tonight?"

I looked at their two eager faces.

"Of course," I said. "Are you planning to sleep over as well?"

The new house rule was that Eve could sleep over but the bedroom door had to stay open. Lena had rolled her eyes into the next century when I told her, but besides that, there had been no arguing.

Eve nodded. "My parents are going on a date tonight."

Lena pulled a face. "Gross."

"I think it's nice that your folks want to go out together," I said.

Eve shrugged. "My dad is always grabbing my mom's butt," she said. "I'm glad they're going to do it somewhere else besides the kitchen."

"I heard you wanted to see me," Ollie said.

He and Gabe had returned.

I wrinkled my face, remembering the disappointing news I was going to have to tell him.

"So," I said. "We've hit a snag with the costumes."

Ollie's eyebrows went up.

"How much of a snag?"

"A little one," I said. "I think. I hope."

Ollie crossed his arms.

"The suits are taking longer than expected," I said. "I won't be able to make a scarf for Ben's costume. It's too time-consuming."

"Oh," Ollie said. "That's fine. The scarf would just be frosting on the cake. We don't *need* it."

Then he glanced over at Lena.

"Of course"—he walked over to her and gave her scarf a little tug—"this one could be perfect. If you'd lend it to us."

Lena pulled the scarf out of his hands.

"No," she said.

Ollie's surprise was obvious—I wasn't sure Lena had *ever* been that short with him.

"Okay," he said, before turning back to me. "No scarf is fine."

"Great," I said. "I'm going to head back to the shop—girls, why don't you meet me there at closing?"

"Okay!" Eve said.

Lena just nodded, fingers wrapped tight around her scarf.

"How are the stacks?" Ollie asked, clearly trying to lighten the mood. "I've heard that a section of the store has become very popular."

It took every ounce of my being not to look at Ben. I knew if I did, I'd be blushing from hairline to toes.

"It's officially retired," I said. "I was able to move some shelves this morning."

Well. Last night. After I'd gotten thoroughly fucked against them.

Ben had helped, both of us sweaty and laughing.

"That's a shame," Gabe said. "I kind of liked it back there."

"Eww," Lena said.

"You're just going to have to find other places to make out," I said. "Like your apartment."

Gabe had his arm around Chani, and they were exchanging glances like two people with a secret. And then . . .

"Before you go," he said, "I have an announcement."

We all gathered, my mother joining us in a semicircle around Gabe and Chani. I had a pretty good feeling what the announcement would be, but I kept my mouth shut.

Gabe held up Chani's hand, displaying the lizard-looking ring.

"We're engaged!" he said.

Congrats came from all corners, and my mom was the first to hug Gabe, tears in her eyes.

"I'm so happy for you two," she said, before turning to Chani and giving her a hug.

"Thank you." Chani was beaming.

"Mazel tov," Ollie said. "You're not the only one learning Yiddish."

Gabe shook his head and pulled the other man in for a hug.

"Happy for you," I heard Ollie say.

"Cheers, you two," Ben said, giving Chani a kiss on the cheek and Gabe a firm handshake.

Then it was my turn. I gave my brother a hug, squeezing him as tightly as I could.

"This is so exciting," I said.

"Thanks," he said, but his eyes were focused on Lena. "What do you think?" he asked her, tentatively approaching.

Lena looked at Eve. Eve nodded and gave her a little push.

"It's cool," Lena said, and then gave Gabe a hug.

He closed his eyes as he squeezed her tight, and I could see years of tension lift from his shoulders.

"Really happy for you, Mr. P!" Eve said.

"For the love of god, call me Gabe," he said.

Chani came up alongside him, nervously looking at Lena. It got a little hushed.

"I'm really excited to be part of the family," Chani said.

There was a long pause.

"Yeah, okay," Lena said, and gave her a nod.

Chani beamed like she'd won a Pulitzer.

I was about to head back to work when Gabe pulled me aside.

"We want to get married at the store," he said. "Would that be okay?"

"You own the place," I reminded him. "Of course it's okay."

He grinned. He was so happy.

"I was also thinking we'd do an engagement party or something in a few weeks," he said.

"Sounds great. Do you want to do it at the store as well?"

"I think we'll do it at Mom's," he said. "But I was wondering . . ."

He paused. He looked nervous.

"What?" I asked.

"Would you speak at the party?"

I hadn't expected that.

"You want me to speak?" I asked. "I'm not a very good public speaker. Why not Ollie?"

"Oh, don't worry," Gabe said. "Ollie will definitely be speaking. Chani's sister as well. But I'd like you to say something. If you're comfortable with that."

I had never been good in front of a crowd. I didn't want to ruin the party by saying something stupid, or worse, boring.

"Just think about it," he said, sensing my hesitation. "It's just friends and family. And . . . I'd really like you to."

"Of course I will."

He gave me a hug.

"Can I also do a PowerPoint with all your baby pictures?" I asked into his shoulder. "And some of those awkward preteen ones?"

"Ha," he said.

"That's a yes," I said.

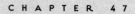

CHAPTER 47

NOW

WAS STOPPED ONCE MORE BEFORE I COULD LEAVE.

"Would it be okay if Mr. Walsh came over for dinner too?" Lena asked, looking at her feet.

It was the last thing I would have expected her to ask.

Ben and Eve were behind her.

"He said he can help me with my audition," Eve said.

I didn't know anything about auditions—I wondered if Lena was going to do the same. Probably not.

"And I might have mentioned that I hadn't tried any of your baking," he said.

"Which is crazy!" Eve said. "Mrs. P is the best baker in Cooper!"

"My publicist," I said, gesturing at her.

"She makes good cookies," Lena added.

"Publicists," I corrected.

"I don't want to be an imposition," Ben said.

Lena was now giving me her "please, Mom" eyes. Like

I'd ever been able to resist those. Not that I had any objections to spending more time with Ben.

"I can take them back to the house," Ben said.

My eyes widened.

"*Not* on Lillian," he quickly corrected. "I can borrow Gabe's truck."

"Lillian?" Lena asked.

"My bike," Ben said.

"You have a motorcycle?" Eve asked, eyes huge.

Ben smiled. "Sure do."

"Can we ride it?" Lena asked, looking at me.

"No," both Ben and I said at the same time.

The girls' disappointment was palpable.

"Ben can take you in the truck," I said. "I'll be back at six-thirty."

THE FIRST THING I noticed when I came home was the bag of cookies on the counter, rather than the three people gathered around it.

"Where did those come from?" I asked. "I haven't made snickerdoodles all week."

Lena looked down at the counter. "I might have hidden some in the pantry," she said.

I could tell that she expected me to be mad, but I just found it adorable. Which she probably would have hated even more.

"Sneaky," I said. "But kind of brilliant."

"That's what I said," Ben added. "And these cookies?" He kissed his fingers. "Bloody fantastic."

Eve giggled and tried to imitate him. "Bloody fantastic."

"Almost," Ben said. "Try it with a little more 'blah' at the front."

Eve tried again.

"Very good," Ben said.

"Is this for the audition?" I asked.

"We're doing *Into the Woods*!" Eve said.

I paused. "Is there a character with an Irish accent?"

"No," Eve said. "But I think it will add a certain je ne suis quoi, if you know what I mean."

I bit my lip to keep from smiling too broadly.

"I do know what you mean," I said.

"She's going to get the lead," Lena said.

"You don't know that." Eve tucked some hair behind her ear.

"Yeah, I do," Lena said.

They smiled shyly at each other. It made my heart glow.

"Why don't you go practice the Witch's rap a few more times and then show me again?" Ben suggested.

"Really?" Eve asked.

"Really."

"We'll be back in thirty minutes!" she said. "Thanks, Ben!"

She grabbed Lena's hand and practically dragged her away from the counter.

"Yeah, thanks, Ben," Lena said, before she was pulled out of the kitchen.

I stared at the swinging door.

"She invited you over for dinner and called you Ben."

He shrugged. "Is that a problem?"

"No," I said. "Not at all."

It shouldn't have been a problem. It should have been great. It was great.

So why did I feel weird about it?

"These cookies are amazing," Ben said, holding one up. "Just as I knew they would be."

"Thanks," I said.

I hadn't expected him to look so good in my kitchen. It was the first time I'd had a man here that wasn't family or family-adjacent. It hadn't even crossed my mind when Lena asked if Ben could join us, but this was kind of a big step. For me.

A big step that didn't feel like a big step.

It felt normal. Nice.

I liked Ben standing here eating cookies.

"You're going to laugh when I tell you this," he said. "But apparently there's this whole paragliding community over in Bozeman."

I let out a dramatic groan. "I was hoping you wouldn't find them."

He laughed.

"Keeping secrets from me?"

"Just the ones that might result in you crashing into a mountain."

"That rarely happens," he said.

"Let me guess," I said. "You're going to check them out?"

"Of course," he said. "Wanna join me? They do tandem flights."

"I'm good," I said.

"One of these days I'm going to get you up in the air. Or under the water. Or maybe just on the back of my bike."

"Good luck," I said. "My thrill seeking starts and ends with the rides at the county fair, and I haven't been there in years."

"We'll have to change that," he said.

"Oh, will we?"

I was playing aloof, but I warmed at the thought of all the things we might do. All the things I'd show him.

"Then again, I do love deep-fried food," Ben said. "And dunk tanks."

"Speaking of, I should probably start dinner," I said. "Though it's sadly not fried, deep or otherwise."

Ben snapped his fingers in faux disappointment.

"Need any help?"

I shook my head. "I've got some frozen meatballs that I can thaw."

"Homemade?"

I gave him a look. "Of course."

He grinned.

I took out the meatballs and placed them in the sink, running water on them.

"What is *that*?" Ben asked.

He was referring to the squeaky sound the faucet was making.

"It's nothing," I said. "I keep meaning to call a plumber."

Ben leaned on the counter, arms crossed.

"It almost feels like you're doing this on purpose," he said. "Where are your tools?"

This time, I knew where they were—in the closet behind the stairs. I remembered seeing them there one of the nights that I'd thought to organize the space, before I'd decided otherwise. That was the place I kept all of Spencer's stuff. The things I couldn't stand to get rid of.

They were dusty and covered with a few spiderwebs.

Spencer had been proud of them—they'd been bought piecemeal with his discount from the hardware store, and when he finally had the full set he wanted, nothing was unfixable. Even if it didn't need to be fixed. He'd replaced the door handle on the upstairs bathroom no fewer than three times.

I held those tools in my hands and didn't want to give them to Ben.

Which was silly. They were just things. Some of them had never even been used.

Having Ben in my kitchen was one thing . . .

"Find any?" Ben's voice filtered through my thoughts.

He pulled the door open wider.

"Oh, this will work great," he said, grabbing a tool from the top of the box, and disappearing.

I put the rest of them down gently and backed out of the closet, shutting the door.

In the kitchen, Ben already had the cabinet doors open and had shimmied under the sink. All I could see was his body, waist down.

For a moment it wasn't Ben at all.

"Do you have a rag I could use?" he asked.

I handed him one.

He worked. I watched.

I missed Spencer.

"Try it now," he said.

I turned the water on. No squeak.

"Thank you," I said as he pulled himself out from under the sink.

He shrugged. "I could teach you how to do it," he said.

"Why would I do that when I have you?"

The moment it was out of my mouth, I felt all my insides plummet to the floor. I gripped the counter, with the worst déjà vu I'd ever experienced. I wanted to throw up.

Ben was beside me immediately.

"Is something wrong?" he asked.

I swallowed hard. "No," I said.

He gave me a look. "And you said *I'm* bad at lying."

"It's nothing," I said.

I couldn't tell him. It was too much. Too soon. The tools. The memories. All of it.

And yet, I was glad he was here.

Ben rubbed my back, the circles wide and gentle. He was good at that.

"Do you need some water? A cool towel?"

I shook my head.

"I'm fine," I said. "Just got a little dizzy."

I could tell he didn't believe me, but he was silent, continuing to rub my back.

That's when I heard footsteps coming down the stairs. Ben stepped back, and I put a smile on my face just in time for Lena and Eve to burst back into the kitchen.

"I'm ready to go again!" Eve said.

"Great," Ben said. "Let's go outside and you can knock my socks off."

The two of them left—I expected Lena to follow them, but she didn't. She stayed in the kitchen. Just me and her.

"Want to help me make dinner?" I asked.

"Sure," she said.

"I've got the meatballs defrosting," I said. "Can you fill the pot with water for the noodles?"

Lena nodded and carried the pot to the sink.

"Hey," she said. "The faucet isn't screaming at us any-more."

"Ben fixed it," I said.

The kitchen was silent except for the running water.

"He's nice," Lena said.

"I think so too," I said, feeling like I was tumbling head-first into something I wasn't completely ready for.

I was scared. But maybe that was okay.

CHAPTER 48

NOW

"AND THAT'S WHEN THEY CHUM THE WATER," BEN said. "Do you know what that is?"

Eve and Lena, eyes wide open, shook their heads in unison.

"That's when they add blood and fish guts and fish bits to the water to attract the sharks," he said. "And let me tell you, it works pretty quickly."

"Oh my god," I said.

"And you're in a cage?" Eve asked.

"With a scuba suit and oxygen," Ben said. "It's bloody incredible."

"Bloody incredible," Eve said.

"Very good," Ben said. "Your accent gets better with each attempt."

Eve beamed.

"Why would you want to be surrounded by sharks?" Lena asked.

She'd been mostly quiet through the meal, listening as Ben regaled us all with stories of his insane, death-defying adventures.

I'd thought paragliding and skydiving was the worst of it.

I was wrong.

The man was a lunatic.

A gorgeous, sexy, captivating lunatic.

"Why not?" he asked.

"Because it's crazy," Lena said.

Ben ate some broccoli. "I might be a little crazy then."

Lena looked like she agreed.

"Have you ever gone spelunking?" Eve asked.

"What is spelunking?" I asked.

Ben's eyes gleamed. "Eve, my darling, it's as if you read my mind. That's next on the list." He turned to me. "Spelunking is like skydiving, except you're jumping into a cave with a parachute."

"*What?*"

"You are crazy," Lena said.

"Yeah!" Eve breathed.

"I mean, technically, spelunking is exploring caves, but you can definitely parachute into them. As long as they're not bottomless pits."

"Anyone want any more spaghetti?" I asked.

"Yes, please," Ben said, holding out his plate.

It was the third time I'd refilled it.

"What were you saying about bottomless pits?" I asked.

He grinned. "Can you blame me?" He looked at the girls. "This is the best meal I've had since I got here."

Eve beamed like he'd complimented *her* cooking, while Lena looked down at the table, a small grin on her face.

I leaned back, watching it all.

It was nice.

Really nice.

Ben wasn't Spencer.

I knew that. And still.

There had been times, when I'd just been chattering on about something, some never-ending monologue about the cheap new plastic bags at the grocery store, or wool prices, or whatever, and I'd look up to find Spencer looking at me.

Not just looking. Staring.

It had made me uncomfortable at first because it was so intense, and I didn't know what to do with a look like that.

A look that said *I am madly, hopelessly in love with you.*

He never stopped looking at me like that.

Now, across the table, Ben was giving me a similar look.

Not as intense as Spencer's had been, but what he was thinking was clear as day.

I like you. I like you a lot.

Maybe this *could* work out.

"Dessert?" I said once dinner was done. "Do you even have room for more?" I asked Ben.

"I always have room for dessert," he said.

"Me too!" said Eve.

Lena nodded.

"Chocolate mousse, coming right up," I said.

Ben rose from his seat. "Can I help?"

"It's basically all done," I said. "Just have to put it in bowls."

"Okay," he said. "But we're doing the dishes."

"Sounds like a deal," I said.

The quiet of the kitchen only made my thoughts louder. Bolder.

What if I gave it a try with Ben? A real try, not sneaking off to his place after hours or meeting in parking lots to go on dates. What if we went out here, in Cooper? Where everyone could see us?

What if he was here, in my kitchen in the mornings?

In my bed at night.

My hands trembled a little as I spooned the mousse into glass cups and added a few pinches of salt.

"Stop," I told them.

Ben and the girls were in the middle of a conversation when I returned.

"Thank you," Ben said, taking the chocolate mousse, before turning back to Lena. "I actually never told her."

"Told her what?" I asked.

"We're talking about coming out," Ben said. "And I was telling them that I never came out to my mom. I was fourteen when she died."

"I'm sorry," Eve said. "About your mom."

"Thanks," Ben said. "I like to think she knew, but I don't think I really knew at that point. I mean, I knew, but I didn't *know*-know, if that makes sense."

Lena nodded emphatically.

"My mom said that she knew," Eve said. "But I think

she just thought she was being cool. My dad gave me a high five."

Ben laughed. "A high five is a pretty good reaction. When I told my father, he pretended he hadn't heard me, and we haven't spoken about it since."

Lena was looking down at her plate. She'd never get a chance to tell Spencer.

"What about you?" Ben asked me. "When did you come out as straight?"

I smiled. "The minute I saw Fox Mulder in his little red Speedo."

"Ew, Mom, gross," Lena said.

Ben took a bite of chocolate mousse and groaned. "Oh my god," he said. "This is the best thing I've ever tasted."

I flushed with pride.

"It's really good, Mom," Lena said.

"So good!" Eve said. Her bowl was already empty.

I went to get her a second helping, and was about to head back into the dining room, when I heard Lena talking to Ben.

"My dad died when I was ten," she said.

"I'm sorry," Ben said. "It sucks to lose a parent. Do you want to talk about him?"

I held my breath and the chocolate mousse. There wasn't an audible response.

"It's okay," Ben said. "If you ever feel like it, you can come talk to me. I don't know exactly what it's like for you, but I know what it's like to lose someone you love."

"Thanks," I heard her small voice say.

My heart squeezed. I loved her so much.

I pushed through the door, announcing myself. "Another chocolate mousse for our guest," I said, setting it down in front of Eve.

"Thanks, Mrs. P!" she said.

"When did you come out to your friends?" Lena asked.

Ben thought about it, his fingers tapping against his chin like some queer Yoda.

"I think they knew when I started kissing boys in front of them," he said.

I could see the shock in both girls' eyes.

"But you can come out whenever you want," he said. "It's your choice who you tell and when you tell."

"What if you don't like keeping secrets?" Eve asked.

The two girls exchanged a look, and it was clear this was something they had been talking about.

"It's not a secret," Lena said. "It's just personal."

"It's part of who we are," Eve countered. "Don't people deserve to know that?"

"Not everyone is going to react like your parents," Lena said. "Or my mom."

"Who are you afraid of?" Eve asked.

"My grandmother won't be pleased," Lena said.

That was an understatement.

Eve looked confused. "I thought your grandmother already knew."

"Not that grandmother," Lena said. "The bad one."

I bit my lip to keep a laugh back. It was hard to feel sorry for Diana—that's what happened when you were a bigot—a gay granddaughter who wanted nothing to do with you. Actions. Consequences.

Eve crossed her arms and leaned back.

"I just think it's cowardly."

Lena frowned.

"Don't you regret not telling your mom?" Eve asked Ben.

He shook his head.

"Regrets are tricky. Because once you start picking apart your life like that, wondering what could have been, you start to realize that everything you have now would be different. And I don't regret where I've ended up."

The way he said it, how he glanced my way as he spoke, felt like he was talking specifically about being here with me. With us. I blushed.

Neither girl noticed because they were staring at him, rapt.

I couldn't blame them—they weren't used to this kind of honest, raw emotion. This nakedness of feeling. Neither was I.

"If I regret anything with my mom it's that I didn't tell her I loved her enough," he said. "Then again, I don't know if there's such a thing as enough when it comes to saying that."

Lena was looking at him almost as if she were seeing him for the first time.

"I'm lucky," Ben said. "My life is full of people that I love. Who love me." He took a bite of mousse. "And *you're* lucky too. Because you're part of a community—a family. Being queer is a gift. I would have figured that out earlier but I didn't know many gay people when I was your age, and that sucked. But you guys." He smiled. "You have two queer elders at your beck and call."

"I don't think Ollie would appreciate being called an elder," I said.

Ben grinned. "Well, he is whether he claims the title or not," he said. "We're all part of something larger—of all those who came before us."

Everyone seemed to absorb that as we finished our mousse. The girls helped Ben in the kitchen, cleaning the dishes and wiping down the counters.

"We're going to my room," Lena said.

"Door open," I reminded her.

She rolled her eyes.

"Thanks for your help, Ben!" Eve said.

"You're going to kill it at that audition," Ben said. "And you better come to the theatre right after and tell me all about it."

"Okay!" Eve said, and flung her arms around him in a hug.

"Yeah, thanks," Lena said.

"Anytime," Ben said. "And hey, if you call Ollie a queer elder the next time you see him, I'll take you spelunking."

"You will not," I said.

"Okay, I'll buy you an ice cream."

Lena smiled. Small, but it was there.

"Okay," she said.

He wasn't going to get a hug, but I didn't think he was expecting one.

"Have a good night." He waved to the girls as they headed upstairs.

Then it was just the two of us.

"This was nice," I said.

"They're such great kids," he said.

"Want to sit on the porch?" I asked.

"I thought you'd never ask."

———

IT WAS WONDERFUL OUT. I could smell the lilacs in the air. It was the best time to be in Montana—spring always made me love Cooper, which was helpful after the usual hateful winter.

"That chocolate mousse was incredible," Ben said. "Life-changing."

"The secret is sea salt," I said.

"Right, your mastery in seasoning."

I smiled. "PhD."

"Forgive me, doctor."

We were sitting on the front stoop, legs pressed together. Without saying anything, Ben reached over, and took my hand.

"You look beautiful tonight," he said.

I raised an eyebrow. "You like women covered in sauce and butter?"

"More than you know."

I smiled.

"I wasn't kidding," he said. "Before, about the whole home-cooked meal thing. I can't remember the last time I've had one, let alone one that good."

"If I'm good for anything . . ." I said.

He squeezed my hand. "You're good for a lot of things."

In the darkness, I blushed.

"My mom was usually too drunk to remember to go to the store, so I took care of food most of the time, and I wasn't great at it. I had to make do with the cheap stuff in the half-off aisles."

I remembered what that had been like.

"I'd never knock the perfection of buttered noodles," I said. "Or ramen."

"Or Spam," he said.

We exchanged a smile.

"Do you do this a lot?" he asked. "Family dinners?"

"We do," I said.

"It's nice."

"You're welcome whenever you're free," I said. "I always make too much anyways."

The thought of him coming over, sitting at the table with us, telling Lena stories, making us laugh, eating all our pasta, made me happy. Comforted.

"There is nothing like small-town hospitality," he said.

"One of the perks."

The stars were out tonight. It was perfect stargazing weather. For a moment, I thought about asking if he'd like to go—if he'd stay out late with me.

But he spoke before I could.

"I should probably head out," he said. "Early morning rehearsal."

I nodded, but he didn't get up.

"How are they going? Rehearsals?"

"Good," he said. "It's a great show. I really missed it."

"Missed what?"

"Theatre," he said. "The chance to connect with people directly. Film and TV are great, but nothing beats a live audience—they bring so much to a performance—and you can't prepare for any of it. Everything is in the moment. Pure. Honest." He looked at me. "I've missed other things too."

My heart leapt.

"Can I take you out tomorrow night?" he asked.

"Okay," I said, sounding breathless.

He grinned. "Great," he said, standing.

I did the same, dusting off the back of my jeans.

"Good night, Lauren," he said, pressing a kiss to my cheek.

"Good night," I said.

CHAPTER 49

NOW

GABE WAS IN A *MOOD*.

I too was in a mood, but while mine was all sunshine and puppies, Gabe's was far more thunderous.

"Will you stop that?" I asked.

He kept pacing up and down in front of the checkout desk. When he ignored me, I stepped out from behind the counter and grabbed his arm.

"What the hell is going on?" I asked.

"Nothing."

"Clearly," I said. "Well, your *nothing* is killing the vibe in here."

He looked around.

"No one is here," he said.

I'd meant that he was killing my vibe, but if I said that, I'd have to explain why I was in such a good mood.

I couldn't wait to see Ben tonight.

"*Almost* no one," I whispered. "But the lunch rush will be starting soon, and I'd prefer not to have my brother stomping around like a cartoon villain while customers are here."

Gabe let out a groan and shoved both hands through his hair.

"Do you want to tell me what's going on?"

"Can't," he said.

"Then can you at least go to the office and have your tantrum there?"

"It's not a tantrum," he said. "I'm dealing with some serious things, okay?"

An unpleasant thought popped into my head.

"Did you and Chani break up?" I asked, really hoping that wasn't the cause.

"What? No," Gabe said, and then gave me a piercing look. "Why? Did she say something?"

"No—"

"Because that would just be the cherry on top of this whole day."

"It's eleven-thirty."

"Argh!" he said, and stomped back to the office, slamming the door behind him.

The store rattled. I sighed.

Until Gabe showed up, my morning had been going rather nicely. I'd set out books and hung up new products on the wall while thinking about Ben. About seeing him tonight. About telling him that I wanted to give this *thing* between us a try. A real try.

I'd even caught myself whistling.

But then Gabe had stormed in like a big, pouty thundercloud.

"FUCK!"

The office door barely muffled him at all.

I gave an apologetic smile to Mrs. Bowen, who had just placed her books down on the counter.

"You know how actors are," I said. "So dramatic."

She gave me a small smile but glanced back at the office door with concern. Once she was gone, my own smile disappeared.

"What the fuck, Gabe?" I flung the door open.

He was sitting on the couch, head in hands.

"What is going on?" I asked, now genuinely concerned.

"I can't talk about it," he said, and looked at his phone. "Goddammit, where is Ollie?"

"Is it something to do with the theatre?" I asked.

Gabe ignored me, presumably calling Ollie again.

"If you don't get your English ass down here in fifteen minutes, I'm coming to you," he said, and then hung up.

I leaned my hips back on the desk, arms crossed.

Gabe looked up at me, his face drawn.

"I should have seen this coming," he said, balling his hand into a fist and giving the couch cushions a solid punch.

"Careful on the furniture, okay?"

"I'll buy you a new one," he said.

Silence reigned. I kept checking behind me to make sure no one was waiting at the counter, while Gabe leaned his head back against the couch cushions and stared at the ceiling.

"This is a fucking mess," he said after a good five minutes.

"I would love to help you out," I said. "But I don't have any idea what is going on."

He gave me a look—a long, searching one, and I was

pretty sure he was just about to tell me what was causing his massive meltdown when his phone rang.

"Ollie? Where have you been?" he all but bellowed into the phone. "You can't be at the theatre—I was just there. Yeah. Yeah. I know—I fucking know. Okay. *Fuck.* I'm on my way."

He hung up and pushed himself off the couch.

"Gotta go," he said.

"Glad I could help," I said.

"You did, actually." He dropped a kiss on my cheek on his way out the door.

I tried to settle back into my good mood, but the afternoon turned out to be quite busy and a little after three, Lena came into the store wearing an expression very much like Gabe had been wearing this morning.

"Great," I muttered to myself. "Hi, honey."

Lena grunted and went into the office, slamming the door behind her.

Like uncle, like niece.

"I have no idea what's going on," Chani said.

I turned, not knowing she was there—she must have been trailing Lena.

"Did you pick her up?"

Chani nodded, car keys twirling around her finger. "She called me."

I wasn't expecting that.

"She called *you?*" I asked, and then quickly apologized. "I didn't mean to sound so incredulous. It's just, she called you?"

Chani gave me a smile. "Trust me, I was just as surprised as you are. I think she tried Gabe, but he wasn't picking up, and then maybe she tried Ollie, but she ended up calling me to come get her from Eve's."

"She was at Eve's?"

"She didn't say anything when she got in the car," Chani said. "I think I heard a thank-you, but whatever happened, she wasn't going to confess to me. I was just the chauffeur."

I let out a sigh. Just when things had started to look up. "I'll have a talk with her about her manners."

"It's okay," Chani said. "I'm honestly flattered she thought of me at all."

I looked at my phone, even though I knew I hadn't missed any calls or texts, and wondered why Lena hadn't reached out to me.

"Are you busy?" I asked.

"Nope," she said.

"Could I ask another favor? Would you mind the counter for a bit? I should go talk to Lena."

"Of course," Chani said.

She looked thrilled to be asked.

"I'd love to say this dysfunction is unusual for us," I said. "But I don't want to lie to you."

She laughed. "Can't spell dysfunctional without fun."

We both winced at the bad joke.

"Why don't you and Gabe come over to dinner tomorrow night?" I asked.

I loved my brother, but I wasn't giving up my night with Ben.

"He'll like that," Chani said. "Sounds really nice."

"Great," I said. "Tomorrow at seven."

"Now go check on Lena," Chani said. "I'll watch the counter."

I opened the office door to find Lena in an almost identical pose to what I'd found when I went looking for Gabe.

What was with today?

"Lena? Honey?"

She didn't lift her head as I closed the door carefully behind me.

"Are you okay? Did something happen?"

"Eve and I broke up," she said, her voice muffled.

Fuck.

I hadn't seen that coming—what had happened between last night and now?

With everyone.

"I'm so sorry," I said, sitting down on the couch next to her. "Do you want to talk about it?"

"She's just being ridiculous!" Lena threw up her hands, her whole body flung back against the cushions. "She wants to tell everyone that we're together and thinks I'm a coward because I don't want to."

Oooof.

"That's really hard," I said.

"Yeah, I know," she said, looking at me with a disdain I'd come to know well. "It's all Ben's fault."

My chest got tight.

I'd been so happy that Lena seemed to be warming up to Ben. Especially now that I was willing to give this whole real-dating thing a try. This was the opposite of good timing.

"He made it sound like being gay is just the best thing in the entire world and that we're like these special unicorns with our own families and elders," Lena said. "But I don't want to be a unicorn. I don't want to stand out. I just want to get through school."

TOTALLY AND COMPLETELY FINE

I put my hand gently on her back. She didn't flinch, which seemed like a good thing.

"Eve just doesn't understand," Lena said. "Everyone likes *her*. She'd probably be fine."

She looked down at the floor.

"But I'm not popular like her. I don't do school activities or whatever. I don't want to be the lead in the school musical. I don't want anyone looking at me."

I knew exactly what that was like.

"Did you tell her all this?"

"Obviously," Lena said. "And she said she didn't want to be in the closet forever and that we should probably take a break."

I could see tears begin to build in her eyes.

"Well, a break isn't necessarily breaking up," I said.

"I'm not going to come out," Lena said. "Not here."

"That's okay," I said.

"No, it's not," she said. "It's like I have to choose between being with Eve and having the whole school know or keeping quiet but being alone."

I felt for her. I knew a little bit about what she was talking about.

Lena wiped her eyes roughly.

"Whatever," she said. "It's whatever."

"Honey—" I tried, but she was already getting up.

"I'm going home," she said.

"Do you want Chani to drive you?"

It wasn't a long walk, but it was a testament to how upset Lena was the way she paused and then quietly said: "Can you ask her?"

CHAPTER 50

NOW

I STOOD OUTSIDE BEN'S DOOR FEELING LIKE THE DAY
had wrung me dry. Between Gabe and Lena, it seemed like
half of my world was on fire, and I had no idea how to
extinguish the flames. And as far as Gabe was concerned, I
still didn't even know what had been set alight.

Part of me just wanted to put my head against the wood
and stay there until things miraculously figured themselves
out, but I also knew that the person behind that door
would probably make me feel better. That made me smile.

I knocked.

But when the door opened, my smile faded immediately.

Because Ben looked terrible.

Like he hadn't slept or eaten. Like he was wearing yesterday's clothes, though since everything he owned was
black, they were probably just wrinkled. He'd clearly been
running his hands through his hair because it was standing
up in all sorts of different directions.

"Hey," he said, his smile forced.

"What is going on today?" I asked, following him into his apartment. "First Gabe, then Lena, and now you. Is there something in the water?"

"What's wrong with Lena?" Ben asked.

I noticed he didn't ask about Gabe.

"She and Eve broke up," I said.

"Oh no." Ben sat down on his bed, looking even more miserable.

"They'll figure it out," I said, even though I had no clue.

"I feel like that's probably my fault too," he said.

I decided not to confirm that for him.

"What else is your fault?"

"Gabe's mood," Ben said.

My stomach was queasy. I had a feeling where this was going, and I was extremely glad I hadn't started tonight's conversation with: "Hey! I know we agreed this was just casual, but I'm falling for you and think you should stay in Cooper for a while. Maybe forever? Now kiss me!"

Because that would have been embarrassing.

"Fran called this morning," he said.

I sat down on the bed next to him.

"I got the job," he said.

Was it possible for your heart to soar and sink at the same time?

I put a big, happy smile on my face. "That's incredible," I said. "Congratulations Bond, James Bond."

I gave him a hug, and he hugged me back, but I could feel the tension in his body.

"They want me back in L.A. as soon as possible," he said. "Signing contracts. Making announcements."

"They're excited about you," I said. "You should be so proud."

"I have to be there the day after tomorrow."

"Oh," I said, and then realized what he was saying. "The play."

No wonder Gabe had been freaking out. They were putting on a two-man show and one of those men was about to jet off for another gig.

"Yeah." Ben's expression was one of misery. "I tried to get Fran to talk to the production—to give me enough time to do the show. They wouldn't budge." He looked at me. "They wanted me on a plane by tomorrow morning, but I convinced them I needed at least forty-eight hours to get everything here sorted."

"Wow," I said.

"Yeah," he said. "Wow."

"At least the pay will be better," I joked.

Ben looked at me.

"It's more than enough for me to pay off my father. To get the house back."

"Oh," I said. "I didn't realize it was that much."

"He's a dick," he said. "He picked a number he thought I'd never be able to reach."

"But now you can," I said.

"Now I can," he echoed.

We sat there, both of us staring at a plain white wall.

I grabbed onto the only glimmer of hope.

"Well," I said. "L.A. isn't *that* far."

Ben dropped his head. "Production is in Australia," he said. "They want me to move there. Four years at least."

"Oh."

"It's a little bit farther than L.A.," he said.

And that was that. He didn't have to say it—this wasn't going to work.

I tried for lightness. "I've heard the skydiving there is amazing."

He didn't say anything. I reached over and took his hand. Gave it a squeeze.

"You were the smart one," Ben said.

"Me?"

He had turned to face me.

"I should have listened," he said. "When you told me this was complicated."

For once in my life, I hated being right.

I should have been prepared for this. Instead, I'd been stupidly falling for him.

Now I was about to be left behind. Again.

It wasn't the same, of course. But loneliness piled on top of loneliness is a heavy burden. And I'd walked right into this one.

I'd done this to myself.

I wanted to cry.

"Well," I said. "I guess tonight is our last date."

"Guess so." The smile he gave me was wry and sad.

At least I wasn't alone in that.

"What would you like to do?" he asked. "Feels like we should do something special."

I thought about it.

"I know the perfect thing," I said.

"Yeah?"

"Take me for a ride, Ben."

CHAPTER 51

NOW

I'D NEVER BEEN ON A MOTORCYCLE BEFORE. ESPECIALLY not at night. My heart pounded as I climbed onto the back behind Ben, my helmet firmly in place.

"Just hold on to me," he said.

There was no question about that. I wrapped my arms around him and leaned into his warmth. The bike sputtered to a start beneath us, and the intensity of the vibration was a little too much at first, but then everything settled—the bike, my shoulders, my stomach.

"Ready?" Ben asked.

"Ready," I said, even though I wasn't.

I didn't think I'd ever be ready.

Story of my life.

A shriek of surprise flew out of me as we took off.

"Oh my god," I said.

"You okay?"

I could barely hear him over the wind. "I'm okay."

I didn't know if he heard me, but no doubt he could tell by the way I pressed my front against his back that I was still on the bike.

My head felt huge and unwieldy in the helmet, but somehow, I managed to rest part of it on his shoulder—or near his shoulder. From behind the visor, I could see Cooper flying by me—nothing more than a blur of lights at this speed.

I'd given him directions to a place outside of town that was known for good stargazing. Of course, the sky was cloudy tonight, so chances were low that anyone else would be there. We'd have the field to ourselves—all that openness.

I was grateful for the helmet—not just for the protection but for how it hid my tears. It wasn't until we were already on the road that I allowed them to fall, wet trails running down the sides of my face.

How could I have been so foolish? I'd known that this was a bad idea from the beginning, but I'd allowed myself to be convinced—by Ben's eyes, his kiss, my own stupidity—that I could handle it. That I'd be fine.

I wasn't fine.

I wanted to howl into the night, scream about how unfair it all was. How cruel the universe was to bring me this man when I couldn't keep him.

It had taken me so long to admit my feelings for Spencer—I'd kept it from myself, worried I'd get hurt. Now, I was worried that I hadn't learned anything at all. That I was too late.

I was going to hurt no matter what.

My tears were dry by the time we reached the field.

Ben helped me off the bike, and we left our helmets propped up on the seat. There was a bag attached to the back. Ben pulled a blanket out of it and laid it down.

It was still cold at night, but snuggled up next to Ben on the blanket, I barely felt the chill.

"I really thought we'd have more time," he said.

"Shhh," I said. "Let's just enjoy this."

He nodded, and I rested my head against him. I couldn't see any stars, but I didn't mind.

It was just us. Nothing—no one—else around.

Sitting up on my knees, I turned to Ben, who pushed himself up to his elbows. Before I could second-guess myself, I took his face in my hands and kissed him. With intent. With tongue.

He groaned, and I began pulling his shirt from his pants.

A hand stilled mine.

"What are you doing?" he asked.

"Something that scares me," I said.

This time when I went for his belt, he didn't stop me.

Instead, he flipped me onto my back, with him on his knees, my thighs pressed against them. With one hand, he reached for the collar of his shirt and pulled the whole thing off in one fluid movement that was far sexier than it should have been.

Not that I cared. This was our last night. I was going to indulge in every feeling, in every thought, in every desire that I had.

I thanked the gods of safe sex for my IUD.

Ben's belt was unbuckled, his jeans just slightly open at the waist. Starting at his belly—enjoying the way his skin jumped under my touch—I ran my hands upward, palms spreading outward as I reached for his shoulders.

The moon made the wispy cotton sky glow.

Ben put his hands on the widest part of my hips, fingers curling around to my ass, and then, with a sharp tug, pulled me forward and up. I was pressed against him—the seams of our jeans lined up perfectly—my toes curling as he rolled his hips to mine.

Locking my ankles around his back, I pulled his mouth to mine and we kissed like that, nearly fully clothed and thrusting against each other with a sweet wildness. My shirt was pulled free, and I felt the night air on my breasts for less than a moment before Ben's hands were there to warm them.

"These fucking tits," he said, before using his lips to trace circles around my nipples—one at a time.

I reached between us for his zipper and ended up knocking my forehead into his chin. We both pulled back with a wince, and then a laugh, me rubbing my forehead ruefully, while he tested his jaw with a grin.

"Maybe we should do this separately," I said.

Quickly we got rid of the rest of our clothes. I barely had a chance to remove my socks before Ben was reaching for me. His body was hot and heavy on mine—the perfect protection from the cold—and his mouth gave soft, biting kisses against my neck.

I threaded my hands into his hair, letting it fall through my fingers before gathering it up again and again. I closed my eyes, trying to capture the sensation forever—the beautiful sensuality of touch.

Ben's hand was tracing the back of my thigh as he pulled one leg up high and tight against his side. Each time we were together, it seemed he made it his mission to find something new that I liked. This move had been the latest discovery.

His mouth moved to my collarbone, his teeth dragging carefully across it. I arched up against him, wanting everything and more.

My body hummed, eager for pleasure, for release. But my mind wanted it to go on forever—wanted to stay in this moment for as long as possible.

I pulled Ben's mouth back to mine, my tongue finding his in a hot, sloppy tangle that had us both panting. With my leg still hooked around his back, I swung the other up, capturing him between my thighs as I pushed my hips up against his.

I'd discovered things he liked as well.

Ben pressed me against the blanket, unfolding me onto the ground. His hand skimmed down my stomach as he inched backward on his knees, eyes blazing in the dim light.

He kissed the inside of my thigh before sliding his hands under my ass and lifting my hips to his mouth. My voice was swallowed up by the night air as he drew his nose across my clit, almost playfully, before pressing the flat of his tongue in its place.

There was his hair again, the soft, smooth strands falling through my fingers. I pushed, and he pulled, as if there were some way we could bring our bodies closer. My legs were around his neck, his arms reaching up past my hips to grasp my hands as I bucked against him.

His tongue went deep, and I could feel his hum of pleasure.

He kissed me until my hips jutted forward, my back arching, body moving of its own accord. My breath was labored, clit throbbing, as he climbed up my body.

I cataloged every groan, every kiss, every touch, determined to remember this. Not all of us had the chance to savor our last time. I wasn't going to lose it again. My fingers drew patterns along his arms as if I could brand him. As if I could leave my mark.

Just as he'd left his.

It was almost too much. The pleasure, the pain.

I took his face and kissed him, chasing away all thought. I felt his cock against my stomach. Felt his hand skate along my waist. Felt the roughness of his leg against mine. Felt. Felt. Felt.

He touched me. One finger, then two.

"Ben," I pleaded.

He kissed me. Kissed me and fucked me with his fingers until I came again.

"I hate you," I said, once I could breathe.

It was easier to say that in jest than to say what I truly felt.

He ran a finger along the line of my jaw before pinching my chin and pulling me in for a kiss. His ring was cold against my skin.

I slipped my hand between us until I found that perfect

cock of his. He groaned, forehead down on my shoulder as I traced his length with my palm. His hands gripped my waist as I guided him inside.

My back against the blanket, I cradled his hips in mine as he moved languidly against me, his mouth making sweet, messy kisses across my lips. Another moment, another feeling to savor, holding his face, my eyes shut as he pressed deep inside.

I curled a hand over the back of his neck, hot for the way I could feel him growl. His hips began to move faster, his fingers sliding downward to find my clit.

"Oh god," I moaned, the words half lost in his mouth.

He pressed his hips forward, replacing his fingers, and I found myself spinning toward delicious pleasure.

"Please." Ben's voice was hot in my ear. "Lauren. Please . . . *fuck*. I want to feel it. Need to feel it. Please, love, please."

The accent was the final fucking straw.

I'd never been more grateful for the vastness of Montana than when Ben's name echoed across a cornfield as I came for the third time.

Apparently, there *were* places to scream in small towns.

He raced to follow, his arms braced by my sides, hips pounding against mine.

"Fuck," he groaned.

His chest was sweaty, his hair damp. His arms were bracketed around me. He pressed his forehead against mine, before tilting his head down and rubbing my nose with his.

I felt my heart shatter into a thousand pieces.

———

BEN STOPPED IN FRONT of the house. Lena's light wasn't on, so I figured she'd probably gone to sleep. I swung my leg over the bike and dismounted, feeling even less steady on my feet than I'd been a few hours ago.

Ben took off his helmet, and I handed him mine.

He looked so gorgeous, sitting there on his bike, hair messy, eyes gleaming.

It seemed impossible that I'd fallen so fast, but here I was.

I didn't want to say goodnight. I didn't want to say goodbye.

"Come to dinner tomorrow night," I blurted out.

Ben looked up, toward Lena's window.

"Is that a good idea?" he asked, clearly worried about her.

"It will be fine," I said. "And you deserve a good meal before you head off to Australia. I hear they put eggs on their burgers."

"Don't knock it till you've tried it," he said.

"Dinner?"

"Dinner," he said.

"Tomorrow at seven?"

"Can't wait," he said.

I knew it was risky—that I was standing in front of my house, in my neighborhood, in my town, out in the open—but I hooked my finger into the neckline of Ben's shirt, catching both his necklaces as I did, and pulled his mouth to mine.

It felt like a goodbye kiss.

When we broke apart, I couldn't look at him. I knew I'd start to cry, and I didn't want that.

"Tomorrow," he said.

It wasn't until he'd driven off, and I was standing in my entryway, that I remembered that he wasn't the only person I'd invited over for dinner tomorrow.

Fuck.

CHAPTER 52

NOW

GABE HADN'T BEEN HAPPY ABOUT THE DINNER MIX-UP, but he decided to come anyway.

"Might as well make it a proper send-off," he said. "Invite Ollie as well."

"I don't want any bloodshed," I told him.

"There won't be," Gabe promised, and then paused. "But maybe you should invite Mom just in case."

I ended up needing to get the extra leaf from the closet so the table would be big enough.

"Can you set the table?" I asked Lena.

She had been sulking around the house all day, but I hadn't said anything. Broken hearts were painful at any age—maybe even more so now, when everything was so new and unknown.

And it wasn't as if I could give her advice on how to repair what had shattered.

She put each plate down with the sigh of someone who was certain they'd never love again. I wanted to wrap my arms around her and tell her that this wouldn't last. That nothing ever lasted. For good and for bad.

I needed to remind myself that.

Chani and Gabe were the first to arrive.

"Everything smells amazing," Chani said.

"Lena helped with the dessert," I said.

I'd made a pavlova.

"Barely," Lena muttered, before escaping back into the dining room.

"How's she doing?" Chani asked. "Did she tell you what's going on?"

I nodded but didn't feel it was my place to say.

"She'll get through it," I said.

"Who will get through what?" Gabe asked, mouth full.

"That is for dinner," I said, pulling the half-eaten roll out of his hand.

"I'm hungry," he said.

I pushed the roll back at him because what was I going to do? Put it back in the basket?

"What's wrong with Lena?" Gabe asked.

"Nothing," I said.

Ollie was the next to arrive.

"I heard the news," I told him. "I'm sorry about the show."

"It will be fine," he said. "Thankfully I know the part. We'll have to adjust our schedule—and I'll need you to make changes to the costumes—but I think we'll pull it off."

"You might even have a bigger audience," I said.

Ollie shrugged. "You know what's ironic?" he asked.

"What?"

"This is the second time James Bond has thrown my life into chaos."

Mom was the next to arrive, and she spent several minutes poking her head into every pot I had going on the stove.

Ben was the last, and the tension in the house rose palpably when he entered.

"Thanks for letting me crash your dinner," he said.

There was silence, and I saw Lena look away. Ben noticed and his face fell. Thankfully, Chani stepped forward and gave him a hug.

"Congrats on the big news," she said.

"Thanks," he said.

That seemed to break the ice.

"You'll be great," Gabe said.

"They're lucky to have you," Ollie said.

Ben looked at me, and I nodded in agreement.

"Hey, Lena," he said, holding up the bag he was carrying. "I got you some ice cream."

She stared blankly at him.

"You know, because of the whole queer elder thing and telling Ollie . . ." He trailed off when it was clear she wasn't going to respond.

"That was your doing?" Ollie asked.

"I'll just go put this in the freezer," Ben said.

"It's pretty crowded in there," I said. "Feel free to move things around."

He disappeared into the kitchen.

"This is going great," Gabe said.

Chani hit him on the arm.

"When do you start filming?" she asked when Ben came back into the room.

"Next month," he said. "But they want me in L.A. to-morrow." He looked at Ollie and Gabe. "I swear I tried to get them to push it back until after the play, but—"

"We know how it is," Ollie said.

Gabe just nodded, and then turned to me.

"How's your speech coming?" Gabe asked.

"Speech?" Ben asked.

"I'm supposed to speak at the engagement party," I said.

"My speech is amazing, by the way," Ollie said. "In case anyone was wondering."

"Mine's not going to be as good as Ollie's," I said.

That got a laugh—a sad trickle of one, but a laugh nonetheless.

"Why don't we grab plates," I said. "Everything is set up in the kitchen."

We all filed in, making a ramshackle line of sorts. Lena was at the front, but just as she was reaching for the chicken, she knocked over the gravy.

A dozen hands scrambled to right the gravy bowl, but some had gotten on the counter. I grabbed a paper towel and dabbed up the mess.

"No harm, no foul," I said, before passing the sullied towel to Lena to throw out.

She stepped on the pedal to open the trash can, looked in, and froze.

Then she reached in.

"What are you doing?" I asked, grossed out.

Lena's face was pale and drawn as she pulled out a famil-iar wrapped bundle.

"Why is this in the trash?" she asked.

It was Spencer's pizza dough. His *last* pizza dough.

Everyone was frozen. Even though I was sure that Chani and Ollie, like Ben, had no idea what this was about, it was clear that it was something.

"I'm sorry," Ben said. "I saw it had gotten moldy, so I tossed it—was it a science experiment or something?"

I came over to Lena immediately and saw that Ben was right. At some point, the Saran Wrap had been punctured and it had been left out long enough to get black spots on it.

"Mom?" Lena asked, her voice small and wavering.

"It's okay," I said, taking the dough from her.

We both looked at it.

"Can't we just put it back?" Lena asked.

"I don't think so," I said.

It was gross—beyond spoiled. I couldn't remember the last time I'd really looked at it.

"I'm sorry, honey," I said, and dropped it back into the trash can.

Lena reacted violently.

"What did you do that for?" She pulled the dough out again and pressed it against her chest.

It had gotten mixed up with the garbage, so she'd inadvertently spread some leftover cottage cheese and fruit across the front of her shirt.

"Lena." I tried to take it from her, but she pulled away.

"I can't believe you're just going to throw it out," she said.

"Lena," Mom tried, but she pulled away from her too, clutching the pizza dough even closer to her.

"There's nothing we can do," I said.

"We could make some more," Ben offered, but it was

absolutely the wrong thing to say and the wrong time to interject.

Lena spun toward him.

"We can't just make some more," she spat. "My *dad* made this."

"Oh," Ben said.

"Lena." Ollie stepped forward, but she just shot him a glare. He withdrew immediately.

"I'm sorry," Ben said. "I didn't know."

"Yeah, because you're not my dad," Lena said. "Just because you're fucking my mom doesn't mean you'll ever be my dad."

It was like a slap in the face.

I could see shock radiate around the room.

I didn't know how Lena had figured it out, but I shouldn't have been surprised. She was always more observant than I gave her credit for.

"Lena!" Mom said. "Language."

Of course, that was the least of our worries right now.

"Please, honey," I said. "Not here—let's go somewhere. Talk about it."

I reached for her, but she pulled away.

"I *hate* you," she said.

Me, but also Ben.

"I'm sorry," I said to him.

"It's fine," Ben said.

"It's not fine!" Lena's voice was rising in volume and pitch. "None of this is fine! Dad is dead and now we can't make pizza, and you don't even care."

My heart cracked.

"Lena—"

"I wish *you* were the one who died," she said.

The room went deathly quiet. Lena's chest was heaving, her eyes wild.

I took a breath in. Then out.

"Me too," I said.

I'd never said it out loud, but it was true.

Lena's face was white, tears running in rivers down her cheeks.

None of our words could be taken back.

With a sob, Lena turned and ran out of the kitchen. I heard the front door slam behind her.

Everyone was silent and still.

"Lauren——" Gabe stepped toward me, but I shook my head.

"Go make sure she's okay," I said.

Ollie went after her, Chani following in his footsteps.

"Are you all right?" Ben asked, his hand between my shoulder blades.

I shrugged off his touch. I didn't deserve it.

I was a monster. A terrible mother.

"She's not in the yard," Ollie said. "I think she went down the alley."

"I'll get the car," Gabe said.

"She can't get that far," Chani said.

"It's a small town," Gabe said. "She's probably headed toward the junction."

"Why would she go that way?" Chani asked. "Isn't it mostly just back roads?"

I knew exactly where she'd gone. My stomach gave a painful, sickening twist.

"One road in particular," I said.

I'd been avoiding it for three years. I didn't want to go. I wasn't ready.

But it didn't matter.

"I know where she is," I said.

"We can go with you," Gabe said.

"No," I said. "It's better if I go alone."

CHAPTER 53

NOW

I DIDN'T KNOW IF IT WAS A STATEWIDE THING OR SPE-
cific to Cooper, but when someone died in a car accident,
the spot was marked with a cross. Speeding was a problem
in Montana. There were always too many crosses.

I'd never gone to see if they'd placed one for Spencer.

They had.

And that's where Lena was.

She was sitting off the intersection in one of two banged-
up old chairs, looking at the white letters that spelled out
Spencer's name across the horizontal section.

I approached slowly.

There was no indication that she even knew I was there,
though she must have. I sat right next to her. The chair was
wobbly and half stuck in the muddy grass, but it didn't fall
over.

We sat there in silence.

What was there to say?

It wasn't until Lena wiped her face with her palms that I realized she was crying.

Even though I couldn't tell if she wanted it, I reached over and pulled her toward me, holding her tight against my chest. I wanted her to feel my heartbeat.

"I'm sorry," I said. "I'm so sorry."

She sobbed into my shirt.

"I miss him so much," she said.

"Me too."

She laid her head on my shoulder. She seemed so small. So young.

"I'm sorry I said, you know, about—" she said. "I didn't mean it."

"I know," I said.

She looked up at me.

"Did you mean it?" she asked.

I put my arm around her. "I know how close you and Dad were. I know you miss him."

"I'd miss you," she said. "If you were gone."

I gave her a squeeze. "I love you," I said. "I love you so much."

"I love you too," she said.

"Do you come here a lot?" I asked, realizing that there was more than just the cross and two chairs. There were stacked piles of rocks and some scraggly looking flowers that had clearly been planted there.

Lena nodded. "Eve helped me bring the chairs," she said. "We found them behind the Finnish Line a while ago."

"I bet we could figure out a way to clean them up a bit," I said. "There are all those tools still in the house. Your dad's tools."

The tools Ben had used.

"If we fixed the chairs"—Lena's words were hesitant—"do you think you'd want to come here once in a while?"

I took a deep breath.

"Is that what you'd like?"

"It's kind of nice sometimes."

She reached down and drew her fingers across the petals of some of the flowers, limply hanging on.

"I like to talk to him when I'm here," she said. "Is that dumb?"

I squeezed my eyes shut.

"Not at all," I said. "I talk to him too. Sometimes."

"I miss Dad." Her voice was teary.

"I do too," I said. "Every day. All the time."

"You do?" she asked.

I nodded.

"Why don't you ever talk about him?"

I paused.

"I don't know," I said. "I think it made me feel like this big, sad, depressing storm cloud sweeping in to ruin everyone's day."

"I feel that way too," Lena said.

"Maybe we need to try something different," I said.

"Like what?"

"Like talking about how we're feeling. Even when we're sad. Especially when we're sad."

There was a long silence.

"Do you think—" Lena paused, started again. "Do you think he'd be proud of me?"

"Yes," I said without hesitation. "He loved you *so* much."

"Do you think he'd still love me even if he knew about . . ." Lena's voice got quieter and quieter. ". . . Eve?"

"Of course," I said fiercely.

"You don't know for sure," she said. "Like, you didn't know what he believed when it came to ghosts or heaven or that stuff."

I now understood what she'd been trying to figure out.

"I know for sure," I said. "Because there is nothing that would have made your father love you any less."

"What about you?" she asked, her voice so small.

"Honey, I love you so much," I said. "I love you more than anything in the entire world."

"Even after . . . what I said?"

"I love you," I said. "I love you, I love you, I love you." Lena was crying again, holding on to me tightly.

"I tried to plant some flowers," she said. "But they keep dying." She looked up at me. "Do you think that's a sign?"

"No," I said. "I think that's the soil."

"Grandma said it's because I'm not praying enough," she said. "That if I brought a Bible out here and read to the flowers, they'd grow. That Dad would know how much I love him."

"Grandma is wrong," I said. "She doesn't know how flowers grow."

"She's the worst," Lena said.

"Yeah," I said. "She kind of is."

That at least made Lena giggle a little.

I breathed in the scent of her hair and found that there was something familiar.

"You smell like your dad," I told her.

She took a bit of her own hair and sniffed. "Yeah?"

I hugged her tighter. "Yeah, it's nice. Really nice."

"Mom?" she asked.

"Yeah?"

"I don't want you to be lonely," she said.

I pressed my lips together. I'd cried enough for one day and apparently, I wasn't done yet.

"I'm okay, honey," I said. "I have you. And Grandma, and Uncle Gabe."

"And Ollie," Lena said. "And Chani."

"And Teddy," I said. "That's a lot of love to have."

Lena was quiet for a moment.

"And Ben?" she asked—the question so tentative. "Do you need that too?"

"He's leaving," I said, reminding her.

"But—"

"It's over," I said. "It's better this way."

Lena looked up at me. I tucked her head under my chin.

"I'll be fine," I said, hoping that it would eventually be true.

CHAPTER 54

NOW

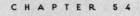

BEN WAS SITTING ON THE PORCH WHEN WE RETURNED, standing as we walked up to the house.

"Why don't you go inside," I told Lena. "You must be hungry."

She nodded and paused for a moment in front of Ben.

"I'm sorry," she said.

"Me too," he said.

Then she disappeared into the house.

Ben shoved his hands into his pockets.

"She's okay," I said.

"Yeah," he said.

He came down to meet me on the bottom step.

We both knew what needed to happen.

What was inevitable.

What we should have prepared for.

I waited for him to say it.

"I think it's best if I go," he said.

I didn't want him to, but I also knew he was right. It would be best. For everyone inside. For him. For me.

"I had a good time," I said.

Wholly insignificant words for what we'd shared, but it made Ben smile.

"I did too," he said. "And you know, if you're ever in Australia . . ." He lifted a hand, miming a phone.

"Of course," I said. "And if you're ever back in the States and want a good meal . . ."

"That would be okay?" he asked.

"Of course," I said, even though I knew it wouldn't be.

But he wasn't going to be coming back.

He lifted a hand and cupped my cheek. I leaned into his palm.

"I'll miss you," I said, trying to hold back my tears.

"I'll miss you too," he murmured.

This was a goodbye kiss. I could feel the finality in it.

Ben dropped his hand and stepped away, but before he got to the gate, he turned to look back at me.

And his eyes . . .

I choked back a sob, placing a hand against my chest. His eyes followed the motion.

"If I've learned anything," he said, "it's that the heart is a miraculous, resilient thing. It's capable of so much. It can even expand if we give it the chance."

I wasn't going to say anything, but I couldn't help myself.

"But why does it have to hurt so much?"

Ben gave me a sad smile.

"I don't mind the pain," he said. "It reminds me that I still have a heart to break."

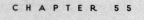

CHAPTER 55

NOW

THE NOTES IN FRONT OF ME—WRITTEN IN MY OWN handwriting—kept swimming in and out of focus. I'd never been a good public speaker. Or speechwriter. Why Gabe had wanted me to do both at his engagement party completely baffled me.

An engagement party that had basically turned into a pre-wedding party, since Gabe and Chani were now getting hitched next week.

Ben had left ten days ago.

I hadn't heard from him since, nor had I texted or called.

A clean break would be best, I'd decided.

I hadn't expected it to hurt as much as it did.

Ollie finished speaking to riotous laughter and applause. I don't know why I'd agreed to go last—whatever I said after Mr. Darcy was going to be a letdown. Chani's sister had been smart, offering to go first.

"And now, my sister, Lauren, has a few things to say," Gabe said.

Fuck.

Allyson, who had come as my date, gave me a little nudge when I didn't move.

"You've got this," she whispered.

I stood, feeling wobbly from my fingers to my knees. Thankfully, it wasn't a big party, so I didn't need a microphone, but I still felt the pressure of all these faces—most of them familiar, some not—staring at me.

"Hi, everyone," I said. "I'm Lauren. Like Gabe said."

My mouth felt dry. I tightened my grip on my note cards, crinkling them in my hands.

"Gabe is my younger brother," I said.

Already, I knew this was a bust. I'd literally just repeated what Gabe had said.

"I've watched Gabe grow up," I said. "From his days as a football star."

Ollie let out a loud snort, which prompted a few titters from the crowd.

"To his college plays and early films, to becoming a big movie star."

This speech was so boring.

"I don't know Chani that well," I said. "But I know that my brother has very good taste, which means that she must be very special."

Chani smiled and looked at Gabe. He beamed at her; their hands entwined.

I thought about the way it had felt to hold Ben's hand.

"Also, Gabe is very stubborn," I said. "It's a family trait."

"That's right, it is," someone in the crowd shouted out.

Everyone laughed. It was the first laugh my speech had gotten.

"He's so stubborn that he refused to admit that he's been in love with Chani for almost ten years now."

I wished Spencer were here with me.

I wished Ben were here with me.

I lowered my note cards. The speech I'd written was nothing. Just a bunch of hollow words and bad jokes, each an attempt to skim the surface of what love really felt like.

"Falling in love sounds easy, right?" I took a deep breath. "It's not. It's work and hardship and tears and pain. The worst thing about love is that you'll never know what it will look like. And you can never imagine what it will become."

My hands started to shake, and I began to feel light-headed. I put a hand to my temple, cool fingers against my hot skin.

"Love is a shape-shifter. It will look different at eighteen than it will at forty than it will at eighty. It will *feel* different. You don't *fall* in love—it isn't something you trip and tumble over. Love is something you need to hurtle yourself into—something you race toward heart first, even if you don't know what will happen. *Especially* if you don't know what will happen."

Black spots appeared in front of my eyes. I tried to shake them away.

"And it's hard work. Because the truth is that *life* is hard work. *Living* is hard work. It's work but it's also joy and laughter and stupid jokes and good timing and a ton of luck and a thousand other things that you won't recognize until they're standing right in front of you. Sometimes you won't even see it until it's gone."

There were confused, worried rumbles from the crowd.

"Lauren?" Gabe stood.

"I'm fine," I said, waving a hand. "I'm just so happy for you two."

"Lauren," Gabe said again, and that's when I realized I was crying.

"I'm just really happy," I blubbered. "That's all. These are happy tears."

They clearly weren't.

Gabe stepped toward me, arms out, but I pulled away from them. This was humiliating, but I couldn't stop weeping. Snot was coming out of my nose. I could barely see through the tears.

"Oh god," I said. "I'm so sorry."

I ran out of the room.

I fled to Mom's basement. I didn't know why. I hadn't been there in years—no one had—it was probably full of spiders.

The old couch was still there, and it still squeaked when I sat down.

That reminded me of Spencer.

Because everything reminded me of Spencer.

And Ben.

And being alone.

I put my face into my hands and sobbed.

The couch squeaked again as Allyson sat down next to me. She took my hand, let me weep, and gave me a tissue when I finally came back to myself. I felt like I'd been wrung dry.

"Did I ruin the party?" I asked, sniffling.

"Ollie gave another speech," she said. "Everything's fine."

"I just need a moment," I said.

"You should tell him how you feel, Mrs. P," Eve said.

I hadn't heard her and Lena come in.

"It's not that simple," I said.

"Yeah, it is," she said with the confidence of a thirteen-year-old in love for the first time. Her hand was linked with Lena's. I didn't know the details, but apparently, they had reconciled. I was glad.

"He hasn't called?" Allyson asked.

I shook my head. "It hasn't been that long," I said.

It felt like ages.

Lena hadn't said anything. She was just holding Eve's hand and looking at the floor.

"We both agreed this was for the best," I said, wiping away my tears. Hopefully for good. "I'll be fine—I'm just feeling emotional today."

Eve gave Lena a small push forward.

"Tell her!" she said. "Tell her what you told me!"

Allyson gestured to Eve. "Maybe we should give them some time," she said.

They left, and Lena came over to the couch.

"C'mere," I said.

She sat down and let me put my arm around her.

"I'm fine," I said. "Don't worry about me. I'll be fine."

"Was it because of me?"

"No, honey," I said. "It's because of a lot of things."

"But I'm one of the things," she said sadly.

I let out a breath.

"He's going to be moving to Australia for four years," I said. "It just didn't make sense."

"What if he didn't move to Australia?" she said. "Would you be together?"

"I don't know," I said.

She nodded. Her expression was so serious. So thoughtful.

"Eve thinks we should give him a chance. Thinks I should give him a chance."

"It seems like things are better between you two," I said.

Lena shrugged, but there was a little smile there.

It was nice. The two of us sitting here.

"I love you," I told her.

"I love you," she said. Then, quietly, "It's okay if you lo— if you like Ben too."

"Oh, honey," I said.

I wanted to tuck her up against my heart. She was trying so hard. Being so kind. So generous.

"If you feel that way, you should tell him," she said.

I pushed her hair back from her face and kissed her forehead. She let me.

"When did you get so wise?" I asked.

She shrugged. "Probably because I'm an old soul," she said. "At least, that's what Eve tells me."

"You are," I said. "A very old soul."

"I think Ben's an old soul too," she said.

"You might be right," I said.

And then, suddenly, all I wanted to do was talk to Ben. Wanted to see him.

Be with him.

My heart leapt into my throat alongside my stomach. I was terrified, but it was okay.

"Whatever happens," I said, "none of it means I love your father any less."

"I know," Lena said. "Are you going to call him?"

I stood, pulling her up along with me.

"Come on," I said. "Let's go see how much a ticket to Australia costs."

CHAPTER 56

NOW

I DIDN'T GET A CHANCE TO BUY THAT TICKET. BECAUSE when we reached the top of the stairs and opened the door, Ben was standing right there.

"Surprise," he said.

I stared.

And then I looked at Lena.

"Did you plan this?"

She shook her head, looking as stunned as I felt.

"Plan what?" Ben said.

"What are you doing here?" I asked.

He looked good. He always looked good. I wanted to bury my face in his neck.

"Can we talk?" he asked.

I took him out to the porch. The engagement/pre-wedding party was happening inside, so we had the soundtrack of laughter and talking as we sat down on the front steps. The same front steps where I'd once spied on Spencer drinking Yoo-hoo with our cat. I looked up toward my old bedroom window, half expecting to see myself there.

But it was empty, of course.

"Lauren," Ben said.

I didn't let him finish. I took his face in my hands and kissed him. On my mother's porch. During a party. Where anyone could see us. I didn't care.

"I have to tell you something," I said.

"Me too," he said.

But we didn't stop kissing. It was so good. So right.

Any hesitation or doubt I might have had flew right out the window.

Who knew what would happen next. Tomorrow. The day after. The year after.

"I want to be with you," I said. "It will be hard, but I think we can make it work."

"Lauren," Ben said.

"I can come visit the set, and you can come to Montana during breaks, and we can try."

"Lauren."

"I just . . . I just think I might be falling in love with you," I said.

"I turned down the movie," he said.

I pulled back.

"What?"

He smiled at me. "I told them no."

I couldn't believe what I was hearing.

"But . . . but it's Bond."

"It's a movie," he said.

"Your career—"

"—will survive," he said. "I'm not quitting—there will

TOTALLY AND COMPLETELY FINE   • 413

be other roles, other jobs. Hopefully ones that won't be on the other side of the globe for years at a time or strip away all of my privacy. Besides, I have a pretty sweet gig already lined up at a brand-new theatre in Cooper, Montana."

"Fran?"

"Fired her," Ben said. "She was thrilled. Wants us to come visit for the holidays."

I couldn't believe what I was hearing. But . . .

"What about the money?" I asked. "Your mom's house?"

He took a deep breath.

"Having the house won't bring her back," he said. "I think I've finally accepted that. And I don't think she'd want me to give up the chance for something special. For someone special."

He tucked my hair back behind my ears.

"I'm talking about you," he said.

I let out a watery little laugh, but I couldn't speak.

I was happy and overwhelmed and terrified and so many other things all at once.

What was I afraid of?

The truth was, everything. Of loving again. Of losing again.

Of everything I couldn't control.

Of falling.

I didn't have to stop being scared—but I was ready to take risks again. That was the thing about being willing to be dropped forty or so feet. You had to trust that you were strapped in—that you'd done all you could to stay safe.

I'd waited so long to allow myself to love Spencer. To love.

I wasn't going to wait this time.

So, I took a breath.

I didn't know what would happen tomorrow or next week or next year.

That was okay.

Now was good.

"Hey," he said, his fingers under my chin, lifting my face to his.

"Hey," I said.

"What were you saying?" he asked. "About maybe falling in love with me?"

"Never mind," I said. "I thought I was talking to the next James Bond."

Ben laughed and put his forehead to mine.

"I think I'm falling in love with you," I whispered again, needing to say it. Needing him to hear it.

"Lauren," he said. "I'm already there."

CHAPTER 57

THEN

"THIS IS A FANTASTIC COOKBOOK," I TOLD SPENCER.

It had been sent to the Cozy the other day and I'd taken it home, hoping to dig into a recipe or two, but I couldn't narrow down which one I wanted to try.

"That's great," he said, patting down his pockets. "Have you seen my keys?"

"Next to the mail," I said. "Oooooh, a new brownie recipe."

"Like anything could top yours," he said, leaning over my shoulder.

"There's always room for improvement."

"Where's Lena?" he asked.

"At my mom's," I said. "She's got an English test tomorrow."

"Smart," he said, giving me a kiss on the cheek. "Okay, I'm off."

I nodded, focused on the book in front of me. At some point, we were going to have to tell Gabe to stop sending

Spencer money for school or he'd never graduate. Which I was pretty sure was his goal.

"I'll stop at the store after class," Spencer said. "So let me know if you want anything."

"Mm-hmm."

"Love you," he said.

"Love you too," I murmured. "Oooh, almond extract, that's unexpected. I don't think we have any in the pantry. Spencer, get me some when you're at the store, okay?"

Nothing.

I looked up.

He was already gone.

Sometimes I wished that I could Vulcan mind meld with Lena and give her all the memories I had of Spencer. But I couldn't. All I could do was tell her about her father— all the stories, all the moments, all the ways we loved each other. All the ways he loved her.

He loved her *so* much.

And he would have blubbered like a baby seeing her tonight. She looked beautiful in her bridesmaid dress, with her hair cut short in a sleek bob that would have made her look at least sixteen if it wasn't for the way she kept tugging at the back of her hem.

The groom couldn't stop smiling. And not just smiling, but smiling and looking over at his wife, who kept smiling and looking at *him*.

"You two are gross," I told Gabe.

His tie matched Chani's sparkly blue dress. Sans sparkles.

"I know," he said. "Isn't it great?"

I wrapped an arm around him. "Yeah," I said. "It is."

The wedding had come together perfectly, which was a good thing because Gabe and Ben and Ollie were going to be opening a show—and a theatre—in two weeks. We were all bracing for the onslaught of press and famous folk, and I was pretty sure that was the reason Gabe and Chani had wanted to get married before all that happened.

Gabe kissed the top of my forehead. "Thanks for being my best man."

"I'm surprised you picked me over Ollie, to be honest," I said.

"He wanted to officiate," Gabe said.

"He did a great job." I looked across the store to where Ollie and his husband were talking to Chani and her friend Katie. Her parents were talking to Mom, and her siblings were talking to Jacinda, who had surprised all of us with her presence—which I assumed was the point.

"He would have settled for nothing less than greatness," Gabe said.

The bookstore was decked out—lots of twinkle lights wrapped around shelves, flowers on every surface, and we'd also managed to make enough room for a small dance floor in the center.

Gabe and I stood there, at the edge of it all, and I closed my eyes for a moment, soaking up the love around me, and also missing Spencer. The way I always missed him.

But it was okay. Feeling both things at once.

I was learning how to do it.

The funny thing was that I was pretty sure Spencer would have really liked Ben. I knew, without a doubt, that he would have been so happy that I was happy.

Music started playing, and Gabe gave my shoulder a squeeze.

"That's my cue," he said.

I didn't recognize the song, but it was an older one—some pop song from years and years ago—and when Gabe reached Chani, she gave him a gentle slap on the arm. He just grinned and pulled her onto the dance floor before dipping her deeply in a move I remembered from his first Bond movie.

"I never knew Gabe could dance off-screen too," Ben said.

He'd come from the refreshment table and handed me some sparkling water with lime. Gabe had insisted he didn't mind having alcohol at the wedding, but the rest of us agreed that a dry wedding would be just as much fun.

"I think this is the extent of his dancing," I said.

Then I took my time taking Ben in.

His suit was blue, hair long and gorgeous, earring glinting in the light. He wore his usual boots, but they were shined to a mirror finish. Just last week he'd signed a year lease for a rental house just outside of town. We were talking about taking a trip in the next year or so. I hadn't told him yet, but I'd also started researching places to go skydiving. I thought by then I might be ready to give it a try.

"I don't have the same moves," he said. "But I've been told my enthusiasm makes up for a lack of skill. Want to dance?"

Before I could answer, we were approached by the second-cutest couple in attendance—Lena and Eve. They'd decided to wait to tell people about their relationship, but when they were in safe spaces, they were as cozy as any couple could be. It was nice to be able to give them a place to do that.

"You guys look great," Ben said.

"Thank you!" Eve said. "Did I tell you that I'm getting fitted for my costume next week?"

"Awesome!" Ben said, the two of them exchanging a high five.

Of course Eve had landed the role of the Witch. Ben had coached her every day until the audition, and I'd heard her Irish accent—it was pretty damn good.

Not as good as Ben's, of course.

"I like teaching," he'd confessed to me. "Maybe I can run some sort of after-school acting program."

I knew he'd be great at it.

He'd also been teaching Lena how to repair things. They used Spencer's tools and started with the rickety chairs that were at the intersection. Fixed the legs, sanded the whole thing, and gave them a new coat of paint.

We were both discovering new things that we liked. With Ben's encouragement, I had started taking an online design class. Just simple stuff, like how to make a pattern, but I liked it. He'd been right—I did like to learn.

I'd also started offering a new service at the Cozy—Pockets for All—where people (women mostly) could bring in articles of clothing that they'd like pockets added to. Allyson, of course, was my best customer and publicist.

She was dating someone she'd met at a speed dating event.

A woman.

"It's all very new," she said. "But I like her a lot."

We had scheduled a double date for next week. Ben was

excited to meet her date, but even more excited about going out to dinner in town with me.

I realized Diana knew about Ben when she left a message for me, screaming that I was desecrating Spencer's name and our marriage and that I was a whore and I'd always been a whore and I'd always be a whore. I deleted the message and blocked her number. Cried about it, but just a little. Then I'd gone to Ben's new place and fucked him until her words faded away and all I could hear was Ben's voice, rough and right, telling me what a good, good girl I was.

I was certain I'd never tire of the way he said my name.

There were times I caught looks from people when I kissed him or held his hand outside of the Cozy. I found that I really didn't care.

Life was short. So fucking short.

And I was going to enjoy every moment I could.

"I have something for you," Lena said.

Her hands were behind her back.

At first, I could tell that Ben thought she was talking to me, so his surprise was evident when she pushed a box at him.

"It's on loan," she said. "For the play."

I watched Ben open the box, and then slowly pull out Spencer's scarf. Lena's scarf.

"This is . . ." Ben's voice cracked, and he cleared his throat. "This is very generous."

He looked like he might cry.

"Thank you," he said.

"It's not a big deal," Lena said. I could tell she was hoping he wouldn't cry.

"I'll take very good care of it," Ben said.

Lena was looking at her feet. Then she looked at me. Then at Ben.

"And I'm learning how to make pizza dough, so if you wanted to come over for pizza sometime, that would be okay," she said.

Before he could answer, Lena was gone, pulling Eve across the room. She barely had time to wave.

"Wow," Ben said, looking down at the scarf.

"Wow indeed," I said, feeling like I was brimming over with happiness.

And I realized that was how time healed.

When you filled it with opportunity and people and love.

I felt so many things at once.

I would always miss my dad. I would always grieve for Spencer.

But my heart was big enough to hold space for them *and* others. It was like Ben had said—the heart expands.

There was even room in it for me.

Messy, tired, angry, sad, scared, confused, unsure me. I didn't have to be perfect to be loved. I could just be myself.

And *that* was totally and completely fine.

ACKNOWLEDGMENTS

I'M GOING TO TELL YOU SOMETHING STUNNINGLY OBVI-
OUS.

It is hard to write a book about grief while you are
grieving.

This book was a bitch to write.

There were times I didn't think it would ever get done.

There were times I didn't think I would ever like it, let
alone love it.

There were times I really, really, really wanted to give up.

I didn't mainly because of two annoyingly persistent
and wonderful women.

My agent, Elizabeth Bewley, who has talked me off
many a (metaphorical) ledge, and is always on hand to give
the exact right pep talk exactly when I need it.

My editor, Shauna Summers, who can see the potential
in a story even before I can see it myself—and who never,
ever lets me take the easy way out.

I might have cursed your names at times, but always followed with a fervent "thank you."

I love being a Dell author—having been around the publishing block a few times, I know a good team when I see it, and you are all the absolute tops. Melissa Folds, Taylor Noel, and Mae Martinez—I adore you.

Thank you to *everyone* at Penguin Random House. Thank you, Kara Welsh, Kim Hovey, Jennifer Hershey, Cara DuBois, Belina Huey, Saige Francis, Meghan O'Leary, Barbara Bachman, and all the other often unseen and talented hands that made this book possible.

I am beyond lucky that so many people judge my books by their covers—because what covers they are! Kasi Turpin for the art, Cassie Vu for the direction. Thank you, thank you!

Thank you to my creative covens for feeding me encouragement and love and, occasionally, tacos. Zan Romanoff, Maurene Goo, Sarah Enni, Doree Shafrir, Kate Spencer, Katie Cotugno, Robin Benway, Falon Ballard, Courtney Kae, Lacie Waldon, Erin La Rosa, Alison Greenberg, Lindsay Grossman, Lauren Airriess, Lauren Cona, and those I might have forgotten because of my mush brain.

Thank you to AAEA: Alice Lawson, Ashley Silver, Eren Joyce, and Allison De Fina. Truly the dream team—making all the things happen.

Thank you, Romancelandia. I love being part of this community—writers and readers and booksellers and everyone. I've been reading romance since I was a preteen—when a reader tells me that one of my books introduced them to the genre, there is no higher honor.

Tal and Daphna—I want to eat all the cannolis with you.

For Sally, Maeve, and the OG Lena.

Thank you to Prozac and Wellbutrin and gabapentin. Edibles. My heating pad. So many plants. The Jewish Council Shop on Magnolia. Daily naps. Hummingbirds, birds, and butterflies. Summer hats. The color green. Heirloom seeds. gb. Thai tea with boba. Treasure hunting with Mike. Dole Whips. Vintage cookbooks. Garden centers. That yellow bag that somehow goes with everything. Tiramisu.

To my family. Mom, Adam, and Abra. Amy and Tim. Feivel, my love.

To our house full of pets. Mozzarella, Susannah, and Geordi. My sweet Basil, who I miss every day.

And John.

John.

John.

I love you.

© JOHN PETAJA

ELISSA SUSSMAN is the bestselling author of *Totally and Completely Fine, Once More with Feeling, Funny You Should Ask,* and several YA novels. Her work has been praised by NPR, *The Washington Post, Cosmopolitan, Publishers Weekly, Booklist,* and other publications. She lives in Los Angeles with her husband and their many pets.

elissasussman.com

Instagram: @Elissa_Sussman

ABOUT THE TYPE

This book was set in Bembo, a typeface based on an old-style Roman face that was used for Cardinal Pietro Bembo's tract *De Aetna* in 1495. Bembo was cut by Francesco Griffo (1450–1518) in the early sixteenth century for Italian Renaissance printer and publisher Aldus Manutius (1449–1515). The Lanston Monotype Company of Philadelphia brought the well-proportioned letterforms of Bembo to the United States in the 1930s.